D0409921

VALIANT HEARTS

"You make bold to come here, barely clad," Gareth said.

Briar Rose stood her ground. In the gold light of the oil lamp Gareth appeared younger, his harsh features softened. With a slight smile she said, "By now you should know how unmannerly I am, despite the best of training."

He leaned forward and kissed her exposed shoulder. "You are an enchantment," he murmured against her neck. "You should go now and leave me be, before I do something foolish."

A dark fire smoldered in her eyes. "I want to stay with you, Gareth."

He hesitated, raw desire conflicting with reason . . . until a groan exploded from him, echoing out into the night. "By the stars, I cannot let you leave!"

Recent Titles by Susan Wiggs from Severn House

THE LILY AND THE LEOPARD
THE RAVEN AND THE ROSE

BRIAR ROSE

SUSAN WIGGS

This title first published in Great Britain 1998 by
SEVERN HOUSE PUBLISHERS LTD of
9–15 High Street, Sutton, Surrey SM1 1DF.
This first hardcover edition published in the U.S.A. 1998 by
SEVERN HOUSE PUBLISHERS INC of
595 Madison Avenue, New York, N.Y. 10022
by arrangement with HarperCollins*Publishers*.

British Library Cataloguing in Publication Data

Wiggs, Susan
Briar rose
1. Love stories
1. Title
813.5'4 [F]

ISBN 0-7278-2200-4

Printed and bound in Great Britain by
MPG Books Ltd, Bodmin, Cornwall.

For my grandparents,
Marie and Harold Banfield—
They know the meaning of
"happily ever after."

1

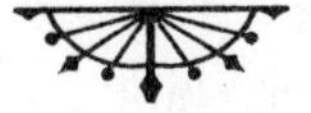

Embraced by the crook of a meander in the River Swale, Castle Briarwood clung to a grassy fell, the stones of its whitewashed keep cutting a sharp profile against the noontide sky. High walls protected the small, thatch-roofed town and church, and the moors rolled out beyond the river.

Briar Rose stood in her solar, pulling a hanging of heavy damask back from the window to look out upon Briarwood, her home. The scent of ripening fruit wafted in from the orchards and chippers trilled in the linden trees. Peasants in the distant fields were at their tilling, driving fat rouncies through the furrows of land, which had been recently harvested of their grain and hay. Somewhat closer, a broad meadow was being prepared as a jousting field.

This, at least, lifted Briar Rose's mood. She let the damask hanging fall and turned back to her solar. Her great chest stood wide open, the rich contents mocking her. It was her trousseau, a lavish assortment of Tripoli silks and cloth of gold, dainty underthings, a mantle lined with squirrel, a robe of lilac velvet trimmed with golden braid.

The garments would not be worn now, not as they should have been. For Briar Rose's betrothed, the frail Hugh, earl of Tesselwaithe, had recently died.

Sighing, Briar Rose turned back to watch the preparation of the jousting lists. Some time later, Janet, a tiring woman, entered the solar.

"My lady," Janet scolded, " 'tis one hour to vespers, and your parents await you in the hall. You've not even begun to get ready."

"Is it so near vespers?" Briar Rose wondered, wrinkling her delicate brow. "I was lost in thought, I suppose."

Janet hugged the girl close. "There now, lovey, I know you grieve for poor Hugh. But no matter; your father will find you a husband."

"I am sixteen and should have been married a year ago," Briar Rose said.

"There is yet time," Janet said consolingly. "But now your lord father craves your presence that you may meet his new wife." Janet took up an ivory comb and began pulling it through the long, jetblack locks that reached fully to the girl's hips.

Briar Rose suffered the familiar ministrations absently, wondering about Acacia, the stepmother she was about to meet. Her own mother, the gentle Mary, lady of Briarwood, had passed away while Briar Rose had been at the house of Lord Henry and Lady Catherine Wexler in Yorkshire, where her schooling had taken place. At Wexler, Briar Rose had learned the refinements of being a lady and the arts of housewifery, that she might make a suitable wife for Hugh.

But, like the trousseau, her education would not be needed now. Sighing, Briar Rose let Janet straighten the folds of her many-layered gowns and chewed dutifully on a sprig of fennel to sweeten her breath.

"Do behave," Janet cautioned, propelling her toward the door. "Laugh prettily and lift your gown to reveal your dainty foot. Here, open your mantle to show your parents how graceful you've become."

Briar Rose composed herself and left the solar with the smooth, gliding walk she'd been taught to affect. She stepped lightly down the narrow stone staircase.

Lord John Padwick and his new wife, Acacia, waited in the great hall, seated on canopied chairs at the head of a massive oaken table, sipping spiced wine from silver chalices. Rushlights and candles impaled on iron spikes lit the hall. At her father's nod, Briar Rose came forward and kissed him—his dear, aging face which wore, as always, a look of almost childlike bewilderment. Then she curtsied deeply and kissed her stepmother.

Against her lips the lady's long, stark cheek felt cold and rendered unnaturally smooth, probably by sheep fat. Acacia was severely beautiful, much younger than her husband. Her smile was fleeting and chilly.

"Is she not every bit as lovely as I told you?" Lord John asked with fatherly pride.

Acacia's cool, green-eyed glance appraised the girl. "She's a mite small and has a fullness in the mouth. Her chin is rather squarish, is it not? I've always thought an oval face was much more attractive. And that hair—why, 'tis black as a crow's wing."

Briar Rose's eyes widened and her temper rose. She studied her stepmother with a frank stare. Acacia might be a beauty, but her looks had been enhanced by artifices. Her hair was plucked to broaden her brow and perhaps it was dyed, for the reddish shade seemed unnaturally bright. It occurred to Briar Rose to mention that vanity was sinful, but in deference to her father she held her tongue.

If Lord John was offended by his wife's comments, he did not show it. He was like an unchanging gray stone; subtle words had always washed over him, leaving no impression. He merely smiled his pleasure at having his daughter with him once again after an absence of two years.

"Briar Rose," Acacia murmured, the name rolling off her tongue like an insult. "What an odd name. How did you ever come to call her that, my lord?"

"Ah, 'tis a pretty story," Lord John said, sipping his wine. "Before the girl was born, a scourge of illness had swept through the shire. Briarwood had fallen into such a state of disrepair that it was fairly overrun by brambles and evil weeds. The fever spared few of us.

"Then, like a miracle—for it was thought my wife was barren—the child came to us. I thought her beautiful, like a sweet rose among the briars, and my wife declared that that was what the babe should be called."

"Hmph." Acacia motioned for one of her waiting damsels. "Have Nurse fetch the Lady Bettina," she instructed, not about to let her own daughter be eclipsed by the newcomer.

Briar Rose's half sister was but a mewling infant, conceived and born during her absence. Acacia made a great show of pointing out the fairness of the skin and eyes, the paleness of the wispy hair.

"She is a fine baby," Briar Rose said dutifully, raising her voice above the infant's cries. Acacia motioned the nurse away when the howling grew overloud.

" 'Tis lucky I am to get daughters," Lord John said, rubbing the front of his short tunic with a satisfied air. "Most men crave sons, but that is not the case for Briarwood."

Briar Rose smiled proudly and glanced over at a long, fading tapestry on the wall, which depicted the legend of Isobel d'Evreux, the first mistress of Briarwood. Two centuries before, that courageous woman had lost her husband during a battle with wild tribes from the north and single-handedly led her knights to victory over the marauders. King Richard was so impressed by Isobel's actions that he granted her seisin and proclaimed that Briarwood Manor should be ruled by her female descendants forever after. He had a crest ring wrought especially for the formal hallmote occasion and vowed that its wearer would be mistress of the manor once she married.

It was an ancient, romantic tradition, and Briar Rose was proud to be a descendant of the fabled Isobel. Being heiress to Briarwood gave her power few women would ever know.

Caught up in these thoughts, she forgot her restrained manners momentarily and blurted out, "My lord, will I marry soon? I had thought the keep would be mine by now. I've many improvements in mind."

Acacia bristled. For more than a year she had ruled over Briarwood, and considered it hers. Yet as soon as the girl was wed—and she was certainly ripe for it, with her blossoming body and eager, blue-violet eyes—the power would be wrested from her.

"I look to marry you well, daughter," Lord John said, oblivious of the venomous glance his wife shot him. "Since Hugh died, the suitors have been many, but I must be careful whom I ally you with."

"Of course, my lord," Briar Rose said, folding her hands demurely in her lap. Absently she began twisting her signet ring. This ring, wrought of gold worn smooth by generations of wear, boasted the crest of Briarwood:

a five-petaled rose with a center of seeds, a symbol of bounty, set upon a base of rocks for solidness.

Acacia looked covetously at the ring. It was the key to Briarwood, for the wearer was recognized as sole heiress. On the day the estate was conferred by the manorial hallmote, the ring would be held up as evidence of ownership.

Ambition for her own daughter burned within Acacia. Padwick's parents had had no female issue, so the manor would pass through him. And if she didn't do something soon, it would pass to this starry-eyed chit. Acacia took a draught of wine, stroked her fur-lined mantle, and swore privately to have the ring—and hence Briarwood—for her Bettina.

Unaware of her stepmother's vow, Briar Rose sat quietly until it was time to proceed to the chapel for vespers. Throughout the Scripture reading she was occupied with private thoughts. She prayed for the soul of her mother, and then for Hugh. She mourned Mary's death but could summon little grief over Hugh's passing.

She'd known him all her life. His parents were nobles in a neighboring shire. Hugh had been a frail, serious boy, more given to chess playing and reading than to active sport. With an impish smile Briar Rose recalled how often she'd shocked her betrothed by galloping her palfrey wildly, swimming in the castle ponds, sometimes even joining the household knights at their war games.

Acacia noticed the smile and her nudge dug deeply, painfully, into Briar Rose's side. The girl immediately grew serious, fixing a pious expression on her face and pulling her chaplet forward to conceal her inner thoughts.

She had come home prepared to love her new mother, yet Acacia seemed so disapproving that it was hard to summon affection. Briar Rose fingered her ring and clung to the idea that soon Acacia would have to give up playing mistress of Briarwood. She'd have the unhappy choice of staying on at the keep in a secondary role or going to Lord John's smaller estate, called Padwick. That damp, crumbling keep overlooked a rocky shore of the Narrow Sea, a day's ride to the southeast. Compared to Briarwood, it was modest and crude.

Briar Rose quickly said a string of Aves to atone for her unkind thoughts and thanked the Blessed Virgin for Briarwood. She lifted her eyes to a rose-gold shaft of light, which angled in through a high oriel. Please, she prayed with every impatient fiber of her young body, please, send me a husband . . .

Excitement kept her from her bed that night. Briar Rose stood wrapped in a robe at her window again, watching the play of firelight in the fields below. Dozens of striped tents housed the tourneyers and their retainers, who were feasting late in anticipation of tomorrow's event.

Not just knights but their squires and standard-bearers and buglers were waiting to enter the lists. The scent of woodsmoke wafted up on a breeze that hinted of autumn's first chill. Briar Rose shivered and smiled. Tomorrow she would take her place in the galleries with all the visiting ladies, for once not relegated to the children's stands, where the youngsters were deviled by watchful nurses.

And perhaps she would take along a silk scarf to toss to one of the knights. Surely among the company below she would find a favorite—a husband . . . Briar Rose laughed aloud. For a girl of noble birth to choose her own mate would certainly raise some eyebrows. But, she thought, swelling with pride, Isobel d'Evreux would understand.

Still smiling to herself, Briar Rose stirred the fire in the grate. Sparks snapped and flew outward, dancing near the hem of her robe. The snores of her waiting damsels issued from outside the chamber door, where they slept on pallets. Briar Rose extinguished her candle with moistened fingertips, dropped her robe, and crept into her great wood-frame bed.

Her dreams carried her away to the jousting field, where from the shaded gallery she saw a great knight upon a swift charger thundering at his foe. The contestants met in an awesome clash of steel and splintering lances, caparisons flying about the horses. Briar Rose gasped. The dream scene was suddenly engulfed by a harsh fog of smoke, obscuring everything, stinging her eyes, constricting her throat. Dizziness welled up within her and she fought for breath, choking . . .

Somewhere between dreaming and wakefulness, she sat up and screamed for Janet. Through a haze of thick, smothering smoke she stumbled naked toward the door. The tiring woman wrapped her mistress in a blanket and propelled her quickly to the screens passage outside.

The rest of the keep was alerted. Servants arrived from all directions, carrying water to the lady's solar. The fire was contained in just a few moments. Briar Rose went in her borrowed blanket to sleep on a truckle bed in her parents' great chamber.

Lord John grumbled about the newfangled chimneys in the house, which Acacia had insisted on adding some months ago. He had a draught of hippocras brought up from the kitchens for his daughter and swathed the girl in furs from his own bed.

Lady Acacia, on the other hand, seemed more angry than worried. She snapped at the servants and at her husband, and turned away peevishly to feign sleep.

* * *

Early the next day Briar Rose ran to her solar, having nearly forgotten last night's episode. Servants were already there, airing the room with damp cloths and spreading fresh rushes and herbs on the floor. Briar Rose clutched her blanket around her and waited for them to finish.

Peter, a boy whose family had served Briarwood for years, was cleaning the grate of the fireplace where the blaze had originated. Hesitantly he motioned Briar Rose to his side.

"There's something I think you should see, my lady," he said, bending over and pointing up into the chimney hole above the grate.

Briar Rose looked. A wad of straw blocked the chimney.

"That would account for all the smoke," Peter told her, " 'Tis a wonder of God you didn't smother."

A chill gripped Briar Rose. Stubbornly she told herself that the straw was left there by accident, to stop draughts from entering the room. She refused to believe that someone had wanted this fire to start. Still she couldn't help thinking that, with all the preparations that had been made for her return, this detail had been neglected. She drew away from the fireplace and instructed Peter to remove the straw.

"You will say nothing of this," she told the boy, hoping that her voice didn't betray her nervousness.

"But my lady—"

"Speak no more of it." Briar Rose was not about to let her day be ruined by the incident. She didn't want it to be whispered about that there was trouble at Briarwood; the keep's reputation must be protected at any cost.

Her bath arrived in a lidded, trunklike tub and the fire was forgotten. Janet scented the water with rosemary and bathed the girl from head to toe, as she had so many years ago when Briar Rose was a child.

"You've not changed all that much," Janet joked, making sport of Briar Rose's small bosom and straight, boyish hips.

"You've a saucy tongue," the girl said, but she laughed. "Anyway, I shall fill out and one day be as beautiful as the King's daughter, Isabella."

Janet's expression softened, her kindly eyes shadowed by her crisp wimple. She cupped Briar Rose's small chin in her work-roughened hand and said, "Don't worry about changing yourself, sweeting. You've your own kind of beauty."

Briar Rose stepped out of the bath. A pair of waiting damsels approached with scented ointments and rubbed her with them.

Briar Rose donned a pair of loose breeches and a chemise and a stiff cotte of linen. Her rich gown of silver-embroidered violet had a graceful, long bodice and dagged sleeves that parted at the elbows. A jeweled girdle was fastened about her waist, accentuating her slimness.

Briar Rose wore her hair in long, coiled plaits under a pretty caul headdress that matched both her gown and the deep blue-violet of her eyes. She felt like a true lady, not just a girl anymore. She was a chrysalis, emerging from the cocoon of childhood to soar, a woman at last.

"I want my father to see me," she cried. Forgetting to affect her smooth lady's gait, Briar Rose bolted from the solar and sailed down the stairs, leaving the keep by the main door. The bailey of Briarwood had always seemed to her to be an enchanted place, and on this August day it was doubly so. Violets, heliotropes, and roses bloomed riotously beside the fishpond and around the dovecote and mews. The whitewashed stonework of the outer wall was lovely and ornate with whimsical wainscoted patterns.

Briar Rose left through the big gate, calling greetings to the workers and guests she met, garnering stares, for now she was a different person from the skinny, hoydenish girl who had left for Wexler two years before. The atmosphere was convivial, as a feast day should be, and many stopped to greet the girl who had returned a lady, to one day become mistress of Briarwood.

Lord John was not to be found at the bustling encampment of the tourneyers. Briar Rose wove in and out of the tents and pavilions, searching for him.

What she found instead caused her to freeze in her tracks. She gasped softly at a knight who stood in her path.

He was busy and didn't notice her, even when she stood stock-still to gape at him. His hair was a mass of spun gold, cropped in the manner of a knight, waving about a perfect, clean-shaven profile. He had a high, handsome brow and gray eyes, a chiseled mouth and chin. His cheekbones were sculpted high, the jaw squarish and firm, unyielding. Although he was undoubtedly young, without a trace of gray in his shining hair, there was an odd, world-weary look about him as he ran his hand down the flange of the lance he was inspecting.

The knight made a quarter turn and Briar Rose swallowed hard, seeing for the first time the whole of his extraordinary Saxon face. One of his eyes, she noticed, was slightly puckered as if from an old battle wound. A more self-conscious man might cover the scar with a patch, but there was no hint of vanity in this knight. He wore his masculinity like a mantle, exuding confidence with every graceful movement he made.

The knight was not yet clad for battle. His powerful legs were encased in gray hose, and the short black tunic barely covered his muscular buttocks. He was with his squire, readying his sword and armor and the trappings of his horse.

On the shield that leaned against a tree was the figure of a black hawk on a field of gray. Briar Rose immediately dubbed him the Hawk, for his rugged features and intense eyes with their repressed predatory look reminded her of that noble bird.

Finally he noticed her, turning as if he felt her stare. "By the rood, what's this?" he asked, bowing slightly.

Briar Rose, who had never in her life been shy, faltered under his hard gaze, with the one eye that slanted so mysteriously.

"I—I was looking for my—for Lord John."

"You've missed him, then. He's gone back to his keep." His eyes held hers with a faintly amused gaze as he asked, "What business do you have with Lord John? Surely the old man's not taken on a mistress! By my troth, I'd wager Lady Acacia is—"

Briar Rose felt a stab of temper. "I beg you, sir, to speak more respectfully of my father."

A look of surprise crossed the handsome, craggy face, and he burst out laughing.

"So you are the Lady Briar Rose. I'd heard Padwick had a daughter, but I never expected one so young or fair. Ah well, 'tis not the first time my tongue has gotten me in trouble."

Briar Rose sniffed. It was a pity the man's manners were not as appealing as his looks.

Abruptly he grabbed her hand, admiring the slender softness of her fingers.

"My lady, I humbly beg your forgiveness. Don't be offended." He punctuated his plea by pressing a kiss of wicked intimacy upon the pulse at her wrist. The look he gave her as he bent over her hand somehow robbed the apology of its sincerity.

Briar Rose snatched her hand away, confused and breathless. She rubbed her wrist where his lips had touched. Looking up, she was dazzled by his smile.

"I suppose," she said, keeping her voice light, "that I shall have to forgive you. It must never be said that the heiress to Briarwood is without compassion."

His eyes—they were gray, flecked with silver—crinkled at the edges. "Proud words, sweeting. You'll make a fine chatelaine one day."

Briar Rose searched his face for a hint of mockery, but his compliment seemed genuine. "Do you think so, sir? I've always wondered if I'll be equal to the task."

"My dear, I've no doubt you're equal to any challenge."

Jesu, but he was handsome! Her heart thumped wildly in her chest as she contemplated her next move.

The man's eyes held hers as she groped for the violet scarf she wore at her belt. She'd brought the scarf along on a whim, but now it seemed as if she'd been expecting to find her champion. She said softly, "I want you to have this, sir, to bring you fortune in battle today."

The knight took the scarf and grinned, revealing even, white teeth and small fans of humor at the sides of his eyes. "A token? How flattering, dear maiden. I am, indeed, honored." There was something cynical in his voice, an almost bitter note, when he turned to his squire. "I'd wager the damsel does not know about me yet, Paulus."

"What is it that I should know, sir?" she asked. "What awful secret are you hiding?"

"I've many secrets, but I've never attempted to hide

my penchant for beautiful women," he said, his voice rich, caressing.

Briar Rose's feigned calmness was completely shattered when the knight stepped closer, exuding a woodsy, leathery scent, and captured her in his arms. He grinned down at her.

"You should be more careful in bestowing your tokens, my lady." Holding the ends of the scarf in his two hands, he brought it behind her waist, capturing her against him by pulling on the ends. "I may not treat this bit of silk with proper respect."

Briar Rose was a prisoner rendered immobile by the tautly held scarf and by the sweet, shivery sensations that ran up and down her spine.

There was little time to wonder at his uncanny effect on her. He bent swiftly and took her mouth with his, drawing the very breath from her. She was too shocked to pull away. He gathered her so close that she could feel the whole length of him like a wall of granite pressing against her. She felt helpless in the unyielding embrace and full of sensations so strange and new that her head seemed to spin.

Jesu, she thought, sweet Jesu . . . She tried to pull away but instead sagged against him, marveling at the firm, insistent pressure of his lips and the liquid heat of his tongue as, shockingly, it crept out to rim her mouth. None of Hugh's chaste, dry kisses—few and far between—or the Briarwood stableboys' stolen pecks could have prepared her for this. Briar Rose realized, as her heart thundered in her ears, that for the first time she was in the arms of a man. A man who knew exactly what he was about.

Her eyes fluttered shut as she began to enjoy the kiss—the racing of her heart, the intoxicating taste and smell of this man. Shyly her hands crept up to his shoulders.

Suddenly she was released. Her lips felt bruised and tender, her limbs as weak as barley stalks.

"Do you still want me to keep your token?" the knight asked, his extraordinary eyes challenging her.

Briar Rose felt spots of color rise to her cheeks. Unable to find her voice, she merely nodded and fled. The man's rich, mocking laughter followed her until she ducked behind the ladies' gallery some yards away.

Briar Rose leaned, recovering, against a wooden pole, her head swimming with new, glorious emotions. She wanted to whoop with joy. She had found her knight, a man she'd never dared dream of until today. She didn't even know his name; to her he was the Hawk, as fierce and fearless as a wild bird. The Hawk . . . Briar Rose vowed that she would be the one to tame him, and in taming him, she would make him her own. And why not? she asked herself. She needed a husband. It was as if her prayer in the chapel had been answered. She planned to tell her father tonight, at the feast, that her search for a husband was over.

The rest of the morning passed in a blur, and before long Briar Rose found herself seated under the canopy of the gallery facing the lists. At her left was Acacia, starkly beautiful in a gown of deep red and gold, and to her right was Lady Harriet Frowley from a keep some miles to the north.

The spectators cheered when the heralds and buglers announced the commencement of the tourney. To the bright music of trumpets and much waving of flags and ribbons, the standard-bearers crossed the field. Then came the parade of combatants, two dozen knights on their brightly caparisoned destriers, their armor gleaming in the sun.

Briar Rose saw her champion once again. Her heart rose in her throat. There was a hawk emblazoned on his shield and breastplate. His helm was closed over his face, but Briar Rose knew the piercing eyes, one of them intriguingly scarred, would be keen and alert. On his sleeve her violet scarf flew like a banner, a delicate wisp against the hard metal of his armor.

Lord John enumerated the contest rules and announced the champions of the *poursuivants.* The Hawk didn't seem to notice the girl who waved so frantically in his direction.

At last the combatants were ready. The week before, they had been matched and seeded according to skill. There was a display of arms in the cloister so that the knights might be easily identified in the heat of battle. Any knights who were found unworthy were ejected, their horses confiscated and spurs cut off.

Friday, Saturday, and Sunday had been set apart for the truce of God, and during that time the challengers rested. On Sunday the ladies chose their favorite, who would preside over the mêlée. The honor had been given to Lord Alain de Wannet, a champion from York.

This morning would begin the culmination of all the preparations. From her place in the ladies' gallery Briar Rose studied the lists. The field was long and broad, surrounded by a double fence with entrance and exit points. Between the two fences, knights and their squires waited.

A hush settled over the crowd. Trumpets blared, and the knight of honor cut the cords to the lists.

"Laissez-aller!" The cry began the long-awaited fight.

War-horses surged forward from either end, and

blunted lances shattered against opposing shields. The crowd came alive and began to cheer. Even Acacia shouted huzzahs and clapped her hands.

Briar Rose sat forward on the bench, straining to see her champion. She caught her lower lip with her teeth, hardly daring to breathe.

The Hawk was in the midst of the fray. He had unhorsed a man already and was riding down another opponent now. He sat his great gray destrier expertly with his lance braced and angled across his body, the better to fell anything that stood in his way. The violet scarf fluttered and Briar Rose feared it would be torn, but the Hawk deflected every blow with his shield.

After some time it appeared that the knights of the opposing team were avoiding him. The Hawk was able to fell each man he went after. Time and time again he clashed and shattered lances against his shield, and before long the lists were littered with fallen knights and the squires who came to their aid.

Finally, when the afternoon heat shimmered over the lists, there were only two combatants left: the Hawk and Lord Alain de Wannet, the knight of honor. Both had abandoned their broken lances and came at each other with maces. The spikes had been blunted, but the heavy weapons were effective nonetheless. By turns the men were the pursued and the pursuer, and the maces swung with mighty force.

"A Wannet! A Wannet!" the crowd cheered. It seemed that everyone except Briar Rose favored the knight of honor.

Growling from behind his helm, which was sinisterly shaped like a hangman's hood, Lord Alain struck the Hawk's mount. The animal squealed and cast its armored burden from its back, raking the air with its front hooves. It was a dishonorable way to unhorse a man, and Briar Rose was surprised when the judges allowed it.

The Hawk did not seem unduly perturbed. His squire scurried out, helped him to his feet, and gave him back his mace. With deadly accuracy the Hawk swung out and brought his opponent down. Wannet fell heavily to the dirt, thrashing his steel-encased limbs and cursing as his squire helped him right himself.

"Let the swordplay begin!" Lord John called. This was the most favored form of combat, man-to-man, two champions pitted against one another.

Lord Alain instructed his squire to remove the blunt from his sword.

"It mustn't be allowed," Briar Rose cried. "They must fight with rebated weapons."

"Nonsense," snapped Lady Harriet. "The rules do not apply in this case."

Briar Rose gave no answer, for she was intent on watching this frightening new development. The Hawk removed his own blunt and the two came swinging together. Metal clanged against metal, ringing like funeral bells.

Lord Alain was a mighty knight, having secured a formidable reputation in France, but from the start it was clear who would win. The Hawk's blows were coolly dealt and accurate while the other's were made in anger. Like a dancer, the Hawk lunged.

The knight of honor fell. The Hawk approached him calmly and touched the point of his sword to the vulnerable mail at his neck.

In the silence that followed, Wannet's angry oath carried across to the stands.

"Whoreson! You've still not forgiven me for winning Celestine from you!"

"That quarrel ended when she drank poison, Wannet, to escape you. Now, will you yield the day to me, or shall we dredge up old enmities before our host?"

Wannet swore again but, grudgingly, he capitulated.

"Who is he?" Briar Rose asked.

"Lord Gareth Hawke, baron of Masterson." Lady Harriet's voice was chilly, as if the very name were distasteful to speak.

Gareth Hawke. The name formed on Briar Rose's lips. It fit him aptly: a man's name, a champion's. It pleased her that she had dubbed him correctly right from the start. She cocked her head.

"He won the day; why is there no cheering?"

"Hawke is champion because he can't afford not to be," Lady Harriet sniffed. "My dear, the man's estate is in a bad way and he needs the money he makes as a tourneyer. Ah, I see you haven't heard the story."

"Nor have I," Acacia said, always eager for a bit of gossip. "Do go on."

"Lord Gareth is quite young, not thirty, yet he's long on experience. In the past he presided over flourishing estates and a good-sized town—Masterson, north of here—and was a favored knight of the shire.

"Now he has fallen from grace. He claims the bishop of Morley Diocese offended him, abducted and murdered his sister, and tried to take some of his lands. So he and his knights invaded the diocese, pillaged its lands and villages, and ransomed the doyen and several priests.

"Naturally the bishop—whom I vow had been wrongfully accused by Hawke—complained to his superiors, and Masterson was placed under the ban. The town has since seen no Mass, no services at all. I'm told it is now a wild, lawless place. Lord Gareth's been reduced to tourneying and mercenary work to keep Masterson alive. He's also a notorious manhunter. 'Tis said he'll root out and murder anyone for a goodly sum."

Briar Rose turned away, her face clouding. It wasn't true, she told herself. The Hawk was an honorable man. It was obvious in the proud, almost arrogant way he carried himself, his strict adherence to the rules of battle during the tourney. If he had indeed committed such atrocities against a diocese, it must have been because he had been deeply offended.

Even now, as he quit the lists with his retinue, helm in hand, his great blond head was tilted up and his cold, gray-eyed stare defied anyone to cross him. Briar Rose couldn't abide the thought of his leaving without being properly honored. As her stepmother and the other women continued to whisper and gossip, she stepped down from the gallery and snatched up one of the garlands that adorned the pavilion. She heard—and ignored—Acacia's shout of outrage as she ran across the dusty, trampled lists toward Lord Gareth.

She shouted his name and he turned. She stopped just a few feet away and dropped into a deep curtsy, laying the garland at his feet.

"My lord," she murmured, blushing.

He grinned. Sweat traced rivulets down the sides of his face and glistened on his brow and upper lip.

"Flowers for the champion?" he asked archly.

"Of course, my lord. It must never be said that Briarwood doesn't know how to treat a champion."

"I see. Then I suppose you must, for the sake of propriety, bestow a kiss of victory."

Briar Rose felt the color rise to her cheeks again. "I've never heard of such a convention, my lord."

He laughed richly. "Nor have I, but perhaps we can begin a new tradition." He stood solidly, his eyes challenging her. He kept his arms at his sides, leaving it to Briar Rose to make the first move.

She was terrified. It was one thing for a man to sweep her into his arms, catching her unawares, but it was something else again to take the role of the aggressor. She hesitated, feeling her breath come quickly, studying that rugged Saxon face. The gray irises of his eyes were rimmed with a dark metallic color that seemed to intensify his gaze.

"Well?" he prompted.

Briar Rose heard Acacia calling her name. Her stepmother wouldn't approve of her consorting with this man. A gleam of defiance leaped to her eyes. She stepped forward, rising high on her toes to reach him, and brushed her lips against his.

Then Acacia was upon her, sending Lord Gareth a murderous gaze and pulling Briar Rose's sleeve.

"What the devil are you thinking of?" the woman exclaimed, leading her away like a disobedient child. "Have you no sense of propriety at all?"

Briar Rose said nothing. She looked back in time to see Lord Gareth's broad, impudent grin and stumbled along behind Acacia.

Lord and Lady Padwick presided over a feast of enormous proportions. Servitors bearing casks of beverages poured from the buttery in a steady stream.

Varied meats had been roasting on spits for days. Beef boiled with onions and cabbage was hoisted from the pot and arrived on a great iron hook.

Delighted guests ate heartily of the plentiful fare, complimenting their host. Briar Rose, however, toyed with the meat and pease on her manchet.

Most of the knights were there, making merry and

being served by their squires, yet Lord Gareth was nowhere to be seen. He should have had the place of honor beside Lord John at the high table, but that seat was occupied by a rather smug Lord Alain de Wannet.

She turned her attention to the minstrels' gallery, where harpers and jongleurs performed. The song was a lively one in French, a playful satire about good King Edward the Third.

A minstrel called Piers Love stepped forward and bowed respectfully before Lord John, a grin on his clever, impish face. "A tribute, my lord, to the lady of the manor." He had a beautiful voice which seemed to caress the air.

Acacia smiled and preened a little, nodding at the minstrel. But Piers didn't see; his merry eyes were fastened on Briar Rose.

Piers strummed lightly on his harp and someone called for silence. Still staring at Briar Rose, he began to sing, his voice clear and bright, trilling slightly.

Briar Rose smiled at Piers and tossed him one of her ribands to thank him for his tribute. She turned to say something to her father but saw that his attention had been diverted by Acacia.

"It's an outrage," the woman was saying, her green eyes narrow and hard. "I demand that you send Piers Love away immediately."

"Really, my dear, it was only a—"

But Acacia continued her tirade, unaware that her voice was rising and could now be heard by all.

"I'll not let my place be usurped by that—that disagreeable chit!"

Lord John sighed wearily. He gave Piers an apologetic look and waved his hand, dismissing the singer.

But Piers only grinned and bowed again. "I shall be

on my way soon, my lord, since your wife no longer favors me. But please, one last song—"

With shouting and stamping, the revelers begged for more from the master. Acacia glared down at them from her seat at the high table. At Padwick's nod, Piers began another song, still holding Briar Rose in his gaze.

At first the soft melody seemed to herald a love ballad, but the words—as impudent and outrageous as Piers himself—belied the lilting tune.

If your stepmother, driven by spite,
Secrets in your food by dark of night
An aconite pill, then is filled with delight
When next morning she sees you turn green.
Care naught for her spells! It'll soon be seen—

Briar Rose shot to her feet. "Enough!" she cried, raising her voice above the laughter of the guests.

"Sir," Briar Rose continued, "you do my lady mother a great injury. I must ask that you apologize."

Although he was hardly contrite, Piers Love bowed low before Acacia and mumbled something unintelligible. He quit the hall slowly, with a spring in his step. Gradually the tension at the high table faded.

Briar Rose shifted restlessly, unable to keep her mind on the conversation. Nearby, some of the visiting ladies gossiped endlessly, even daring to whisper of Lord Alain de Wannet's young wife, who had killed herself the year before. It was said that the lovely, fragile Celestine had been dreadfully unhappy in her marriage. But Briar Rose cared nothing for rumors. All she could think about as she gazed down at the brightly arrayed women and dashing knights was Gareth Hawke, the conspicuously absent champion.

She declined to join in the rounds of singing and

dancing after the feast. Acacia frowned at this unmannerly breach of etiquette. But Lord John was indulgent, admitted the girl did look a little flushed, and excused her.

Fetching a mantle to shield her from the chill of the late summer evening, Briar Rose fled from the keep. Her slippered feet carried her across the flambeaux-lit bailey and stole past an inattentive sentry at the eastern gatehouse.

Just a few fires smoldered in the encampment tonight, for most of the knights and their retinues were celebrating in the hall. Her heart thumping with a mixture of delicious anticipation and trepidation, Briar Rose wound her way down the grassy fells.

He was there, at the same tent he'd occupied earlier. Only this time he was alone in the deserted camp.

Briar Rose fought a sudden urge to flee. Shadows from a flickering fire gave his face with that scarred eye a dangerous, almost sinister cast. A mercenary, a manhunter. Briar Rose watched as Gareth did a curious thing. He walked some yards away with a bucket and set it before his charger, performing a duty that should have been done by a groom. Chiding herself, Briar Rose decided that there was nothing dangerous about this man.

She stepped from the shadows into the circle of firelight and waited for him to return. It was unthinkable for a young lady to venture out alone at night, in search of a man. But Briar Rose's legendary ancestress, Isobel d'Evreux, had done the unthinkable in her day.

The knight returned shortly and Briar Rose straightened her shoulders.

"Lord Gareth." She dropped into a curtsy and then recovered.

His eyes, dark and flashing in the firelight, widened slightly. "I'm surprised to see you again, my sweet."

Briar Rose's breath came quickly. "I've come to offer my felicitations. You fought valiantly today." His doublet was of homespun, looped with gleaming stones taken, no doubt, from the granite hills of his northern homeland. Briar Rose had a strange urge to reach out and finger the polished stones. She clasped her hands determinedly behind her back.

"For that I thank you," Lord Gareth said. "And for the token as well. It may have brought me luck."

"It was more than luck that helped you win the day," Briar Rose said. "You're a skilled and noble warrior."

A note of cynicism crept into the knight's deep voice. "Skilled, perhaps, but hardly noble. I won because I needed the prizes."

"I've heard that Masterson is troubled," Briar Rose said.

"More than you know, dear girl." Gareth turned away, shunning her dewy-eyed concern. He didn't need the pity of this tiny girl-woman with her breathless admiration and pretty rosebud mouth.

"The gossip I heard about you is cruel," she persisted.

Deeply bitter, he said, "No doubt it's richly deserved. I am under the ban, cast out by the Church as an indiscriminate plunderer. Lepers are probably better tolerated than I."

"Can you not reverse the ban?"

He laughed harshly. "No, dear maid, I cannot. I've the whole diocese of Morley against me, and all their knights, not to mention Lord Alain de Wannet, an enemy made some years ago."

"Because of Celestine?" Briar Rose asked.

"So you've heard that gossip as well," Gareth mused, something soft and wistful passing across his face.

"Who was she?"

Gareth grimaced. Briar Rose couldn't possibly know what memories her question evoked. Celestine had been everything to him at one time. But Wannet's superior wealth and influence had won out and Gareth had lost the gentle, quiet girl. He couldn't speak of such things to Briar Rose. He shrugged.

"Wannet and I both offered for Celestine and 'twas he who won her. He made the girl miserable and she took her own life."

Briar Rose suspected that there was much more to this tale, but she knew better than to pry. She turned the subject back to Gareth's censure. "Is there any chance your attack on Morley will be forgiven, my lord?" she asked.

He shook his head. "I'd never be able to prove that the diocese is a den of godlessness."

Briar Rose drew in her breath. What Lord Gareth was saying was close to blasphemy.

He laughed at her discomfiture. "You see, my girl? Can I ever convince anyone that the priests of Morley are guilty of selling indulgences, adorning themselves like popinjays, keeping concubines, and practicing simony? No, of course, you don't believe me; no one will."

" 'Tis hard," Briar Rose said pensively, "for anyone to think ill of the Church. But if it's true, why can't you prove it? Go to King Edward himself—"

"Hah! You are naive, little one, hopelessly so. Bishop Talwork is intimate with the king, who has never favored me. Even before this came about, he censured me for showing mercy to the Scots in the border wars. And all I did then was agree on some boundaries."

Lord Gareth turned away again and began rolling up the flies of his tent. He wished the girl would go away;

he had more pressing things to do than to pass the time in idle if enticing flirtation. He'd already said too much.

"Are you leaving so soon?" she asked.

"Aye, I'm off at dawn. I've already taken the prizes and sold them back to their rightful owners. There is naught left to do."

"But the feast—"

"Do you think they would have me in their midst?"

"I would," Briar Rose assured him.

Gareth raised the eyebrow above his scarred eye. "Is that so, my lady? What would your parents think?"

Briar Rose looked away, studying the patterns of the moonlight on the colorful canvas of a nearby tent. "My father has never denied me anything."

Gareth could well imagine that Lord John was indulgent where his beautiful daughter was concerned.

She lifted her chin. "Please, Gareth, do come to the hall."

"What would it serve? I've better things to do with my time than to mingle where I'm not wanted."

"But such a grand feast has been prepared! There's a troupe of acrobats and dancing and—"

Gareth shook his head. Something about this young, sweet Briar Rose caused a stirring in his blood and he caught himself foolishly wishing that things could be different, that he could court her properly and do justice to her beauty and position. He thrust the unsettling longing aside.

"There's no place in my life for such things, my lady. Not now." His gaze raking over her slender form, he added regretfully, "Go and dance with all the knights, Briar Rose. Find someone with less woeful tales to tell."

"But I—"

"Go on with you." His eyes smoldered in the firelight. "Go, before I'm tempted to forget you are mistress of the keep." Insolently, he chased her off with a gentle slap to her backside.

Despite the impudence of his action, Briar Rose retreated only a few feet. She stopped and turned, planting her feet.

"I am no child, Lord Gareth, to be sent off to bed."

His hard-eyed gaze swept over her slim body, which was outlined by the moon's silvery glow. "I couldn't agree with you more, my lady," he murmured, and quickly he closed the space between them. He moved to gather her to him.

Briar Rose stepped back. In sooth, she wanted nothing more than to feel his strong arms about her, but she knew such closeness would render her weak and helpless, as she had been this morning. The odd loss of control bothered her. She pressed her hands against the polished stones on his chest.

Keeping her voice even, she said, "Neither am I a knight's plaything, my lord."

He threw back his head and laughed. "Of course not, sweeting. I've already guessed you've a good head on your shoulders. Which makes me wonder why you insist on consorting with the likes of me. Shouldn't you be back at the feast, batting your eyes at Wannet, the most eligible widower in the northern shires?"

She heard the angry twist in his voice as he said the name. Clearly the bitterness over Celestine ran deep.

"Would you foist me on a man you hold in such low esteem, my lord?" she asked.

"I'm the only one who thinks ill of Wannet. He has many friends, including the duke of Lancaster. You could do worse for yourself, Briar Rose."

"Yet I could do better, my lord," she said softly.

"Be careful, little one, lest I read an invitation in your words."

Briar Rose shivered in the chilly breeze and looked up at the silver-rimmed moon. Somewhere in the distant trees a nightingale called.

"Perhaps it *is* an invitation you hear, my lord."

Gareth felt a strange stab of emotion. He found the rapt expression on her face utterly captivating. He couldn't remember the last time he'd been so stirred by the sight of a woman. But then he couldn't remember ever meeting a woman so strikingly lovely, seemingly guileless, who disdained the rumors she'd heard and came to him, flouting all the constraints of etiquette.

She had an intriguing face, small, squarish, with a delightful little nose. The soft, sooty sweep of her lashes caressed her milk-white skin as she blinked at him in the moonlight. Deep eyes, intelligent eyes, a mirror to the person within. And those lips—full, ripe as a summer cherry, begging to be tasted.

As he studied her, Gareth felt the heat of raw desire radiating through him. It was a dangerous attraction he felt toward this woman, this Briar Rose. He was in enough trouble already without offending the daughter of a peer of the realm. It was best, he decided, to let her know from the start that he was a rogue, a pariah, a man who had nothing to offer save the bit of gold he earned on his adventures.

"You'd best get back to the keep," he told her, his voice low and slightly threatening.

"But I . . ." Briar Rose set her chin and stood firm. "This is my home. I go where I want and see whom I please."

"You do, do you?" Inwardly Gareth cursed. She was a tenacious little thing, not at all intimidated by his warning. Very well, he thought.

With no attempt at gentleness he seized her, crushing her against him. As the breath left her, Gareth pressed his mouth down to hers, tasting its sweetness yet trying to ignore the stirring within him. He felt her mouth soften, felt her sway toward him. He knew then that she had no fear of his kisses. But there were other ways to frighten a maiden. Slowly he fitted a hand between them and brushed aside her mantle. Then his hands went behind. The bodice of her rich gown was damnably complicated, but he managed to loosen the fastenings.

Her breasts were thinly covered by a chemise. It was no playacting that Gareth did as he moved his hands over the sweet mounds of her breasts and then lifted his mouth from hers.

"You should have heeded my warning," he reminded her, his eyes glittering silver. He lowered the chemise so that her flesh was completely bare to the chilly night breeze and to his roving hands.

Briar Rose gasped and pulled away, gathering her mantle about her.

"Rogue!" she said, outraged that he would make so bold with her. When he laughed insolently and reached for her again, she ran all the way back to the keep, her face burning with humiliation. She should have listened to him. He *was* a rogue. And to send her away with such insolence . . . She slowed to a walk, feeling her temper cool in the night air. As the sensations Gareth had evoked faded, she was able to think more clearly. He *must* care. Hadn't he accepted her token, even taken her in his arms and kissed her? It hadn't been a courtly kiss; there wasn't anything polite about it. It was certainly not the action of a man intent on shunning her.

"Dear man," she whispered, realizing the truth. She leaned against the cool stone of the keep. "You think that by putting me off you are protecting me." Suddenly she ached for him, getting his things together alone while in the hall the feast went noisily on. Once again she hurried across the bailey, this time full of hope and confidence. He must think me such a goose, running away like that, she thought. She decided to tell Gareth that she loved him—for what other name could she give to this fluttering of her heart, this wild heat that spread through her at the very thought of him? It didn't matter that he was under the ban—

"We all supposed you'd retired," Lord Alain de Wannet said, stepping from the shadows to block her path.

Briar Rose mumbled an excuse and pushed past him, ducking beneath a drooping vine. His arm snaked out and caught hers and she could smell the spirits on his breath. Despite his loss today, Alain was in a jovial mood.

"Come back inside with me, sweet Rose," he said firmly. "Your father would not want you out wandering at this hour." He propelled her to the hall. Briar Rose was repelled by his overly familiar touch, the hungry look on his bearded face in the glow of the flambeaux.

She was burning to see Gareth, but there was no way to do that now with Alain clinging to her, watching her every move. Very well, she thought, I have until dawn to find Gareth. She made a great show of yawning and, pleading fatigue, climbed to her solar, much to the chagrin of Lord Alain. He stood in the soft-scented night air, shaking his head.

She was an impertinent wench, and it occurred to him to complain to Lord John about her manners, but then he changed his mind. Young Briar Rose had recently lost her fiancé and would need a husband. Briarwood was modest by Lord Alain's standards, but it was aptly situated by the Swale and might be a fine bit to add to his own holdings. There was some nonsense about the place falling to the girl and her female issue and not to a man, as it properly should, but Alain was confident he could deal with that. The King had been prodding him to marry since his wife had died last year, her unborn child with her . . .

A canny smile curved his moist red lips as he stroked his pointed beard and turned over the possibilities in his mind. An idea quickly took shape, and Alain saw himself as the new lord of Briarwood. When the time was right, he'd speak to Lord John, who doubtless would be grateful that one so eminent would be interested in his daughter.

In the solar above, Janet helped her mistress to bed. She combed the girl's long black locks and stirred the fire. Briar Rose climbed obediently into bed to wait until it was safe to steal out and find Gareth again.

Then Corynne, one of Acacia's waiting damsels, arrived bearing a salver with a goblet upon it. "Compliments of your lady mother," the maid said. "She thought the draught might soothe you after all the excitement."

Briar Rose propped herself up, surprised. Was Acacia, after all, softening toward her? She smiled her thanks and took the goblet. Its contents smelled of apples and spices and she drained it quickly. Corynne pulled the drapes around the bed and withdrew with the salver and empty goblet.

The draught left a lingering, slightly metallic taste, but it helped Briar Rose's nerves. It wouldn't be easy to face Gareth and speak so frankly with him; she'd need all her courage. It wasn't every day a girl confessed that she had lost her heart to a man, that she wanted him to offer for her. But, she thought, a smile curving her lips, she was kin to Isobel d'Evreux, who had always spoken her mind. Briar Rose settled back to await the dawn.

When the hall was silent save for the blubbering snores of the sleeping guests, she'd slip away to the encampment.

Yet, despite her eagerness, she began to feel a heaviness in her limbs. It seemed an effort just to lift the covers of the uncommonly warm bed. Her mind drifted idly and she found herself remembering Piers Love's last song: "If your stepmother, driven by spite, secrets in your food . . ." What was it? Ah, yes, "an aconite pill . . ." And then a bubbling pain thundered through her vitals and she felt as though her very life was burning away.

With a mighty effort she heaved the drapes aside and forced herself to retch into the chamber pot. Her throat burned; her mind whirled helplessly.

Burning . . . the fire . . . and now the apple draught.

"Poison . . ." Briar Rose gasped, reaching for her calling bell. She dashed it to the floor, hearing it clatter loudly as she collapsed, hanging halfway off the bed.

2

Janet alerted the household with a shriek. Within minutes a rider was dispatched to the village of Briarwood to fetch the physician.

Acacia had brought Godfrey Pelham to the marriage with her, insisting that the town needed a real doctor instead of relying on midwives and wandering barbers. By the time he arrived, the solar floor had been cleaned and Briar Rose was wrapped in homespun cambric, sleeping fitfully. She awoke when the doctor and his haughty servant approached.

Godfrey Pelham was a man who took full advantage of the extra luxury the sumptuary laws allowed him because of his status. His red velvet gown was generously cut and his florid face was framed by a furred hood. He wore embroidered gloves and a belt of silver around his ample girth and even had a set of golden spurs that clicked lightly on the stone floor.

Briar Rose smiled feebly. She felt sick unto death, yet she could not help but consider the doctor's presumptuous accoutrements, and the steep fees the man must charge in order to have it all. As he made no move to examine her, Briar Rose said in a weak voice, " 'Twas something I drank."

Godfrey Pelham nodded as if he had known this all along and instructed his servant to prepare a remedy. It was a concoction of bethroot ground with oil of roses. The heady odor repelled Briar Rose.

"Take it away," she said and turned her head to one side. Janet brought her water. She sipped a little of it.

Godfrey thought to insist but then seemed to consider the status of his patient. It wouldn't do to cross the future mistress of Briarwood, especially when her father was so anxious to pay for her recovery. Shrugging, the doctor put aside the first remedy and brought forth a skin flask of goat's milk.

Briar Rose found this more appealing and drank a thin stream from the flask. The rich liquid seemed to coat and quiet her churning innards. She lay back and after a while felt the color returning to her cheeks.

"Lord be praised," Janet murmured, dropping to her knees. She began to pray in earnest, and the physician went to collect his fee.

"Janet," Briar Rose said, suddenly remembering something. "What time is it?"

The tiring woman wrinkled her brow for a moment. "Prime was rung some hours ago. Yes, 'tis well past the hour of prime."

"And well past sunrise, then," Briar Rose said, deflating.

"What is it, lady?"

"I was to see someone—well, it will have to wait. Send me my father, Janet, and beg Acacia to come also."

Lord and Lady Padwick hurried to the bedside. Lord John was dressed in a tunic and robe of muted brown as if he'd prepared himself for ill news. Acacia, in contrast, wore a lavish gown of yellow marbled silk and a tall, bright headdress. She looked positively festive, Briar Rose thought darkly.

"The physician gave me milk," Briar Rose explained. "It seems to have settled my stomach."

"You gave me grave worry," Lord John said, taking her small hand in his. "I can see, though, that you're on the mend already. God be thanked for that."

"The girl looks well enough," Acacia said. "Come, John, we've guests awaiting us." She moved to the door without another glance at Briar Rose.

"Stay a little," the girl whispered to her father. "Please . . ."

"I'll be along presently," he said to Acacia. "Wait for me in the hall."

"Really, John, this is most unmannerly—"

Briar Rose tried again. "Father—"

Lord John looked about in confusion, seemingly pulled in two different directions.

"Are you coming, John?" Acacia prodded.

He heaved a tired sigh. "In a moment, my dear."

Defeated, Acacia left, slamming the door behind her. At Briar Rose's nod, Janet withdrew.

Lord John looked so old, so haggard. Briar Rose didn't know how to soften the blow, so she said simply, "Acacia means me ill."

"Nonsense, darling girl. 'Tis only her manner. She has a sharp tongue and is quick to find fault."

" 'Tis more than that, my lord. She would like to have me dead and gone so that she may have Briarwood for her own baby daughter."

The lines around his mouth deepened. "That's a dark accusation for you to make against my wife."

"I make it after much consideration, my lord. 'Tis no

happy thing to learn that my own stepmother would do me harm."

Lord John's graying brows drew together. "Go on," he prompted, forcing himself to listen to his daughter, who wasn't given to making idle accusations.

Briar Rose wished she could protect her father. He was a stranger to evil, innocent as a child. "Your lady loves Briarwood well. She'd not take kindly to giving her place here to me or to moving to Padwick."

"Aye, that's true enough. My Acacia is proud and likes comfort."

"She knows that when I wed, I'll come into full ownership of this place. And I shall marry soon unless Acacia finds a way to stop me. My lord, I think she means to do away with me."

"How can that be?" Lord John inquired.

"The fire two nights past was no accident," Briar Rose said, wishing fervently that it had been. " 'Twas started by a swatch of straw stuffed up into the chimney. Peter found it."

"That would account for all the smoke," Lord John conceded.

"I would have smothered had I not awakened. Then last night Corynne brought me a draught from Acacia. That was what made me ill. Had I not spilled it back out soon after imbibing it, it would have killed me."

"Are you saying, Briar Rose, that the draught was poisoned?"

"Yea, my lord."

Briar Rose saw the bleak acceptance on her father's face. She squeezed his hand. "My lord, I feared to tell you this, but I feared even more what would happen did I not tell you. I am a coward—"

"No, you did right to say this." Lord John exhaled heavily. "Other men are in the habit of punishing their wives, yet I have never raised a hand to a woman. Now I'm afraid I must. I shall lock Acacia in the west tower and send a priest to instruct her in her penance."

"You cannot," Briar Rose objected. "We have no evidence save my word, and Acacia can easily deny it. Already I gather she has made allies of Father Sabius and Friar George."

Lord John shook his head. "Briar Rose, if she has done this monstrous thing, then I must deal with her severely."

"What would it serve, my lord?" She drew her knees up and hugged them to her chest. "Let the matter go. If you confront Acacia, it will only stir up gossip among our guests. I won't have people whispering of strife at Briarwood. Acacia is artful enough to make you and me look like fools."

Lord John nodded reluctantly. "Practical girl, you're right of course. Very well then, I shall protect you until you are safely married. Lord Alain de Wannet let it be known last night that he is interested in negotiating a match—"

"No!" Briar Rose cried, cringing at the thought of the wily knight with his pointy beard and wet red mouth. And then there were the whispers about the fate of his first wife . . .

"I won't even consider it, my lord." Color flooded to her cheeks. "I've found the man I want to marry."

"What would your dear mother say," Lord John chuckled, "did she know you've taken it upon yourself to make a match?"

"It wouldn't surprise her at all. I am descended from Isobel d'Evreux, who proved a woman is every bit as worthy as a man."

Her father laughed aloud. "If I think you've chosen

wisely," he said, "it will spare me a lot of looking. Who is the man you've decided to favor?"

Briar Rose hesitated for only a moment. "Lord Gareth Hawke, baron of Masterson."

The smile faded from Lord John's face. *Hawke* . . . He cleared his throat. "You couldn't have chosen a man of poorer repute, daughter. Not only does Hawke lack wealth, he is also devoid of all honor, and has been under that ban for nearly two years."

"I know that, my lord. I know all, yet I love him still. I would have him in spite of everything."

"Love! How can you say you love a man when you hardly know him?"

Briar Rose's eyes grew softly pensive and a smile shaped her lips. "I knew the moment I saw him. It was as if something had reached out and called me to him. I felt it in my heart. I know it as surely as I know the sun will rise tomorrow."

"And what does Hawke say to this?"

"I've told him nothing of my feelings." She swallowed hard. "He didn't seem as taken with me as I was with him, but he will love me one day, I swear it."

Lord John shook his head.

"No doubt the man would dearly love to get Briarwood in his clutches," he remarked darkly. "You mustn't let him, my girl. He would sap its wealth and turn it into a godless cesspond."

"I think not. Lord Gareth has but fallen on hard times, which I'm certain will pass."

"Not so long as he is under the ban. Tell me, Briar Rose, would you be able to live without services? No vespers or compline, no Mass celebrated, the holy days ignored, the belfries forever silent? Would you bring that on your own people?"

Briar Rose thought of the hardworking villagers who

lived their lives in the shadow of Briarwood's church, measuring their days by the Mass, doing all they did for the glory of God.

Then she considered Lord Gareth, his thick fair hair and flinty gray eyes, the lips that had recently taken possession of hers, even as the man had claimed her very heart.

"If my husband is under the ban, then so shall I be," she told her father obstinately.

"You'd not even be wed in the Church!"

"You could get a special dispensation from the bishop. He does rely heavily on your generosity, my lord."

"I simply refuse to give my consent," Lord John said resolutely. It was the first time he'd denied his daughter anything. He couldn't help softening when a pair of shining tears sprang to her eyes. "Ah, Briar Rose, you do tug at my heart. Very well then, we shall compromise. You may marry the man when his name is cleared, but not before."

Briar Rose started to object, something inside her straining with impatience, but she held it back. She owed a great deal to the people of Briarwood.

"I shall wait and wed no other, no matter how long it takes," she vowed, forgetting her previous impatience to be married. As a draught of finest welkyn ale destroys one's taste for plain beer, Gareth had spoiled all other men for her. She dashed the tears from her cheeks and began to dream of the day the ban would be lifted and Lord Gareth Hawke would be hers. It never occurred to her that he would want otherwise; how could he not want her when she loved him so desperately, with all the fullness of her heart? It was unthinkable that he'd not reciprocate her feelings.

* * *

For the next few days Lord John kept a watchful eye on his wife. Where before he had admired Acacia's stern command of the household, he now saw her actions as overly acquisitive, even presumptuous.

One day he saw her cuff a servant and rebuke him for a minor blunder, and realized that perhaps, indeed, the green-eyed vixen was capable of harming Briar Rose. Acacia wanted Briarwood badly.

Behind the drapes of their massive bedstead one night Lord John said, "Padwick is not so prosperous or modern, yet it is the home of my fathers and I love it well. 'Twould be best to remove ourselves there when Briar Rose marries."

"Nonsense, John," Acacia snapped, her voice a hiss in the dark. "The girl is disagreeable and unlovely; who would marry her?"

"If you believe that, then why do you feel so threatened by the lass?"

Acacia laughed harshly. "I? Threatened by your daughter? Come now, John, where did you get that idea?"

He moved the drapes aside to stare at her keenly, and something in his gaze caused her to shiver. "It occurred to me when I realized that you attempted to take her life. Don't look so surprised, my lady. The fire was deliberate; there was straw stopping up the chimney. And Briar Rose was given poison by your maid, Corynne."

Acacia composed herself in the face of her husband's accusations. Damn the girl. John had been so easy and compliant before she'd returned. She managed to look offended. "The girl is trying to turn you against me, John. But I am your wife, not some peasant who's poached a deer. I'll not allow you to mistreat me."

"I daresay you will not. But one more 'accident,' Acacia, will not be tolerated."

She resisted the urge to sigh with relief. So John was still a weakling, even after that willful girl tried to influence him. Inwardly she vowed to be much more careful in her future dealings with Briar Rose.

" 'Tis well that young Tesselwaithe died before marrying the chit," she said smugly. "She probably would make a poor wife. Surely you've not found her a match already."

Lord John thought back on his conversation with Briar Rose. The girl had made her own choice and she was stubborn enough to hold to it. The idea of his daughter married to the fierce Gareth Hawke made him cringe. The man was little better than a common outlaw. Yet he was forceful and handsome to look upon and capable of showing great charm. A spirited girl like Briar Rose might easily fancy herself in love with the man.

Finally he answered his wife's query. "I've not yet approved of a match for my daughter, but she looks to wed and was quite taken with Gareth Hawke."

Acacia had a sudden image of the knight in his rough northern garb, hacking his way through the tournament lists. She smiled maliciously into the dark. Hawke was the worst possible choice, but perhaps Briar Rose deserved such a man. Yet it would not do to have the girl wed.

"It mustn't be allowed," she said stridently. "My lord, have you no pride? Would you see your daughter wed to an outlaw?"

"I have forbidden it, so you can relax for the time being, Acacia. But if Hawke is pardoned, I'll change my mind."

Acacia swallowed, stifling an objection. The chit had

no right! She was spoiled and willful and would bring the estate to ruin. Clenching her fists, Acacia lay silent until she heard her husband's breathing even out. It was time someone shattered Briar Rose's illusions about Gareth Hawke. Acacia would take great pleasure in doing so.

Moving with feline stealth, she slipped from the bed and wrapped her lithe form in a cambric robe. Her bare feet made no sound as she padded from the chamber.

A sliver of light issued from Briar Rose's chamber. Acacia entered without knocking.

If Briar Rose was surprised by this late-night visit, she gave no sign of it. She simply turned and fixed a cool, violet-eyed stare on her stepmother.

With only a hint of deference, she inclined her head. "Good evening, lady."

Acacia would have preferred that the girl quail before her, but that was not to be. Here was one person at Briarwood who did not fear her. Well then, she'd humble her husband's daughter soon enough. Her lips thinned into a half smile of greeting.

"Lord John tells me you look to wed."

"I do, my lady."

"So it's true. You yearn to steal Briarwood from us."

"I do not steal what is rightfully mine, madam."

"And who, indeed, would wed a disagreeable chit such as you?" Acacia asked. "You'd best get used to the idea that your hopes died with young Hugh."

Forgetting discretion, Briar Rose shot back, "Not so, madam. I shall marry Lord Gareth Hawke—"

Acacia's harsh laughter interrupted her. " 'Tis a fine choice you've made, girl. An outlaw, a common mercenary—oh, it is too much!"

Briar Rose pursed her lips and turned away from her stepmother's taunts.

Acacia's fingers felt like talons as they bit into the girl's shoulders. "You shall never marry Hawke. Your father will not allow it. Now, do be reasonable and give me the ring. 'Tis all I need to make my place here secure. The people need that, you know. They need to feel a certain continuity. Already they've grown to love me. All they know of you is that you're a spoiled child, determined to send the whole manor into ruin. Here, give it over."

Briar Rose's fist clenched with a will of its own. She covered the golden crest ring with her other hand and wrenched away from her stepmother's grip. "You'll never have it," she said fiercely, her eyes flashing dark and dangerous in the lamplight. "The only way you'll get this ring is by cutting it off my finger when I'm dead. And that, my lady, will not happen. Now, if you do not leave me now, I shall scream for my father."

Acacia saw no problem in that. Her husband was as pliant as potting clay in her hands. It was the girl herself, this ebony-haired vixen with her witch-dark eyes, who frightened her.

Despite Acacia's animosity, Briar Rose was glad to be home. It was a soft summer day with autumn's hint in the breeze that swept down the fells from the north.

She found her father in the garden by the dovecote, sitting on a stone bench before a backdrop of climbing roses. The birds cooed with their soft, liquid voices. Bees droned with a steady hum, adding movement to the riot of color the late summer flowers created.

Briar Rose kissed her father and sat with him. She thought he seemed worried and melancholy.

He took her face and cradled it between his hands, studying the violet depths of her eyes. "Is there anything

I adore above you, my daughter?" he asked, his voice quavering like that of an old man.

"There is Acacia, and the infant, Bettina."

"They are mine, 'tis true. Yet you are of me and your fair mother, and that is something I can never forget."

Her heart filled. "Father, I love you."

"And I you, sweetest. That is why it pains me so to send you away."

Briar Rose pulled back, her eyes wide and incredulous. "Send me away? But I've only just returned from Wexler."

"It's not safe for you here. Acacia is jealous and would do you harm. You'll be going to a secret place in the north where she will never find you."

"My lord, no! Briarwood is my home; I belong here. Why do you not take Acacia off to Padwick?"

"Alas, I cannot leave this keep until you have a husband."

Briar Rose clenched her fists in frustration. If she wanted Briarwood right away, she would have to accept Wannet or some grizzled old baron or earl, and if she waited for Lord Gareth Hawke, that wait would be spent in some barren northern place. She was silent and thoughtful as she reasoned out the dilemma. The second choice was preferable, she decided at last, for the first meant a lifetime of unhappiness instead of mere months.

"Where is this place you would send me, my lord?"

" 'Tis the convent of St. Agatha, near Ninebanks. Janet has a sister there."

"A nunnery!" Briar Rose had a swift image of dark cloisters, interminable Masses and penances, and mysterious, silent nuns.

"You might profit from staying there. Naturally you would be instructed in the faith and in housewifery as well." Lord John stroked his daughter's silky hair and added teasingly, "Perhaps, too, the nuns may even do something about your sharp tongue and impulsive behavior."

"My lord, I do try—"

"I know, Briar Rose. I say that in jest; I would not have you other than you are."

Briar Rose embraced him, now resigned to her temporary fate.

A high moon lit the inside of the keep, slanting in through the narrow windows. Briar Rose and Janet left the living galleries via the great staircase, moving like wraiths on silent feet. In their hands they held their shoes and the bundles of belongings they would take with them.

In the stables Lord John waited with Sir Simeon, captain of the Briarwood knights, who was to accompany the lady and her tiring woman. There was no one else to see them off and no one had been told of their leaving.

Smiling bravely through a sheen of tears, Briar Rose bade her father farewell and let him help her into the seat of her dainty gray palfrey mare.

"Are you sure, Briar Rose, that you want to wait for him?" her father asked.

"Very sure, my lord."

"But it could be months, years—"

"I know. But I love him, Father."

The tiny party left through the east gate, two good palfreys and a sturdy jennet, moving with haste through the shadowy bastions and towers of the castle. They were soon on a barely trodden country path where elm trees loomed up over them with dark, armlike branches arching over the road.

" 'Tis a place where ghosties hide," Janet whispered. "And the blinking fireflies be not insects, but the souls of dead children who have not been baptized."

"Hush now, woman," Simeon hissed, shaking a meaty fist in Janet's direction. "What good does it to fill our lady's head with such nonsense?"

The tiring woman settled into disgruntled silence. Briar Rose smiled beneath the hood of her mantle. She knew what an effort it was for Janet to hold her tongue. They traveled through a fragrant forest, dark and misty and alive with night sounds. They journeyed long into the next day, not stopping until their mounts grew stubborn.

They'd gone four days to the north when Briar Rose noticed that the landscape had changed. The green forests with their wildflower floors were behind them. This new country was a place of worn hills and craggy stands of rock. Gray-brown gritstone clung to the northern fells, which were creased by watered corries. A lone kestrel hung in the cool rushing air, its wings and tail outstretched. The sun shone less brightly, and the wind seemed to blow stronger from the north.

At dusk Simeon announced that they must find shelter for the night. In the distance they saw a walled town dominated by a massive castle. Against a background of worn slopes and aging trees its gray walls rose sheer from a placid moat, which was carpeted with dying water lilies. Swans and dabchicks glided through the waters, swirling the reflection of the towers and machicolated gates. The adjoining town seemed to huddle for safety around the castle.

The travelers approached by way of an angled bridge, passing through the main gate.

" 'Tis best to proceed straight through," a passing carter warned Simeon, curling his gnarled old hands around the handles of his flatbed cart. "Masterson is not a likely place for such as you to tarry."

Her heart thumping, Briar Rose suddenly began to look about. So this was Masterson, the home of Lord Gareth Hawke, her love, the man she'd vowed to marry.

Offal littered the streets and swine and rats ran among the refuse. The passersby all seemed to have a look of drawn resignation and hungry, dull eyes. They passed the church, which at one time must have been lovely. Now its edifice was unwashed and sooty from coal smoke, the bell tower silent. Until now she hadn't realized exactly what a church ban meant. Silently she blessed her father for his wisdom in making her wait for him. Never could she bring this blackness upon her own people.

"Is Lord Hawke at home?" she asked the carter.

"Bah, he's off soldiering somewhere or settling someone's debts to bring us money. Might as well be fighting dragons, for all the good it'll do." Bright eyes, barely visible within their folds of aging flesh, narrowed at her. "Why do you ask, lady? Has the master broken your heart, as he has so many others? Or he used to, rather. Not many women are interested in him now that he's out of favor."

"I . . ." Briar Rose pursed her lips. "Never mind."

They crossed a narrow, malodorous alleyway where three bawds in cheap, colorful raiment called to Simeon.

"What's your pleasure, sir?" they asked. "Will you dally with one of us?"

Briar Rose saw Simeon's big, rough-featured face turn an odd shade of crimson as he kept his eyes trained straight ahead. She realized vaguely that the bawds had offered him something sexual and expected to be paid for it. She frowned her disapproval. This whole place had an air of dishevelment, of lawlessness. Briar Rose's back stiffened. Gareth's people were victims of the bishop of Morley, who had taken their lifeblood from them by placing them under the ban.

As they started to leave the town, she heard shouting from behind and a thundering of hooves. Twisting in the saddle, Briar Rose saw a flash of black and gray, a flying cloak, a blond mane bent low over the neck of a powerful horse.

"Jesu!" she breathed, awestruck by the sight of Gareth Hawke.

Simeon mistook her exclamation for fear. "Come, my lady, we must try to outride him."

"We're not moving," she said obstinately. "Lord Hawke has returned and I wish to speak with him."

While Simeon frowned, Janet prayed and wrung her hands. Only Briar Rose waited placidly, her heart quickening as Lord Gareth approached, followed by his squire and another man who had a dark, sharp-featured face and rode like an acrobat.

Gareth knew immediately that the trio waiting in front of the northern gate was not of Masterson. The mounts were too glossy and well-fed and the knight's tunic bore foreign colors: rose and violet crossed by silver. Frowning, Gareth wondered where he'd seen the colors before.

And then it came to him. Briarwood. He motioned to his companions and slowed his horse to a walk. The woman tossed back the hood of her mantle, revealing a glossy raven mane.

Damn! Gareth thought. What the devil is the girl doing here? He set his jaw. He'd been haunted by her for days as he and his squire and agent rode the shires.

He hadn't been able to shake the image of Briar Rose, staring at him in admiration, offering her felicitations after the tournament, causing his body to ache for her. Gareth had fought the haunting images, knowing that it was foolish to dream of possessing her.

Yet here she was, sitting her palfrey proudly, watching him with those wide, blue-violet eyes. If he'd been on foot, the look she gave him would have made his knees buckle.

At last he reached her. He fixed a mocking grin on his face and bowed. "My lady."

She smiled sweetly. "Lord Hawke. I was disappointed to hear you weren't at home. What a happy coincidence that you've arrived."

His brow darkened. "What the hell are you doing here? This is no place for you."

The knight put up a hand. "We're only passing through, my lord. We'll be on our way—"

"No," Briar Rose said quickly. "There's not much light left. Perhaps, Lord Gareth, you would offer us the comfort of your keep for the night."

He sent her a cynical look. "If it's comfort you're after, you've come to the wrong place. But I can feed you and your mounts and perhaps find a pallet somewhere that doesn't reek too offensively."

"We're well-used to hard travel, my lord."

He looked at her for a long moment. Then, with a jerk of his head, he led them to the keep.

Briar Rose sat in a small cell-like chamber above the great hall, having eaten her fill of a plain but hearty meal. Janet was already snoring on a pallet, but sleep eluded Briar Rose. She'd hardly spoken to Gareth. He had hosted the evening meal and then disappeared with his squire, Paulus, and Giles, the other man he'd ridden in with. Apparently he had no interest in seeing Briar Rose.

She pursed her lips. Perhaps he didn't want to offend her, and so kept his distance.

"We'll see about that, my lord," she murmured, shrugging into her mantle. She left the chamber and went down to the hall. A servant told her where to find the master. She went out to the bailey and mounted to the sentry walk, which ran along the wall.

The waning moon was a sliver in a murky sky and at first Briar Rose saw nothing, but soon she made out a dark shape some yards away. Her feet carried her to his side. He was leaning on the wall, his elbows resting atop it, staring out across the moat and beyond, to the hilly reaches of his estate. There was a decided droop in his shoulders as if a heavy burden were upon him. And yet his profile looked so sharp, so noble, that Briar Rose couldn't imagine anything defeating him.

Somewhere, she found her voice. "Lord Gareth . . ."

He swung about to face her, his face unreadable.

"I—I wanted to see you before we leave at dawn."

He nodded. "I couldn't get a word out of your man Simeon. Where are you going?"

She didn't hesitate. "To the convent of St. Agatha's, beyond Ninebanks. I'm to stay there until—until—" Briar Rose swallowed, unable to continue. It was one thing to dream of making him her husband, but to actually speak to him of it was much more difficult.

"Until what?" he prompted.

"Until I marry," she finished, not daring to add that it was he she wanted.

"That shouldn't take long, my lady. You're young

and quite maddeningly beautiful, and well-endowed by Briarwood."

"I'm very discriminating, my lord, in considering a husband."

He chuckled. "More discriminating, I hope, than you've been in seeking my company."

Briar Rose planted her hands at her hips. "Why do you constantly speak ill of yourself, my lord? Can you not simply accept the fact that I want to be with you?" She blushed at her own words.

Gareth frowned. "I speak ill of myself because there is nothing good to be said of Gareth Hawke, not anymore. I live the life of an outlaw. In the past two years I've done things that doubtless made my ancestors of Masterson writhe with shame in their graves."

"Wh-what sort of things?"

He grinned darkly. The scarred eye slanted down at her. "You're a bright lass. Surely you can imagine what a man might do in desperation."

"Murder?"

"I've killed before."

Briar Rose swallowed hard. "Thievery?"

"Most certainly."

"Rape?"

He grinned broadly. "Now that, my girl, is a crime I've not been accused of." In one swift movement, he pulled her against him. "Yet."

Briar Rose gasped. Although the now-familiar scent and feel of him filled her with giddy sensations, she was alarmed. He'd admitted to the most heinous of crimes, and was insinuating that he'd not be averse to rape.

"Gareth—"

He kissed her deeply, roughly, his hands roving up and down the length of her. Briar Rose felt both fear and desire warring within her. She loved the feel of his arms around her; she knew she wanted him as a woman wants a man. But not like this, not without his commitment . . . Yet the feelings he aroused in her were too strong to be denied. When his tongue slid between her lips, she opened them. His tongue darted into the secret recesses of her mouth, tasting, filling her with a need she barely understood.

But as he had before, Gareth ended the kiss and set her aside. She looked at him in confusion.

He smiled, almost kindly. "Not even a hardened criminal could defile a maid like you," he said gruffly. "Go on with you, little Briar Rose."

She found herself longing for the warmth of his embrace. "What's the matter, Gareth? Don't you like being with me?"

Anger flared in his eyes. "To be honest, no, sweeting. I don't like how I feel when I'm with you. I don't like the things you say to me. You make me think too hard, on things I'd rather forget."

Things he'd rather forget . . . Briar Rose swallowed a hard lump in her throat. "Is there someone else, Gareth? Is that it?"

"By the rood, Briar Rose, if I were pining for a woman, would I be moved to kiss you every time we meet?"

"Then what?"

"You remind me of all that I lack, if you must know. Decency, piety, wealth—Jesu, 'tis like dangling a ripe fruit before a starving man."

He took her by the shoulders, gently this time, and propelled her to the stone steps. "Go away, little Briar Rose. Go off to your convent, and think no more of me."

* * *

The walled nunnery with its silent, cloistered corridors sat upon a wind-whipped knoll, a day's ride from castle or town. Mute robed nuns glided by, to chapel, to cell, to refectory, their faces hooded by black and brown cauls.

The abbess who received Briar Rose was an irritable woman called Mother Sofalia. She snatched up the letter of introduction and took possession of the sack of gold that Lord John had sent.

She then perused the bit of parchment for a long time, her lips moving silently. She said, "You have been given to us for protection."

"That is so, Mother."

"Your stepmother does not love you well."

"No, Mother." Briar Rose gazed steadily at the woman.

"You've an insolent stare, girl. And a look of wantonness about you."

Janet stepped in then, dipping a little in courtesy. "She's a good girl, Mother; just high-spirited, like many her age. But she's quick to learn, Mother, and sings a pretty note, too. She—"

"Silence!" The abbess thundered the command. "So long as the endowments come regularly from Lord Padwick, the girl shall have a place here. But she'll behave; I'll see to that. Go now, both of you, to your cells and send your man to sleep in the tithe barn."

In the morning Briar Rose and Janet were allowed to visit with Janet's sister, who was called Marguerite.

While the long-estranged siblings talked, Briar Rose looked around the convent. They were in the broad courtyard among rock roses and foxglove and curative herbs. Farther away were the vegetable garden and orchard; Briar Rose had been told she would be working there when she wasn't busy with her prayers or lessons in the scriptorium.

Despite the animated conversation of Janet and Dame Marguerite, the girl's mood plummeted. Life would be so dull here, so colorless without parties and riding and minstrelry at table, without archery and games of chess and hoodman blind. Briar Rose sighed and shifted restlessly.

"This one has an air of melancholy about her," Dame Marguerite observed.

" 'Tis hard, you know, for one born to comfort and ease to have this thrust upon her," Janet explained.

Dame Marguerite took both of Briar Rose's hands in hers and said, "Yet I sense something else in your discontent, girl." Dame Marguerite took Briar Rose's face in her hands.

"You're a beautiful young woman, obviously bright and well-bred. You've led a charmed life, my dear. Things have been easy for you, perhaps too easy."

Briar Rose frowned. "What do you mean, Dame?"

"Just that you mustn't expect things to be so always. It's part of growing up, sweeting. The Lord has put trials in your way to test your strength."

Briar Rose swallowed, a look of pain chasing across her face.

"Don't despair," Marguerite said. "If you surmount your troubles, you'll be the better for it. It's a curious thing, happiness. It means so much more if it is earned."

"Earned, Dame?"

"Indeed. You can't expect it to simply fall into your lap. Before anything can be given to you, you must give something of yourself."

"I don't understand."

"You will. Janet tells me you're in love with a man, a

knight. But what have you ever given to him? What part of yourself have you risked for his sake?"

"I . . ." These were hard, searching questions. "Nothing," Briar Rose finished weakly. "But what can I do? What have I to give?"

"You'll have to discover that for yourself, sweeting. It's not enough to simply love someone and expect your happiness to come from that alone. Love is a powerful thing, but it's not the only thing. There is sharing, sacrifice, self-denial. It can be painful, Briar Rose, but if you're strong, you'll find it's worth it in the end."

Briar Rose lay that night and pondered Dame Marguerite's words. She knew better than to expect some clear sign from above. The answers would come subtly, through some back door of her mind. But she did see the merit in the nun's advice. Perhaps it was her help she must give to Gareth. Yes, maybe that was it. She would help him regain something he'd lost—his honor—and he in turn would help her get what was hers . . . Briarwood, her home.

The wind blew down from the northern fells, cold and disquieting. She was too tired to plan, to reason it all out. But she knew she'd have plenty of time here at St. Agatha's to reflect on it.

3

Curfew had been sounded in the city of York and the cover fires flickered against a sky of deep twilight blue. Shadows chased over the city's walls, darkening the bars of the great imposing gates that protected the town.

David Feversham drew the hangings across the window of his small office in the Shambles district, lit a tallow candle with a twig from the tiny fire, and turned back to his guest.

His dark, somewhat exotic features were drawn into an expression of profound worry. On his chest Feversham wore the circular yellow patch that marked him as a Jew. This weighed heavily on him as he said, "Think you, Lord Gareth, that the baron of Stepton might be induced to repay me? Mind you, I'd not be so impatient were it not for my family. The baby is grievous ill and the rest haven't been able to sleep for hunger."

"How much does Stepton owe you?"

Feversham toyed with the laces of his tunic and lowered his eyes. "Nearly a hundred pounds. It's all here in this promissory note. I thought it a safe loan." The solicitor shrugged his narrow shoulders. "But you know how it goes with one of my faith. People are willing to borrow from us yet not all of them feel obliged to pay us back."

Gareth felt a strange sort of kinship with the nervous little Jew. They were both outcasts; both wanted nothing beyond simple justice and some means of getting by in the world. And each man, it seemed, was possessed of a deep, abiding faith which no one understood or respected.

The knight, who was not able to stand his full stature in the timber-framed office, settled back on his stool and said, "You've offered me a goodly sum to persuade Stepton to pay you."

"It's worth that much to me." The banker pushed a leather purse across the table toward Gareth. "This is all I can spare for now, my lord. But I've made a promissory note to pay you in full once Stepton has honored our agreement."

Gareth made no move to take the purse. He merely folded his arms across his chest and said, "I shall not accept any payment now, sir. If I fail at this task, I do not deserve it; if I succeed, then I'll take the full amount on delivery."

Gareth left the solicitor's office and made directly for Stepton, which was on the northern edge of York.

The house was vast, its walls stretching several hundred yards down the lane, and it sat solidly on an oak-shaded hill. As he rode closer on his palfrey Gareth's anger rose, for he didn't see the signs of poverty and decay he'd expected, a condition which would have excused the baron's failure to pay his creditor.

The walls were freshly whitewashed, the grounds clipped and pruned. The gateman Gareth approached had an ample belly and a look of lazy contentment. Recognizing the newcomer as a knight, the sentry granted him passage to the courtyard.

Rather than giving his mount over to a lad for stabling, Gareth tethered the animal back at the gate, where his squire waited in the shadows. If this Stepton proved troublesome, he'd need to leave in a hurry. He went to the hall to await the baron. The long room was richly appointed with hangings and tapestries, pikes crossed above the dais, a service of heavy silver on the sideboard. A servant came with a mug of hot spiced wine, which Gareth refused. He was not here to trade social pleasantries with his host.

At last the baron appeared, wrapped in a mantle of finest velvet, and the two men stared for a moment while recognition dawned.

"Lord Gareth," the host said at last, inclining his head. His dark eyes grew cold with anger. Gareth guessed he was remembering his humiliation on the field at Briarwood.

"Lord Alain. I didn't know Stepton was yours."

Alain made an expansive gesture with his arm. "Stepton; Wannet, where I was born; Eagleton in the south—they are all mine."

"You've more wealth than I thought."

"It's not seemly to speak of such things."

Gareth narrowed his keen gray eyes and said, "It pleases me to see that you prosper."

Alain smiled indulgently. "You will, of course, stay the night, Gareth."

"I'm on an errand of business. There's no need for you to play host to me. I'm here to collect the sum you owe the solicitor David Feversham."

Alain looked blank.

"You did have business with him," Gareth prompted.

A little tic leaped at Alain's jawline and he clenched his hands. "My business was with the Jew; 'tis none of your affair."

"That may have been true at one time, but I've accepted the task of collecting the sum." Gareth stretched his legs out and crossed them at the ankles, relaxed and confident in the face of Alain's discomfiture. "I'm sure you can find the required amount in your coffers."

Alain slammed his fist down on the table. "By the saints, Hawke, you'll not have it! Let the heathen lawyer wait!"

Unaffected by his host's anger, Gareth said calmly, "He has waited long enough, Alain."

"I refuse to pay. Especially to a low-living outcast such as yourself. Doing a Jew's business is filthy work, Gareth. I thought you had more honor than that."

Gareth shrugged. "You're hardly one to speak of honor, my lord. You managed to put it about that Celestine took her own life because she was unstable of mind, while we both know full well that she was quite healthy."

"I have no fear of your accusations, Hawke."

Gareth fought an overwhelming impulse to drive his fist into Alain's smirking face. Alain was right. People would never believe the word of a disgraced outlaw over that of an honored knight. He closed the part of his mind that carried the memory of Celestine. "If you'll just get the money, my lord, I'll be on my way."

"A Jew's lackey," Alain snarled. "You've stooped quite low, my friend."

Gareth schooled himself to ignore the jibe. He had expected resistance. Moving slowly, he rose and rounded the table until he stood behind Alain. "Let's go, my lord, to your counting chamber."

Tiny hairs on the back of Alain's neck rose at the sound of the command. He opened his mouth to call for a guard, but before he could speak, Gareth's arm had snaked out and sealed off his windpipe. He disliked using force in his endeavors, but Wannet was proving difficult.

"What would they say at court, Alain, should they learn you don't honor your debts?"

Wannet's face flushed deep red, both from Gareth's choking grasp and from the fear that his dishonesty would bring him disfavor with the royal family. He struggled briefly in the unyielding hold and then went limp, opening his hands in a mute gesture of capitulation.

Gareth didn't fail to notice his malevolent gaze, however, and he released his captive slowly, ever watchful of a surprise move.

Gareth followed him out of the hall, keeping a short, pointed dagger pressed against Alain's back. The baron of Stepton held his tongue even when they passed some of the household servants.

Gareth nudged him into the counting chamber, where two skinny clerks labored over their ledgers.

"I've private business with this, ah, gentleman," Alain said through gritted teeth.

The clerks scurried away.

"The key to my strongbox is here, on my belt," Alain said.

Gareth stepped clear, never relaxing his watchful attitude. "Go and open the box," he instructed.

With great reluctance and barely suppressed rage, Alain fetched the sum in gold pieces and gave them to Gareth.

"Censure is too light a punishment for you. I'll see you hanged from the gibbet, Hawke."

Gareth flashed a grin at him and was gone.

The night was deceptively quiet. Gareth sat alert against a tree in a forest just north of the Plain of York, studying the sounds and tensing at each tiny rustle or breaking of a twig. His squire, Paulus, slept soundly, having sated himself with the meal and ale provided by a grateful David Feversham, who had vowed unending loyalty to Gareth.

If Wannet's men were to strike, it would be at a time like the present, when darkness cloaked the countryside. Gareth had no doubt that the angry baron had sent someone, probably a band of anonymous ruffians rather than his own men. He only hoped they'd left York in good time to avoid them. He sat in waiting silence until the gray light of dawn appeared and then he awoke Paulus.

Autumn mists shrouded the gentle ripple of hills. Making fair time, squire and knight passed through hamlets and villages, pushing northward and westward for Masterson.

"It's well that we hurry," Paulus remarked. "The harvest will be well under way by now."

Gareth's broad shoulders slumped a little. Last he'd heard, the grain crops hadn't fared well, for it had been a summer alternately plagued by drought and deluge.

They covered as many leagues that day as their mounts would bear, propelled both by what lay ahead of them and by what threatened from behind. On the second night they settled in a wooded coppice alongside the rocky bed of the river Swale and slept by turns in the cold night. It was then that Alain de Wannet's men fell upon them.

On a dusty, starlit road, knight and squire met three strong fighting men. There were no rules governing the swordplay here, only the desperate need to fell or be felled. Gareth fought with the cool skill of a seasoned warrior, warding off blows with his shield and swinging his sword at the dark shapes that came at him.

He unhorsed one of his attackers with a heavy blow and dealt another a cut to the shoulder. Then, together, he and Paulus felled the third.

"Dismount, sir!" the squire cried, full of the heady taste of victory. "We can finish them!"

Gareth frowned at Paulus's shortness of breath. Squinting in the starlight, he noted a spreading patch of darkness on his squire's forearm. He'd not embarrass the young man by pointing it out, but he knew Paulus wasn't fit for fighting.

"You're too impetuous," Gareth said, wheeling his horse westward. "We've no armor and are yet vulnerable. Besides, lad, where's the honor in finishing such an unbalanced fight? Let them return to Stepton with their tails between their legs." He caught the reins of one of the attacker's horses while another one galloped off in a panic.

Paulus scowled at the attackers, who were struggling to their feet. Following his master's lead, he caught the last of the wandering horses and with it in tow, set off at a trot.

Gareth noticed that the blood had soaked Paulus's glove. They'd have to find somewhere to stop. They forded the river Swale and came to a walled town. Gareth alerted the sentry. The gatekeeper examined Gareth's shield.

"Briarwood welcomes you," the keeper said, his

voice gravelly from sleep. "Proceed to the bailey yonder."

Briarwood . . . Gareth set his jaw. He'd never thought to return here, but now that he had, an image that had haunted the secret places of his mind burst into his consciousness.

Briar Rose, the girl with the ruby lips and dewy eyes, had never quite left his memory. Perhaps she was above somewhere, having her long raven locks combed out by her women. But no, only three weeks ago she'd been at Masterson on her way to a nunnery. Gareth refused to admit that he felt anything like disappointment.

The remainder of the night was passed in the hall in Briarwood keep, by a fire that had burned to embers.

Lord John Padwick came to greet Gareth in the morning. Clearly he was not pleased to have this particular knight under his roof.

"I am loath to impose upon you, sir, but there was trouble last night." Gareth nodded at his wounded squire, who was flirting with a serving wench at the foot of the hall. "I'll take my leave today."

"Nonsense," Lady Acacia said briskly, sweeping into the hall with a regal air. "You must tarry here; I insist on it." She flashed Gareth a dazzling smile.

Gareth took her proffered hand and raised it to his lips. "I'm humbled by your kindness, my lady, but I'm not fit company for you. I must go." His bitterness at being shunned by his peers had lessened to resignation.

Acacia drew her mouth into a pout. "Stay, Lord Gareth, or I shall be insulted. One more night is all I ask."

Gareth glanced at Lord John, who shrugged noncommittally. He said, "If it pleases you, my lady."

"It does, thank you. And now I'll go to the kitchens to see that a festive supper is prepared." She fixed a satisfied smiled on her face and left John and Gareth to stare after her and wonder.

"Your pardon," Gareth said to John. "I didn't know how to answer the lady."

"Of course we must do as she says," John answered. "Though her manner makes me wonder. Acacia is always so concerned with appearances . . . It surprises me that she'd have you under her roof."

Lord John's honesty failed to arouse Gareth's anger. It was true that Acacia had social ambitions and it seemed unlikely she would tolerate someone who was under the ban. But women were fickle creatures, Gareth reminded himself. Perhaps this northern estate seemed lonely and remote to the vibrant Acacia and she craved whatever company she could get.

John, too, seemed to be considering his wife's motives. His lined face clouded and he voiced a fear that had been lurking unpleasantly in the back of his mind.

"My wife is much younger than I," he said, his unwavering stare fixed on his guest. "She may be eager to have a handsome swain like yourself about the house."

Gareth replied evenly, "I am no lady's lapdog, my lord. I stay only to do your wife a courtesy, nothing more."

John let out his breath audibly. He believed Gareth and trusted that Acacia would not find a willing playmate in him. With a more comradely air he invited, "Come out to the fields with me. A new well house has just been built on the eastern tract."

Feeling as though he'd just passed some sort of test, Gareth followed his host from the keep.

For supper that evening there was roasted capon and boar's meat, too, for Lord John's huntsmen had been successful the week before. The lady of the castle insisted on sharing her goblet of spiced wine with Gareth and she plied him with rich puddings and cheeses from the buttery. Rare sweetmeats—dates, figs, candied quince—ended the meal, and the small gathering tarried late into the night, listening to music and song from the minstrels' gallery.

Gareth smiled congenially and said, "Briarwood is a fine place, my lord."

Lord John acknowledged the compliment with a nod, but said, "It's not always been so. Before the birth of my daughter, times were hard."

"Briar Rose?" Gareth's eyes kindled. Ever since he'd arrived he'd not been able to help thinking about the girl who had, against all propriety, favored him with her attention and the first kind words he'd heard in nearly two years. Although he'd accepted his loss of status among the peerage, something within him cried out for understanding, and Briar Rose had been the only one to offer him that. He was not so jaded that he hadn't been touched by the instant liking the girl had taken to him.

"Our daughter's name is Bettina and she is still a babe," Acacia said, cutting off her husband's reply. She gave Lord John an angry glance. If he trusted her so little that he would hide Briar Rose from her, then Acacia would not deign to acknowledge the girl's existence. "Tell me, Lord Gareth, have you been to court of late? I should so like to hear some news of our King Edward and his Lady Philippa from the Lowlands."

"I'm no longer welcome at court," Gareth said curtly. "I was barred when the ban was put on me."

Acacia made a clucking sound with her tongue and gave her guest more wine. She noticed that her husband was now deep in conversation with his bailiff and took the opportunity to speak privately with Gareth.

"I've a matter of some importance to discuss with you," she whispered. "I must see you later in my chambers. My maid Corynne will come for you." Acacia's green eyes glittered momentarily, like two hard, bright emeralds. "It is something that may well profit us both," she added, giving Gareth one of the most artificial smiles he'd ever seen. Then she rose from the table, yawned delicately, and bade a general good-night.

"The hour is late," Lord John said after his wife had left, and soon he, too, quit the great hall.

Gareth stayed in the hall where he'd slept the night before. He sat in an alcove by the window, his elbow resting on one knee, wondering about Lady Acacia. What was it he'd seen in her eyes at supper? Not lust, but something akin to that. The look in the green eyes had been avid, almost cruel, and chilling in its penetrating sharpness. He decided at first that it was best to pass the night alone, and leave quietly in the morning. There was tension in this place, and secrecy, and Gareth had no desire to enmesh himself in it. But then, thinking of Lord John, who had been kind to him in spite of his initial disapproval, he hesitated. The man was no match for his scheming wife and might need to know what she was planning. Too, there was the mystery of Briar Rose, who seemed to have been put out of her own house. Although he told himself it wasn't his concern, Gareth longed to know why.

That night a woman with a sputtering candle to light the way led him to the lady's private chamber, which adjoined the room where Lord John slept.

Acacia's slender form was draped in a voluminous white bliaut. She came forth with a gliding step to greet her visitor. Devoid now of tinted artifices, her face looked rather too pale and her unadorned hair hung in limp hanks about her narrow cheeks. Oddly, Gareth felt a bit more sympathetic toward this less opulent Acacia.

"Don't keep me in suspense any longer, my lady," he said. "Tell me what it is you must say in private."

Acacia sat in a leather chair by the hearth, where the firelight and shadows carved deep hollows in her features, and motioned for her visitor to do the same. "It's a matter of extreme delicacy, Lord Gareth."

"You know me for a discreet man."

"Indeed. I also know that Masterson is failing and that you've had to resort to certain mercenary deeds in order to support it."

"You've studied me well, madam."

"Of necessity, Lord Gareth. You see, I have a task for you to perform. If you succeed, it will earn you the sum of two hundred pounds."

The lady's voice never wavered when she named the extraordinary amount. Gareth sat silent and stared at her, his eyes hard as flint. He'd killed for lesser sums.

"You've captured my interest, madam. Pray, tell me more."

Acacia fixed a peculiar expression on her face. A wistful sadness tugged at the corners of her mouth, yet her eyes still glittered with sharpness. She heaved a sigh and said, "Alas, Lord Gareth, this happy home you see is to be no more unless something is done to stop my stepdaughter's treachery."

"I didn't know Lord John's firstborn was a troublesome lass."

The hardness of Acacia's eyes grew more pronounced. "She may be called Briar Rose, but do not bc fooled by such a pretty-sounding name. The girl is wicked and scheming, with a soul as black as the hair on her head. She hates me, my lord, and wishes to turn me out of Briarwood along with my poor baby daughter."

Gareth tried to reconcile his memory of the sweet, wide-eyed beauty he'd met with the picture Acacia painted. He could not. Still, he knew virtually nothing of the girl . . .

"Can your husband not control her?"

"He will not. In his eyes the chit can do no wrong. She is clever; make no mistake. You shall have to remember how she manipulates as you deal with her."

"I beg your pardon, madam, but I've yet to agree to anything at all."

"I believe you to be a man of good heart, Lord Gareth, despite your reputation. When you hear my plight, you shall be honor-bound to help me."

"Do let me judge that for myself, my lady." But even as he spoke, Gareth felt the lure of the two hundred pounds tugging at him. There was little he would not do to secure such a sum. Masterson needed it badly, especially in this year of poor harvest. The people required bread and the knights and yeomen who served him were growing impatient with their lack of pay. They would soon defect to some other keep if Gareth did not act. And Masterson, defenseless, would fall into the clutches of the bishop of Morley.

Acacia smiled privately at her cleverness in naming such a vast amount, which she could easily afford. A small price to pay for securing Briarwood for her daughter. She finished recounting her tale to Lord Gareth, telling him of the unique tradition, begun by Isobel d'Evreux, of passing the estate to a daughter, and of the crest ring which was worn by the true heiress.

"I want that ring for my Bettina," she finished.

"But as the eldest daughter, does not Briar Rose have a right to the estate?"

"There is a precedent for the inheritance to pass to a younger girl. Isobel actually left Briarwood to her second daughter, deeming the first incapable of doing it justice. I ask you, my lord, is it right for such an evil woman to take my home from me—the only home Bettina has ever known?"

"What, then, will become of Briar Rose?"

"Ah, she's a wily one, and some consider her comely. She'll have no trouble finding herself a place in some comfortable keep with a man who will have her."

"I've no doubt of that," Gareth agreed, recalling Briar Rose's beauty, her intriguing aura of innocence mingling with untried sensuality.

Acacia looked irritated. "I don't know what it is about the chit that moves men to poetry and song. She's not at all pretty, with her mass of sin-black hair and strange-colored eyes."

"No, she isn't pretty, Acacia. She's much more than that." Gareth watched the lady's face and found that his suspicions about her were true. She felt threatened by her stepdaughter.

Her eyes flashed and narrowed like a cat's. "Don't tell me you, too, have fallen under her spell, my lord."

Gareth laughed humorlessly. "No need to worry. I've learned my place since being censured."

Acacia sighed with relief. She sensed that it was time for Hawke to show his true colors. Knowing his dire need for money, she expected that greed would win out.

"Let's get to the matter at hand, my lord. I'll give you half the bounty in advance."

Gareth's mouth hardened. Lord, but Masterson needed the money. Still, he held back. He didn't trust Acacia. He raked a hand through his hair.

"Come now, you'd be a fool to turn me down. I know your needs. And what I ask is so simple—"

"Perhaps you'd better tell me just what it is you would have me do."

"Find my stepdaughter, Lord Gareth. It shouldn't be hard for a man of your skill and cunning. All you have to do is bring me the crest ring. You'd not be doing anything wrong. The ring doesn't belong to the girl anyway."

"It sounds like stealing to me, madam."

"I seek only to protect my own daughter."

Gareth pressed his lips together. He found the lady's dramatics distasteful.

Hurriedly Acacia said, "You don't have to harm my stepdaughter, Lord Gareth. Just get me the ring; 'twill be proof enough of ownership."

Gareth shifted uncomfortably in his hearthside chair. Unsettling images of his village and keep, floundering and failing in the north, flitted through his mind. He sat silent for a long time, watching the flames leap in the grate and listening to the crackle of burning logs. Over and over again he said to himself, I've only to get this ring and two hundred pounds will be mine. He thought of the succor the money would bring to his people. It would be an utter relief to see that they trusted him as in times past . . .

Yet he knew he couldn't steal from Briar Rose. Not when the girl's blue-violet eyes haunted him and her rose-red lips smiled at him in his dreams. Not when she alone had faith in him after the fiasco at Morley. He glanced at Acacia, saw the smile etched on her stark face. He knew if he refused her, she'd find someone else to do the deed. Some lowly cutthroat who'd think nothing of killing Briar Rose to earn his reward.

Paradoxically, the girl would be safer if Gareth agreed to become Acacia's lackey. She'd not be harmed, nor would her inheritance be taken from her. Gareth knew Acacia had no inkling of his thoughts; if she had, she'd withdraw her offer. But she was prepared to gamble a great sum on his greed.

Finally Gareth said, "I'll find the girl."

Acacia smiled, catlike. "I'm placing all my trust in you, my lord."

Better me, he thought, than some ruffian who would mistreat Briar Rose.

"My maid will bring you half the amount in gold."

So it was done. For good or ill, Gareth would meet Briar Rose once again. God help the girl, he thought.

Gareth didn't return to his quarters right away. He paced the corridors of the keep, wondering what he'd gotten himself into. There was something unsavory about the whole business, something Acacia was holding back from him.

That feeling was borne out when, in the silence of the sleeping household, he heard a hissing voice which he knew belonged to Acacia. He'd been standing in the screens passage mulling over his thoughts when he heard Acacia summon the maid Corynne.

Stepping back into the shadows, he watched them descend the wide central staircase. He waited a few seconds, then followed the small glow of their candle to Lord John's offices.

"He's agreed to it," Acacia whispered, bringing forth a key.

Corynne nodded eagerly at her mistress and watched her delve into a coffer of gold and silver coins.

"Aye, 'tis as good as mine, if Hawke's reputation is to be credited," Acacia continued. "By Christmastide the girl will be dead and this keep will belong to my Bettina."

Corynne gaped. "Dead, my lady?"

"Of course. Hawke will surely have to kill the chit to get the ring. And that is best for all concerned. I don't want her meddling about here for years to come." Acacia shut the coffer, locked it, and suddenly began to laugh, stifling her mirth with a hand over her mouth.

"My lady?" Corynne questioned, a worried look creasing her narrow brow.

"I was just thinking of Briar Rose's dismay when she discovers that Gareth Hawke, the man she's chosen to marry, is willing to steal from her for a bounty."

Gareth froze, his heart thundering in his ears. At first he thought he hadn't heard correctly, but Acacia's harsh whisper had been clear. He shook his head. So the headstrong girl had set her misguided sights on him. No wonder Lord John had hidden her away. Gareth didn't blame the man. He was hardly fit for a lady like Briar Rose, no matter what she thought she wanted for herself.

He wanted to wash his hands of the whole situation. But it was too late for that now.

He was startled when morning sounds awoke him; he'd not realized he'd been asleep. The noises of men leaving for the fields, of the scullery preparing the day's meals, of servants tackling their myriad duties, echoed through the halls of Briarwood and told Gareth that it was time to approach Lord John.

It pained him to do so. As the two men walked inside the bailey among the late flowers and lazy bees, Lord John was in a pensive mood. Just as Gareth was about to speak there was a tiny mewing sound behind them. It was the nurse, with a small babe swaddled in her arms.

"Pardon, my lord," she said hastily. "I didn't mean for the wee one to disturb you."

John smiled softly, his eyes crinkling about the edges. "I've never found the sounds of children disturbing." He held out his arms and the nurse gave him the baby. Gareth could see the old man's heart fill with love for the child. Lord John seemed like a child himself, innocent despite his years, smiling, guileless.

"Not the beauty my first one was," Padwick remarked, allowing a tiny fist to curl about his finger. "But my Bettina has a charm all her own."

Gareth cleared his throat. "Why isn't Briar Rose in residence here, my lord?"

The smile disappeared. "It is a family matter."

"I'm afraid, my lord, that I know far too much about the situation. Your wife resents the girl greatly."

"I can do nothing about that, Gareth."

"But you must, my lord. Acacia is out to harm Briar Rose."

"Maybe so, but the girl is in hiding."

"She tried to hire me to find her, my lord."

Lord John's attention was snatched from the baby. His face was ashen with shock as he led Gareth away to privacy.

"Last night?"

"Aye, my lord. She promised me a great deal of money in return for bringing her some sort of ring that Briar Rose possesses."

"Ah yes, the crest of Briarwood. And what did you say to my wife?"

"Only that I would find the girl. As I mean to, my lord."

Lord John's brow creased. "So you are thc hunter you're reputed to be. I'd hoped it wasn't true."

"Hear me out, my lord. I must go to your daughter or

Acacia will hire someone else to do it. Someone who may care nothing for the girl's welfare."

Lord John was silent for a long time. The bees droned on and the scent of ripe apples wafted up from the orchards. He sent Gareth a measuring look.

"Are you saying that you do care for Briar Rose?"

"Inasmuch as I would care for any innocent creature who is in danger."

"She fancies herself in love with you. Did you know that?"

"I heard Acacia speak of it to one of her women."

"And what do you intend to do about that?"

"Nothing, my lord. I expect your daughter will soon find that her infatuation is unwise. It would be best if she never saw me again. But I can hardly allow Acacia to send someone after her who will steal from her, perhaps kill her."

Again that pensive silence. And then, "What are your chances of mainpern, Lord Gareth?"

He shrugged. "I know better than to pursue it. Bishop Talwork is an intimate of the King. I'll get no pardon there."

"Yet you believe you deserve one?"

Gareth swallowed a burning lump of anger. "Aye, my lord. Talwork lords over a corrupt diocese and his appetite for more land and power is insatiable. I attacked him only because he provoked me."

"Have you no friends at court to speak on your behalf?"

"No one dares. And I don't blame them. Is it so important to you, my lord?"

"Indeed it is. You see, I'd like you to marry my daughter, Gareth."

He stopped walking, stunned by the request. "Lord John, I'm hardly in a position—"

Padwick spoke as if he hadn't heard. "She's a good lass, stubborn and temperamental, but she should settle nicely. Now, there is one thing you must promise before you wed her."

"My lord, I've not agreed—"

Padwick waved off the protest. "You must keep the marriage a secret so that Briarwood will not be brought under the ban."

Gareth grew impatient. "It's foolishness, I tell you!"

"But it is the only solution. You're right about Acacia. She'll never give up. I want you to protect the girl by marrying her, by keeping her safe until you're mainperned. At that time I'll be proud to have you as my son-in-law."

Gareth clenched his fists. In his own way Lord John was every bit as stubborn as his daughter.

"I'll go to Briar Rose, my lord, and take her to safety. No harm will come to her so long as she is in my care. But I'll not marry her."

"I'll have to settle for that much, then. But don't be surprised if Briar Rose is more demanding than I."

"What about the crest?" Gareth asked, relieved that Padwick had apparently abandoned the ridiculous idea of marriage.

"I think it is best that you take it. Briar Rose will never be safe so long as it is on her finger. Take it, Gareth, and send it to me. Acacia will never be the wiser."

"I doubt the girl will give it up so easily."

Padwick smiled a little. "She'll fight you to the death over it. However, you must take it for her own good. But please, Gareth, do not tell her you're acting on my instructions. She wouldn't understand. She'd think I'd given in to Acacia and hate me for it. I couldn't live with that."

"And what will she think of me, my lord?"

"I wouldn't worry about it. She worships you."

Gareth shook his head. It was all growing so twisted, these matters that should have nothing to do with him. But he felt somehow beholden to Padwick and to the unsuspecting girl who hid in a convent from her stepmother's malice.

"I should be going," he said at last. "My squire will bring you the money your wife gave me."

Lord John shook his head. "Keep it. Consider it a dower gift."

"No, my lord. I don't intend to marry the girl."

"Then keep it as a bounty for the ring."

"I may not be able to get it, my lord. Perhaps you'd better wait until you receive the crest."

Padwick smiled again. "For a man on the brink of ruin, you're damned reluctant to accept money."

"I only take what I earn."

"Very well, here's what you're to do. I've a friend by the name of Wyatt who lives in Stillgarth, a league south of Masterson. I'll instruct him to pay you as soon as you present him with the ring. But remember, my daughter must not know of my part in this."

Gareth nodded, although he was uneasy with the plan.

"What about Acacia, my lord? She's expecting me to bring the crest to her by Christmas."

Lord John squared his shoulders, a noble attempt at hardness that just barely succeeded. "I'll deal with her," he said determinedly. "Now, you must go. I'll prepare a letter for Wyatt in Stillgarth."

"Very well, my lord."

"And Gareth . . ." Padwick's voice quavered a little.

"Yes?"

"Be good to my girl."

Gareth nodded and went to the stables, calling for his squire and horse.

He traveled alone, having sent Paulus on to Masterson. It was swifter that way, and more confidential as well. In the autumn chill that now gripped the northlands, Gareth rode across wide heaths blanketed with drying heather, into the marshy fens and through a forest to Linnet. From there, Lord John had explained, he could reach the nunnery of St. Agatha's in a day.

He took his rest in the village, staying like a common wayfarer at an inn called The Yellow Stag. Ever alert for thieves and cutpurses, he supped on cold shoulder of mutton and coarse bread and slept lightly, dagger in hand.

It seemed he had only just dropped off to sleep when harsh whispers awakened him. Gareth shared the great room with half a dozen other travelers, most of whom were snoring.

"His Excellency desires yet more holdings," one man said in cultured tones. "We may have to take Gilshire."

"Lord, not that place," his companion replied. " 'Tis nigh as strong as Masterson."

The first speaker chuckled. "I think, my dear Griffith, that we'll not find Masterson the mighty keep it once was."

"What? What do you mean?"

"Remember, Hawke has been under the ban. I understand his best knights are deserting him like rats from a sinking ship. The people are no doubt restless; poor, pious folk, waiting for the toll of the church bell that never comes."

"His Excellency will be pleased, if what you report is true."

"We'll bring him even better tidings. By next Eastertide, Masterson will belong to him."

The two whispered and plotted awhile longer as Gareth seethed and felt his insides twist with impotent rage. Talwork's men. So it wasn't enough for the bishop to murder his sister and bring the estate to its knees; Talwork coveted the keep and lands and would have them for his already huge diocese.

No, Gareth vowed to himself, Masterson would not be taken. Not while there was a single breath left in his body.

As if plagued by demons—and indeed he was, for now he knew Talwork's men were closing in—Gareth rode straight to the nunnery of St. Agatha.

The sister at the gate was a surly and snappish thing who turned him away, saying there was no such girl as this Briar Rose at St. Agatha's. She declared the letter he carried from Lord John to be a forgery.

Gareth had expected this. With an air of feigned acceptance he mounted his palfrey and rode back to the stand of linden trees from which he'd first emerged. He tethered his mount and waited a bit, then in stealth crept back to the walled convent.

This time he avoided the gate and made for the rubble-built eastern wall. On the other side he could see the tops of a few apple trees, and it somehow occurred to him that young Briar Rose might go there to sit and while away the crisp, sunny afternoon.

The mortar in the wall was poor and it crumbled as Gareth tried to scale it. He swore and dusted his chafed fingers on his tunic and finally used all the strength in his brawny arms to pull himself to the top of the wall.

As expected, he found himself looking down on a small orchard. Fragrant apples hung on the trees, ripe for harvest. Off to one side was a good-sized garden patch, still green with the tops of turnips and onions and wispy mustard gone to seed.

All was quiet. There was a crude stone bench below, but it was vacant. A ladder stood unattended beneath a tree and only the sound of a bee or two, buzzing daringly late into the harvest season, could be heard.

Gareth sat atop the wall, waiting patiently as a cat. Had it not been for the worries that had been planted the previous night, he might have enjoyed the rest. The sun was so warm as to penetrate the chill, and the smells of ripe apples and fresh-cut straw were pleasant and comforting. Gareth leaned his broad back against a strut. The sun slid low and he heard vespers being sung in the distant chapel.

His wait atop the wall was proving fruitless. He had just decided to return to the sheltered coppice and revisit the convent at nightfall when a certain noise caught his ear.

It was a sound quite incongruous in a nunnery: the patter of running feet. Gareth tried to imagine one of the severe, berobed sisters hurrying along the cobbled cloisters, and could not.

The sound came closer and Gareth stiffened. It was the girl; there was no mistaking her. She was tiny, looking even smaller as he gazed down from his high perch, and she ran like the wind. To quicken her pace she had picked up the front of her skirts to reveal incredibly dainty, slippered feet. Her hair—inky black in the golden light of sunset, flew out behind her, the great long strands escaping from her coif.

"Wicked girl," said a deep, rasping voice. "How dare you try to escape me."

The girl stopped short. She did indeed look both wicked and defiant, her head thrown back proudly and her dark eyes smoldering. She waited, hands on hips, for the nun to approach her, never moving an inch herself.

"Now," said the nun, her face flushed an angry red, "perhaps you can tell me where you thought you were going."

"To the orchard," the girl replied in clipped tones. Gareth was more than a little surprised at the aplomb with which she faced the formidable-looking nun.

"And what, pray, were you intending to do there?"

Briar Rose rolled her eyes impatiently and said, "*Breathe*. After doing penance all morning and working at lessons all afternoon—not to mention carrying wood to the kitchen in between—I suddenly felt the need to sit alone out here and simply breathe the sweetness of God's own air."

The nun responded by boxing the girl's ears. "Wicked, profane girl," she said, punctuating each word with a blow, "you knew I had need of you and your needle tonight."

Briar Rose stood firm. If the beating hurt her, she never flinched. As defiant as ever, she said, "You know I am clumsy and useless with the needle; why do you insist that I work at it night after night?" More quietly she added, "Dame Marguerite never made such demands on me."

"Bah!" The exclamation was spat like an oath. "Marguerite was stupid and useless," the nun continued, "filling your head with superstitious nonsense. 'Tis a good thing, I think, that she was taken by a fistula. She did you ill, girl, whether you know it or not."

The coil of fury that Gareth had seen tensing in the girl suddenly unfurled. Briar Rose shoved the angry nun back with her hands and exploded. "You call me wicked, Dame Michaela, yet I say *you* are the evil one. You're glad that dear Marguerite is dead, for you thought her the favorite of the abbess, and you were always jealous. Well, now she is gone, and Mother Sofalia loves you no better than before, because you're a horrid person and a horrid nun!"

Dame Michaela's face went purple with rage, her eyes bulging so that Gareth, who had watched the exchange in astonishment, feared they might pop out of their sockets. He himself nearly flinched when the nun's clenched hand shot out and caught Briar Rose savagely on the side of the head.

"Filthy chit!" Michaela boomed, her voice shattering the evening stillness. "You and your foul lies—God help you, you shall be doing penance and eating gruel and water in the dark for the rest of your days." The nun snatched a handful of the girl's silky black hair and began yanking her away from the orchard. "First off, my fine lady, I'll have you shorn of this mane you prize so highly. You don't need it now that Marguerite isn't here to fawn over it. And then—"

"No!" Briar Rose screamed, finally afraid now that Michaela's rage had turned into sheer madness. Leaving a good portion of dark strands in the nun's hands, she tore herself away and ran to the orchard.

With an agility that amazed Gareth, she availed herself of the ladder and hoisted herself up into the tree nearest the wall, climbing with the speed and agility of a squirrel. By the time Gareth realized what the girl meant to do, she had already reached the uppermost branches.

Hurriedly, before she gained the wall, Gareth dropped to the ground. He found himself wanting to cheer her on, silently urging her to escape before Dame Michaela's screeching brought someone to detain her.

Briar Rose dropped to the ground beside him with a gentle thud. When she saw him, her face registered only momentary surprise.

Then, Gareth saw with an odd pang, it was as if the sun had reappeared in all its brightness on the horizon. For Briar Rose gave him a smile of such dazzling brilliance that he nearly dropped to his knees before her.

4

"I knew you would come," she said, and pressed her small body against his broad frame, her eyes brimming with gratitude.

Gareth's mind whirled with the wonder of her young beauty. Her welcome reminded him—unpleasantly—that she was expecting a husband, and not a man hired to protect her, however good his intentions were.

There was no time to explain what he was about. Another shriek from Dame Michaela on the other side of the wall seemed to stir the girl out of her almost reverent exploration of the front of his tunic.

"We must away," she said, her eyes wide and fearful. "The last time they caught me outside the walls, I was kept in my cell doing penance for two days."

The thought of anyone caging this wild, beautiful creature filled Gareth with inordinate anger. "Come," he said, taking her hand firmly in his.

They set off at a run, lifting their legs high over the tall autumn grasses, and did not slow until they reached the leaf-hooded coppice where Gareth's mount was tethered.

And there, Gareth resolved, he would explain to the girl. He could feel the heavy gold ring on her hand, nestled so trustingly in his. He knew that, after he had told her the terms of his censure, she'd not want to marry him. As he ran he tried not to think about his task, tried not to notice those wide violet eyes that were so lovely, so discomfitingly adoring . . .

The horse lay dead—slain—in the coppice. Its once beautiful flanks had been cruelly gouged, beaten mercilessly until the flesh resembled a pulpy mass of gore.

Briar Rose stopped, frozen by horror, and gasped. "Oh, Gareth!"

Stunned by this wanton violence, he dropped to his knees beside the carcass. Bayard . . . that had been the palfrey's name. The beast had been valiant and loyal, bearing his master for miles over the years, never faltering. A more noble beast could not be had for any amount of gold.

Briar Rose retreated a few steps, instinctively reluctant to intrude on this scene of pain and loss. The great man knelt over his horse, his height seemingly diminished and the usual proud tilt of his head dipped poignantly. She fought an urge to reach out to him, to offer what little comfort she could. This man was in many ways still a stranger to her and might be offended by the intimacy of such a gesture.

Gareth didn't tarry long over his grieving. He shook his head as if to clear it and straightened.

"Talwork's men," he muttered, thinking aloud.

Briar Rose's eyes widened. "The bishop, you mean?"

He turned and stared at her as if surprised to see her there. "Aye, this mischief was done by men of the cloth.

The horse was murdered with maces. Clerics do not kill by the blade of the sword; the Bible forbids it."

"They may still be about," Briar Rose said. "Gareth, they might harm you . . ."

He shook his head. "Talwork's men are cowards. This is meant as a warning only, a show of power. I came across a few of them in Linnet. I would guess that, now they've found me, they'll be back in stronger numbers."

Briar Rose nodded and stood silent. Until now, Gareth's problems with Morley Diocese hadn't been quite so real. But, looking at the carnage before her, she became suddenly aware of the gravity of the situation. Besides being censured, Gareth was faced with the wrath of a corrupt, vindictive bishop who had all the power of the Church behind him.

She shivered. A cold wind rustled through the leaves, tearing them from their branches and casting them to the ground. Finally Gareth bent and gathered up what little he could salvage from his plundered saddle pack. He spent a few moments covering the fallen horse with large stones and branches to shield it from scavengers. He gave the sad mound a last, lingering look and Briar Rose thought she heard a word or two of prayer from him. Then he trudged away, motioning for Briar Rose to follow.

They crossed a meadow of dried grasses and entered a broad forest, following a barely trodden path, picking their way through brambles and drying thistleweed. When the evening light waned to darkness, Gareth finally halted.

"We'll pass the night here."

Briar Rose listened to the night sounds, the nightingale's song and the lonely cry of a curlew. With the sun had gone the warmth, and she shivered.

Gareth saw her faint shudder. "We cannot have a fire," he apologized. "We've both nuns and friars to hide from."

"Of course, Gareth."

By the light of a waxing moon he studied her face. Her expression was sympathetic and troubled. He saw her moisten her lips and move her hands nervously against her homespun surcoat.

"What shall we do, Gareth?" she asked in a small voice.

"What indeed," he responded, his voice sharp in the evening quiet. "It occurs to me that I've done you no great favor in taking you from St. Agatha's." He lowered himself slowly to the forest floor and leaned against the lichened trunk of a tree.

Briar Rose seated herself beside him, close enough so he could feel the warmth of her body and smell the herbs with which she'd rinsed her hair. "But you have, Gareth," she said. "I was going insane in that place; the nuns were so mean and strict. Only Dame Marguerite made my days bearable. She taught me so much about myself. I was a selfish thing; I still am. But I will learn, Gareth. For you, I'll become a better person."

The more Gareth heard from the girl, the more he questioned the wisdom of his plan. She was so impossibly naive, so maddeningly ignorant of the danger she was in. Perhaps it would have been better to leave her waiting and hoping at the convent and trust that she was safely hidden from Acacia. Yet it would have been simple for anyone who knew what he was about to locate her, only a matter of time before some other hireling was sent.

Briar Rose settled against a tree. Before long she began to chuckle, and then laugh aloud. Though he couldn't see her eyes in the darkness, Gareth knew they were full of sparkling exuberance.

"I was just thinking of Dame Michaela," she said merrily. "What a shrew she was. I was beginning to think I'd spend the rest of my days at St. Agatha's."

"Was it really as bad as that?"

"Indeed, it was," Briar Rose averred. "At first I didn't mind, because of Dame Marguerite. But she died after I'd been there only two weeks. The other nuns were snappish as terriers and used the rod often on me. It seemed the work would never end—sweeping, cleaning, carrying wood and water." She leaned closer to the presence beside her and said fervently, "Oh, Gareth, I'm so glad you came for me."

Guilt was something he rarely felt, but the sincere trust of Briar Rose ate at him and made him wonder if he was growing soft. In response to her misplaced gratitude he patted her small hand.

She ignored his reticence. He had struck her from the first as a silent, undemonstrative type and she rather liked him this way. She said, "So tell me, Gareth Hawke, what prompted you to come. Oh, say that the ban has been lifted!"

"It hasn't. You saw what Talwork's men did. If anything, they are more determined than ever to plague me."

Briar Rose concluded with a thrill of her heart that he'd not been able to stay away for wanting her. "My father must not know we are together, not yet. I promised him we'd not become betrothed until your name is cleared."

Gareth looked away. Lord John had been adamant in not wanting the girl to know he had any part in sending Gareth to protect her. And Gareth had promised to guard his secret. But the girl's reference to a betrothal bothered him. He didn't know what was more cruel, to allow her to romanticize about him or to give her the truth straight away. There was a danger in the latter. Disillusioned, Briar Rose might do something reckless, run away, back into Acacia's clutches. He cleared his throat.

"You are presuming a lot about me. And about your father."

"He'll not know that I've left St. Agatha's. So long as he sends endowments there, the nuns will be loath to tell him I'm missing." She asked again, "What shall we do?"

Gareth spent a long moment in reflection. How would she react, he wondered, to the truth? He could tell her that Acacia had hired him to steal her ring, that her father had intervened, that Gareth had agreed to earn a bounty, that his sole purpose was to protect her from someone even less honorable who would do Acacia's bidding. But there was something about the girl, a sweet vulnerability that made him reluctant to hurt her.

Gareth merely shrugged. "Our first matter is to get out of these parts. Not only are we in danger of being pursued by nuns and friars; the men of Lord Alain de Wannet are also out for my hide."

"Alain—but why?"

"It all started when we were both lads, vying for a woman. Then I bested him at the Briarwood tourney. Later, when I forced him to settle up a debt, he directed all his wrath at me. I've no doubt our paths will cross again."

"I dislike Alain de Wannet," Briar Rose said.

Gareth grinned at her. "Somehow, dear maid, I can't imagine anything resembling dislike to be lodged in your heart."

"I can hate as well as I can love."

He was surprised by the passion in her voice. "So tell me, how has Wannet offended you?"

"He hasn't, actually. In fact, he offered to marry me. But I wouldn't even consider it. I didn't like his presumptuousness, nor his covetousness of Briarwood. I'm prepared to share my estate with a husband, but one who would love and respect it as I do and not make it into some sort of northern fortress, as Alain undoubtedly would. Besides, I . . ." She hesitated, unable to find the words to tell him that she wanted no other man but him.

As if he'd sensed her thoughts, Gareth didn't press for her to continue. He crossed his leg over his knee and idly began spinning one of his spurs.

"You're right about Wannet. He's not for you, or for any decent lady. But neither am I."

She turned and pressed her hands to his chest. Gareth nearly winced at the warm feeling that welled up in him at her touch.

"What will it take, my lord," she inquired, "for me to convince you that you *are* worthy?"

"Go to sleep. We've a bit of a trek ahead of us."

She settled into disgruntled silence. She thought of their predicament, fleeing from nuns and friars and powerful barons, not knowing what lay ahead. Yet here beside Gareth's warm bulk, she felt safe. He was self-assured, seemingly invincible.

"I feel as if nothing ill could befall me so long as I'm with you," she said.

Gareth clenched his jaw and wiped a distracted hand over his face. He'd known from the start that dealing with Briar Rose wouldn't be easy. By her very nature—her gentle compliance, her tacit worship of him—Briar Rose was causing more problems than she could possibly know.

In a voice bursting with hope and certainty she said, "Oh, Gareth, it will be so good once we're wed. There shall be feasts for every holy day, and then some! And before long the children will come—daughters for Briarwood and sons for Masterson. Gareth, we shall be so—"

"Enough!" he interrupted gruffly, unable to bear any more of her misbegotten plans. "You are quite hopelessly naive, Briar Rose. Do you know how foolish your talk sounds? A woman like you shouldn't even think of life with one such as I."

Yet he'd been strangely affected by her girlish dream. How agreeable it would be to wed a lovely, adoring lady and gain the estate as her dowry. He recalled considering marriage another time, before the problems with Morley Diocese, and after his heart had mended from the loss of Celestine. He'd even gone to King Edward and bade His Grace's advice on a suitable match. At that time Masterson was a well-placed, profitable estate, and the King had put forth some effort in finding a match to consolidate his vassals in the north, where the Scots plagued the borders.

There had been meetings with his fast friend, Kenneth Shelby of Tynegate, whose sister had been wed at twelve and widowed at fifteen. Rowena was beautiful and she adored Gareth, but the moment he fell on hard times she had, much to her brother's chagrin, abandoned the betrothal. In sooth, Gareth couldn't blame her.

He smiled ruefully into the dark. Before the ban, King Edward would have smiled on a union of Briarwood and Masterson. Now, though, it was out of the question.

Briar Rose sat in contrite silence. Then she moved closer to him and laid her head against his arm.

His muscles tensed under the pressure of her head. Gareth felt an uncanny urge to gather her close and let her sleep in the crook of his elbow. He resisted the impulse to bring his arms around her small shoulders and didn't relax until her breathing evened out and he knew she was asleep.

In sleep, Gareth defied his own vow to hold the girl at arm's length. Some time during the night he'd drawn her to him, warming her against the chill. He felt a strongly protective inclination when it came to the girl, a feeling he'd not had since his sister, Mary, had been abducted by Talwork's men. He grimaced. Soft as a lamb, he was getting. The sooner he found something to do with the girl and she forgot her unfortunate infatuation with him, the better.

Briar Rose's eyes fluttered open and her first glimpse that morning was of Gareth's face, frowning in deep concern over something. He looked tired, she noted. The scarred eye drooped slightly more than usual, and lines creased his cheeks and jaw, causing him to look older than his years.

Impulsively she put out her small hand and caressed one of his tanned cheeks, letting her fingers trail down the side of his neck to his bulky shoulder. "Good morrow, my love," she said softly, her violet eyes luminous in the misty morning light.

He jerked away as if stung by her gentle touch. With a swift motion that belied the stiffness in his joints, he leaped up and began brushing himself off, making ready to leave.

Briar Rose roused herself. When Gareth offered no assistance, she drew herself up and straightened her crumpled gray surcoat.

"It's time we left," Gareth said, not looking her way. "We've a bit of a walk if we're to make Ninebanks today."

"I'm thirsty," Briar Rose said, miffed by his indifference to her discomfort. "And I've not yet said my morning prayers."

"Come along, then; there's a stream over here."

The water felt shockingly cold at first, yet it enlivened Briar Rose as she splashed it on her face and drank from her cupped hands. Then, kneeling in the dry leaves, she said her prayers.

The Latin words, spoken in her soft, melodious voice, sounded both familiar and alien to Gareth. *"Ave Maria in gratia plena . . ."* The prayer was imprinted on his memory, and he responded to and almost joined in with the girl when she finished the Ave and began to murmur a Pater Noster. Yet it had been so long since he'd prayed or been allowed to attend Mass that he felt himself an outsider, like the heathen he'd been branded. His face was angry when Briar Rose turned to him and announced that she was ready to leave.

Leaves trickled down, singly, on the silent pair as they walked through the forest. Briar Rose kept her eyes fastened to Gareth's broad back and wondered at his low mood. Naturally, he was still feeling the loss of his prized palfrey, but something else seemed to plague him as well. She dared not comment or complain that she was hungry. He didn't seem to be a man who would have sympathy for her plight, which was so insignificant in light of his own woes.

She looked instead to the future, when she would be his wife. Startling herself, she realized she was staring at his muscular thighs and buttocks, which were barely concealed by the short woolen tunic he wore. It gave her to wonder about the more intimate aspects of marriage.

At their very first meeting she had been drawn to him. Something about his looks and demeanor filled her with a longing she didn't understand. She felt a strong urge to touch him, to run her hands over his firm limbs and breathe in the unique, male scent of him. It was a passion Briar Rose had never known before. She knew that when the time came she would be Gareth's willing bedmate.

When they emerged onto a rutted track, Gareth turned to her. Caught in the midst of her amorous thoughts, Briar Rose blushed deeply and looked away.

If Gareth noticed, he ignored it. "We're nigh onto Ninebanks," he announced. "We can get supper and perhaps a bed for the night there."

And then what? Briar Rose wondered. But she merely nodded and joined him on the road.

They walked until the sun began to lower in the west. Ahead, a single spire pierced the sky above the town. Their arrival was barely noticed by the busy townfolk; it was fairing time in Ninebanks.

It was an unlikely place for a fair of such size, but Gareth pointed out that Ninebanks had a good river flowing by it and ample roads for travelers. Even at this late hour a few peasants staggered onto the square in front of the church, loaded down with goods.

Purveyors haggled over fresh and smoked fish, the sharp smells of which assailed Briar Rose's nostrils. Farther down a row of stalls was an array of butcher's meat and booths displaying honey, salt, oils, and wine. Gareth strode past this area, his eyes flicking restlessly over the surging, noisy crowd.

When Briar Rose lingered over the bolts of exquisitely embroidered silk and Arras material, he gave her hand an impatient tug. She went dutifully with him, telling herself that his empty stomach and the discomforts he'd suffered the night before had made his temper short.

A bold tradesman in garish dress approached them. "Good day to you, sir." He had a secretive, hissing voice and a mouthful of misshapen teeth.

"Good day." Gareth spared the tradesman only the merest glance and continued walking.

"Is the lady your wife, then?" the tradesman persisted.

"No."

"Ah then, perhaps you may be willing to give her over to me for a goodly price. You look none too pleased with the wench yourself, sir."

The man's lecherous stare perused Briar Rose hungrily and she shrank away from him.

Gareth's response to the tradesman's suggestion was swift and brutal. His hand snaked out and caught the man by the collar, which he twisted until the fellow was gasping for breath.

"Take yourself and your foul intentions elsewhere, or I'll deprive you of your reason for wanting the girl in the first place."

He relaxed his grip and the tradesman scurried fearfully away into the crowd.

"Thank you, Gareth," Briar Rose said softly putting her mouth to his ear.

He jerked away, stung by her gratitude, and wondered that he'd allowed the man to anger him. He should have treated the lecher's suggestion like a bawdy joke and sent him on his way with a deprecating remark. Yet the very thought of someone wanting Briar Rose in that way infuriated him.

Ashamed of his overly strong reaction, he continued

striding past the vendors until he found a woman with a basket of meat pasties. The woman's hands and person looked none too clean and she refused to part with more than four pasties for Gareth's coin, but Briar Rose was too hungry to care. She wolfed down her portion and followed it with mead from a flask that Gareth had bought while she was eating.

"Delicious," she told him, brushing a crumb from her lips.

Gareth shrugged. "I imagine you're used to much daintier fare."

Her temper rose. He simply didn't understand how much she loved him, that things like the food she ate didn't matter one bit so long as it was food consumed in his company.

"I'm not the spoiled child you make me out to be, Gareth Hawke. I've not acquired a taste for cosseting."

He grinned at her show of spirit. "I daresay you've not, Briar Rose. You travel like a seasoned squire, although you're a much more attractive companion than my Paulus."

In that moment of levity, Gareth's hawk-sharp eyes never rested. He scanned the crowd and Briar Rose saw him stiffen. Her gaze followed his and she saw the cause of his concern. Coming up the row, striding with jangling spurs and offhanded self-assurance, was a trio of knights with the red Wannet eagle emblazoned on their chests.

Wordlessly Gareth pulled the girl into a shadowed alley, where top-heavy buildings leaned out and obscured the sky.

"Are they looking for us?" she whispered.

"For me, at any rate."

The knights swaggered by, joking raucously yet seemingly alert to their surroundings. They stopped to hail another pair of men, and the five stood together, conferring on some matter.

"Who are they, Gareth?"

"Those are the men from Morley. One, I suspect, is called Griffith. I had a slight brush with him some nights back."

Briar Rose moistened her lips. "Gareth, I'm frightened."

Without thinking, he put his arm protectively around her shoulders. "We'll get away from this place as soon as the way is clear."

The knights lingered in the square until the merchants began to roll up the flaps of their stalls and load their wares onto carts. Weary peasants hefted their bundles and left at twilight.

Gareth took Briar Rose by the hand and led her away from Ninebanks, where they wouldn't find haven after all. Soon they were back on the rutted road they'd left only a short while before.

"Where do we go now, Gareth?"

He found himself admiring the girl's staunchness. No complaint, even when she had every reason to grumble, only curiosity about what was to befall her next. As kindly as he could, Gareth answered, "I fear we're to pass another night in the woods."

Gareth awoke and scrambled, cursing, to his feet when he discovered Briar Rose was missing. He must have dropped off to sleep around dawn after a tense, lengthy vigil. Now the sun was high over the trees and the hollowed-out spot where the girl had lain was cold.

With the swift, economic movements of a man accustomed to hasty departures, Gareth gathered up his few belongings. He followed a faintly trodden path, rubbing the sleep from his eyes and scowling at the roughness of his grizzled cheeks. Hearing a rush of water nearby, he veered off to find the source.

There was a deep, eddying stream cutting a path through the elm and linden trees. Gareth hesitated when he saw a figure in the distance, a flash of gray and the blue-black sheen of the sun on Briar Rose's head.

As he watched, Briar Rose set down a small bundle of berries she had been gathering in her coif. Then, to his amazement, the girl shed her clothes, dropping her gray surcoat and undertunic and peeling off her stockings until she was clad only in a thin, knee-length chemise.

No mere girl, but a woman, Gareth realized with an uncomfortable start. Her breasts beneath their filmy covering swung enticingly as she stepped through the river grasses. Her legs were slender and topped by the pretty swell of rounded buttocks. A breeze blew against her and Gareth saw the flatness of her belly and the shadow of the dark hair below it.

Fighting the urge to go to Briar Rose and press that lithe body close to his own, he hung back and watched her test the water with a small bare foot. He heard her gasp at the chill, and then with an effort of will she waded in up to her hips.

Presently, Gareth grew annoyed at himself. What was he doing, shrinking in the shadows as if in mortal fear of this slip of a female? He squared his shoulders and strode from the woods, reaching the water's edge just as Briar Rose was dipping the great length of her hair into the stream.

She jumped when he appeared so suddenly, towering over her with a stone-faced countenance. But she recovered quickly and said with a playful formal curtsy, "Good morrow, my lord."

She exhibited no missish modesty but opened her arms. "Come bathe yourself, Gareth. The water's none too warm." She was as fresh and natural as a wildflower, her face blooming with a wide smile.

He was drawn to her, and to the babbling, crystal water. Suddenly his troubles seemed lighter as he allowed himself the indulgence of a bath. He removed his tunic and unlaced his cloth hose, then took off his chemise. His broad chest, lightly furred with straw-colored hair, bore the scars of many battles, and Briar Rose studied him closely.

A sparkle appeared in her eyes and she grinned. "You've not removed your braies," she told him.

He gave her a mocking frown. "Nor shall I, madam. 'Tis not a fitting sight for a lady's eyes."

She giggled and splashed him. He roared at the shock of cold water and waded in after her. She kicked nimbly away, but he caught and dunked her, squirming and struggling, under the surface.

She resurfaced, gasping, and swam away again, delighted by Gareth's playfulness. Her body tingled with the chill of the water and with something more, an excitement she'd never felt before. Her feelings for Gareth were becoming more obvious day by day. She felt so alive with him, so full of hope, even though they'd been living like fugitives. There was something magical about the moments they spent together.

Slowed by her thoughts, Briar Rose wasn't ready for Gareth's next attack. He surged up from behind and grasped her about the waist.

She twisted around to face him. "You're not playing fair, sir," she complained good-naturedly.

"There are no rules in this kind of game," Gareth said, his voice low and husky and close to her ear.

Briar Rose gasped softly as she felt him press her

against him, one hand straying to her hips. He captured her surprised lips with his, swiftly at first, and then lengthening the moment into a lingering embrace.

At first Briar Rose stiffened, appalled by the sensations that rushed through her. Then an irresistible languor crept over her, drawing her toward Gareth, the gliding hands that tamed her limbs, his seeking mouth and tongue, which slid between her lips. Need, compelling and confusing, coursed through her. She was overwhelmed by her feelings and by the power of Gareth himself.

He must have felt something too, for when he dragged his mouth from hers, his eyes had grown smoky, his voice ragged.

"I believe," he said, "that we'd best quit before one of us loses at this game."

But Briar Rose didn't want to stop. Gareth had awakened something in her that cried out for completion. She reached for him again. Laughing, he dunked her under and swam away.

For a small portion of the morning their plight was forgotten. Gareth couldn't remember the last time he'd felt so free of troubles. Briar Rose's irrepressible sense of fun pervaded him thoroughly; he chased her through the swirling waters and called taunts to her and reveled in the almost musical sound of her laughter.

Briar Rose, too, enjoyed the diversion. Here was another side of Gareth's enigmatic personality. He was the playmate she'd craved since girlhood. Unlike Hugh, who had watched in shrinking disapproval when she used to cavort in the castle ponds at Briarwood, Gareth entered into her gaming like a young boy. Only when she began to shiver uncontrollably and her hands and feet grew waterlogged did Briar Rose beg for mercy. Chuckling, Gareth allowed her to wade ashore with slogging steps and tried hard to tear his eyes from the sight of her body, outlined to frank perfection by the wet chemise.

They relaxed in the drying autumn grasses, clad only in their undergarments, and let the sun warm them. They ate the blackberries Briar Rose had gathered, laughing when the sweet purple juice stained their fingers and lips. She delighted in placing berries at his lips, watching his tongue come up to take them into his mouth. There was something dreadfully sensual about the simple act, and Briar Rose felt herself growing soft and warm somewhere deep inside. Her eyelids drooped.

Gareth groaned aloud. "God's wounds, woman, stop looking at me that way. If you don't, I might give in to the temptation to have you right here and now, in the grass."

She felt a thrill of anticipation. She was unschooled in the arts of love, but somehow she'd made Gareth desire her. Boldly she placed a berry between her lips and put her face down to his.

She transferred the berry to his lips, their mouths brushing together in a moment of shattering sensuality.

With another groan, Gareth pulled her on top of him, no longer able to battle the feelings she evoked in him. The berry burst and spurted juice between them as he crushed his mouth to hers, tasting, hungering. Briar Rose felt light-headed and giddy in his arms, full of delicious sensations. When she felt his hold slacken, disappointment welled up in her.

Determinedly she pressed downward again and licked the juice from his lips, slowly running her tongue over his mouth.

"Sweet Christ," he said, trying to keep his hands from straying to her breasts and thighs.

"What's the matter, Gareth?"

Somewhere he found the will to set her aside, before he did something they'd both end up regretting.

"I wonder," he said mildly, "if I could be wrong about you. I thought you a maid, an innocent, yet you behave like the most practiced courtesan."

Briar Rose sat up. "How dare you say such a thing? You are the first man I've ever been with like this."

"Am I, Briar Rose? Where did you learn to kiss a man like that?"

" 'Twas not something I learned, Gareth. I am discovering how to love you and if you don't believe that, then there's no point in arguing about it."

He swallowed and looked away. She was honest with him. In sooth, he wished it were otherwise, that she wasn't a woman of honor. He lay back on the grass, covering his eyes with his arm.

"I believe you, Briar Rose. But I also think you don't know me well enough to decide that you love me."

"I'll judge that for myself," she said tartly, although now there was no anger in her voice. They lay quietly for a time, enjoying the sun and the fresh smells and the sound of rushing water.

"Are you ready?" Gareth asked at length. "I'd not reckoned on this delay."

"Ah, but I notice you did not object too strongly."

"That I didn't. I confess I had a few days' grime on me. But let's not tarry. We're being pursued, my girl."

Her brow puckered in a small frown. "Is it always this way with you, Gareth? Must you ever be looking over your shoulder?"

"That's how it's been ever since Bishop Talwork began eyeing Masterson. He'll not rest until he gains it."

"Can you not just give it to him?" Briar Rose asked impatiently. "Briarwood is enough for us—"

" 'Tis a matter you do not understand," he snapped. "I am not a man who gives in easily."

Chastened, Briar Rose dressed in silence and followed him through the woods. They made fair time that day, and by evening felt they had put enough distance between themselves and their pursuers to build a fire to warm themselves at night.

With the patience and cunning of a seasoned hunter, Gareth trapped and skinned a fat rabbit and they shared the spitted meat before retiring on a bed of fallen leaves.

While drifting off to sleep, Briar Rose thanked him. He was embarrassed by her gratitude. " 'Twas only that we needed food," he said.

"You are good to me; you will always be, won't you?"

Her question plagued him and he made no response. He merely squeezed her hand, feeling the heavy ring there, and told her to go to sleep.

Briar Rose was not fully awake when she heard an ominous noise at dawn. A twig broke under the foot of an animal with a heavy tread. Shifting her position, she saw that it was a mounted man approaching them. The Wannet eagle on his chest, bright red against a field of azure, stood out like a banner in the drab autumn woods.

The fire had died down, yet the trickle of smoke that climbed from the ashes must have alerted the hunter. Tensing, Briar Rose watched in mute fear as he was joined by two comrades.

Gareth continued to sleep soundly. Odd, for he was such a light sleeper. Briar Rose considered rousing him but knew it would avail nothing. He had only his dagger, no match for the gleaming swords and prickly maces of the other knights. Thinking quickly, she straightened up and covered his sleeping form with her surcoat, thus concealing the black and gray hawk on his tunic.

Gareth awoke and lay motionless when he heard

voices. He stayed relaxed, feigning sleep, and listened closely. His hidden hand closed around the dagger at his belt, and he awaited his chance. Before he could hiss at Briar Rose to run for cover in a nearby ditch, he heard her speak.

She greeted the men in an artfully feigned brogue, imitating one of the novices at St. Agatha's who hailed from the borderlands.

"Good day to ye, my lords," she piped, and in his mind's eye Gareth saw her dip courteously in their direction. What the devil was the girl up to now?

"And who might that one be?" asked a deep, Yorkish voice.

"Bah!" Briar Rose spat insolently on the ground. " 'Tis my ne'er-do-well 'usband, and a rotted drunkard 'e is, my lords. Canna do aught with 'im, leastways not until 'e sleeps off the ale."

The visitors chuckled at the girl. "We're after a great blond one, not unlike that man of yours."

"Ye can take 'im, and with me best wishes, my lords. Bah, I've no use at all for the sot."

"Alas, you'll have to keep him," one of the men said. "We're out for a knight who has a scarred eye and wears the sign of the gray hawk. Perhaps you've seen him."

"Nay, my lords. I've time but for to chase down this lout o' mine. I dinna ken yer hawk."

"We're off, then, and good fortune to you!"

"Bah! And a fat lot o' it I'll be needin'!" Briar Rose called after them as they cantered away.

She watched until the gleaming rumps of their horses disappeared, and then allowed herself to expel a sigh of relief. Then she looked down at Gareth, and knew by the tenseness of his shoulders that he was no longer asleep. Looking closer, she saw that he was shaking from head to toe.

"Gareth, do get up. They've gone."

The shaking did not abate. Laboriously Gareth rolled over, and then Briar Rose saw the reason for his trembling. He laughed aloud now, uproariously and uncontrollably.

Briar Rose frowned again. "I didn't mean for it to be that amusing, Gareth."

Her anger seemed to enliven him further. Laughter rumbled from deep within him, sounding rich and melodious, and at last Briar Rose succumbed too. She knew this was a rare thing for her to witness; Gareth was not a man easily amused and wasn't often given to frivolity.

When he recovered he chuckled, "You did handle them well, Briar Rose."

"It was the best I could do; they were upon us so suddenly."

He cupped her small, squarish chin with a gentle hand. "I do thank you. This day would have gotten off to a much poorer start if I'd had to fend off three knights. You've a quick wit, girl."

Briar Rose blushed. He was always sparing with his praise, but the rarity of his compliments made them more meaningful.

Gareth studied her, her cheeks so prettily pink and her eyes sparkling like a pair of dew-kissed violets. Something tugged at his heart when she met his steady gaze, and the lips she turned up to him looked delicious . . . inviting. With an effort he tore his eyes away.

"How would you like to have a good meal and spend this evening with the roof of a keep over your head?" he asked.

"Oh, Gareth, could we?" Though she hadn't complained, Briar Rose felt stiff and begrimed and weary of running.

"I've a friend—one of few who still tolerates my company—who has a small manor not far from here. Tynegate, it's called, on the river Tyne."

"I should like that very much."

They left their makeshift camp and walked for some time in companionable silence until they came to the river. Following the bank, they made their way to a modest stone keep whose southern wall was adjacent to the river itself.

" 'Tis the home of Sir Kenneth Shelby. We fought together in the border wars," Gareth explained.

The gate was open long before they reached it. A lad scampered to alert the household, and when the visitors entered the great hall, Sir Kenneth was waiting.

Of an age with Gareth, though nowhere near him in size, Kenneth Shelby had a winning smile and dark good looks, with brows slashing upward above velvety brown eyes. He greeted Gareth with familiar warmth and welcomed Briar Rose graciously.

"Gareth has brought many a wayfarer to Tynegate," he said, "though none so fair as you."

Briar Rose felt the color rise in her cheeks. "Thank you, Sir Kenneth."

A young woman appeared. She could only be Kenneth's sister, Briar Rose guessed, for she resembled him closely, being dark-haired and brown-eyed and small of stature. Yet the resemblance ended there. Rowena Shelby was youthful, yet there was a hardness about her pretty features as though she had been disappointed by life too many times. She seemed ill-tempered and impatient; it showed in her fleeting appraisal of Briar Rose and in the snappish order she issued to a waiting damsel.

But the welcome she gave Gareth was warm enough, Briar Rose noticed with a slight, unpleasant twinge. Rowena's rather pinched countenance softened and she greeted Gareth with a kiss and a lingering embrace, laying her cheek against his broad chest. Briar Rose found herself wishing that the banns of her betrothal had been posted so that she could make a formal announcement to Kenneth and his sister.

"So tell me about this lovely thing," Kenneth said to Gareth, indicating Briar Rose. "Another damsel you've rescued from a dire situation?"

Gareth laughed easily, relaxing now that he was in the company of friends. "Hardly. As a matter of fact, Briar Rose was much safer back in a convent called St. Agatha's, some days west of here."

"Safer, perhaps," she added, "but thoroughly miserable."

"The life of a novice did not suit you then?" Rowena asked, arching her delicate brow. Her darting eyes didn't fail to miss the ripeness of the girl's small figure or the fullness of her rosebud mouth. "You don't seem the pious type. You hardly look like one to be pledged to Agatha. Was she not the one who gave her life rather than her virginity?"

Rowena was goading her and Briar Rose knew it. She decided to make light of the taunt and said, "Hardly a worthy cause for martyrdom, I've always thought."

Gareth seemed amused by the exchange. The two women had matching wits and temperaments. Like a pair of cats they appraised one another and finally settled into an attitude of tenuous, mutual tolerance.

Tynegate was small but thoroughly modern, for Kenneth was a seasoned courtier who avidly followed all the trends he learned from other nobles. Many of his improvements were patterned after the work of John Lewyn, the great mason-architect. His fireplaces were new and well-ventilated and the windows of the great hall boasted small pieces of expensive colored glass. The upper part was divided into a number of apartments, a great advancement from the days when the entire household slept together in the hall.

Briar Rose and Gareth were each led to private solars. As Briar Rose stood surveying the heavy draperies of the alcove bed, a pair of servants brought in a good-sized wooden hip bath and filled it with jars of warm, herb-scented water.

Then Kenneth came, bearing a bundle of clothing. He had a clean white lady's chemise and a flowing houppelande dress that was piped with gold braid. There was even a tall, steeple-shaped headdress with a filmy veil.

The clothing was worn and threadbare in places and none so fine as Briar Rose had once had, but it was sumptuous compared to what she'd been made to wear at St. Agatha's.

"You are too kind," she told Kenneth.

"These belonged to Rowena; she hasn't worn them lately." He smiled. "I think you'll find that my sister is a woman of high style. She follows the trends at court rigorously and casts off anything that has fallen from Princess Isabella's favor."

"This is terribly generous of her." Briar Rose began to wonder if her first impression of Rowena might have been wrong.

"Of course," Kenneth said hastily. "Well, I must see to the hall and kitchens. We so seldom have visitors here."

A serving girl bathed Briar Rose, deftly washing her and dipping her hair in a special rosemary solution. She exclaimed over the length and silky texture of it while drying it gently with linen serviettes.

Finally, clean and groomed and gowned, Briar Rose made her way to the great hall. Her appearance caused a small stir among those who were already there. The deep red of the gown enhanced her pale smooth skin and matched the color of her smiling lips.

Kenneth gallantly kissed her hand and led her to the seat on his right. "The dress becomes you," he said.

Briar Rose thanked him. Then she leaned over and said to Rowena, "You are more than kind to lend me this."

Rowena gave her a chilly look. "My brother borrowed the garments without my knowledge."

Briar Rose's face fell. "I'm sorry . . ."

"Never mind. At least Kenneth had the sense to find some castoffs. And the red, I think, suits you better than the somber gray you had on."

"Thank you anyway," Briar Rose said. Then she greeted Gareth. He had stood for her entrance and she'd had a glimpse of clean hose and a padded jupon, which must have belonged to Kenneth, for it was tight about the shoulders and chest.

" 'Tis a finer night than the last few," she remarked.

He smiled politely, his rugged good looks enhanced now that he was clean-shaven and combed. Briar Rose was filled with pride at the sight of him.

One of the butlers stepped forward and, acting as surveyor of ceremonies, bade the newcomers welcome with a song. Though the servitors at Tynegate were few, they knew their etiquette. Tynegate even had musicians of sorts, who played a gay tune on horns and lutes while singing a long ballad.

Briar Rose complimented the lead singer on his rich tenor voice, which vibrated through the hall with liquid beauty. The young man bowed nearly to the floor in recognition of her praise. Then he took a perfect red rose from an urn below the high table, a late summer bloom that had been preserved. Placing it before Briar

Rose, he strummed his lute softly, his adoring eyes never leaving her face.

Look on this rose, O Rose, And looking laugh on me,
And in thy laughter's ring the nightingale shall sing.
Take thou this rose, O Rose,
since love's own flower it is,
And by that rose thy lover captive is.

Her face grew warm. She held the flower to her cheek for a moment before setting it beside her manchet. She looked about, seeing Kenneth's broad grin and Gareth's pensive smile and Rowena's eyes hardening with impatience.

The song dissolved into another one, a merry country tune.

"We try to affect some semblance of civilization even in these northern parts," Kenneth said.

Rowena sniffed. "I shall be glad to get back to Windsor. It is so awfully dull hereabouts."

"There now," said Kenneth, patting her hand, "we've work to do here. 'Tis poor management to be absent overmuch."

"You seem young to be lord of your own keep," Briar Rose remarked. "You do a fine job of it."

Kenneth smiled ruefully. "These days, I do. But before—"

"Never mind that," Gareth interjected. "By the Mass, Kenneth, let the lady compliment you."

Kenneth laughed and gave his friend a look that was admiring, almost loving. "I don't mind letting Briar Rose know that I owe the prosperity of this keep to you." He sipped some wine from the mazer he was sharing and said, "Gareth is poor about accepting praise. Were it not for him and his knights some years back, I would have lost Tynegate to Morley Diocese."

Briar Rose began to see that Bishop Talwork had a monstrous appetite for acquisition. "You do not favor Morley either, then."

"Not at all. They would have overrun this place, but Gareth arrived and our combined forces saved us." Kenneth's face softened. "I'll not forget how he helped me."

"We're all indebted to you for that," Rowena said to Gareth, and squeezed his hand. She gave him a look that brimmed with meaning. "I remember how frightened I was, Gareth, and how sweetly you comforted me through the night after the attack."

Briar Rose felt vaguely put out by the forces that bound these three so closely. Gareth's past life was closed to her; she shared so little with him as yet. But, she vowed silently, all that will soon change. We two will be inseparable, and make our own memories. She gave Gareth a smile, hoping by her expression to communicate this thought to him. He looked quickly away and made a light remark to Rowena.

"It's been a long time," he said with a rakish smile. "How are things at court? Have you broken many hearts lately?"

"Ah, you're a tease," Rowena said, laughing.

"As I remember, you always had a half a dozen swains slavering after you."

"She still does," Kenneth added.

"No doubt you reject them as cruelly as ever," Gareth said. "Come now, who are you holding out for? Do you have some secret liaison with one of the royal cousins?"

Rowena launched into a gossipy tale about Joan, the Fair Maid of Kent, who had captivated the Black Prince.

This talk of court—the feasting, the displays of archery and horsemanship, the many plots and rivalries that went on—caused Briar Rose's heart to sink. She felt gawky and young, impossibly provincial, for she'd never witnessed the pageantry of King Edward's court.

Finally the meal was over and the dancing began. To a tune played by a piper and lutenist, the castle staff at the lower tables whirled and reeled in a peasant jig. With a deep bow Kenneth begged Briar Rose to dance the jota with him. He was an able partner, light of foot and gay. The two made a handsome pair, he with his dark good looks and she flushed and brilliant as she moved through the steps.

Gareth had been about to offer his hand to Rowena out of courtesy. He found himself staring instead at the red rose on the table, and then at Briar Rose herself. She was entrancing in her beauty and artless grace. The flowing houppelande swayed about her figure. Every so often Gareth caught a glimpse of her trim ankle and dainty slippered foot. Her ruby mouth was parted in a becoming smile and her eyes sparkled with amusement. It was a rare comeliness that Briar Rose possessed, all the more appealing because she was unconscious of it.

Kenneth was looking at her in a way that told of kindling desires, and Gareth's jaw clenched at the unpleasant jolt it gave him. Before long this Briar Rose, this girl-woman, would forget her impetuous fascination with him and look to more suitable men—like Kenneth. Gareth knew he would lose her soon. Tynegate was a good place for her to stay until she made an advantageous marriage. It was unlikely that Acacia—or anyone she hired—would find her here, and Lord John would be satisfied with Tynegate's security.

Rowena tugged at his sleeve and gave him a pouting look. She had not failed to notice the intense stare he directed at Briar Rose. He'd never looked at Rowena in that way, with tenderness softening his rugged features and his eyes burning with passion.

"Do let's dance," Rowena insisted, and finally Gareth obliged.

The piper's tune ended and another, slower song was struck up. Without thinking, Gareth bowed his thanks to Rowena and claimed Briar Rose's small hand with his own.

She smiled at him, instantly forgiving him for having ignored her during the meal. She was glad for the musician's pensive, melancholy air, for in this dance the partners strode close together, hands clasped.

Gareth's hand rested in the small of her back, warm and protective. He gazed down at her with eyes that seemed softened by some emotion, his mouth set in a serious line.

His movements were rough yet controlled and Briar Rose matched them effortlessly. The other dancers seemed to fade away until they became a vague blur of color in the background. All that existed for Briar Rose was the music, and Gareth himself. Each time they were close it seemed her passion for him grew stronger. She loved the feel of him beneath her hands, the firm texture of muscle beneath flesh. His scent alone—woods and leather and clean maleness—was enough to drive her to distraction.

She looked up at his craggy Saxon face. It was not youthful despite his age, but wise and rugged and unreadable. Briar Rose wished for a moment that she might penetrate that calm, as she had that one time when they'd bathed in the stream together. But, she reflected with a patience she'd not known she possessed, he was a man with weighty troubles and was not easily given to levity.

When the dance ended, Gareth led her back to the high table. There was an almost regretful look in his eyes when he relinquished her hand. Briar Rose whispered her thanks and sat down to sip a draught of creamy lamb's wool.

Rowena shot her a glowering look, but Briar Rose only smiled. Rowena was shrewd and vain and acquisitive, fearful of having her position usurped by another. Briar Rose was confident that Rowena didn't have serious designs on Gareth, for she appeared to abhor anything that was even faintly improper. Still, she couldn't abide the fact that Gareth might prefer another.

But Rowena was her hostess tonight and Briar Rose chided herself for her unkind thoughts. She gave her a charming smile and said, "The lamb's wool is delicious. I daresay I've never tasted such sweet cider and cream."

Rowena shrugged delicately and said, "We were saving the cider for the Catherning in November, but Kenneth insisted on serving it tonight."

"I see." Briar Rose set aside her mazer and declined a second helping of the froth-topped drink.

Gareth, who had watched the exchange with mild amusement, leaned over and whispered to Kenneth, "Being at court has refined your sister's manners."

"Likewise her claws, I fear," Kenneth answered.

Rowena had turned her attention back to Gareth, in whom she still found a private fascination. No man at court, not even the royal princes and their noble kin, possessed such stunning rough looks or that intriguing, aloof manner. Cloaking her prying words with an artful smile, she asked, "How goes it with you, Gareth? We've talked all evening of our doings, yet you've said nothing of your own."

"Little has changed since we were together last year

at Michaelmas," Gareth admitted. "I am still under the ban."

"Can you do nothing to change things?"

"It appears not. I've sent several missives to the King, but I doubt my requests ever actually reach him. I'm not the one to tell him of the corruption and criminality at Morley. He'll have to hear that from someone impartial whose word he has no reason to doubt."

Kenneth and Rowena sat for a moment in uncomfortable silence. Kenneth tried to explain. "I rarely have audience with His Grace or his advisers. Besides, why would they listen to me?"

Gareth patted his friend's hand. "No need for you to walk the fence for my sake, Kenneth. Be careful what you say. If the wrong word reaches the wrong ears, you yourself may be put out of favor."

Rowena shuddered visibly at the thought of being disgraced. "Have you nothing but melancholy news, Gareth? Come, let's lighten things a bit. Tell us of your tourneys and such."

It was customary for knights to boast of their conquests in the lists, but Gareth no longer took pride in his victories. "Tourneys are all the same," he said. "If the host is not completely averse to my reputation, I do my part for what I can gain from it."

"He's a fine champion," Briar Rose interjected. "He won the day at Briarwood last summer." Even if Gareth didn't take pride in his accomplishments, she did, and fiercely. She squared her shoulders and added, " 'Twas my token he wore that day."

Rowena forced a smile. "No doubt it brought him great fortune," she commented wryly. Then she exaggerated a sigh and studied her delicate hands. "Alas, it seems Gareth has had nothing but ill luck since our betrothal was abandoned."

Briar Rose felt as if she'd been punched in the stomach. "Betrothal?" she said, her voice low, as if she didn't want to believe what she heard. She waited in tense silence for Gareth's response.

He said nothing, but Kenneth shot his sister an angry glance. "I'm afraid Rowena has things a bit turned around. The betrothal was canceled after Gareth was censured."

"You were betrothed?" Briar Rose repeated, feeling her heart begin to ache. Perhaps she'd been wrong about Gareth after all. Perhaps the bitterness that clung to him was due to his being disappointed in love, first by the girl called Celestine and then by Rowena.

Seeing her distress, Kenneth was quick to intervene. "It wasn't a love match, Briar Rose, although I would have been pleased to have Gareth as my brother."

"Kenneth presumes to know much about the situation," Rowena purred. "Yet he doesn't know everything, does he, Gareth?"

Briar Rose wished he'd say something to put her agonized thoughts to rest, but still Gareth held his silence.

She was miffed by his seeming indifference and hotly embarrassed that she hadn't known of the betrothal beforehand. She recalled that once Lady Wexler had lectured her on the importance of appearing cool and self-possessed at all times, never showing emotion, especially to strangers. Now Briar Rose wished she had heeded the lesson, for Rowena was looking at her with the most maddening gloat, like a cat who had just discovered a secret entrance to the buttery.

Briar Rose decided then that she must take the offensive. She'd get no help from Gareth so she squared her shoulders. "Tell me, Rowena, why didn't the two of you marry?"

"I thought that was obvious. I couldn't very well become the wife of a man who'd been censured."

"But if the two of you were in love, Gareth's status shouldn't have mattered."

"Of course it matters. Love and marriage are two different things. Love is a thing freely given, while marriage is a business contract. Why, at court I see young girls married to impossibly old men. Surely they must take on lovers, if only to preserve their own sanity. Perhaps that will be my lot. I'll get properly married and then Gareth and I—"

"That will do, Rowena," Kenneth cut in. "Bawdy talk is common enough at Windsor and London, but we provincial folk find it offensive."

Briar Rose sent her host a look of gratitude. Then, embarrassingly, she yawned.

"Our dear guest is tired, Rowena," Kenneth said. "She is probably not used to the late hours we keep at Tynegate."

Feeling uncomfortably like a child being sent off to bed, Briar Rose left the great hall. She wanted to tell Gareth good-night, but she knew what she would see if she turned back. Rowena with her canny stare, Kenneth's amused, slightly cynical smile, and Gareth's stony gray eyes. Stepping around a seneschal who slept where he had drunkenly fallen, she kept her eyes straight ahead.

Kenneth nodded meaningfully at Rowena, who went off with her women, looking offended. But she knew he and Gareth had matters to discuss—things that were not for her inquisitive ears. And, despite her sophistication, Rowena had been bred to obey the lord of the keep.

When she had gone, Kenneth said, "I must apologize for my sister."

Gareth chuckled. "Never mind. Briar Rose is not one to allow herself to be trodden upon. Her pride shone through all of Rowena's taunts."

Kenneth looked at him sharply, seeing an unaccustomed gentleness in his craggy features. "What's going on, Gareth? How is it you're traveling with the lady of Briarwood?"

Gareth took a long draw on his mazer. And then it came pouring out, the whole tangled story of Acacia's treachery and Lord John's secret intervention; Briar Rose's unflagging loyalty and her expectations which must, of necessity, remain unfulfilled.

Kenneth gave a low whistle. " 'Tis some fix you're in, my friend."

Nodding grimly, Gareth said, "But how could I refuse Padwick's money? Masterson is near ruin. The people are sick and starving and my knights—if any of them remain—are threatening mutiny."

"I'd have done the same. 'Tis no easy thing, seeing one's people suffer. But now you've the girl on your hands. What do you propose to do about her? She cannot go back to Briarwood if her stepmother is the dragon you describe."

Gareth grinned ironically. "Her father suggested I marry the girl, but, of course, that's out of the question. Yet she needs a husband, Kenneth. Not some weakling, but a man who will protect her and what is hers." Gareth looked levelly at his friend. "What about you, Kenneth? She seemed to like you, and I'm sure King Edward would approve of the match."

Kenneth was sorely tempted. He needed a wife, and Briar Rose not only possessed a rich estate, she was beautiful and charming besides. Yet something in Gareth's manner gave him pause. He'd never known his friend to be a sentimental type, but there was a light in Gareth's eyes, a softness that was more probably strength.

"You don't want me to marry the lass, Gareth," Kenneth said.

"What the devil do you mean by that? 'Tis as good a plan—"

"But what of you, my friend? Could we still be close as brothers if I wed the very woman you love?"

"What nonsense you speak, Kenneth." The speed of Gareth's denial rendered his words unconvincing. "She's a good lass and I've stuck my neck out to protect her from her stepmother. But *love?*"

"It complicates things; love always does. But 'tis not something to be choked off like a dammed river. Admit it, Gareth. Even when you were betrothed to my sister, you never felt what you're feeling now. If things were different, you'd marry Briar Rose."

"If!" Gareth grabbed his mazer and clenched his fist around its base. "I cannot change what is. So let's not speak of it again." He drained his mazer. "Love!" The word was a curse on his tongue.

"Even if I were willing," Kenneth continued, "what of the girl? She's not a docile one and I doubt she'd have me. You're a great blond lout of a fellow, Gareth, but women like you; don't ask me why. Briar Rose's heart is set on you."

" 'Tis an affliction she'll recover from."

"There is one other solution. You could marry her. Wait a minute before you object, Gareth. 'Tis not so preposterous as it sounds. I know you cannot be wed by the Church, but there's a magistrate nearby who owes me a favor. He'd grant you a civil ceremony."

"Ridiculous! Briarwood would then be tainted by my censure, too, and soon be as poor as Masterson."

"Then we'll do exactly what Padwick suggested. We'll keep your marriage a secret until the ban is lifted. The king has a short memory and doesn't hold a grudge for long. In the meantime you can keep the girl safe with you and not allow her to be plagued by her stepmother, or by fortune hunters."

"It would make *me* a fortune hunter, Kenneth."

"Nonsense. The girl clearly adores you—"

"That'll change when she learns why I fetched her."

Kenneth shook his head. "She'll forgive you."

"You don't know her, my friend. She is extremely loyal to Briarwood."

"Then tell me a better plan, Gareth. Tell me how else you're going to get Briar Rose to stay with you after she learns you've been hired to take her ring. If you don't wed her, she'll probably do something foolish, like return to her stepmother's clutches. Yet if she was your wife, she'd be obliged to stay with you until the danger has passed."

Kenneth waited, and the silence drew out between them. Most of the people at the feast had retired or collapsed onto the floor, drunk with wine and revelry. A few servants dozed on their feet, slumping against the sideboards.

"There is none," Gareth said at last, his voice echoing through the hall. "If Briar Rose is to be safe, she'll need to marry someone trustworthy." Gareth's mouth lifted in a crooked grin. "Little as I have, I can at least offer her my protection. I'll put the idea to her in the morning."

Kenneth lifted his mazer in salute. "You're doing the right thing, Gareth."

"I doubt it, my friend."

* * *

Feeling as clumsy and inept as a stripling lad, Gareth went to Briar Rose the next day as she was walking in the well-kept courtyard. She stopped under an arbor when she saw him. Her face lit up. Gareth was stabbed by her beauty, which was framed by the changing leaves on low-hanging limbs.

"Kenneth and I talked last night," he said without preamble. "We think it would be best for you and I to marry straight away."

Briar Rose froze and stared. Her heart rose to her throat. She hadn't known what to expect after the previous night's revelations, but even in her most hopeful moments she hadn't dared to wish for this. It wasn't the flowery proposal on bended knee that she'd imagined so many times, but then Gareth was not that kind of man. Yet in his way he was saying what she had long yearned to hear, and that was enough.

With a cry of joy she flung herself at him and covered his face with kisses.

Gently but firmly he set her away from him. "Hold a minute, girl. You've not heard me out. We cannot be married by the Church. A magistrate will preside. Very few must know of it so Briarwood won't be affected by my censure."

Briar Rose was subdued, yet still her eyes shone brightly. "I'd like to shout it from the rooftops. But I understand, Gareth."

"We shall have to live at Masterson."

She nodded agreeably.

"And another thing." Gareth groped for the words. "I think it best that the marriage not be consummated until our vows are repeated at the church porch."

She looked stricken. "But . . . *why?*"

"Anything could happen, Briar Rose. If it appears that I am to be under the ban for many years, you'll want an annulment. It will be easy enough to get if we've not—"

"Really, Gareth, aren't you being overly cautious?"

His face was hard as granite. "Will you accept these terms or not?"

She was too close to realizing her dream to argue with him. Later, however, she knew she'd contest his last condition, and vigorously. And so she asked, "Where is the magistrate?"

"He's waiting in Kenneth's offices. Shall we go?"

As she followed him docilely to the keep, Gareth breathed a sigh of relief. There was another reason for his not wanting to consummate the union. He'd already taken responsibility for her safety; he didn't want the added burden of her heart as well.

Briar Rose would ever remember her wedding day as one that defied all of her girlish imaginings. The air in the silent little office was bleak and chilly. Seated at an escritoire, the magistrate looked bored as his stylus scratched over the parchment. Kenneth and Rowena witnessed the deed. No vows were spoken. It was more like a wool-trader's bargain than a union of two lives. The magistrate dripped wax over the signatures and stamped it, and the deed was done. It hadn't taken more than five minutes.

Only Kenneth was affected by the act. He stepped forward, kissed Briar Rose, and wished her well.

She looked down at her brown surcoat—borrowed from the chest in her room—and bit her lip. She had just given herself in marriage to the man she loved, but where were the chiming bells, the well-wishers, the priests and clerics, the grand nuptial feast? Where was her fabulous dress and flowing hair and Gareth's rich lord's clothing? She felt drab . . . as if she'd been cheated in some way.

"You're more lovely than a princess," Kenneth whispered to her. "A gown of spun gold and pearls would not enhance your beauty."

She forced herself to smile, acknowledging his kindness. He alone read her thoughts and was trying to allay her disappointment. She stole a glance at Gareth, whose fair brows were knit in a hard expression. Suddenly Briar Rose threw her shoulders back and shoved aside her heartsickness. She had no right to expect more than Gareth could give. She'd not allow herself to be childish and petulant. Hadn't Sister Marguerite warned her that happiness was gained through hardship and sacrifice?

Placing a hand on Gareth's arm, she said, "There, we are done now. Perhaps we could go to the hall for some wine."

Gareth nodded, looking somewhat relieved. The four of them had wine and ale and a meal of sausage and pudding and a delicate lark's tongue pie. Rowena seemed amused by the sham of a wedding, but her brother's stern looks kept her sharp tongue in check.

Finally Kenneth and Gareth withdrew to the stables to look over Kenneth's new stock, as if it were any other day. The ladies were left to themselves. Briar Rose was treated to a tour of the castle, and forced herself to admire Rowena's needlework in the solar. She was grateful when the long, strange day finally came to an end and it was time to retire.

In her chamber she was given a worn bliaut of cambric to wear, and a single wick burning in a bowl of oil for light. The room was small and sparsely furnished, hardly inviting except when compared to where Briar Rose had made her pallet during her travels with Gareth.

"Your own clothes are there," the waiting damsel told her, indicating a row of pegs behind the door. "They've been laundered fresh for you."

"Thank you," Briar Rose murmured.

The maid shuffled her feet as if waiting for something.

"If there anything else?"

"Er . . . my lady said I was to get those clothes from you."

Angry flames of blue kindled in Briar Rose's eyes as she tore the brown surcoat over her head, pulling with it a few strands of hair. With quick, irritated movements she cast off the tunic and chemise. When she was completely naked, she thrust the bundle at the maid, who bowed in deference to her fiery anger and started to withdraw.

"Wait," Briar Rose commanded. She snatched up the bliaut and added it to the woman's bundle. "Take this as well, and tell Lady Rowena that I'd best be left naked. Imagine her worrying that I'd abscond with her bliaut!"

The maid winced. "Pardon, my lady," she said nervously. "Take the gown and wear it, do. 'Tis one of my own; Lady Rowena offers naught."

Briar Rose's face softened. "There now," she said, "you don't have to do that."

"Wear it, or I shall be sore miffed," the maid insisted.

There was a knock at the door. Briar Rose held the gown up to cover herself and a pair of servants entered with the hip bath.

"I thought you might like a bath," the maid explained. "It being your wedding night and all." Briar

Rose stared, and the woman smiled knowingly. " 'Tis a secret, of course, but you know how it is in big households . . ."

"I see." Feeling slightly ridiculous, Briar Rose submitted to the maid's ministrations. She tried not to imagine how it could have been at Briarwood with Janet and her women bathing her, anointing her with fragrant oils, readying her for her husband with just the right combination of ceremony and good-natured bawdiness. Yet the Tynegate maid was skillful with the scented water and comb and managed to make Briar Rose feel pampered and special despite the circumstances.

Finally she was left alone to stand beside the small fire in the grate, gazing and thinking. Despite a feeling of overwhelming fatigue, sleep eluded Briar Rose. She took to the bed, lying beneath the woolen and fur covers, staring idly at the flame in the oil lamp.

She was a married lady now, although she didn't feel like one. Her husband was keeping her at arm's length when at this moment he should be holding her close to his heart.

Alone in her shadowy, cold room, she experienced again the sense she'd had all day of being cheated. Had she not followed Gareth for days, never complaining, never questioning? And what did she get in return? Nothing but a dream that was still no more than a dream.

She kicked the covers aside and stood, the flagged floor cold on her feet. She couldn't abide Gareth's idea of a chaste marriage. She was through grasping at the few small things he offered her, like scraps to a dog. It was time she did something for her own happiness.

The rose the singer had given her the previous night was in a horn vessel at the window ledge. Briar Rose took this and tucked it into her hair. It was the only ornament available. She hoped Gareth wouldn't miss its significance.

Moving like a wraith along the darkened corridor, she found Gareth's chamber. A thin sliver of light fell from the partially closed door. Briar Rose slipped in.

His name was on her lips, but she held silent for a long moment. Gareth had discarded his jupon and stood by the window in his chemise. His head was bowed and his broad shoulders sloped downward. His mood seemed low and weighty, as if the responsibilities he carried were almost too heavy to bear. Briar Rose's heart cried out in sympathy for him. She'd meant to demand her due from him, to compel him to treat her like a wife, but she hesitated to bring up the subject. Perhaps they could just talk awhile . . .

"Gareth." All the emotion she felt was in her whispered utterance.

He spun about, startled. With a sweep of his eyes he took in her loose hair and thinly clad body. Gruffly he asked, "What is it?"

"I—I couldn't sleep." Briar Rose laughed nervously. "Nor did I rest well last night. Perhaps I've grown used to the open night."

His eyes flicked over her, dispassionately noting the rose that bloomed beside her face. His face was granite-hard and there was a glint in his gray eyes that hinted at anger. Every muscle of his long body looked tense.

Briar Rose took a deep breath. It was best to speak of things that were not so charged with feelings, at least for the present. She pressed on. "Gareth, I was thinking on a matter . . . on your interdict. Is it true, what you and Kenneth have said about Morley?"

"By the rood, have you forgotten what they did to my horse? And there are other things, the very crimes I had threatened to expose. Whoring and simony and the selling of indulgences are commonplace there."

"King Edward would be appalled, did he know of it."

"No doubt."

"Then he must be told."

"So I thought. And look where it's gotten me." Gareth's voice was tight and bitter.

"Gareth, I would like to speak with the king."

He shook his head. "I'm afraid that cannot be. 'Twould be your word against Talwork's, whom His Majesty holds in high esteem. You'd likely be laughed out of court, or sent to the stocks for slanderous words."

Briar Rose crossed to the window and stood very close to him. "Take me to court, Gareth. At least let me try."

As with a will of its own, his arm encircled her. "I fear your kindness is misplaced." He turned his stony stare out to the autumn night and his arm tightened about her shoulders.

She followed his gaze. The stars sprayed across the sky like silver studs on a shield of black. Somewhere in the darkness, a nightingale called. Moving her arm about his waist, she said, "Gareth, you are worthy of the very best I have. Please, let me try . . ." Suddenly her idea about going to court was eclipsed by his closeness, the warmth pulsating through his strong body, the feel of him beneath her hands. Briar Rose was jolted into remembering why she had come in the first place.

She pulled the flower from her hair. Repeating phrases from the song she'd heard last night, she caressed the front of his tunic with it.

" 'Take thou this rose . . . since love's own flower it

is, and by that rose . . .' " She raised the blossom to his lips, ever so gently. " 'Thy lover captive is.' "

A groan of agony was wrenched from deep in his throat. In the flashing moment before his mouth descended on hers, Briar Rose saw his shadowed features contorted in an expression of inner pain.

The kiss was long, all-consuming, as if Gareth were trying to drink his fill from her very soul. His arms were taut bands about her and his tongue probed boldly, sending shivers of emotion through her.

Briar Rose felt a warm hunger in her loins. Her heart thumped wildly in her chest as she pressed closer, wrapping her arms about him and feeling his muscled back under her hands.

His body seemed to leap to life; she could feel the strength of his passion, the hammering of his heart.

Finally Gareth pulled his mouth away and stared intently at her flushed face and moist, full lips.

"You make bold to come here, barely clad," he said.

Briar Rose caressed his cheek. In the gold light of the oil lamp he appeared younger, his harsh features softened. With a slight smile she said, "By now you should know how unmannerly I am, despite the best of training." She shrugged, and the overlarge bliaut fell aside, revealing a soft white shoulder.

Drawn by the tantalizing smoothness of that exposed flesh, Gareth leaned forward and kissed it. "You are an enchantment," he murmured against her neck. "You should go now and leave me be, before I do something foolish."

"I don't wish to go, Gareth."

He held her close. "My nightingale. You are a dark little bird who comes to me in the night."

"Let me stay, do."

Briar Rose punctuated her plea with feather-light

kisses on the warm hollows of his neck. Her small hands caressed his back and the sides of his hips and then twined into his mane of golden-yellow hair, pulling his head down to hers.

A dark fire smoldered in her eyes. "I want to stay with you, Gareth."

He hesitated, raw desire conflicting with reason. Her hands and lips continued to urge him until a groan exploded from him, echoing out into the night. He pulled her hard against his frame.

"By the stars, I cannot let you leave!"

He was caught up in the magic of her sweet lips, entranced by the spell she wove so artlessly. Passion and regret mingled as he gathered her up and laid her on the bed.

Waves of anticipation thrilled through her. Her every sense seemed to be heightened. The flesh where he had touched her tingled. The bed robes beneath her smelled of the lavender and herbs they had been kept in, and the light from the lamp and hearth fire cast a muted glow over the room and on Gareth's tall form as he stood over her, staring with passion-bright eyes.

She held her arms out to him and he came to her, powerless to keep to his vow against taking her. His hands stroked her body while he kissed her fiercely. The embrace locked their reclining figures together, weaving their limbs into a silken tangle.

Briar Rose gloried in the rush of new sensations. Her heart swelled with love for Gareth. She matched his every kiss with one of equal fervor and let instinct guide her. Without conscious thought, she ran her hand along his inner thigh in a way that tormented him with pleasure.

Finally his kisses aroused her to a peak of desire. She found herself wanting more, demanding more. When he pulled back, he saw this in the blue-violet flames of her eyes.

"You'll never be the same, Briar Rose, if you let me continue."

"Gareth, I haven't been the same since the day I first saw you."

The look she gave him, so soft, so welcoming, drove all reservations from his mind. He knew he had her eager consent and it no longer mattered that he was playing her false. Only the faintest fading voice warned him that she would not be here if she knew the truth.

As she looked upon him with love and desire, Gareth's resistance crumbled. He was gentle with her, and slow. Tenderness tonight was the only thing he could give her freely.

She still held the rose loosely in her hand. It was a symbol of her submission to him, and yet it was also the symbol of her gentle captivity of his heart. Smiling, Gareth took the flower. He slid the hem of her gown upward, gliding the rose over every inch of flesh as he uncovered it, her slim ankles, the feminine curve of her calf, the backs of her knees. Her thighs were smooth as cream. The sight of her caused Gareth's head to reel with passion. Her breasts were firm and heaving under the caressing flower.

At last, after a long, exquisite agony of waiting, he cast the bliaut to the rush-covered floor.

She helped him remove his chemise and hose, and finally his braies. His naked body took her breath away. Muscled and hard with healed scars, broad-shouldered slim-hipped, he made a picture of maleness that inflamed her to new heights.

Now they touched intimately, flesh upon flesh, pressing their bodies together. Briar Rose felt a fluttering of her heart. Vaguely she remembered what Lady Wexler had told her of marriage, that the wife was forced to suffer her husband's monstrous appetite and should bear it with silent submission.

There was nothing at all monstrous about Gareth, big and rough though he was. He touched her gently, respecting her innocence. His hands moved over her breasts, fingers trailing about her nipples and then lower, over her taut middle, to the soft, untried folds of her womanhood. She made a small sound, a whisper of protest, and stiffened slightly at the shocking intimacy of his light-fingered caresses.

He was leading her down a path she'd never trodden, knowing little about where it ended. The pleasure she felt was frankly carnal, something Lady Wexler had lectured against, yet a firestorm raged through her, making a mockery of all the proper training she'd had.

Gareth was awestruck by the innocent beauty who shuddered and quaked in his arms. Passion seemed to pour from her, from the small, fluttering hands that played over his burning flesh, and the moist rosebud mouth that whispered his name like a prayer and clung to his lips.

He'd never felt such joy in readying a woman for love. "Deflowering," some called it, yet it was impossible for Gareth to regard it as such. On the contrary, his wife was like the rose she'd offered him, on the verge of blooming, needing only his caresses to bring her to full, glorious awakening.

Gareth had some inexplicable urge to possess every minute detail of her. Propping himself up on one elbow, he started with light, feathery kisses on her smooth brow, her low-lidded eyes, the tiny, throbbing pulse at her temple. He moved his mouth down the silken skin of her neck, over a smooth shoulder, and down her arm, tasting the flesh in the crook of her elbow and then each finger, one by one, eliciting a series of gasps from her moistened lips.

The feel of her virginal flesh ignited a fire in Gareth that made him feel like a hot-blooded youth again, in a frenzy of passion. But unlike a youth he took his time, for Briar Rose's sake. No matter what the future brought, he wanted her first experience in love to be beautiful.

Only when she was practically tearing at his flesh and Gareth's hand grew moist with her readiness did he know the moment was right.

Briar Rose stared up into his face as he loomed above her. Although a shiver of trepidation rippled through her, she loved everything she was feeling, the heat induced by his fingers, the tingling of her skin, the fierce adoration in her heart.

Gareth swept downward to kiss her breasts and then her mouth, drinking in her sweetness. She felt his hands prepare the way and then, slowly, carefully, he sheathed himself in her.

There was a flash of pain and she cried out, but not in protest. Despite the tearing sensation, she felt warm and secure in Gareth's arms; she trusted him. Her lips clung to his as her arms and legs wrapped themselves around him.

"Relax, sweet nightingale," he mumbled against her lips, beginning to move, slowly at first, and then increasing the tempo. It was a rhythm that some part of her seemed to know, deep in the core of her heart. The pain ebbed away and soon became something even more agonizing, a pleasure so intense that tears squeezed from beneath her tightly closed eyes.

What had begun as a vague heat and a stirring in her loins blossomed into a frenzy of desire. The fire in her blood became a raging blaze. She clutched at Gareth's body and uttered his name breathlessly.

The pinnacle of pleasure was so sweet that she could never have anticipated it in her wildest dreams.

She cried out sharply and with her legs hugged Gareth to her. With a rush of joy she felt him take his release, and clamped her mouth on his to prolong the moment of sweetness. They stayed together, still intimately coupled.

"My dearest, most precious husband," she whispered at last. "I had no idea . . ."

"You were made for love, my nightingale," he told her huskily, his voice raw with emotion.

" 'Twas you who showed me that."

Her gratitude seized his heart. Guilt washed over him, a bitter draught after he'd tasted the sweetness of her love. He cursed himself vilely, hating what he had done in a moment of weakness. He should have sent her, and the blasted rose that now lay crushed on the bed, away. He should never have taken the offering of herself, which she had made so freely, in ignorance of his true character.

She trailed her fingers lightly up the length of his chest and he saw it: the crest ring he'd been contracted to send to her father. He must explain himself, and soon, before there was another episode like this and he became further mired in this glorious, impossible emotional entanglement.

How Briar Rose would hate him. It would shatter her hopeful young heart when she discovered the man she claimed to love was but a common thief.

How would she remember him? he wondered as she curled herself next to him and fell asleep. As her first lover, or as one who had betrayed her trust for a sack of gold?

6

In the bailey of Tynegate a mule brayed at dawn and workers came yawning from their quarters to start the day. The chapel bell rang, summoning the residents of the keep to prayers.

Briar Rose stretched long and mumbled to protest the early hour. A biting cold pervaded the room and she curled her body closer to Gareth. She inhaled deeply, breathing the warm smell of lavender and the less tangible scent of love, of bodies lying close. A smile of utter contentment curved her lips. What bliss it was to awaken in the arms of the man she loved. Last night could have been a dream; it was that splendid, that magical. Yet no dream could equal what she had experienced. Gareth stirred, awakening slowly beside her, holding her with tenderness as the last moments of sleep fell away.

"Is that the chapel bell?" he asked. He looked wonderful, his blond mane tousled, eyes blinking in the light.

"Aye, ringing prime." She snuggled closer and

sighed. "Ah, Gareth, it's so cold outside this bed, I'm not at all eager to leave it. But Kenneth will be looking for us at Mass."

"For you, perhaps, but not for me. I am banned from services, remember?" He came fully awake as the old, bitter frustration rushed back at him.

"I shall stay here, then, and make my excuses later." Already she had begun running her hands sensuously down the length of his body, feeling it stir to life at her touch. She was hungry for him, more than ever now that she knew the joy his lovemaking could bring.

Gareth thrust her away. "Listen to yourself, girl," he snapped, ignoring her hungry eyes and the lips he had bruised with his passion the night before. "Will you sink to my level, then? Forget all you've learned for the sake of a few lusty moments?"

Briar Rose drew back, spurned. "Gareth, I only wanted to . . ."

He looked away, not wanting to see the passionate woman he had made her. Staring grimly at the cold stone wall of the chamber, he said, "Get yourself up, and to Mass, Briar Rose. And then it will be time to leave for Masterson."

With reluctant obedience she slid out from beneath the covers and, shivering, found the bliaut she had so ecstatically abandoned only a few hours before. She shrugged into it, stepping lightly on the cold flagged floor. The rose she'd brought with her last night lay near the bed, its petals fallen, only the bare stalk intact.

She paused at the door. "Gareth, what ails you this morning? Is it something I have done? Or . . . or did I fail you in some way last night?"

His eyes narrowed at her. "For bounty's sake, Briar Rose, don't give me that whipped dog look. It doesn't become you." She turned away, looking small and contrite, and, more gently, he added, "You've done nothing amiss, girl. Least of all last night. Now, be off with you, or you'll miss prayers."

After prime, they started off again, this time rested and fed and carrying a sack of provisions from Tynegate's kitchens. Kenneth had offered them mounts, but Gareth had refused. He didn't like being indebted, even to a good friend.

Briar Rose didn't mind Gareth's silence. It was enough that they were together, that she could walk beside him and steal glances at his strong-featured face. She thought about the night before, remembering with waves of warmth how he'd held and kissed her.

But by midday she grew weary of the tedium. The landscape was rugged and unchanging, yellowing meadows interspersed with stands of barren autumn trees. When they paused for a rest and a small meal of dark bread and potted cheese, Briar Rose discarded her coif and wandered through the tall grass at the roadside. There were some clumps of laceweed drying in the weak sun. As Gareth sat watching, she gathered sprigs of it to weave into a garland.

Gareth chewed on a crust of bread and wet his palate with sour wine from a flask. His gaze was drawn to the girl. She bent gracefully and pulled a bit of the weed from its stalk. Her face today was more lovely than he had ever seen it. It was soft and serene, the face of a woman fulfilled. That ate at Gareth, for what he had done, false though it was, had made her that way.

How would that beautiful face look when she learned the reason he had taken her from St. Agatha's? The smooth brow would darken into a frown and the violet eyes would smolder. The lips that were presently set in a secretive smile would be twisted by rage. Although Gareth had never seen that side of Briar Rose, he knew instinctively that she was a woman who could hate as fiercely as she loved . . .

"Do you like it?"

She had fashioned a crown from the laceweed and set it on her head in place of the coif. On her the garland looked charming, the delicate dried white blossoms framing her smiling face.

Gareth merely grunted and stood. " 'Tis time we moved on."

Briar Rose fell in step with him, hurrying to match his strides. "Is it very far to Masterson, Gareth?"

"No. We'll stay at Linnet tonight and reach Masterson tomorrow."

She kicked at a pebble in the road. "My memories of Masterson are quite dim."

"The less you saw of it, the better."

Briar Rose winced at the bitterness she heard in his voice. "The town was in a poor state," she said carefully. "But Gareth, I saw how it must have been at one time, what it could be again, if only—"

"It's a sewer, festering with corruption," he snapped. "Those who are lucky have the means to take flight; the rest stay and prey on one another."

She kicked at another stone in the path. "Then let me help you. My mother's jewels could be traded for grain and gold to pay your knights."

"I will not let you do that, Briar Rose. Where is the honor in it?" He tried not to think about his part in her father's scheme.

She turned on him then, eyes flashing. "Where is the honor in refusing my help, Gareth Hawke? Is it so honorable to allow one's own people to suffer?"

He grasped her upper arm hard and spun her around

to face him. In a low, fierce voice he said, "Enough of your meddling, girl! I shall reckon with this in my own way." He let her go with a shake and strode forward, furious with the knowledge that his methods were just as dubious as hers.

They came to Linnet at sunset. The town was no more than a cluster of thatched houses and a slumping old wayfarers' inn called The Yellow Stag.

Wearing a soiled apron and coif, the alewife came to serve them at a low table.

"We'll have a meal, and something to drink," Gareth told her.

"I'll see your coin first, if you please."

"I've money to pay."

"So you might. But we've had our share of knights like you, sir. Most have naught but a rusty sword and some emblem on their chests."

Gareth's jaw clenched—he'd been here only a few nights before—but he slapped a pair of coins on the table. The alewife snatched them up and pocketed them.

A few peasants in grimy shirts and breeches sat hunched over clay mugs of ale. A pair of aging men sat by the fire, rubbing their grizzled chins as they studied the pegboard they were playing. In a shadowed corner of the low-beamed room were three men wearing hooded cloaks and speaking in hushed tones.

A group of raucous youths ambled in, laughing and joking among themselves. "Dorrie!" one of them shouted at the alewife. "A round for me and my mates, and be quick about it."

"I'll not be serving you, Cully," she retorted, speaking over her shoulder. "You've not done an honest day's work since your folks turned you out."

Cully laughed, his handsome face ruddy from the

wind. He crossed the room to the alewife and put his arm around her waist.

"True enough, Dorrie, my sweet, but sometimes a *dis*honest day's work is far more profitable." He pulled a length of silver chain from his tunic and dangled it before her eyes. "We've been to the fair in Ninebanks."

"I don't hold with stealing," the woman said, although she gazed at the bauble in admiration.

"Nonsense, woman. It wasn't my fault a certain well-dressed gentleman at the fair failed to clasp his chain properly. Why, it practically slipped into my hand!"

The woman snatched the chain and pocketed it. "I'll draw your ale."

Cully turned with an air of triumph. It was then that he spied Briar Rose.

"Lord in heaven," he breathed, his eyes widening in amazement. "What's this, an angel fallen into our midst?"

Gareth saw a blush creep up to Briar Rose's cheeks. "You're making the lady uncomfortable, my friend," he said. His voice was mild, but there was an ominous undercurrent to his statement.

The young man didn't seem to notice. "A lady, you say, sir?" His gaze flicked over her gray homespun garb. Then he spotted the crest ring on her hand. "That's a good bit of gold you have there, my lady."

Briar Rose closed her fist around the ring and clutched it to her chest.

"That's enough, Cully." One of the others drew him off to a table. This one, at least, had seen danger in Gareth's flint-eyed stare. Raising his hat, he added, "Sorry, sir. My younger brother has no manners."

The alewife brought them mugs of ale. "That's Harry," she murmured. "Good as the day is long;

Cully's always been a thorn in his side. I'll be right along with your supper."

Gareth nodded. His eyes wandered to the three quiet men in the corner. They had been singularly disinterested in the exchange, or at least had pretended to be.

Unlike Gareth, Briar Rose showed no interest in the other patrons. She was hungry and thirsty and still irritated with Gareth. The game stew that the woman brought them was surprisingly good. The ale was bitter but cool, the bread quite edible when soaked in the stew.

Gareth watched Briar Rose eat. Indeed, she did look like a rose amid briars and weeds, her delicate beauty and manner of eating at odds with the coarse surroundings. With both regret and relief he told himself she would soon be at Masterson. This wandering life was not for her, no matter how little she complained of it.

"Thank you for the meal," she said quietly, dabbing at her mouth with a corner of her surcoat.

" 'Twas hardly dainty fare."

For the first time since they'd quarreled, Briar Rose smiled. "I had not a dainty appetite."

Gareth placed his hand under her chin and stroked it gently with his thumb. "Poor girl. You must be tired of being dragged over half the countryside."

"Not so long as I'm with you, Gareth. My love, do forgive my meddling earlier. It pains my heart to be at odds with you."

"There's no apology due." Gareth looked away and signaled to the alewife. "We need a bed for the night. A room to ourselves, if you have it."

Gareth stooped under the sloping roof beams of the loft the alewife had offered them. " 'Tis worse, I think, than the woods we've slept in," he said apologetically.

There was nothing in the loft but a straw pallet and

some mouldering blankets in a heap. But the straw was fresh and fragrant and thickly lain, and Briar Rose lowered herself to it with a sigh.

Gareth had gotten a tallow candle stub from the alewife's boy. It burned unevenly, casting an uncertain glow about the room. By this light Briar Rose removed her shoes and surcoat.

"Ah, I'd forgotten this," she said, laughing a little and pulling the laceweed garland from her hair. "The people downstairs must have thought me quite daft. No wonder they were staring so."

"I doubt it was the garland they were staring at." Gareth pulled out a gleaming tendril of her hair and ran his fingers down the silken length.

"Is my hair too long?" Briar Rose questioned. "I noticed that Rowena's was cropped shorter. Perhaps it is a style she learned at court."

"Don't change a thing about yourself, Briar Rose," Gareth said gently, setting the tress aside.

She smiled. "I'm glad that I please you, Gareth. You ask so little of me—"

"I've no right to ask for anything."

"Yet, my dearest, you've no right to reject what I offer." She moved into his arms and, taking his troubled face between her hands, kissed him full on the mouth.

A great weariness overtook Gareth. She was a little slip of a thing, yet there was something powerful in her effect on him. Although a small buzz of warning went off in his head, he thrust it aside, knowing he hadn't the will to combat Briar Rose's ardor. Besides, he told himself darkly, she'd turn away from him soon enough, once she understood what he was really about. With a long sigh he surrendered to her completely, giving himself over to the comfort she offered.

They lingered long over the kiss, enveloped by the

fresh scent of straw and bathed by candlelight. Briar Rose knew then that the quarrel was over and she abandoned herself to the joy of making love to Gareth. With deft fingers she unfastened his tunic and moved it slowly, sensuously, down the length of his torso. Remembering last night, when he had undressed her in such a tender way, she did likewise now. As his chemise fell away she kissed the flesh of his neck and shoulders, and then his belly and thighs as she removed his hose and braies.

Under her evocative ministrations she could feel him relax. It thrilled her to have this power over him, to be able to show him how very much she loved him. While he waited and watched through lidded eyes, she got out of her clothes and lay down beside him.

The straw prickled under her naked back, but it only served to heighten the warm, tingling sensations that danced upon her flesh. Gareth's hands were gentle as he stroked her body, his fingers circling and teasing the tips of her breasts. Under his lips a pulse leaped at her throat and heat radiated from her loins until she began thrusting herself against him.

She stroked and fondled him, her arousal growing even as his did. They were of one mind, giving and taking pleasure and sighing with the deep, sweet emotions they felt in their hearts. Briar Rose gasped when his hand touched her intimately, and then his mouth. On a wave of ecstasy she closed her eyes and dropped her head, moving it from side to side as her body writhed with a will of its own.

His touch was sweet torment, bringing her to a crest of pleasure and then, maddeningly, moving away.

"Rogue," she whispered through clenched teeth. "How you torment me with your pretty tricks."

He laughed low in his throat, enjoying the game, playing her like a musician at his harp.

Briar Rose realized what he was doing and, not to be bested by him, began a game of her own. She pressed his shoulders until he lay back on the pallet, and trailed a line of kisses over his face and down his neck. Then she kissed his chest and belly and thighs, circling his manhood, barely brushing it with her lips and letting the wavy length of her hair trail like a gossamer curtain over his legs.

Gareth groaned and called her a witch. Cupping her firm buttocks with his hands, he placed her atop him. Briar Rose drew in her breath as pleasure rocketed through her. She threw back her head and closed her eyes and took up a rhythm with her hips. She rode with wild abandon until her passion crested, swiftly followed by Gareth's. They kissed hungrily, embracing hard, and finally Briar Rose lay down beside him.

"I cannot imagine a night without you," she told him, tracing the line of his jaw with her finger. "I must have been only half alive before."

"That's not so, Briar Rose. Do not take on about us. There is much you don't know which may separate us."

"Fool! Do you think, Gareth Hawke, that I would let you go now that we are married and have found such joy as this?"

"That's a claim you may find cause to regret, my nightingale."

"Stop this talk, Gareth, and go to sleep. Truly, I think you almost wish for me to stop loving you. And that is something I will not—cannot—do." She moved close and hugged him, reminding them both of the intimate bond they shared. Sighing with contentment, she drifted off to sleep.

Gareth was troubled. Her words echoed in his mind:

You wish for me to stop loving you. And he did wish it, yet at the same time he dreaded it more than death.

Dawn rolled in with a cold, damp fog that pervaded the loft. Gareth looked at the sleeping girl. He cursed his weakness when it came to her. His resolve to keep their marriage chaste had failed him twice. Their intimacy would only complicate things, but Gareth found his wife impossible to resist.

The air in the loft was still, chilly, heavy with the scent of straw. Gareth felt a need to get away, to breathe the open air. Glancing again at Briar Rose, who was still sleeping heavily, he climbed down the ladder.

Linnet was barely astir, he noticed as he strode along the road to the edge of the village. Shrouded by mist, the sheaves of grain stood like waiting soldiers, silent and ready. Every tenth bundle had a green stick protruding from it like a war spear. This was what the king's tax collectors would take as their due.

Gareth sat by the roadside and buried his face in his hands. He, too, had given a tenth of his revenues to the Crown, but a tenth of what he had was precious little. A niggling voice at the back of his mind told him he needed the prize Lord John held out to him. The gold could buy seed for the coming spring planting, pay his knights their due so they would be ready to defend Masterson, and feed the hungry families of peasants and artisans.

Yet how could he betray Briar Rose? Could he, now, take her small, trusting hand in his and slip the ring from her finger, as Padwick had instructed? She would never understand. She'd be devastated, shattered . . .

Gareth wiped his face with his hand, feeling unkempt when he touched the new growth there. A band of bedraggled wayfarers approached. They were not the usual assortment of sturdy beggars who were such a common sight in northern villages, but sickly individuals who dragged their feet as if each step were an enormous effort.

They didn't know him, didn't see the embroidered hawk that was concealed by his cloak. One man, whose gaunt face and yellowed eyes were drawn and guarded, spoke. "Good my lord, have you a coin or two to spare us?"

Gareth handed him a few coins from his purse. "This will get you a meal and a drink at yonder inn."

The man took the money with a trembling hand. "Bless you, sir. May the good saints bless you."

One of the other beggars, who wore a bandage around a septic wound on his leg, attempted to mumble his thanks. He had not even the strength to incline his head; when he tried to do so, he pitched forward, hitting the road with a muffled exclamation of pain.

The others did their best to right him, but they, too, were weak and couldn't bring him to his feet.

"Up with you, Gus," they prompted. He made a feeble attempt to rise and collapsed again.

Gareth stepped forward and, placing his arms around the man's chest, pulled him to his feet.

"Lean on me. 'Tis but a short piece to The Yellow Stag." Slowly the group made its way to the inn, the crippled man helped along by Gareth.

They roused the alewife, who grumblingly set to warming the stew, drawing ale, and preparing bowls of gruel.

Gareth made ready to leave. He turned at the door and asked, "From where do you hail?"

" 'Tis not a place you'd care to visit, my lord. A town by the name of Masterson, and damned for all time, it is."

Face flaming with impotent rage, Gareth left by the

back door. Pain knifed through him, cold and sharp. He'd been away for some weeks, safe from witnessing the town's daily strife. Now it all came flooding back to him. People who depended on him were starving, dying. He leaned against the ladder to the loft, chest heaving, eyes smarting. He knew then, with a leaden feeling in the pit of his stomach, that he had to act. There was no more putting it off. He hoisted himself up to the loft.

Briar Rose still slept, her face a picture of dreamy contentment: the brow smooth, the lips bowed into a small smile. Her right hand lay beside her face, relaxed and slightly open like a child's. The heavy ring on her forefinger gleamed like a beacon in the straw.

Gareth hesitated in a moment of profound regret. Two factions warred within him, wrenching his emotions. On the one side was Masterson, floundering, failing, the people dying, he himself hunted by diocese men. And then there was Briar Rose, trusting, adoring, his all-too-willing wife and lover. There was really no decision to be made. The beggars had made him see what he must do, even at the cost of losing Briar Rose.

Gareth knelt and slipped the ring from the sleeping girl's finger. It fit loosely; she'd lost weight during their travels. Silently Gareth vowed to make it up to her someday, although he knew it was too much to hope for her forgiveness. Perhaps Lord John would confess the scheme to her. He took some coins from his purse to give to Harry, intending to ask the young man to conduct Briar Rose safely to Tynegate. He left the rest with her and climbed down, hating and cursing himself.

He roused Harry and spoke briefly with him. "Tell no one where you are going," he warned. "My wife's safety is in your hands, my friend. Do not fail me."

"I won't, sir. I dare not."

"Godspeed, Harry." Gareth rose to leave. "And tell

my wife . . . tell her I . . ." He swallowed. There were no words that would make Briar Rose understand his deception.

"Never mind," he said curtly, and left the inn.

Slanting fingers of sunlight came through the gaps in the loft, having burned away the morning mist. A single beam crossed Briar Rose's face and she protested sleepily. Eyes closed, she reached for Gareth.

He was not there. She sat up and rubbed the sleep from her eyes. His clothes were gone, his side of the pallet long cold. Her brow wrinkled, then softened as she recalled the previous night. He'd never leave her after that. He was probably down in the tavern breaking his fast and speaking to other wayfarers about the roads.

Briar Rose smiled and stretched, feeling no shame as she remembered their lovemaking. For all Gareth's roughness and seeming indifference, he was thoughtful, allowing her to sleep as long as she pleased. He'd never confessed his love to her, as she had to him so many times, but his actions told her that he cared. Eager to see him, she dressed hurriedly and dragged her fingers through her tangled hair before donning her coif.

Her fingers . . . Eyes growing wide and confused, she paused to look at her hands. Her ring was gone! Working calmly at first, she began to search methodically through the straw, looking for a telltale gleam of gold.

With rising panic she realized that the ring was not there. She felt naked and violated, as if the ring had been part of her flesh rather than something she wore.

She gathered up Gareth's belongings and sprang from the loft. It occurred to her that a thief had come and taken the ring while she slept. But then, how could that be, when a purse of coins was there too, lying out in plain sight?

The thief must have been a bungler or drunk, Briar Rose decided, forcing herself to relax. If so, Gareth would have scant trouble finding him and taking back the ring.

She entered the tavern. By the dim light of the hearth fire she saw only a quartet of beggars at one of the tables. They looked up and watched her with sickly eyes.

Briar Rose said, "I am looking for a knight. Have you seen him?"

"The great blond one?"

"Aye. Where is he?"

"He's gone."

Briar Rose tapped her foot. "I know that. But where?"

"East on the road, I reckon. We didn't ask where."

"And when was that?"

A shrug. "Some time ago. 'Twas an odd turn, too. Three others—dark, secret ones—left just after him."

Briar Rose pursed her lips and turned away from the beggars. The alewife came from the kitchen, wiping her hands on her stained apron.

"Where has my lord gone?" Briar Rose demanded.

"I wouldn't expect him back if I were you. Many's the girl what's been left behind by a pretty young man like that one. You're lucky he paid for your bed."

Briar Rose's glance was caught by a gleam of silver at the woman's throat. She remembered Cully, then, who had blithely admitted stealing it.

"Where is the youth called Cully?" she demanded.

"Still abed, I reckon."

Briar Rose ran to the large chamber behind the taproom, intent on confronting the thief. "Lord have mercy on his rotted hide," she hissed as she squinted in the dimness.

He wasn't there. Cursing, Briar Rose crossed back through the taproom. She burst from the tavern into the sunlight. The alewife's boy jumped back in surprise, spilling the grain he'd been feeding to a small flock of hens. Briar Rose nearly tripped over him and whirled about, words of anger on her lips. But, seeing the lad's frightened stare, she softened a little and helped him scoop up the grain.

"There now," she said, "I didn't mean to startle you." She managed to smile when he bobbed his head in thanks, even though she could feel the precious seconds pass.

At the front of the dooryard was one of the young men who'd been at the tavern last night. Briar Rose remembered that the alewife had called him Harry.

"Where is your brother?" she demanded.

"I thought he was still asleep."

She stamped her foot furiously in the dust. "He's stolen my ring."

Harry swallowed. "Are you sure, mistress?"

"Just tell me where he might have gone." The road stretched east and west. Harry looked blank. Then he brightened. "Mistress," he said, placing his hand on her sleeve. "You're to come with me."

"I'll do no such thing," she said, pulling away.

"Your husband asked me to see you to Tynegate."

"Why would he do a thing like that?"

"I didn't ask, mistress, but he was sore concerned for your safety."

She recalled what one of the beggars had said: Three others—dark, secret ones—left after him. Of course that was it. Gareth had left alone to draw off the men who stalked them.

The fool. The damned, noble fool. How could he even think she'd lamely follow Harry to Tynegate? Her first impulse was to find Gareth. But there was still the matter of her ring.

"Will you come, mistress?" Harry asked.

"Certainly not." She pointed to the west. "You'd best set yourself to finding your brother. Because if I come across him first, he'll be the worse for it."

The high sun mocked Gareth's bleakness as he plodded on. The ring secreted in the lining of his tunic weighed heavily there, pressing on his heart. Images of Briar Rose—laughing at some jest, or speaking in her quick, earnest way, or aflame with passion—flashed through his mind. The trusting way she'd looked at him, her eyes brimming with love and pride—he felt lower than the snakes that slept the winter away beneath the rocks that littered the fells.

Many times that day he turned and pointed his feet westward. It was still not too late to go back to her, to restore the ring to her finger, to beg her forgiveness. And then, clenching his jaw with resolution, he forced himself back toward Masterson. At the day's end he'd reach his home, if, God willing, he was able to elude the bishop's men, who were undoubtedly on his trail.

Yet even the thought that Briar Rose would be safe with Kenneth, and the Masterson knights paid with Padwick's bounty, didn't lighten his spirits. He was but a beggar knight, no better than the vagabonds he'd helped this morning, wandering in poverty with nothing—no horse, no sword, not two coins to rub together.

He met no one on the road. It was as if all the people

in this northern shire shunned him, not wanting to be tainted by him. Of course, winter was approaching and the tinkers and wayfarers had settled somewhere for the cold season, but Gareth didn't see it that way. He was a knight under the ban, a collector of other men's debts, a lackey of noblemen, a common thief. He walked with his head bowed.

Hoofbeats. Gareth spun around to see three figures approaching, riding hard on the dusty track. Retreating to the roadside, Gareth squinted against the blazing autumn sun. The riders' cloaks flew out and the hoods had fallen back to reveal two tonsured heads. Clerics. Talwork's men, and the third was undoubtedly a knight of Morley Diocese. So they had found him. Gareth wondered what had taken them so long. He thanked God that Briar Rose was safely on her way to Tynegate.

Gareth surveyed his surroundings with a fleeting glance. This was the heart of the north country, with its stunted trees and drifting moors. Dull gritstone boulders clung to the fells. It was open and desolate; there was nowhere a man could hide.

Besides, it was not his way to hide from danger, but to meet it face on. He stepped back onto the road, straddling the mound in the middle, throwing back the folds of his cloak to reveal the hawk emblazoned on his chest. He drew his dagger and waited.

The riders' horses slid to a stop before him. The wind howled down the desolate moors. One of the clerics spoke.

"We have searched long for you, Lord Hawke."

Griffith. He recognized the voice.

Gareth planted his hands on his hips. "Had you been better hunters, you would have found me days ago."

Griffith's hand moved to a stout wooden club that hung on the knotted scourge at his waist. The other cleric had a mace; this was doubtless the instrument that had killed Gareth's palfrey.

"His Excellency Bishop Talwork desires concessions from you, Lord Hawke. He may be willing to lift the ban if you cooperate," said Griffith. His eyes in the heavy-jowled face were small and colorless.

"Liar!" Gareth exploded. "Talwork will do nothing of the sort. He wants my town and my keep and all of my land, and knows he must kill me to take it."

Griffith looked at the other cleric and then at the knight. "Brother Andrus, Sir Charles," he said, " 'Tis regretful, but we must act."

In a flash of wood and prickly steel and the blade of a sword, they were upon him. The three made a clumsy trio, hacking and lashing wildly. Gareth evaded their blows, light on his feet despite his great height. A strong kick sent Griffith sprawling to the dusty track. Gareth ducked beneath Andrus's swinging mace and spun to face Charles, who, as a trained knight with a sword, posed the greater menace.

He had small, darting eyes, snarling lips, and a diocese knight's hatred of more privileged, landed men. He advanced on Gareth, sword singing as it sliced through the air. As Gareth leaped back, Griffith's club descended from behind in a crushing blow to the shoulder.

Gritting his teeth against the pain, Gareth stabbed upward with his dagger and cut the cleric in the arm. Griffith howled and staggered back to lean against his horse as he tried to staunch the bleeding.

Andrus swung his mace then, an ill-aimed, clumsy blow that grazed Gareth's arm. The pain of it, and the smell of his own blood, caused his temper to explode.

"I am no hapless beast," he growled, "tethered to a tree as my horse was."

Andrus laughed harshly. "It matters not. You'll end

the same as the palfrey." He swung out again and the backlash of the weapon caused him to reel and fall to the ground.

Sir Charles, with his more elegant weapon, advanced again, circling Gareth cautiously.

"I know of you, Lord Hawke," he said. "You are a hard warrior, but not without a sword." Charles thrust forward and his blade bit into Gareth's side.

Gareth felt the warmth of his blood as it seeped through the wound, through his clothing, dangerously copious. His head began to thud; his vision blurred. Everything slowed down, lilting, dreamlike.

A snarl from Sir Charles jolted him back into action. He kicked aside another blow and pressed in, to crack his fist against the other man's jaw. Sir Charles's sword cut Gareth again, near the first wound.

Gareth sank to his knees, a look of confusion on his face. With a clarity that only the gravely wounded possess he suddenly saw the pointlessness of their fighting.

He spoke to his enemies, the words coming from somewhere deep inside, as of their own accord.

"What is it you've gained today?" he asked. The blood seeped. Gareth wavered and coughed. "Will you, Charles, be a landed knight now that you've finished me? And—and you, Griffith, a higher station perhaps? What is your reward, Andrus? A bauble for your valor?" He laughed, but the laugh sounded more like choking. "Nay, that is not Talwork's way. He'll not divide his power."

The three men were still, witnessing his pain. At last Griffith spoke.

"Finish him."

A grouse rattled harshly in the moor grasses. Gareth's mind seemed to separate from his body. As if from a distance he watched Griffith advance on him and deliver a stunning blow to his ear with the club. He saw, rather than felt, Andrus's mace graze his back. And finally, from that place apart from his body, he witnessed the beginning of his own demise.

He tried to steady himself, but the seeping blood spilled, weakening him. He pitched forward and tasted the dust in his slack mouth.

Still separate, still floating, he felt his pulse being tested and heard the men speak.

"Nearly gone. He'll be scavengers' fare within the hour."

"One last stab, perhaps?"

"No need. We are not butchers."

"What prize shall we take His Excellency?" Griffith asked, his mouth twisted in a tight smile of victory.

"His head, perhaps, or an ear?"

"No, not that. 'Twould be putrid before we reached Morley. Besides, it's not seemly for diocese men to be hacking up corpses."

Brother Andrus bent and took hold of Gareth's shredded tunic. With a sharp tug he pulled the hawk insignia from it. Holding the torn emblem aloft he said, "This will do."

"What of the girl back at the inn?" Charles asked. "I'm not too proud to have a piece of Hawke's whore."

Gareth's mind screamed a protest. Briar Rose! Sweet Christ, not Briar Rose! But he was mute with weakness. The scream didn't reach his lips. Please God, he prayed silently, let her be safely on her way to Tynegate.

"There's no time," Griffith said. "His Excellency awaits us."

Gareth heard the thudding of hooves and knew they'd left him for dead. The grouse rattled again. The wind howled.

And then, with a dusty sigh, he slipped into the deep velvet void of unconsciousness.

Briar Rose shivered as she hurried along. Somewhere on this dusty track Gareth walked, and he was being followed by men who were out for blood.

In the afternoon, when her shadow was long in front of her and the moors flamed orange in the waning light, she came atop a rise in the path. Below, yards ahead, was a black shape. Briar Rose ran toward it, hoping and dreading.

She reached him, stumbled, and dropped to her knees beside him. Panic rose in her throat at the sight of his bloodied torso and ashen, inert face. She forced her trembling to stop. He needed her and all the calm she could muster, not some impotent, hysterical female.

"Gareth." She took out the wine flask, moistened the corner of his cloak, and pressed the cloth to his cold forehead.

Then, working gingerly, she pulled his torn tunic aside. "Sons of sheep," she swore. "Dastards." They had taken the emblem of the hawk and no doubt thought they'd taken Gareth's life along with it. But his youth and health served him well. A pulse throbbed, slowly, faintly, at the side of his neck.

The chemise was caked to his wounds by drying blood. Using more of the wine, she wet the fabric and pulled it away. She bit her lip at what she saw. Deep gashes, an angry pair of them, creased his left side. The flesh around them was cleanly cut, though, and the bleeding had slowed. Perhaps, then, there was hope for Gareth.

Briar Rose cleaned the wounds and bound them with a strip of fabric from the hem of her surcoat. The cloth had torn unevenly and it took all of her strength to raise Gareth's body, but, biting her lip and sweating with exertion, she did the job and finally sat back, feeling the tension in her back and in her churning innards.

She covered him with his dusty cloak and placed his head in her lap to bathe his face again. Even colored by evening sunlight, it was deathly pale. Briar Rose's tears of despair mingled with the cold perspiration on his brow.

His eyes opened, hesitantly at first, and then willfully.

"Sweet, merciful God, thank you," she whispered.

"Briar Rose . . ." His voice was raspy, disbelieving.

"I'm here, my darling."

"But I—I left you—"

"Shh. I know. And I know why. Dear, noble Gareth, you should have taken me with you instead of trying to face your enemies alone."

He rocked his head from side to side in her lap. His body began to tremble.

"There, you're cold. I'll get your tunic around you." She set his head down gently and took up the garment. "It's badly torn, but warm still."

She began tucking it around his shivering form, then stopped when she felt something hard in the inner lining. "What's this?" she said, half to herself.

The object dropped to the ground.

"My ring!" Briar Rose stared at Gareth with wide, unbelieving eyes—tormented eyes.

7

She groped for her voice. "I don't understand, Gareth. Why did you take this?"

His face was clouded by pain and self-loathing. "I—"

"You stole it from me!" Briar Rose's eyes flashed, then softened when she saw the agony he was in. "Gareth, I told you I have jewels at Briarwood much more valuable than my ring. You had only to ask, and I would have given them all to you." There was something pathetic about what he had done—taking, rather than humbling himself to ask for what he needed.

His voice was a harsh whisper. " 'Twas not for myself that I took it."

Briar Rose slipped the ring on her right forefinger, relieved to feel the familiar weight of it there.

"I know," she said. " 'Twas for Masterson; everything you do is for Masterson." She eyed him shrewdly. "And that, my husband, is why you shall allow me to help you now—in my own way, as you should have from the start."

Gareth could already see the calculations taking

place behind her violet eyes. She would go to the King as she'd been wanting to do and make a fool of herself, perhaps get herself censured, too. He couldn't let her do that. He groaned and shifted in her lap. His strength was slowly returning. Best to get the hurt over now and let her stop deceiving herself about him.

" 'Tis the ring that I needed." His words sounded hard-bitten and angry. "That, and only that. Nothing else will suffice." He watched her face darken; she was as beautiful in anger as he had known she would be. "You were foolish to trust me, Briar Rose. You should have listened to those who warned you about me."

She shook her head in mute denial of the bitter realization that dawned on her. Foolish, Gareth called her, but it was much worse than that. She had been blind and stupid, and he cruel and heartless. Her face burned as she recalled the many times she had lavished adoration on him. He had made a mockery of that love.

Her voice was cold and toneless when she said, "You didn't come to St. Agatha's, then, because love brought you there."

"No." He winced from the pain in his side and from the shame of what he had done to her. "Briar Rose, I never told you that, I never—"

"But you allowed me to believe what I would. You took from me what I alone possess! The symbol of my home!"

He nodded bleakly, his face still ashen. "I never meant to hurt you. You were the victim of my own weakness."

A cold wind came up from the moors, lifting strands of Briar Rose's hair and swirling them about her face. Eyes flashing, she said, "I am a victim no more, Gareth Hawke. I know what you are now and I shall always hate you for it. Always, do you hear me?"

She leaped to her feet and stared down at him. "I'll leave you now. It matters not to me whether you recover and drag yourself to that mound of offal you call Masterson, or whether you die and the carrion birds find you." She spoke it like a curse, and whirled away.

Gareth gazed through pain-filled eyes at her retreating form, feeling all hope seep out of him. With Briar Rose went the last shreds of his honor. And with her also, blowing away like the puffs of dust her small feet kicked up, went a piece of his heart.

Briar Rose clenched her fist around the ring that was now back where it belonged. She almost wished she hadn't recovered the crest; the pain of getting it had shattered her to her very soul. There was nothing that Gareth could have done to hurt her more. In the space of a few moments, he had transformed her from a loving, trusting girl into a woman who could hate, who would grow hard with that hatred, as hard as the stone that lined the road. She had no idea where the road led. She knew only that she had to get away from him, away from the ugly sham her love had become.

Still, she felt an odd tugging, a wrenching of her heart. He'd betrayed her and deserved nothing but her hatred, yet she was troubled by his present state. She'd left him to die like a wounded dog on the road.

Her pace slowed. She couldn't go on. She knew his wan, defeated face would haunt her all her days if she did not help him now. He had mocked her, stolen her very soul, but that was still not reason enough to condemn him to a slow, solitary death. In her mind's eye she saw Dame Marguerite's sweet face, exhorting her to learn compassion.

Briar Rose turned and retraced her steps. She decided to wait with him. There was food in the sack from Tynegate to fortify him, perhaps enough so that he could get to Masterson. Before reaching him, she slipped her ring off and fitted it into the hem of her surcoat. Weak as he was, Gareth might still try to take it.

He lay where she had left him, his good eye staring at the sinking sun, the scarred one nearly closed. She knelt, rifled through the sack, and brought out a crust of bread and a hunk of cheese.

"I'll not let you die," she told him coldly. "Eat, and we shall see if you're able to walk."

He obeyed, touched and shamed that she'd returned to his side when he deserved no more than her scorn and neglect.

Hoofbeats sounded. Briar Rose stiffened and terror clutched at her heart. Men from Wannet or Morley—had they come back to see that they'd killed Gareth? She felt helpless. He was as good as dead if that was what the riders wanted.

After a short wait she saw that it was only one rider, a knight. He appeared over a rise in the east, his shape bronzed by the western sun. He was riding hard toward them. Some instinct caused Briar Rose to reach out and grasp Gareth's shoulder.

"Who is it?" she asked, her heart thumping.

Gareth propped himself up on one elbow, wincing, and squinted at the rider. Relief flooded his face. " 'Tis Cedric, one of my knights."

Cedric reached them and leaped from his horse. "There are five of us out looking for you, my lord," he said. "It's lucky I found you so quickly." He saw instantly that Gareth was wounded. "Who . . . ?"

"Talwork's men. Two clerics and a knight."

"Is it very bad, my lord?"

"I'll make it. What news, Cedric?"

"We've had word from Giles, who was at Morley. He

thinks they mean to attack Masterson. The keep may be under siege within the week."

Gareth closed his eyes for a moment. "We can hold them, but it won't be easy."

Cedric looked away. "There is a problem, my lord, with the men."

Gareth frowned at Cedric's uneasiness. "Tell me."

"They want their pay. They'll not fight unless they get it. Already some are talking of leaving."

Gareth lay back and let an exhausted sigh escape his lips. In his mind he saw an image of Masterson, his family's home for over a hundred years. Its walls had never been breached.

The idea of his keep and town overrun by roistering clerics and unruly diocese knights tortured him. He could not abide the thought. Perhaps, after all, he'd have to earn his bounty. In desperation he clutched at Cedric and drew the knight's ear down to his mouth.

"The girl . . ." he mumbled. "Seize her."

Briar Rose, who had listened to the exchange while trying not to feel anguish for Gareth, suddenly found her wrists in the grasp of Cedric's calloused hands.

Dispassionately, obeying Gareth without question, he bound her wrists in front of her with a leather thong and tethered her like a prisoner to his saddle. She was furious, humiliated. She bestowed every curse she knew on Gareth.

Ignoring her, Cedric and Gareth conferred for a short time in hushed tones and she saw the knight glance over his shoulder at her, looking at her hands. She thanked God that she'd thought to hide her ring.

"I can force her to give me the thing and we'll be done with her," Cedric suggested.

"Too dangerous," Gareth answered. "She's heard

too much. We cannot let her wander away." He managed a self-deprecating grin. "Besides, lad, she's my wife."

Cedric stared at her in amazement, but he held his questions. Gareth made him swear he'd not reveal their marriage. Gingerly he helped his lord into the saddle. He walked ahead and Briar Rose stumbled behind. She directed a look of pure venom at Gareth's back, hoping her stare would penetrate the ice she knew must surround his heart.

In the space of a few hours she had seen her dreams turned to dust, seen the man she thought she loved for what he really was. She had been used, humiliated, and now was being treated like the lowest prisoner. If her predicament hadn't been so ridiculous, she would have given way to tears. But she was bitter beyond tears, beyond words. There was nothing left to feel but the harsh bile of hatred.

As she walked along the road and felt the chill blowing down through darkening corries, her mind whirled with agonizing thoughts. She glanced at the hem of her gown where the ring brushed against her ankle and wondered why Gareth coveted it so. It was wrought of a good-sized hunk of gold, to be sure, but the price it would bring was not nearly enough to save Masterson, as Gareth seemed to think it would.

And then it came to her. *Acacia.* In her hunger to make her daughter heiress to Briarwood, the woman must have made Gareth her lackey. No doubt she'd offered him a huge sum to bring the ring to her.

"How much was it, Gareth?" Briar Rose asked in a voice dripping with venom. "How much did my stepmother give you to steal my ring and my heritage from me?"

He said nothing, but she saw his back stiffen as if she had just lodged a dagger there.

It was all the answer she needed.

Night had fallen by the time the troubled, dusty trio reached Masterson. A sentry in the barbican had only a disrespectful grunt for his returning master.

They crossed the outer ward to the stables, where the horses barely subsisted on thin hay. A scruffy-haired lad in ragged clothing assisted Cedric in bringing Gareth down from the horse. He peered curiously at Briar Rose and looked away when she glared at him.

Her wrists were still bound, but Cedric had untethered her. She noticed that Gareth had gone to the stall of his destrier. He seemed to forget her as he glowered over the unkempt state of the war-horse.

Briar Rose took a chance. Her bound hands were clumsy, but she managed to work the ring out of her hem. Bending swiftly, she secreted it beneath a chunk of stone that lay in a corner of the stable floor. And there it would stay until she could leave this godforsaken place.

Cedric went on his way. For the first time since she'd been taken prisoner, Gareth looked at Briar Rose and spoke.

"You'll be taken to a solar in the southern tower."

She sniffed. "It will be locked, no doubt."

"Aye."

"I am a prisoner, then."

"I'll try not to treat you as such, Briar Rose." He unbound her hands, working gently. He noticed that the ring was missing. "It may be hidden now, but I will have it, make no mistake," he reminded her bitterly.

As soon as her hands were free, Briar Rose cracked her open palm against his cheek, watching his pain, surprised at herself for imparting it. "I'll never give it to you," she cried. "Never!"

It was a vow she repeated to herself again and again as a tiring woman and two guards accompanied her up a sinuous stairway in the south tower. The ring was a symbol of the only thing she had left, the only thing worth living for. Men were wastrels; they came and left as fleetingly as fair weather, but Briarwood endured. It would be her life; she would have room for nothing else.

Kate, the tiring woman, opened an iron-studded door and showed her into the solar.

"This was a favorite retreat of the Lady Mary, God rest her sweet soul," Kate said with a glimmer of sadness in her pale eyes.

Briar Rose looked at her oddly.

"Is something amiss, my lady?"

"No. Mary was my mother's name."

"This was Lord Hawke's dear sister." Kate sighed loudly and the corners of her mouth pulled down. "Things were different in her day. We even had a royal visit or two. The bailey had rich gardens then and the town was prosperous. I was Lady Mary's personal maid, her favorite. Ah, she was kind. Taught me manners and gentled my speech and didn't once beat me or even raise her voice." Kate sighed again. "Now things've changed. This solar is one of the few good rooms we have left. I see to it myself, for her sake."

The tiring woman left after telling Briar Rose that a meal and water for washing would be brought. The heavy door closed with a thud that resounded down the length of the tower, followed by a silence that was broken only by the crackle of the fire in a brazier.

Briar Rose turned away from the door, feeling tired and bleak. She looked around the room and had to admit that Kate was right: it was a good one, and well-kept. The stone walls were cleanly whitewashed and the flagged floor was swept. The oaken furniture had been waxed and polished to a bright shine. The coverlet on the bed and the drapes that surrounded it were the very finest, red damask embroidered with whimsical small animals and birds and flowers.

But these comforts meant little to Briar Rose. She was a prisoner here and no amount of luxury could conceal the fact that the solar was just a glittering cage. Moving restlessly, she went to the tall, narrow window. She looked out and saw that she was high above the torchlit bailey. Too high to even think of escaping.

Kate returned with a salver laden with dried fruits and nuts, a generous slab of cheese, some sliced meat, and a large mug of mulled wine. A pair of lads bearing a basin of water followed, casting curious glances at their lord's guest. They gawked so long that Kate finally shooed them away.

"The chamber jar is there," she said, indicating a clay basin in the corner. "And there are some shifts and a gown or two in the chest. I'll be back in the morning."

Again she left, the door closing with that resounding thud and the iron bolt being thrown from the outside.

The great hall was a scene of disorder. The long tables were lined with unkempt knights and castle folk; the rushes on the floor were strewn with scraps of food that hounds fought over, snapping and growling at each other.

The fare was neither plentiful nor dainty. There were trenchers of coarse dark bread upon which was ladled a watery stew of beans, turnips, and bits of meat. Wine and dark ale flowed from kegs on the sideboards and the wenches were busy running to and fro, keeping the mazers filled. There was some loud joking and cursing, but little frivolity.

Then the master arrived and a hush fell over the raucous crowd. Gareth had bathed and dressed in fresh clothing, wearing his homespun tunic looped with polished stones from the northern hills. His face, scrubbed and cleanly shaven, looked haggard and pale. He would have preferred to take a small meal in his chamber and give way early to the fatigue his wounds had caused.

But there were matters pressing and the men were restless enough already. They needed a master to lead them, not a malingering wounded lord who hid behind the drapes of his bedstead. Gareth moved stiffly to his customary seat, a high-backed chair overlooking the hall, and Paulus helped him sit down.

The castle barber had looked at the deep slashes in his side and offered to wrap them again, but Gareth had refused his services. Absurdly, he didn't want Briar Rose's crude work removed. It was perhaps the last thing she'd given him freely; anything more he would have to take.

He drank deeply from his wine goblet and then set it down, having no appetite for the food. He surveyed the hall, his sharp eyes taking in the state of his knights and people. The poor harvests last year and this were taking their toll.

Finally he addressed his knights. "Good men of Masterson," he boomed, ignoring the fact that the effort pulled painfully at the wounds in his side.

A chorus of halfhearted greetings erupted from the crowd.

"You've all heard the tidings that Giles brought," Gareth continued. "In a few days we will be under siege by forces from Morley. I suspect they may be strong this time. They'll be joined by the men of Lord Alain de Wannet."

"Another of your enemies, my lord?" a man asked.

"Aye, lately renewed, I fear."

"Then there is no hope for us. You shall have to capitulate, my lord."

Gareth's face reddened and he clenched his fist around the stem of his pewter goblet. He knew what the knights were thinking. Lacking pay, they would refuse to defend Masterson. With luck, that might at least spare the town from being sacked.

But he would not—could not—give up. He squared his shoulders and proclaimed, "Morley's unholy marauders shall never prevail at Masterson!"

The squire Paulus and some of the younger knights cheered. They loved their master, with his awesome size and scars of bravery. But the older men, most of whom had families to feed, chafed under Gareth's intensity.

One of them stood and faced him boldly. "Those are words of courage, my lord," he said. "But we cannot eat courage."

"Aye!" chorused many of the others. Gareth knew all too well what his men were suffering. And he knew what he must do.

"Within a short time," he said, "I'll have your pay, and money to buy stores." He motioned to Paulus, who stepped forward and placed a small, locked coffer before him. With a key from his baldric he opened it and tilted the box up so the men could see the cache of coins within.

A waiting silence fell over the hall. Gareth let them look for a time, and then said, "This is a small sum I earned in York. Come morning, each of you may collect a share of it from the bailiff. It's not much, but as I said, there will soon be more." Silently he added, If my wife can be coerced into giving up her ring.

The bold knight who had complained earlier raised his clay mug high. "Our master has never gone back on a promise. Here's to Lord Hawke!"

"Here, here!" the others echoed. "God help the poor dastards of Morley and Wannet!"

Gareth sat back and allowed himself a slight smile. There were few men as loyal as those who served him. They'd been pushed to their limit, yet had returned to him readily. He still had their trust. He'd have to make good on his promise.

Although gratified by the happy mood in the hall, Gareth couldn't suppress an uncomfortable pang of guilt. He'd promised them Padwick's gold.

He wondered about Briar Rose. He could imagine her now, fuming high in Mary's solar, hating him. He wished fervently that he could set her free, but now there was too much at stake. She would have to relinquish the ring, and soon, and he'd have to see to that himself.

Briar Rose passed a day and a night locked in the solar at the top of what the castle folk called Mary's Tower. Her boredom reached a depth that nearly drove her to distraction. She paced incessantly, stared out the window at the town and road beyond, and snapped at the servants who waited on her.

She'd thought her stay at St. Agatha's had been a trial, but this confinement was intolerable. There was nothing to do but wait and fume. During the day she saw men in the bailey at their war games and archery practice. She recognized Cedric, with his big shoulders and flaming hair, and recalled his warning of the imminent siege.

Gareth's men were surprisingly skilled and well-armed. The archers found their target—a cow's skull set on a distant post—from both stationary positions and from astride their horses. The swordsmen and pike-staffers were merciless in their blunted-weapon combat. The mounted men battered the quintain, spinning the dummy wildly on its post. A few of the knights were skillful enough to thrust their lance tips into a dangling loop as their chargers thundered past.

In other quarters men prepared the dreaded Greek fire from naphtha, sulphur, and quicklime. For the first time she realized that a battle was really going to take place. Men would die, property would be destroyed. She'd heard of attacks that lasted for weeks. What would become of her?

Loud shouts of greeting summoned Briar Rose back to the window on the third day. The men were at their drills as usual, but now their mood seemed high, expectant. Then Gareth appeared from the keep to accept their spirited welcome.

They treated him like a prince, Briar Rose noticed with a sharp twinge of bitterness. They hardly seemed like men on the verge of mutiny, as Cedric had feared. Somehow Gareth had changed their minds. Of course, she thought bitterly, remembering. He was planning on taking her ring to sell to Acacia. He must have promised them the money.

She scowled down at him as he moved among his men, spurs spinning as he walked. He was regal, striding in his black tabard with an air of self-assurance, giving no hint that he'd been gravely injured just three days before.

The knights spent the better part of three hours performing for their lord, showing him the feats and battle arts they had been practicing. Gareth watched and nodded approval from time to time, occasionally offering a word of advice or encouragement.

"They do well at their gaming, do they not?"

Briar Rose whirled at the sound of the voice. "Kate. I didn't hear you come in."

The woman dipped her head. "Beg pardon, my lady. I didn't mean to startle you." She set the salver she was carrying on the table. "There's some boiled oxtail and a good bit of fresh-baked bread. The fare usually improves when the master is at home."

"Thank you, Kate." Briar Rose made no move to eat. She turned back to the window. Gareth's presence below drew her interest like a beacon. No, she told herself firmly. 'Tis only that I hate him and am fascinated by him as one is by one's sworn enemy.

Kate had followed her to the window. "Three days ago," she said, "I wouldn't have given a prayer for Masterson. But now that Lord Hawke has arrived and has promised the men their pay, they are ready to stand and fight."

Briar Rose stiffened her back and pursed her lips. Her eyes flashed as she stared down at Gareth. The arrogance, the utter gall he displayed in spending Acacia's coin before he'd earned it rankled her deeply.

She sat down at the window seat and stared out at the darkening terrain. Masterson was in the heart of the wild north country and, high in the tower, she felt as though she were at the top of a crag with a hawk's view of the surroundings.

The town was gathered about the keep. A deep, cold-looking stream cut across the front of the town, forming a partial moat beyond the proper moat of the keep and watering the fields beyond. Under better circumstances it could be a grand, well-protected place.

Briar Rose suddenly realized that Gareth saw it that way, too. And he was doing everything he could to restore Masterson to its former prosperity.

Including marrying her. Bitterness closed around her heart. What a fool she'd been, thinking he'd gone to St. Agatha's to find his love. She should have seen from the start that he'd wed her only to get close enough to steal from her. It would only be a matter of time before he began bleeding Briarwood of its riches in order to endow Masterson.

That night, as she was going through her few belongings, Briar Rose found the folded bit of parchment that had been hastily thrust into the sack from Tynegate, almost as an afterthought. The record of her marriage. It was a harsh reminder of that awful day, when she'd happily agreed to the lowliest of ceremonies, trying not to feel cheated of a grand wedding. Her first impulse was to destroy the offensive document, to cast it into the embers in the grate. But she checked herself. She'd need the record when she sought an annulment, which she vowed to do at the first opportunity. Even consummated, the marriage had been made on such shaky grounds that there was ample cause for dissolving it.

She looked around and saw that Kate had withdrawn. The meal was still on the table. The rich scent of the broth both revolted and tantalized her. With a violent sweep of her hand Briar Rose cast the tray to the floor and savored with a tight smile the great clatter it made.

Much later, Kate and a timid girl arrived to clear the mess away and place another meal on the table. They made no comment. They both shrank from Briar Rose, whose anger had barely abated. Kate lit a candle and a bowl lamp while the girl stirred the fire in the brazier. Then they made themselves scarce, their whispers starting even before they'd closed the door completely.

Briar Rose looked at the evening meal with hungry eyes. The roasted meat in its fragrant mustard sauce smelled divine, as did the hot spiced wine and warm bread. She steeled herself against the gnawing pangs in her belly and again swept the meal to the floor.

The loud crash was still echoing through the tower when the door opened. Gareth stepped inside, his face expressionless as he took in the scene, studying the heated defiance in Briar Rose's eyes.

He smiled sardonically. "Our humble fare at Masterson does not tempt you?"

"Swine!" Briar Rose spat at him. "Get out!"

He shrugged and ignored her demand, and when a scratching sounded at the door he opened it. Paulus and two boys entered, bearing yet another tray that was heavily laden with an elaborate meal. Silently they left, taking the broken and spilled utensils and vessels with them.

Gareth righted the two chairs. "Will you dine with me, Briar Rose?"

"I'd sooner dine with pigs." She refused the chair he offered her.

"Then, with your permission . . . ?" He dipped his hands in the aquamanile and dried them on a linen serviette. With obvious relish he pulled a tender leg from the succulent roast capon and served himself a generous helping of pudding.

Briar Rose backed away and stared at him with fury in her eyes. He seemed not at all concerned that she would not eat. In fact, he studiously ignored her until he had taken his fill and finished the meal with a deep draught of wine.

"There's plenty for the two of us, Briar Rose. I thought we'd have a meal together as husband and wife."

"I'm not hungry," she lied.

"You've not eaten since last night."

"Nor do I intend to, so long as I am a prisoner here."

He eyed her dubiously. "That may be some time."

Briar Rose tilted her chin up. "I disagree. It should take Wannet and Morley but a few hours to overtake your precious keep, and they will free me."

Gareth clenched his jaw to hide his irritation at her taunts. "We're ready for them."

"Ah, yes, your men are eager to fight now that you've promised them money. I wonder, Gareth, if they know where you'll get the gold. Do they know it's from my stepmother, and that you've not yet earned it?"

His eyes widened. He had to remind himself that Briar Rose was just a girl, even though her mind worked with a keen incisiveness that belied her years. Although she had wrongly guessed who had commissioned him to get the ring, the knowing look in her eyes mocked him.

"I will earn it," he said quietly.

Briar Rose longed to rush at him and scratch the insolent expression from his face, but she held the impulse in check. Even seated as he was, relaxed before the fire, he exuded a power she knew she could not best. She said defiantly, "You shall not! The ring is hidden, and I'll carry that secret to my death if need be."

"I think not, Briar Rose," he answered. "I'll be paid. I've promised my men. When the time comes, I'll have the ring."

"Never! I'd sooner die than give it to you."

He studied her furious countenance with a mixture of regret and annoyance. She was so different now from the delicate, loving woman he'd once known. Her spirited good nature had soured to ire and the eyes that had looked at him with adoration were now as hard and brilliant as sapphires. Her beauty was every bit as vibrant as it had always been and Gareth found that his hunger for her hadn't abated.

She noticed the warm look that crept into his eyes. In the firelight, in his black and gray finery, he was unutterably handsome. A few days ago she would have thrilled to that look. Now it infuriated her.

"You'll not be needing the ring, Gareth," she stated. "Your enemies will kill you."

"No doubt they mean to."

"When it happens, it will not be soon enough for me." Her eyes took on a distant look. "When I'm free, I'll go directly to my father and tell him what Acacia tried to do. He will cast her out, and there will be no more problems for me."

Gareth shook his head, smiling ruefully. "You've made it all so simple, Briar Rose. Yet even if Morley and Wannet manage to overtake me, your safety is far from assured. I doubt you've ever seen a company of warriors who are drunk with victory. They'd not relinquish such a prize as you."

"When they learn who I am, they'll not lay a finger on me."

"I would that it were true, but in a castle that has been besieged all the residents are fair game."

"You will not succeed in frightening me, Gareth. Nothing can be so bad as what you've already done."

He quirked an eyebrow at her. "Am I to assume, then, that you prefer rape to your stay in this tower?"

Forgetting caution, she flew at him with no thought but to scratch the knowing smirk from his face. She pummeled his chest with her fists and scratched at his cheeks and eyes. She cursed and kicked him, called him all manner of names.

Gareth had risen from his chair to meet her onslaught. He caught her wrists and wrestled her back to the bed. The two of them fell in a tangled heap upon the furs.

His face loomed over hers, very close, his breathing labored. As she struggled beneath him he said, "You've worse in store for you, Briar Rose, if you continue to fight me."

"Pig!" she spat at him. "You've no right to treat me this way. Let me go this instant."

She seemed better possessed of herself now so Gareth began to relax his grip on her wrists. But even as he did she started her struggles again, reaching out with her nails to rake at his face.

"You fight like a vixen, Briar Rose. If, indeed, Wannet and Morley prevail, that will serve you well."

"They are not my enemies. I will not fight them."

Gareth's brow darkened. "You're a fool, then. Either that, or you're looking forward to being raped."

She writhed under him with a new spark of anger in her eyes. The polished stones that decorated his chest pressed into the flesh of her heaving bosom, and her hands had begun to go numb from his tight grasp on her wrists. Hot, humiliating tears gathered in her eyes when she thought of the other times they had lain together like this. So close, touching intimately . . . But then he'd been gentle, a husband, a lover, so unlike this brute who pinioned her now.

Briar Rose blinked the tears away and swallowed the hard knot in her throat. Through clenched teeth she said, "What you've done to me, Gareth Hawke, is worse than the foulest rape. You've taken everything from me."

"I've done only what is necessary."

"Oh?" she inquired caustically. "And taking me to wife—bedding me—was necessary?"

Her eyes were as hard as the stones on his tunic, but he was close enough to smell the soft fragrance of her hair and skin and feel the beating of her heart. "You wanted that, Briar Rose. Do not deny that you wanted it."

She clenched her teeth in frustration. "I wanted your love, Gareth. I trusted you and I thought you loved me! I thought—I—" She choked on her words and the tears spilled forth at last. Her body went limp beneath him.

Suddenly his hands loosed their hold on her wrists and became, once again, those compelling instruments of pleasure that she had come to know, and crave. He murmured softly into her ear.

"Please don't cry, nightingale. Don't cry anymore . . ." He bowed his head and gently kissed the tears from her cheeks, drawing the salty drops from her skin. Then his mouth traveled to hers, moving over her lips, rubbing from side to side until she gasped and, incredibly, against all reason, began to respond.

She whispered his name, half in protest, half in supplication. It was sweet agony she felt, her body glorying in his taste, his touch, his scent, while her mind screamed out at his falseness. How could he still make her feel this way, as if she were precious to him, despite the fact that he'd stolen everything from her?

From somewhere deep inside, she summoned the will to fight him again. She tore her mouth from his and pressed with all her might on his chest. Gareth studied her for a moment before rising from the bed.

Briar Rose lay still, trying not to think, but her mind gave her no rest. Nothing had changed. Gareth was still her enemy, however much her body craved him, and she'd been wrong, wrong to weaken. As he moved to kiss her once again, she turned aside.

"I think you should leave," she said, her voice cold.

Something in his eyes made her falter for a moment, but she found her will again.

"I mean it, Gareth. You—you found me in a weak moment. It will not happen again. The next time you take me, it will have to be by force, or not at all."

His eyes hardened to flint. He stood and pulled the furs up over her.

"As you wish," he said tonelessly, and left.

The next day morning broke over a silent, deserted town and a tensely waiting keep. When Briar Rose heard none of the usual sounds in the bailey, she hurried to the window. Gareth's archers were stationed at the archières, and the other knights paced the length of the crenellated walls. The gates in front of the great barbican were drawn up and crossed by stout beams, guarded by nervous-looking sentinels.

Briar Rose snatched up a robe and wrapped herself against the chill. She returned to the window, squinting out at the thick fog on the moors. Her heart raced; the day of the siege had come.

There was a clicking as the door latch was thrown. Kate entered with a band of the most bedraggled-looking children Briar Rose had ever seen.

"Pardon, my lady," Kate said, "but the hall and all the chambers are full. This lot will have to weather the siege up here."

Briar Rose regarded the silent, wide-eyed children for a moment. "Of course." She stepped aside. "Do come in and let's stoke this fire. I feel the winter strongly this morning."

Kate bustled away, probably to fetch a tot of wine, which she indulged in often, claiming it calmed her nerves. A lad in tattered clothes scampered to add a few logs to the fire while another fanned the embers vigorously until they climbed to a blaze. The rest of the children huddled near the door, eyeing Briar Rose with a mixture of fear and curiosity.

For a moment she forgot the preparations outside. Without exception, the children wore soiled clothes and had thin faces and wide, hungry eyes. With a stab of guilt Briar Rose recalled the two meals she'd recently dashed to the floor.

"Come warm yourselves by the fire," she invited. No one moved. "Come on, then," she prompted again.

A tiny girl who clutched a fraying straw doll took a hesitant step forward. A boy, who looked to be her brother, jerked her back.

"No, Moll," he hissed. "Remember yourself."

Briar Rose began to feel uncomfortable under their unsmiling, unblinking scrutiny. "Let the child come," she said, "and the rest of you, too."

Moll approached and this time the others followed, one by one, until they were all assembled around the brazier. Still, they remained unnaturally quiet. Briar Rose asked, "What ails you children?"

One of the boys bobbed his head. "The master himself said we was not to bother you, my lady. Said you was a great lady and not to be deviled by the likes of us."

Briar Rose pursed her lips. So Gareth had made her out to be the ogre. She'd not let this image stand. She smiled warmly. "It's no bother for me to share my lonely tower with you. I was beginning to despair of the solitude. Now, why don't you start by telling me your names?"

Odd names, they were. Moll, Rab, Gert, Haw, Sol, and Meg. Short, clipped names, as if no one had cared enough to bestow prettier ones on them. Everything about the children spoke of neglect, from their lice-ridden heads to their tattered shoes. In their pale eyes was a knowledge of hardships such as children should never have to endure.

But their young hearts were not quite hardened, and Briar Rose soon had them at their ease. She regaled them with stories of her home and childhood until they were laughing and begging for more. When Kate appeared with a tray of food, Briar Rose saw to it that the children ate their fill.

"Why did she throw the latch?" Rab asked around a mouthful of bread and cheese.

Briar Rose's eyes narrowed. "To keep me in."

"You aren't allowed to leave?"

"No, Rab."

"But why?"

"Because Lord Hawke wishes it that way."

"I thought you was his guest."

"I suppose I am."

"But I—" The boy broke off and stopped his chewing. Far away a horn blared and there was a faint sound of beating hooves.

Briar Rose sprang to the window. The men at the walls were alert, listening and watching from between the merlons. The thick fog still blanketed the countryside, obscuring the roads and fields.

After what seemed like an eternity a pair of standards appeared in the distance. Briar Rose immediately recognized the Wannet eagle. The other was a golden serpent guarding a crucifix: the Morley emblem.

The host was not large, but well-armed, mounted on good horses or on foot, with a siege engine lumbering in their midst. Briar Rose searched for a glimpse of Lord Alain but didn't see him. He'd sent an able-looking captain in his place, a grandly armored man on a caparisoned destrier. Pursing her lips, Briar Rose realized that Wannet was not about to trouble himself with Masterson, no doubt thinking it an easy take, since Gareth would be presumed dead.

Little Moll clutched her doll to her breast and whimpered. Briar Rose hushed her and gathered her into her lap, trying not to let the child feel her tenseness.

The battle began with a spray of arrows. Men with longbows and crossbows came forward and showered the walls of Masterson with their deadly accurate projectiles. A few of the defenders at the battlements died quickly.

Briar Rose caught her breath when she spied Gareth. He looked magnificent this morning, larger somehow, as he strode up and down the battlements, shouting orders and calling warnings to his men. The way he moved, it was hard to believe that his side was striped with recent sword wounds. Briar Rose felt her throat tighten each time he passed one of the merlons, where arrows shot through unimpeded. Have a care, she told him silently, and then checked her thoughts of concern for him.

As the morning wore away, Wannet and Morley advanced on the walls. A hail of missiles fell on them as they worked to span the moat with a causeway of earth, stones, and even the bodies of their dead. The siege engine was set up and positioned to hurl rock and iron and flaming missiles at the drawn-up gate.

Enemy archers cleared a path for foot soldiers with ladders and axes. The men of Masterson fought doggedly, but it seemed that every time they felled one of the invaders, two more appeared in his place.

By afternoon the enemy was preparing to breach the walls. Gareth's knights brought forth vats of Greek fire and prepared to pour the volatile mixture down on their foes.

All her life Briar Rose had heard tales of fierce battles, from visitors to Briarwood and in the songs of traveling minstrels. But the stories had exalted war, glorified the warriors. Now she found that the reality was a far cry from the romantic ballads of bravery. Men, some of them only boys, were killing one another, and it was ugly, shocking. There was nothing glorious in the way they died, faces smashed by soaring debris, bodies spiked with arrows, drowning in the moat after falling between the crenellated teeth of the battlements.

A screech from behind made Briar Rose jump. The girl called Meg, who had been watching in tense silence, leaned so far out the window that Briar Rose had to drag her forcibly back.

"Heath!" Meg cried. "My Heath is killed!" She lunged again toward the window.

Briar Rose held her so hard that her arms began to tremble. In every quarter men lay dead or dying, felled by arrows or spears. Meg's eyes were fastened on an archer whose body slumped over the wall, an arrow lodged in his neck.

The girl continued to screech and keen for a long time until it appeared her energy was drained. Briar Rose held her through it all, murmuring soothing words and never releasing her grasp around Meg's shoulders.

"There now," she crooned, when Meg's screaming abated to hopeless whimpers. "Was he your brother?"

Meg stared at her with wild, wet eyes. She began to laugh then, an eerie, mirthless sound. "My brother!" she choked. "By the saints, he was my husband!"

Briar Rose wasn't sure she'd heard correctly. For lack

of anything better to say she asked, "How old are you, Meg? Surely not old enough to be a wife."

Meg's eyes narrowed. "Sixteen, I am. Old enough to know a man's love and to carry his babe in me."

Briar Rose's heart went out to the girl. Through the grime and tears and ill-fitting clothes she saw the truth. Meg was, indeed, a woman, and pregnant. "When Kate returns," she said over her shoulder to the others, "tell her to bring a strong draught for Meg." Then she turned her attention to the sobbing girl and held her, rocking, for a long while.

The battle raged on outside. At close range the invaders were dropping in greater numbers, being felled by spears and arrows and now by hot oil and missiles and fiery balls of oil-soaked straw. The noise made by dying men was bone-chilling.

The siege engine had spanned the moat to the drawn-up gate. It pounded relentlessly with great crushing blows. Behind, a host of cavalrymen waited to make their entrance. Gareth leaped from his station at the wall to mount his forces in the outer ward. His squire helped him into full armor and onto a destrier, and Briar Rose suddenly knew what he was expecting.

Already the crossbeams on the gate were splintering and the iron hinges began to give. Gareth's mounted knights positioned themselves at either side, ready to meet their enemies. A band of boys brought a vat of Greek fire to the murder holes above the passageway and prepared to dump the stuff on the incoming foes.

The gate groaned under the assault of the siege engine and finally the hinges tore free. The gate fell with a dusty thud and Wannet and Morley poured in. They gave loud shouts and savage battle cries, sounds which covered the screams of the men and horses who perished under the murder holes.

Gareth and his men fell upon the host, crashing their lances against shields, swinging swords and maces at the heads of foot soldiers, trampling all who stood in their way.

Briar Rose clutched at the stone window frame and her teeth bit into her lower lip hard enough to draw blood. She held this position, transfixed by the savagery of the battle.

Gareth was like a black demon, cutting and hacking his way through the ranks of the mounted knights. There was some commotion among the Morley and Wannet men. Briar Rose guessed it was because they'd supposed Gareth dead.

The knights of Masterson, the squires, archers, and fighting men, shared their lord's unrelenting ferocity. They plunged headlong at their attackers, beating them back mercilessly. And, incredibly, against all odds, they vanquished them.

Looking haggard but victorious, Gareth appeared in the solar where Briar Rose was being held. Night had descended and all the children save a weepy-eyed Meg were asleep on the bed.

"It's safe for them to go now. Kate should have already come for them."

Briar Rose stifled the flood of relief she felt at seeing Gareth alive and whole. The battle had ended in the outer ward and the final moments had been difficult to see, with the banners down, trampled underfoot, and the smoke from flaming missiles billowing up. She'd lost sight of Gareth at the last, when he'd been unhorsed. Now that she was satisfied that he lived, however, she'd not allow him to guess her fears.

She lifted her chin in defiance. "I want to keep the children with me."

"They must go."

"No! Gareth, they're only babes."

He grinned at her crookedly and winced only a bit from his wounds and aching limbs. "Since when have you found it in your heart to care for the lowest urchins of Masterson, my lady?"

Briar Rose glowered at him. "Since I realized how horribly they've been neglected. They were near starving when they arrived."

"I'll give them something from the kitchens and send them on their way."

"You'll do no such thing, Gareth Hawke. They'll have at least one night here and a meal in the morning, and then I will consider allowing them to leave."

Gareth stepped closer with a gleam in his eye. His arms came out and caught Briar Rose in a rough embrace. " 'Tis well they sleep, then," he told her huskily, "for what I have in mind is not fit for a child's eyes."

His kiss stifled her protest and took her breath away. She steeled herself against the tempting impulse to melt into his arms and let her primitive, undisciplined instincts take over. Although his tongue teased her lips, inviting them to open, she battled the weakness.

When he finally lifted his mouth from hers, she said, "You smell of sweat and smoke and blood."

"That offends you?"

"Aye, and you're drunk," she accused.

His laugh was a great, unbridled roar. "That I am, my sweet! Come now, will you begrudge me this one indulgence? Today we drove off not one but two enemies, and I'd say that is cause for revelry. Are you not happy for me?"

Briar Rose pursed her lips. "If you remember, Lord Hawke, I was hoping for a victory for the other side."

He didn't look in the least stricken by her comment. At the moment nothing could mar his jubilant mood. Morley and Wannet had been too confident, sending a poorly organized force small enough to be beaten in mere hours rather than weeks, as he'd feared. He'd shown that Masterson was still a force to be reckoned with. One only had to look into the great hall and the streets of the town to see what effect that had on the inhabitants.

"You should see the celebration below," he told Briar Rose. "We've not had such revelry here in ages. My men are fair to bursting with joy. They're drinking and dancing . . ." He reached out and traced the line of her unsmiling lips with a finger. "And wenching . . ."

She jerked away from him. "Then I suggest you join them. I, for one, do not share your enthusiasm. Find another wench."

Finally his smile faded. "Do you mean that, Briar Rose?"

She tossed her head and lied, "Aye, I do." Inwardly she cringed. The very idea of Gareth with another woman turned her heart to ice. She saw hurt in his eyes, a reflection of her own pain. She drove her stab deeper by saying, "Everyone at Masterson isn't as jubilant as you. Look at Meg, there, in the corner. She lost a husband today. And there are others like her, whose husbands, sons, fathers, and brothers are dead in your service."

For the first time since Gareth had entered the solar Meg dared to speak. She lowered her reddened eyes deferentially. "It's true that I grieve, my lord, but do not take it as disloyalty. 'Tis a fine thing that you won the day." Meg's respect for Gareth was so apparent that Briar Rose was angered further.

"I don't know what it is about you, Gareth, but you seem to have everyone under your spell."

"My people know I am for them. What little I have I share with them."

"At one time I believed that. But a lot of my beliefs about you have changed."

He looked suddenly bleak and sober. So that was her final word. "So be it," he muttered, going to the door. He stopped and embraced Meg, promising her a place of honor for her Heath in the crypt and a year's pay. Before he left, he looked back at Briar Rose. He was sure he'd imagined the softening of her eyes.

Two days later Gareth realized that the siege had changed everything for Briar Rose. Now he did not need her, nor her accursed ring.

Sitting in the armory, Gareth viewed the spoils of victory. The armor, horses, weapons, and prisoners that had been seized were worth a small fortune. It was more than adequate to see Masterson through to the next year's harvest. If that harvest was good, then the estate would be well on its way to new prosperity. Morley's attack had turned out to be a blessing in disguise.

Eager to see Briar Rose's reaction to his good fortune, he left the armory. As he was crossing the bailey, his man Giles clattered up through the gate and hailed him.

"Congratulations on your victory. I only wish I'd been here for the siege."

Gareth flashed a grin at him. " 'Twas your shrewd warning that gave us time to prepare for it. Thanks to you we weren't taken by surprise."

Giles dismounted and gave his horse over to a stable lad. "I did no more than my duty, Lord Hawke."

"There are few scouts who can wheedle information from the most unlikely of sources like you do. I've heard you called the Fox of Masterson, and for good reason."

Giles's smile spread from ear to ear. He was good, and he knew it. In the service of Lord Hawke he had masqueraded as a beggar, a raving idiot, a monk, even a high-born nobleman.

Gareth would have liked to stay and talk, but the business with Briar Rose was pressing. There was no point in making her endure imprisonment any longer.

Giles stopped him. "I must tell you where I've been, my lord, and what I've heard."

"And so you shall, as soon as I've dispensed with a matter of some importance."

It was part of Giles's great talent that he had the uncanny ability to read people as if their heads were made of glass. "My lord, if you mean to settle things with your wife, you'd best hear me out. My news concerns her."

"So you know of her," he said.

"Aye. But you know I'll keep your secret. Now, shall we go somewhere private to talk?"

Gareth had a small withdrawing room just behind the hall. They sat before a low fire, sipping mulled wine and stretching their feet out to warm them.

"My travels have taken me to Castle Briarwood and Stepton, where Alain de Wannet is passing the Catherning," Giles began.

"Ah, so that's why the coward wasn't present for the siege."

Giles nodded. "The poor girl in the tower is in more trouble than she knows."

"I mean to remedy that, Giles. As soon as I've heard you out."

"But you're not the threat, Lord Hawke. Not any longer." Giles sipped his wine, looking ill-at-ease. "The stepmother, Acacia, has somehow discovered that you're acting on Padwick's orders. She spoke freely of it when I pretended to be a sympathetic courtier. She's guessed that you have no intention of carrying out her request."

"Acacia is right in that. But neither will I fulfill Padwick's wishes. At first I was convinced that he was the best person to take charge of the crest. Now I realize that it belongs to Briar Rose. God knows, she has little else to cling to. I mean to send her to Tynegate unharmed, with her ring. She'll be free to seek an annulment, which I expect she'll do as soon as possible." Gareth tried not to wince as he said it. He'd known from the start that marrying Briar Rose was a mistake. A mistake made by a fool who'd allowed himself to become besotted by a pair of ruby lips and shining violet eyes.

"My lord, if you allow that, you may well wash your hands of this whole affair. But Acacia is desperate. She's in league with Alain de Wannet and means to have the girl killed."

"Has Wannet agreed to this scheme?"

"He has, in a sense. As far as Acacia knows, he has hired a huntsman to do the deed. But Alain has other plans for the girl."

"Go on."

"He means to find her himself. Your civil marriage to Briar Rose could easily be invalidated by a well-paid solicitor. Then he'll marry her and take Briarwood for his own. Acacia knows nothing of this. Wannet will betray the betrayer, so to speak."

Gareth sat for a long while glaring into the fire. Finally he asked, "Does anyone know that the girl is here?"

"No, my lord. Masterson is probably the safest place she could be."

"You were right to tell me this, Giles. I cannot release her now, can I?"

"Not unless you'd like to see her captured and married against her will, or killed."

"By the rood, Giles, she hates me enough already!"

"Aye, but 'tis a choice of whether you would have her hate you in safety, or love you in peril."

"Where are you taking me?" Briar Rose demanded as Gareth led her down the winding tower stairs. "If you think I'm about to tell you where my ring is—"

He raised an eyebrow. "You don't trust me, do you?"

She tossed her head. "You've given me scant reason for trust."

"I thought you might like to get out on this fine afternoon."

Briar Rose couldn't argue with that. After the children had left the tower, she thought she'd go mad from boredom. The October day was cold, but the sun was bright, the sky blue and clear. She followed Gareth across the bailey to the stableyard. He nodded to the head groom, who quickly went to do his bidding.

"She is yours," Gareth said, indicating the horse the groom brought out.

Briar Rose clasped her hands. The white mare, outfitted with an elegant saddle, had a a proudly arching neck and prancing, eager feet.

"The stable lads have dubbed her Dame Blanche," Gareth said. "Of course, you're free to change it if—"

"She's quite a lady," Briar Rose said, reaching out to stroke the smooth, glossy neck. "That's a fitting name for her."

Gareth's newly won gelding was midnight black, even more spirited than the mare. "This is Abelard," he told Briar Rose. "He'll never replace Bayard, but the knight who lost him to me is a sight poorer now. Shall we go, then?"

Briar Rose considered refusing, for being with Gareth was sheer torture, but the thought of returning to the tower was intolerable. At her nod Gareth helped her into the saddle. Dame Blanche danced sideways a little, then settled as Briar Rose took a firm hold on the reins.

"You sit her well; she looks to have been bred expressly for you," Gareth said.

She thought the same of him and Abelard, but nothing could have compelled her to pay him such a rich compliment.

The northern landscape was rough, ideal for riding hard. Briar Rose gloried in an exhilarating sense of freedom. The tension of her confinement fell away and she laughed aloud.

Gareth spurred off toward the north and motioned for her to follow. She hesitated for just a moment, considering flight in the opposite direction. But there was no road in sight and she had nothing to take with her. She was determined to escape, but only after careful preparation.

Gareth led her up above the moors where a crisp wind sang down between great crevices in the rocks. The horses climbed with sure feet until they came to a crashing stream that seemed to burst from the hillside.

They dismounted to let the horses drink from a pool that collected at the base of the cascade.

"What is this place?" Briar Rose asked when she had caught her breath.

"It has no name. I've been coming here since I was a lad."

She spread her woolen skirts—borrowed from the chest in Mary's Tower—and sat down. Gareth lowered himself beside her and watched her for a long moment.

She was a charming sight, with long tendrils of hair escaping from her braid and the color high in her cheeks.

"I sense less animosity from you today," he ventured.

Her eyes darkened. "That may be so, Gareth. When we last saw each other, you were drunk and your demands angered me. Today you have given me something freely, and for that I thank you."

Gareth grinned at the recollection of his mood after the siege. "I was overbearing, to be sure, but I had good reason to be that way. We won a fortune in arms and armor, horses and weapons. There are a few well-placed prisoners we intend to ransom. In fact, some have already had their kinfolk buy their freedom."

"So soon?" Briar Rose smiled coldly. "My, but you are impatient."

He caught her sarcasm. "I thought you'd be glad to hear I'm not as needy as I was when we arrived."

A calculating gleam came into Briar Rose's eyes. "You know, Gareth, my father would pay dearly for my release if he but knew where I was."

Her father would probably be only too happy to know that she was at Masterson. "You're not a military prisoner," he said. "I'd like you to think you're not a captive at all, but my wife, the baroness of Masterson."

"I refuse to be your wife. You married me falsely. I want our marriage annulled."

Although he'd expected as much, Gareth felt an arrow of pain shoot through him. "You'll have it," he growled, masking his pain with anger. "In due time."

"Gareth, why must you keep me here? Are you so greedy that you still want my ring for Acacia's bounty?"

He shook his head. "I don't want that from you, Briar Rose, not anymore. But I cannot let you leave."

Her eyes sparkled. "Liar! You do still want it!"

"No. Truly, Briar Rose, I want nothing from you, only to know that you're safe from harm. I've had news that your stepmother has a new plot against you. She and Alain de Wannet are partners now. She wishes for him to eliminate you and he's let her believe he'll do the deed. But in sooth he wants to find you in order to marry you and add Briarwood to his holdings."

"I can well believe that Acacia means me ill, but I doubt Lord Alain would deign to involve himself in her scheming. I know he's your enemy, Gareth, but that's still not cause for you to slander him."

"Did he not offer for you last summer?"

"Yes, but he didn't press his suit. Why should he, when he can have his choice of many ladies better endowed than I?"

Gareth faced her vehemence with expressionless silence, waiting for her anger to ebb. And always there was that attraction he felt toward her, such as he had known with no other woman. It was maddening, both a strength and a weakness.

The silence between them was tense, broken only by the sound of the water rushing into the pool and the whistling of the wind. The torrent glazed and polished the rocks, creating a scene of magical beauty. Gareth studied her profile, her chin tilted up proudly, those sweet lips pressed together in anger. A low growl of frustration rumbled from his throat and he captured Briar Rose in his arms, laying her back on the dry grass. He spoke her name, breathed the intoxicating fragrance of her hair and skin.

She was taken completely by surprise. While her mind screamed out that she hated this man for what he'd done, her treacherous body responded, remembering of its own accord the bliss she'd known in his arms. Heat spread from her loins to her limbs, and when their lips met, a burning hunger claimed her.

It was as if she'd never stopped loving him. Her body wanted—demanded—his caresses. His tongue curled deftly into her mouth and she welcomed it and pressed her body closer. She made no resistance when his hand reached into her cloak and cupped her breast, fondling it through her woolen clothing.

When at last he lifted his lips from hers, Briar Rose looked deep into his eyes. Sweet Christ, how she'd loved him, with those eyes of silver-rimmed gray, that magnificent Saxon face . . . His falseness, his dishonorable treatment of her, were almost too much to bear. And just now he'd compounded the hurt by lying to her again, contriving some fanciful story about Acacia and Alain, expecting her to believe it and stay happily in her tower prison. She summoned every shred of her strength and said, "Gareth, release me."

His eyes turned as hard and cold as the gritstone rocks that surrounded them. With a muttered oath he thrust her aside.

"I want to leave Masterson," she reminded him.

"I'll not release you to your stepmother's treachery."

She laughed harshly. "Acacia can do me no more ill than you already have. I'm not afraid of her."

"God's blood, Briar Rose, you're in danger, can't you see that?"

"I'd rather face it than stay with you."

He stood and untethered the horses. "I'm afraid you have no choice."

She passed a week without seeing him. Despite his threat, she was allowed a little freedom. But always she was watched by Kate, or one of the guards, or the great flame-haired knight called Cedric, who accompanied her on her daily rides. There was no hope of escape so long as Gareth's people shadowed her every move.

She burned with rage every time she thought of Gareth Hawke. She wished she could feel indifferent to him and keep her pain at bay, but she could not. Her hatred was no less intense than her love had been. It twisted and writhed like a live thing within her, robbing her of appetite and sleep.

Now there was no question in her mind. She had to get away or she would go mad. Despair was eating away at her; it threatened to destroy her, if she didn't starve herself first.

Carefully she laid out a plan. Her new freedom allowed her to study, surreptitiously, the workings of Castle Masterson. She learned the routine of the sentinels outside. She made friends with a stable lad called Hal. And she thought hard about Kate, her most constant watcher. The woman had a dangerous weakness for wine.

Briar Rose chose a bright October afternoon to make her flight. She rose as usual and was surprised to discover that she no longer missed the morning services as she had when she'd first come to Masterson. She chided herself for her impiety and blamed it on Gareth, although Friar George had been accusing her of such neglect for years. She stopped for a moment and prayed hastily, whispering the words she'd known since childhood, asking the grace of God to speed her in all her works.

She chose a few items from the chest in her room. There was not much to be had, only an extra shift and chemise and a small vial of rose oil, which she took to trade for a bit of food along the way. The things would not likely be missed.

When Kate came, Briar Rose surprised her with an invitation to join in a drink of wine. Before long, Kate's mood became cheery and besotted.

"Call for another jug, Kate. This one's about done," Briar Rose suggested.

Kate gladly obliged and was soon draped over one of the chairs. "Things look better around the place, don't they, madam? 'Twould be doubly fine if the master were in better spirits."

Briar Rose raised her eyebrows. "He is unhappy?"

"Aye." Kate winked broadly. "You've not let him near you. He may have need of companionship."

"He should have no trouble finding it." Briar Rose clenched her fists but kept her face impassive.

"Oh, aye. And willing ones, too. But the master wants none of them."

Briar Rose tried not to think of Gareth, for inevitably it caused the pain of having loved and been betrayed by him to come rushing back. She asked, "What about you, Kate? Are you not married?"

Kate took a long drink of her wine and Briar Rose refilled her mug. "No, my lady. I'm content as I am."

"And so shall I be," Briar Rose vowed.

"Och, you mustn't say that, my lady. Why, just look at you—so pretty and ripe for a man's love."

Briar Rose flushed. "You compliment me overmuch, Kate." Her eyes misted and she forgot that Kate was there. "There was a time, though, when I would have given everything willingly—my whole heart and soul—to a man. Now I know to keep to myself, and not risk another betrayal."

"He's not betrayed you, my lady!" Kate exclaimed.

Briar Rose faced her with raised eyebrows. "Kate, you don't know what you're talking about."

"There's something between you; we've all seen it. I know not why you shun each other."

"There is nothing between us save bitterness and distrust," Briar Rose insisted.

"On your part, perhaps, but his lordship loves you."

"And this is how he treats one he loves? As a captive in a cage?"

"My lady, his lordship has good reason."

"Bah!" Briar Rose spat. "He is a brute."

"He loves you, I say!"

"You're mistaken. Not even when he tricked me into marrying him did he dare tell me that. 'Twould have been too great a lie, even for him."

"It doesn't surprise me that the master hasn't spoken of his feelings."

"Gareth Hawke has no feelings but lust and ambition."

Kate raised an eyebrow crookedly. "Oh? And which was it, lust or ambition, that made him gift you with that horse you're always riding?"

"He did that to placate me, thinking I'd not be so disagreeable a prisoner if I had a diversion."

"Then what of this room?" Kate gestured around her. "It has been used by no one since Lady Mary was killed." The woman's eyes clouded. "We all loved her, but none so much as the master himself. He'd not allow you to be here, to sleep in her bed and wear her clothes, if he didn't care for you."

Briar Rose refused to be swayed by what she knew to be the sottish sentimentality of a woman who'd drunk too much. To this last nonsense she made no response.

She glared and looked away. Now was not the time for her to start thinking about Gareth, wondering about the true sentiments that lurked behind his granite eyes. That mattered not; he'd wronged her and she would have no more to do with him or any other man.

Some time later, she left Kate snoring in the chair. She pulled a long, fur-lined cloak about her, secreting a bundle inside it, and locked the tiring woman in the solar.

Hal proved as easy to deal with as Kate had been. His young face, appealingly freckled, split into a broad grin when she approached him in the stables.

"Which mount will your escort be taking, my lady?" he asked.

She held his eyes firmly with hers. "I'll be riding alone today, Hal."

A shadow of doubt crossed his face. "My lady, the master said—"

"I'll go alone. Lord Hawke's knights are tired of acting the nursemaid to me." She gave the lad her most artful smile. "Come, Hal, do I not seem like one who can look after myself?"

"You . . . of course, my lady."

"Good. Then take Dame out to the yard for me." When the boy had gone, she ran to a dark corner of the stables and retrieved her ring. Her finger welcomed its familiar heaviness.

"You will be careful, my lady?" Hal questioned anxiously as he helped her into the saddle.

"I'll be fine," she said.

She crossed the narrow causeway that spanned the moat and went down into the town.

She met the questioning looks of the people with a smile, trying her best to look as if she were out for her usual ride. It was all she could do to keep her mount at a sedate pacc when her every instinct urged her to flee.

She nodded at a group of children who were playing at stickball. Oddly, she felt a tug at her heart. She'd grown to like the folk.

At last Briar Rose left the town behind. She took the eastern road, an ill-traveled path that led she knew not where. Her objective was not ahead of her but behind, and she had accomplished it. She had escaped Gareth Hawke.

9

"Gone!" Gareth roared, pouring all his pent-up rage into the word. Kate cringed miserably before him and nodded her head.

"Fool woman," he said, pacing the solar. "If my sister hadn't loved you so dearly, I'd cast you out this minute."

The absence of Briar Rose had hit Gareth like a surprise blow to the gut. He forced himself to speak calmly, though. The tiring woman was already near hysteria.

"Speak then, Kate. When did the lady take her leave?"

"I—I cannot say precisely, my lord. Lady Briar Rose, she plied me with the wine and—and I fear I fell asleep."

Gareth gripped the back of a chair. "Think, woman. When?"

" 'Twas—'twas yesterday, my lord. In the afternoon, I think."

Yesterday! Gareth's spurs jangled as he bounded down the twisted tower stairs. He should not have neglected Briar Rose so. Her rejection when they were last together had angered him, but he should have expected that.

He should have acted more the husband, even in the face of her fury. He'd gone to the tower to make amends. He'd even brought a lovely rabbit-lined hood as a peace offering. But he'd been too late.

He sprinted across the bailey and, panting, entered the stables. "Kervin!" he shouted, summoning the head groom. "Where are you, man?"

The groom appeared shortly. "What's your pleasure, my lord?"

Gareth grasped his shirtfront. "Find your lads so I can question them."

Concerned now, Kervin ducked out and called impatiently. Within a few moments the lads were assembled before their master.

Gareth eyed them fiercely, his very stare setting them atremble. "Where is the white palfrey?"

The boys glanced at one another. Gareth fixed his stare on Hal. He lowered his voice to an ominous whisper. "Well, boy? Answer me!"

Hal blanched beneath his freckles. "The lady t-took her out yesterday, my lord."

"Alone!"

"Aye, sir. She promised 'twould be all right. She said she'd be back—"

"And you let her go, fool!" Gareth raised his hand to cuff the boy, then remembered himself. "Saddle Abelard for me," he muttered, and went to ready himself.

A robed figure on horseback slowly approached the woman who came up the road on a gleaming white palfrey. He removed his brown hood to reveal a tonsured head.

This was Hawke's woman; there was no mistaking her. She was doubtless a lady, her complexion flawless, the lips highly colored, her long hair gleaming richly over the fabric of her mantle. Features so delicate were rare. And Hawke, in his infinite greed, had taken this prize for himself. The cleric didn't know what she was doing here, a day's ride from Masterson, but he knew he'd stumbled upon something extremely useful.

Briar Rose glanced up to see the cleric looking at her with a strange smile. "Good evening, Friar," she said.

He bobbed his head. "Good evening, mistress. But a cold one it is. Tell me, what brings you here alone?"

"I am traveling south."

"At this time of year? Most wayfarers more seasoned than you have already found residences for winter."

"Well, I shall not, until I reach my destination."

"Do let me help you, then, mistress. You look none too warm and I'll wager you've naught to eat. Let me take you to get a rest and a warm meal."

She hesitated only a moment. Then she followed him along the road, where evening was bringing a thin coating of frost to the sere fields.

"You are kind, Friar," she said.

" 'Friar' is a name I seldom go by," he told her, pulling up his hood. "Please, mistress, call me Griffith."

Griffith asked what Briar Rose considered a good number of questions—where she came from, where she had been, whom she'd seen. She answered him as evasively as possible. Some instinct told her to protect her secret.

The cleric brought her to a town with a large market, a strong-looking keep in the distance, and farther on, an abbey surrounded by fields of grazing sheep. The whole place had the look of prosperity, the tithe barns full, people bustling about. Yet there was something that Briar Rose couldn't find a name for. The people they passed regarded her with wary, troubled eyes, and even the fat wool merchants and goodwives wore no smiles as they went about their business.

They went to the abbey refectory where they were served a meal of mutton shoulder, bread, wine, and apples. The surroundings, long rough-hewn tables and carved stonework along the dank walls, made Briar Rose inexplicably nervous.

"I didn't realize wenches did such work," she remarked, eyeing several girls who hefted the great platters of food and wooden kegs of wine. They stared back, dull-eyed and unsmiling.

Griffith made no response. Briar Rose turned her glance to him and wondered at the profusion of jewels with which he was adorned. On the front of his robe he wore a gold and ruby amulet depicting a snake coiled about a crucifix. Aside from the tonsured head and brown robe with its knotted scourge, Griffith had the look of an eminent physician rather than a cleric.

Her thoughts turned inexorably to Gareth Hawke. She wondered what he was doing, what he was feeling right now. Was he as hurt and confused as she had been when she found out the truth? Did he grieve over what might have been, just as she had?

Griffith watched the dark shadows that passed behind her strangely beautiful, violet eyes. He burned to know just who she was, where she was going, why she was hurrying so and hiding so much.

"You'll stay the night," he said, startling her out of her reverie.

Briar Rose blinked away the thoughts of Gareth.

"Thank you. I must see to my mount now," Briar Rose said. "I'm afraid I've no coin for the almonry—"

Griffith pushed himself back from the table. As he was doing so, a serving wench carrying a tray passed behind him. They collided and the tray went crashing to the floor.

The girl shrank back. Griffith advanced on her, hand raised high. He brought his fist down hard on her shoulder and with the other beat her on the sides of the face. Her head snapped back and forth, her stringy hair whipping wildly.

Briar Rose was stunned by the viciousness of the assault. Then she quickly leaped at the pair. She grabbed at Griffith's flailing arm and held it fast.

Griffith bellowed for help. A guard appeared and the two men restrained her.

"Shame on you," she exclaimed at Griffith. " 'Twas your own clumsiness that caused the girl to drop the tray. You had no call to attack her."

Griffith smiled darkly at the guard. "This one has proven to be as meddlesome as the last of Hawke's women. But I must say, she has a good deal more spirit."

The first icy finger of fear touched the base of her spine. His serpent amulet gleamed dully at her and suddenly she remembered where she'd seen it before: on a banner flying over the host that had besieged Masterson.

"We're well-acquainted with the women of Masterson," Griffith said. "The last one caused us a good deal of trouble. Now we're better prepared. Your presence here, dear lady, will serve to reverse the wrongs Hawke has done us."

He explained no further.

Briar Rose stopped struggling when she realized her

efforts against the burly guard were useless. Besides, Griffith's cryptic remarks about Gareth had piqued her curiosity. She walked out of the refectory, nodding to the girl whom Griffith had beaten. The girl mouthed her thanks.

They followed a cloistered outer hallway, passing thick wooden doors and hooded clerics who glided silently by. At the end of the hallway they came to an arched door, which two sentries opened to allow them entry.

The receiving room was opulent with rich tapestries and wall hangings, candelabra fitted with slender beeswax tapers, and gilt-framed icons of important-looking holy men.

Two pages opened a rear door and a red-robed man stepped out. From the gray that streaked his temples Briar Rose guessed that he was of middle years, although he had a youthful, vital look to him. His skin was ruddy and unblemished, stretched taut over the pronounced bones of his face, and his dark eyes were clear and bright.

He seated himself on a tall-backed, cushioned chair. Gargoyles and griffins were carved into the chair, their leering faces and sinuous tongues seeming to mock Briar Rose. She shivered and looked away, then squared her shoulders and tilted her chin up. There was no point in showing fear to these men.

Griffith gave her a shove that sent her sprawling. "To your knees, woman. This is His Excellency, Bishop Talwork of Morley Diocese."

Briar Rose shivered and stared blankly at the stone wall of the basement cell. There was a constant drip-dripping as water beaded on the wall and then fell to the filthy floor. Briar Rose was glad for the darkness in the cell; were she able to see, she knew she'd see the half dozen scuttling rats that were her cellmates.

She drew her knees up to her chest to huddle against the pervasive cold and the ghastly squeaks of rodents. Soon she began to long for that other prison, Mary's Tower at Masterson.

Sighing, she reflected that she had never truly known freedom. Her childhood at Briarwood had been sheltered, she was watched over by a virtual army of nurses, tutors, and waiting women who monitored her every move and chastised her whenever she'd attempted to break free of them. At Wexler she'd been even more restricted, and at St. Agatha's she was walled in and ordered about like the commonest servant.

It angered her to think that her lot in life was forever to be a captive. Would she always be kept by someone else? She set her jaw determinedly and whispered "No" into the darkness. Somehow she would get away from this place.

She indulged in these thoughts for some time, taking refuge from the reality of her plight. When the door was unbolted, the noise startled her and she leaped to her feet.

At first she was blinded by the light of a smoky tallow candle; then she was able to discern a young face. It was the woman Griffith had beaten. Behind her was a guard.

"I've brought you something to eat, mistress, and a cloak to warm you," the young woman said.

Briar Rose took the wooden tray and set it on the floor. "Thank you," she said.

The young woman looked questioningly at the guard, who shrugged noncommittally and stepped out into the dark hallway. "I am Maeve. Thank you for what you did today. I regret that your actions landed you here."

"I think I would have been brought here no matter what," she assured the girl. "But what of you?"

Maeve grimaced. "I was captured along with my mistress and several others during a siege on my home of Masterson."

"Masterson! Then your mistress was Lady Mary!"

"Aye, poor soul. She died here."

Briar Rose hastened to explain her connection to Masterson. Maeve begged for news and seemed especially curious about the flame-haired knight called Cedric.

"We were betrothed," Maeve said. "I still hope to marry him one day if I can ever get away from this place, and if he'll still have me after—after—" She buried her face in her hands.

Briar Rose shivered to think what Maeve had endured here. She took the woman's hands in hers and said, "What's happened is no fault of your own, Cedric knows that. If anything, he'll love you more for surviving your ordeal."

"What sweet encouragement you give me, mistress!"

The guard at the door cleared his throat. "Time to go," he said. "Vespers are about to be sung."

Maeve smiled bitterly. "Ironic, isn't it? They sin against us daily, yet they insist we attend Mass to keep our souls clean."

Briar Rose sat motionless as the door was shut and locked. Tears gathered in her eyes, and to avoid uncontrollable sobs she burst out laughing. The harsh, bitter noise she made was heard by no one save the vermin in the dank basement.

It was night, although Briar Rose had no way of knowing that, imprisoned deep in the bowels of the abbey. A guard came just as she awoke from a fitful sleep and conducted her up a twisted staircase and along a cold, rushlit corridor.

Once again Briar Rose found herself in the receiving room of Bishop Talwork. This time, however, she did not appear nearly so proud or defiant.

The bishop glared at her pale face and red, swollen eyes. "You must be sorry you were so uncooperative earlier, young lady. 'Twould have saved you a visit to our loneliest cell."

Something in the bishop's manner—his arrogance and the cruel twist of his lips—infuriated Briar Rose beyond caution. "I have nothing to say to you until you promise to let me go."

Talwork smiled icily. "I cannot. At least, not until I find out some things about you."

"Is it your common practice, then, to take in wayfarers and treat them in such a manner?"

"Of course not. But you see, my dear, you're hardly just any wayfarer. A woman alone—that is curious enough in itself. And on top of that you are quite obviously gently bred and we know you are associated with Gareth Hawke."

"Not by choice." She had forgotten how eagerly she'd left St. Agatha's with him, wed him at Tynegate, and given herself to him, compelled by her own heart.

"Nevertheless, we have a great interest in him, and therefore in you. Now, suppose you begin by telling us who you are."

Earlier, Briar Rose had considered revealing herself. As powerful as Talwork was, he would act with caution in mistreating one of her rank. But her conversation with Maeve had led her to doubt that it would be any help. Hadn't they captured Mary Hawke, who was of noble birth, and caused that lady's death?

She said, "You may call me Rose."

Talwork quirked an eyebrow at her. "Just Rose? Never mind, 'tis a start. How long were you at Masterson?"

"Longer than I cared to be."

"You will answer, please."

"No."

Bishop Talwork leaned forward and his eyes flashed in anger. "Young lady, I am accustomed to being addressed as 'Your Excellency.' "

Briar Rose sent him a stony stare. "That is a title I reserve for men of the Church whom I hold in esteem."

He clutched the carved armrests of his thronelike seat. The others in the room began whispering among themselves, obviously shocked by the girl's daring disrespect.

"Such impertinence will not serve you well here."

"If you cannot tolerate me, then let me go on my way."

"Tell me the state Lord Hawke is in."

Briar Rose allowed herself a smirk of satisfaction. "You thought your men had killed him, didn't you? No wonder you were so surprised to find he was well enough to defend Masterson."

"I admit I was given the wrong information from my subordinates. I was told he met with a fatal accident."

"Bah!" Briar Rose spat. " 'Twas no accident, as you well know. Gar—Lord Hawke was set upon by your men, on your orders."

"Your defense of a man deemed an outlaw by the Church is heresy."

"I want no part of your feud with Lord Hawke. I don't see what you hope to gain by detaining me here."

"You're of great value to us," Talwork said. "You are the bait that will lure Lord Hawke from his lair. 'Tis known that you are his whore. I expect him to come charging recklessly in to fetch you any time now."

Briar Rose closed her eyes and sighed. The sight of Gareth would indeed be welcome. Much as she tried to hate him, he was at least human, and not some cold, ambitious creature like Talwork.

"He has scant reason to secure my safety," she said.

"You've little faith in your champion."

"There's good reason for that. You'll have to look elsewhere for your bait."

At a tavern called The Cross and Serpent Giles joined Gareth in a mug of ale.

"What news?" Gareth questioned impatiently.

"She is there, my lord, in the abbey."

It was just as he'd feared—Briar Rose had ridden straight into the clutches of the bishop of Morley. "We'll have to move quickly."

"I agree, my lord, but we must be cautious. I have grave doubts about the outcome of a confrontation."

"What do you mean by that, Giles?"

"The information was too easily gotten, my lord."

Gareth allowed himself a fleeting smile. " 'Tis only that you're so very clever."

"For that compliment, I thank you, Lord Hawke. But I still say you were meant to find out about Lady Briar Rose. The men in the abbey were far too free in their talk of how Hawke's woman had come to them. 'Twas as if they'd been instructed to be open about it."

"What purpose would that serve?"

"To get you here, so Talwork can finish the job he's bungled time and time again."

"It's a tired old ploy, but its effectiveness cannot be disputed."

"True, my lord."

Gareth drained the ale in his mug and slammed the vessel down on the table. "Damn the woman anyway!" he exclaimed. "See what her foolishness has gotten her?" But in his mind the blame shifted to himself. He'd made Briar Rose miserable. Yet something told him that she'd never have been content, not so long as she was forbidden to leave.

He sighed heavily. "We'll move tonight. There's no reason to delay."

Giles eyed his master nervously. "They'll be expecting you, my lord."

"Then we shall have to outwit them."

Briar Rose blinked in sleepy confusion at the torch that bobbed in her cell. It seemed she had only just fallen asleep, after lying for hours, listening to the incessant scratchings of rats and shivering in the chilly dampness.

"Come," the guard commanded, and she stood and shook the stiffness from her limbs.

Briar Rose wondered if the bishop ever slept. As she rubbed her eyes with a corner of her cloak, she guessed what Talwork was about. He was obviously hoping to wear her down by depriving her of sleep and subjecting her to long, dark hours in her miserable cell. His unending questions would begin again, just as they had earlier: How many knights served Lord Hawke? What were his plans for winter? And above all, how had he been so well-informed about the siege?

They were questions to which she had no answers. She told Talwork this over and over, but he didn't believe her.

The guard didn't lead her to the receiving room as she'd expected. He took her instead to the refectory.

The long, high-raftered room hummed with activity. The remains of a bountiful meal were on the tables and scattered across the rush-strewn floor. Knights and clerics drank together, served by tired-looking wenches. Briar Rose's throat constricted when she saw Maeve being accosted by two men. With a great show of lascivious humor they wrestled the young woman to a table, laying her amid picked-over bones and dirty trenchers.

Briar Rose forced herself to look away. She began to understand Gareth's hatred of Talwork.

The guard conducted her out the rear door of the refectory. She was glad to leave the noise and horror behind her. But her revulsion returned when she surveyed the chamber to which the guard had brought her.

It was a place such as those she'd heard about in fearsome tales, although she'd never thought to see one. It was a chamber of inquiry. A fire blazed in the grate. Spiked iron boots, thumbscrews, whips, and brands hung on the walls, and a vat of some evil concoction bubbled over the hearth fire.

Talwork came in with a sweep of his grand robe, accompanied by Griffith and another robed cleric whom they called Andrus.

Briar Rose regarded his cloak with a jaundiced eye. "Red velvet and ermine?" she questioned. "Isn't your manner of dress rather ostentatious for the occasion of tormenting a female?"

Talwork slapped her, causing her head to snap to one side. "That is not for you to judge, wench," he snarled. He nodded at the instruments on the wall. "Before long you'll beg to tell me your secrets."

"Fool!" Briar Rose spat, her face stinging where he'd slapped her. "Your barbaric methods will do you no good."

Talwork laughed mirthlessly. "We'll see about that."

His ruby rings glinted like drops of blood in the firelight. He circled slowly, eyeing her up and down. "Now, where shall we begin? Lord Hawke has left his mark, that's clear enough. He's left his brand of defiance on you."

The bishop went to the grate and selected a long iron brand. The end, a rendition of the Morley cross and serpent like the one on the amulets he and Griffith wore, glowed bright orange. Briar Rose shrank from it.

"I, too, will leave my mark upon you, wench. Griffith, Andrus . . ."

The other two men captured Briar Rose and held her still.

"Where shall we brand her?" Talwork asked.

"Here, Your Excellency," Griffith said, pulling the hem of her shift up high over her thigh. "That way, no one will ever be fooled into believing she's as pure and virginal as she appears."

The brand glowed, and she could see every detail of the Morley emblem. As it descended to her flesh, her scream echoed through the halls of the abbey.

She was still reeling from the sizzling pain, staring at the livid emblem as blisters rose up on her flesh, when another robed cleric entered. His face was obscured by his deep hood.

"What is it?" Talwork inquired, barely glancing at the newcomer.

"He is here, Your Excellency. Lord Hawke is at Morley. He's gone to the keep."

Talwork spun and gaped at the man, barely concealing his triumph. "Come with me," he said to Griffith and Andrus. And to the other, "Stay here with the wench." The three left the chamber in a flurry of robes.

Briar Rose glared at the man who had been left to

guard her. She still felt weak from the burn on her thigh, but she managed to hiss, "A pox on you all. You'll not find Gareth Hawke an easy mark."

"I daresay they won't, mistress," the man said in a surprisingly friendly fashion. He stooped and picked up her tattered cloak and wrapped it about her shoulders. "Come quickly and keep quiet. The way has been cleared, but I don't know how long that will last."

Briar Rose followed him out to the corridor. Through a haze of pain she realized that this man was helping her escape. They wound through the cloisters, crossed a frost-covered garden, and exited through a door in the stone wall.

Stars winked in the northern sky and a waning moon lit the outlying fields. Briar Rose inhaled the sharp, cold air, her first breath of freedom. As she scanned the purplish dawn on the horizon, she saw a large cloaked shape topped by a mane of windblown hair. A strangled shout of joy leaped to her throat. It was Gareth, standing in the distance with his squire and four horses, whose breath made great puffs in the chilly air.

She ignored the pain of her burn, was oblivious to the jagged, frozen ground beneath her running feet. In seconds she was in his arms, her face buried in the comforting warmth of his broad chest, sobbing out her relief, sobbing his name.

He crushed her close, stroking her tangled hair and whispering, "There, nightingale, you're safe now."

She wiped the tears from her cheeks. The horror of what might have happened to her become evident. Gareth and his clever assistant, whom she now knew was Giles, had saved her from torture and degradation, from becoming another abused inmate in that seething nest called Morley.

"It was—s-so horrible—" she began.

He kissed her gently on the forehead. "Never mind, sweeting. Come, we must go quickly before they discover that Giles's report was a hoax."

They rode for several hours, speaking little. Paulus rode in the rear, sending dark looks at Briar Rose, appalled at the risk they'd taken for a woman who would not even let her husband into her bed. Giles was wary, casting his gaze about, his ear cocked for the sound of pursuers. Gareth rode abreast with Briar Rose, wishing he could find the words to describe how he'd felt when he'd learned she was a prisoner at Morley, and when she'd gone tumbling into his arms. Briar Rose trembled with cold and with the searing pain of the fresh brand on her thigh. The night was bitterly cold and at one point the stars were obliterated by clouds and it began to sleet again. The riders sat hunched in their saddles, bent over to garner what warmth they could from the bodies of their plodding horses.

Gareth glanced over at Briar Rose and his heart ached for her. She had withdrawn into herself; he could only guess at what she'd endured at Morley. She had emerged from the ordeal whole, but she was young and vulnerable and may have been marked in ways that the eye couldn't discern.

He saw her shiver. "Take my cloak," he said, starting to unlace it.

"No. No, thank you."

"Take it. I insist."

"No!" Her refusal was sharp and final.

Gareth shrugged back into the garment and wished there were something to say that would comfort her. But after that one moment of vulnerability when she'd run to him, she seemed intent on proving that she didn't need him.

They reached Masterson the next evening, having climbed the high moors to avoid the road.

Briar Rose ached in every bone from the long ride. She longed for the comfort of her solar, knowing that a steaming bath would be drawn for her.

And so it was, only moments after they reached the keep. She sank gratefully into the tub with its hinged lid, cringing as her limbs began to thaw with a tingling sensation.

Kate came in with a pile of clean linens and clothing. The tiring woman's attitude was brisk and businesslike. "Are there enough serviettes for you, my lady?"

Briar Rose looked at the generous pile and nodded.

"Very well, I'll send for your meal."

Briar Rose wrapped herself in a cambric robe and stepped from the tub. Kate took up a fine-toothed wooden comb and raked it through Briar Rose's hair with a vengeance.

"See here, Kate," she said, taking the comb, "I know I took advantage of you and I don't doubt that it landed you in trouble with Lord Hawke. But I was kept here against my will. Surely you cannot fault me for attempting to escape."

Kate only blinked. "The idea! And he wanting nothing more than to take care of you—"

"You're wrong, Kate." She was so awfully tired. "If you're to be my keeper, I think it would behoove us both to remain civil with one another."

"As you wish, my lady," Kate replied coldly.

"That's not much of a start."

Kate's normally pale, impassive face grew livid with anger. "You have caused me no end of trouble. Bah! And to think I felt sorry for you—grieved for you, even—when we suspected you'd been taken by Talwork's men! Yet here you are, whole and remorseless, while—while—" Kate choked on her words and tears filled her eyes.

"Go on, Kate, finish what you were saying."

Kate shook her head miserably. "Never mind, I've said too much." Unconsciously she ran her hand down the draperies that surrounded the bed.

Briar Rose had a sudden insight. "You grieve for Lady Mary yet, don't you, Kate? And you resent me for having survived Morley, while she died there."

"I—yes. Perhaps that is it."

"Oh, Kate." Briar Rose stepped forward to embrace the woman fondly.

As she did, her robe fell open and the blistered brand on her thigh was revealed. Kate regarded the mark with horror.

"You poor child," she said suddenly. "Why didn't you tell me what they'd done to you?" She sprang into action, lifting her skirts to run down the tower stairs in search of poultices and salves to soothe the wound on her new mistress.

* * *

When Briar Rose heard a man's heavy tread outside her door the next day, she braced herself for a confrontation with Gareth.

There was an oval of polished metal that served as a looking-glass—a rare luxury from better times—on a shelf by the door. Briar Rose glanced at herself in it. She wished she'd taken the time this morning to plait her hair, but it hung to her thighs in wild disarray. She wore a plain chemise and woolen surcoat which must have once belonged to a young girl, for the garments were short enough to reveal her slim ankles and slippered feet.

Gareth pulled the door open and stepped inside, wearing a tentative half smile that threatened to melt Briar Rose's heart.

She hardened it and said, "I see you do not extend the courtesy of knocking."

Gareth raised an eyebrow above his scarred eye. At one time that had been an endearing expression; now it rankled her. "Forgive me," he said. "I wasn't thinking."

"Then perhaps you shall in the future."

"Perhaps I shall." He held out a bundle to her. "I bought this for you some days ago. Imagine my chagrin when you weren't here to receive it."

It was a hood of finest wool, scalloped about the edges, lined with fluffy winter rabbit fur. She laid it on the bed and murmured her thanks, wishing he hadn't made the gesture. It was so much easier to dislike him when he treated her badly.

"I thought it would keep you warm on your rides," he said.

"Escorted rides."

"Of course."

Briar Rose's temper flared. "I know of no man more stubborn and persistent than you, Gareth Hawke. When will you learn what a useless enterprise you've undertaken in keeping me here?"

He stepped forward, undaunted by her ire, and caressed her cheek with astonishing tenderness. "I'd say that it's been far from useless."

She slapped his hand away before he could see the tremors that rippled through her at his touch. She shrank away from him and from the treacherous feelings his nearness aroused in her.

But he'd seen. She could tell by the way he was looking at her.

"Yield to me, nightingale," he said softly.

She stepped back further. "You'll get nothing from me, Gareth Hawke, but the back of my hand if you try to touch me again. I know what you're trying to do."

"Oh?" he asked, his eyes flashing dangerously. "Do tell. I'm interested."

"You're trying to beguile me into giving you my ring. Perhaps you think to control Briarwood, too. I won't let you. My husband you may be, but perhaps even that can be remedied once I prove you wed me under false pretenses and without a proper contract."

Gareth set his jaw. He took both her hands in his, firmly, so she could not wrench away. " 'Tis not the ring that interests me, Briar Rose. Not anymore. I tried to explain that to you."

She fumed, unable to escape his grasp. "Then let me go, Gareth."

He gazed deep into her eyes, and as always, she was struck by his rugged handsomeness and that compelling way he had of looking at her.

"Would that I could release you in good conscience."

"What's that supposed to mean?"

"It would be dangerous for you to go off by yourself now. Acacia—"

Briar Rose had heard the lies before. She tossed her head. "What a pitiful manipulator you are, Gareth. Your motives are as clear as glass. You hope to frighten me into being your willing wife so that in a weak moment I will surrender my ring and my inheritance to you."

Gareth shook his head. "Even when Acacia first made her proposition to me, I had no intention of cooperating. I only pretended to so that she wouldn't send another after you. I took the ring from you in Linnet because Masterson was on the verge of collapse, but I would have seen it returned to you."

"More lies!" Briar Rose snapped.

Anger shimmered again in Gareth's slate-gray eyes. "Do you think, madam, that you'd be able to keep the ring from me if I really wanted it?"

He loomed over her and she was struck by the sheer size of him and the power he exuded. But she threw her head back proudly.

"I'll die before I give in to you."

"You've nothing to worry about. I don't need the money anymore." His eyes kindled with barely checked rage and something more that caused Briar Rose to shiver. " 'Tis not the ring, or Briarwood that I want from you." There was an edge to his voice that made her realize that she'd finally pushed him too far.

With breathtaking speed his one arm encircled her waist and the other hand tilted her chin upward. His kiss was deep and unrelenting, sapping her resistance, causing a shameful tide of heat to flood her loins. His tongue plundered her mouth, seeking to crumble her will.

Briar Rose made a sound of mingling rage and hunger in the back of her throat. Passion welled up in her, but still she resisted, holding the hem of her surcoat firmly against his seeking hands. Impatient with her resistance, he gave the garment a sharp tug. His fist grazed the healing brand on her thigh.

Briar Rose's cry of pain came unbidden. He brushed aside her hands, which clawed the surcoat down around her legs. Gareth wrestled the fabric upward.

The brand stood out on the whiteness of her thigh, a livid imprint of cruelty. Briar Rose's breath caught at the blaze of anger that crossed his face.

"The bishop's handiwork," he muttered.

"Aye."

Gareth ground his fist into his hand. "The despoiler," he said through clenched teeth. " 'Tis not enough that he plagues me constantly; he must also mark the things I hold dear."

At one time Briar Rose would have responded with joy to Gareth's admission of feeling for her, but she was still furious at him for playing upon her weakness. He seemed to know that his kisses could drug her into a state of total surrender. Almost. Summoning all her will, she turned from him.

"The wound will heal," she said.

Gareth reached for her again, but a single shake of her head put him off. "I'd like to be alone now," she told him coldly.

Gareth knew he had a husband's right to take her, and the strength to force her legs apart and plunge into her as he ached to do. But he stayed the impulse, almost trembling with the effort. She'd never forgive him if he forced her now. He went to the door, then turned and spoke with mock formality. "Madam, I concede this battle to you. But do not imagine that I have given up the war."

A clay dish shattered against the door after he closed it. Briar Rose flung herself back on the bed as a hundred thoughts swirled through her mind. His departure had left her feeling bereft and unfulfilled, and she almost wished she'd given in to him. Her body still felt warm and languorous from his touch; she hungered for him in spite of everything. Still, she knew better than to mistake what she felt for love.

She glanced down at the healing wound on her thigh. Aloud she murmured, "You, too, have marked me, Gareth Hawke, just as Talwork said. You've branded me with a woman's longings."

Two days later, the burn had healed enough for Briar Rose to ride comfortably.

Kate arrived with a cloth-wrapped bundle, which she unfurled with a grin. "The master's had the women sewing on this day and night," she said.

Briar Rose ran a tentative hand over the length of the flowing mantle. It was of velvet, in an iridescent blue-violet shade that matched the color of her eyes. Costly on its own, it was also lined with softest winter-white rabbit fur.

"Take it away," she told Kate. "And tell Lord Hawke that his money would be better spent feeding his people and buying warm clothing for the children."

"Your pardon, my lady, but the mantle was remade from one of his lordship's mother's. And the fur was gotten by hunters in Masterson forests. It cost him nothing save the willing labor of his people."

"I'll not have it," Briar Rose insisted. "The woolen robe I was given at Morley will suffice."

Kate shuffled her feet. "Beg pardon, my lady, but it's

been taken away. 'Twas teeming with vermin so we burned it."

Briar Rose seethed. One by one, Gareth was taking her few belongings from her; soon all she had would come from his hands alone, making her his dependent. With quick, angry movements she took up the mantle and shrugged into it, ignoring how gloriously soft and warm it felt draped around her. She also donned the fur-lined hood. If she was going to flaunt Gareth's gifts, she may as well flaunt them all.

When she went to the stables, Hal gawked at her.

Briar Rose recalled how she'd tricked him. "I hope things didn't go too badly for you, Hal."

He looked at the ground. "Och, the master—he was plenty mad."

"I'm sorry. Did he beat you badly?"

Hal's eyes widened. "Lord no, my lady! Lord Hawke'd never lay a hand on me. Never has, on any of us."

"Then how were you punished?"

"Punished? 'Twas sore enough punishment that I behaved the dupe. His lordship knew I was flailing myself more than his hand ever could."

This surprised Briar Rose. Gareth was a hard man. She'd assumed he was heavy-handed with his servants.

She eyed Hal shrewdly. "I wonder if there's a chance of my having a solitary ride today."

"Nay, my lady. Sir Cedric will escort you."

As soon as they reached the open moors, they broke into a wild gallop. The sharp cold air seared Briar Rose's lungs and placed spots of healthy color high on her cheeks. Her new mantle flowed out behind her, draping down over Dame's backside. They rode far into the afternoon and finally directed their sweating mounts homeward.

They entered the town at a more sedate pace, nodding to the people they passed. A young woman in a dirty apron was feeding a small flock of chickens in her dooryard. When she saw Cedric, her face broke into a grin.

"You have an admirer," Briar Rose said teasingly.

"Oh, aye." Cedric's mind was clearly not on the young woman.

"By the way, Cedric, someone at Morley asked after you."

Cedric gave her his full attention and his plain-featured face seemed to come to life. "Maeve?"

"Aye. She misses you greatly."

Cedric closed his eyes and sighed. "Sweet God, I thought she'd perished along with her mistress. How fares she?"

Briar Rose averted her eyes. It would be cruel to worry Cedric with the truth: "Maeve is a servant at Morley," she said carefully. " 'Tis no easy life, but at least she's not ill."

Cedric nodded bleakly. "I'd give my sword arm to have her with me. If I thought I had a chance against those bastards, I'd fetch her myself."

Briar Rose vowed to find Giles and speak to him right away. He'd gotten her out safely enough; why not Maeve?

They passed the church with its silent bells and then the smithy where the forges were in full operation.

Then she saw a familiar face. "Meg!" The girl was hurrying down the street, a basket of dried herring under her arm.

Meg dipped respectfully and murmured, "My lady."

Her pregnancy was more apparent now. Her belly was swollen, yet her face appeared thin and wan.

"You don't look well, Meg," Briar Rose said.

"Never mind, my lady. The young ones, they've got the fever. It's been a strain caring for them."

"That duty shouldn't fall to you, Meg. Not in your state. Can your mother not nurse them?"

"Och, nay. She passed away before the harvest."

Briar Rose dismounted and fell in step with Meg, leading her palfrey by the reins. "Let's see if there's anything we can do."

The house was little more than a wattle-and-daub hovel with a thatched roof. A hooded opening in the top allowed a filament of smoke to escape. Inside, the only light came from the central fire. There was but one room with five pallets, a table, and shelves with a few crude, patched cooking utensils. Briar Rose wrinkled her nose at the mingling odors of unwashed bodies and sickness, but she delved in and built up the fire.

The five children were burning with fever.

"By the Mass," Briar Rose murmured.

"They've worsened, my lady."

Briar Rose took the young woman's hand and squeezed it reassuringly. "I'll send help. Blankets and food and the barber from the keep. He'll bring you some remedies. Look for him tonight."

That evening she had two projects in mind when she told Kate she'd like to see Gareth. The most pressing was Meg and her younger brothers and sisters. She expected no resistance from Gareth on that.

The second project posed a more delicate problem. It would not be easy to convince Gareth to go to Morley again to fetch Maeve. Perhaps, Briar Rose decided, she would have to think on that one.

He was in the hall, brooding over a mug of cider. As always Briar Rose's breath caught at the sight of him. She felt her heart constrict at the poignant angle of his head and the way he traced his finger idly over the wet ring the mug had left on the trestle table. Why can't you love me? she asked silently. Why must you let your bitterness and ambition get in the way?

"Gareth." The word came softly from her.

He turned and frowned at her. It was the first civility he'd heard from her in days. Damn the woman, she was as changeable as the wind on the moors, shifting from ferocity to gentleness from one moment to the next.

She moistened her lips. "I've something to ask you."

He was intrigued by the abrupt change in her. "Ask, then. I can do no worse than refuse." A corner of his mouth lifted ironically It was impossible to deny Briar Rose anything; didn't she know that?

Her eyes grew moist with compassion. "Oh, do not say no, Gareth, please. 'Tis Meg, the young woman who was here with her brothers and sisters during the siege. The youngsters are sick with fever and they've had only the poorest care. They need blankets and proper food and remedies. Gareth, please help them!"

He stared at her in amazement. She had never begged on her own account, yet for a poor young widow like Meg she would humble herself.

He opened his palms. "Well, I suppose something must be done about it, then."

Briar Rose waited, holding her breath.

He smiled at her. She was no longer the spoiled, self-centered girl he'd once known. "I'll send the barber with food and warm covers and a maid from the keep to help with the nursing."

She ran forward, crying out his name, and astonished him by flinging herself into his arms and kissing him unabashedly on the mouth.

As she wound her fingers into his great mane of hair, Briar Rose knew that if he wanted her now, he could have her. Already she felt a warm stirring within her and her knees began to weaken.

It was Gareth who broke the embrace, though reluctantly. He looked deep into her eyes.

"You tempt me sorely, nightingale, but if Meg is as bad off as you say, I'd best see to things."

"Of course," Briar Rose said quickly, embarrassed by her display, by her readiness to give in to Gareth. She walked to the door with him and squeezed his hand. It was so easy to love him when he was like this. She wished he was always so caring.

"Thank you, Gareth," she said softly.

That night, for the first time since she'd arrived at Masterson, she didn't hear the familiar sound of the bolt being thrown.

11

For the next week Briar Rose made daily visits to Meg's house. Her gratification was sweet when she saw a rapid improvement in the children. The good food and clothing alone would have been remedy enough, and this coupled with the rich herbal draughts and purges the barber brought healed them quickly.

By the end of the week Briar Rose no longer stopped while on her daily rides. Meg and the children were out in the dooryard, waving at her. Word of her kindness to the family got about town.

Slowly she was becoming a part of Masterson. She stopped for frequent chats with the townswomen and often bantered with the guards.

When it was clear that Meg's family was well, she turned her attention to Cedric's plight. As she came to know the man, she was able to see the anguish he was in. His love for Maeve was evident in every phrase he spoke about her.

"She's a good woman, is my Maeve," he would say frequently. "She's never done wrong to a soul."

Perhaps it was her own ravaged heart that made her

want to bring them together, as if to prove to herself that love was not some made-up fancy that always led to disenchantment. She sat pondering the problem in her solar one day in early November.

It had been easy to convince Gareth to lend aid to Meg, but this was a much more delicate situation. There was real danger in it and he'd likely refuse to jeopardize his men or himself for the sake of a serving wench. There was a place in his heart that was startlingly soft, but Briar Rose doubted he could be pushed that far.

She narrowed her eyes at the fire. There was one other possibility: Giles. He proudly called himself a spy, a master of deceit and trickery, the Fox of Masterson. He was a man who thrived on challenge; he'd not be able to refuse a task of such tantalizing difficulty.

She found him that afternoon in the armory.

Giles turned, unruffled as always by a sudden appearance. "Have you decided to take an interest in arms, my lady?"

She eyed the splayed-out arrays of spears and arrows that hung on the walls. "I've always been interested in such things, Giles. In fact, I even know something of their use. Much as my father always said he was blessed for having a daughter, I think he secretly yearned for a son."

"I'm sure you were a delightful pupil."

She took down a light archer's bow and flexed it. "At one time I could hit a mark at half a hundred yards. I still think it a finer pastime than spinning and needlework."

Briar Rose replaced the bow and faced him squarely. "I need help, Giles. There is a young woman called Maeve who resides at Morley. Do you know her?"

"She was the Lady Mary's servant. She was presumed dead."

"She lives, Giles, but do you know what her life is like? She's treated like a slave, forced to do the meanest tasks for those who hold her against her will. I fear she won't last much longer under such treatment."

"Morley's a hard place for a wench."

"Cedric misses her so, I think he'll not hold off much longer. Since I told him she was alive, and pining for him, he may try to free her."

A nervous light came into Giles's eyes.

"Let's fetch her, Giles. You and I together can do it." Briar Rose held her breath and waited for his reaction.

"Folly!" he said. "Be reasonable, my lady. There's naught you and I can do."

"Come now, Giles, you know better than that."

"We both know Lord Gareth would never sanction this escapade."

"That's precisely why he mustn't hear of the plan until the deed is done. We'll be successful, Giles, and he won't argue with that."

"No." Giles's denial was flat.

Briar Rose shrugged, feigning indifference. "You're not up to the task, then. Very well, I shall go ahead with it on my own. I'm sure Sir Cedric won't be at all reluctant to help me." She started to walk away.

Giles gave in as she'd known he would. "You're a determined woman, my lady."

"Then you'll fetch Maeve from Morley?" Briar Rose tried not to look too triumphant.

"Aye, I'll do it."

"And I shall go with you, Giles. I'm a good rider, and fair enough with weapons—"

"That I cannot allow. You'd be missed immediately, and then heaven save us from Lord Hawke. I shall do it alone."

"Tonight?"

Giles couldn't suppress a smile at her impatience. "Aye, tonight. I think it best that no one know where I've gone. I trust that if Lord Hawke asks about me, you'll know how to divert his attention, my lady."

"I do have a certain way of doing that, Giles."

A day passed, and then another. Briar Rose tried not to show her worry. When evening descended on the second day, she knew it would be a long night of impatient waiting. She paced, wondering where Kate was with her evening meal.

The tiring woman never arrived. Instead, Gareth came. Briar Rose held her breath, watching him to see if he'd somehow guessed what she'd done. But he only smiled.

"Dine with us in the hall, Briar Rose," he said.

As always, his presence stirred her. He looked particularly handsome tonight in a short woolen tunic of silver-blue with matching hose and soft leather boots. His hair gleamed in the waning light.

She weighed her choices. She could have her meal sent up as usual and spend the evening waiting and pacing and wondering about Giles, but perhaps she'd be less agitated if she went to the hall.

"Very well," she said. "I'll come. Give me a little time to get ready."

Gareth left her to change her clothing and arrange her hair. She did this with special care, lingering over brushing out her long locks and combing them into a net coif. She donned a gown from the chest and checked her appearance in the small polished metal oval. For once she was satisfied with what she saw: rosy cheeks that glowed with vigor from her daily rides, curling tendrils of hair that framed her face, and a figure that seemed somehow more rounded and womanly than it had last summer.

When she entered the hall, a servitor led her to the seat at Gareth's right, in the middle of the high table. She colored under the curious stares of the onlookers.

Gareth smiled charmingly. "What an air of grace you lend to Masterson, my lady."

"Thank you."

"The gown looks well on you. I've not seen it since—" He stopped, seeming to have difficulty finishing the thought.

"Since your sister wore it?"

"Aye." There was an aching sadness in his eyes. "But 'tis good to see something of my sister about the place."

Briar Rose nodded understandingly. "After my mother passed away, I took pleasure in wearing her things. Somehow it seemed to bring her closer to me."

A rare truce had gone up between them. For the time being Briar Rose accepted the fact of her captivity; she was beginning to enjoy the good spirits and animated conversation that went on in the hall.

When a piper stepped out to play a lively tune, she turned to smile at Gareth. "That was excellent. I don't remember when I've had better."

Gareth took her hand and gave it a squeeze. "We are not totally barbaric at Masterson."

She pulled back quickly from him, aware of the scrutiny of the others in the hall. "Please, Gareth. Everyone is watching."

He threw back his head and laughed. "Heaven forbid that anyone should suspect me of harboring affection for you."

Miffed, Briar Rose held out her goblet for more wine. "I don't want them to think I am softening toward you."

He reached out and stroked her cheek. "Ah, but at one time you were very soft toward me."

She jerked away, her eyes flashing. "That was before I discovered what a blackguard you are."

Still he smiled, refusing for once to let her infuriate him. "And to think, my nightingale, that if I hadn't spirited you away, you'd still be safely in the clutches of Dame Michaela."

Briar Rose cringed at the memory of the nun who had treated her so roughly.

Gareth left off his teasing for a moment as he looked around the hall. "Where is Giles? I've not seen him since yesterday. No, 'twas the day before."

Briar Rose knew she mustn't let him wonder too long. "Gareth, if I'm to live here, I think you should show me about the keep. The lord's chamber, for instance . . ."

His eyes widened at her mercurial change in attitude. "Come along, then," he said, helping her from her seat. " 'Twould give me great pleasure to show it to you."

Pleased at her success in distracting him, Briar Rose followed Gareth out of the hall. She was so intent on keeping his thoughts away from Giles that she barely noticed the stream of bawdy, knowing remarks that followed in their wake.

The lord's chamber, behind the gallery above the hall, was as fine as any she'd seen. The flagged floor gleamed dully from meticulous sweeping and the walls were covered with rich old tapestries depicting whimsical scenes of courtly love and the military exploits of Gareth's ancestors. A pair of oblong windows looked out over the bailey and a fire danced in the grate. The grand bedstead, tables, and chairs were of carved oak and the hangings around the bed were minutely embroidered with silk thread. Candles ensconced on the walls cast a warm, golden glow over the whole room.

A gleam of color on one wall caught her eye. A small design glittered like a many-colored jewel, lit from behind by a candle.

"Gareth," Briar Rose said, approaching the light. "What's this? I've never seen anything so beautiful."

It was a design in colored glass, a rendition of the Masterson hawk.

Gareth came to stand behind her. "It was to be a window for the chapel. I designed it myself and commissioned a glazier in York to cut the pieces. I assembled the pieces myself in these lead strips and an artisan from town painted on the details."

Briar Rose studied the work, surprised to discover that Gareth had this talent. The window was beautifully done in rich royal blues and oranges and golds, the hawk seeming to sweep from a crag, soaring heavenward. It was a picture of fierce pride and unabashed ambition.

"Why did you never finish it?" she asked softly.

Gareth's eyes darkened. "A chapel that's banned from services needs no pretty window."

"But it's so lovely, you should—"

"Never mind," Gareth said, and she heard the anguish in his voice. Every day he must look at his work and recall all that could have been. Briar Rose's hand came up as if to soothe the pain from his brow, but she stopped herself in midmotion.

Gareth grinned, reading her mind. "Mustn't forget yourself, nightingale. It wouldn't do for you to pity me too much."

He crossed the room and pulled the heavy brocade hangings across the windows.

" 'Tis monstrous cold tonight," he explained.

Briar Rose only nodded. Her eyes were fastened on

Gareth, the magnificent breadth of his shoulders, the powerful sinews of his thighs. He turned in time to see the way she was looking at him.

He spoke her name softly, compellingly, and his rich voice filled her with longing. She was afflicted by some strange languor that caused her mind to work sluggishly and her limbs to feel leaden. Perhaps it was the wine that made her forget her frequent vows to resist him.

She knew what was about to happen. She knew she'd not do a thing to stop it. The tension throbbed between them. Then Gareth was standing over her and taking her in his arms. When he pressed his lips to hers, all rational thought fled. She forgot Giles, forgot that she was in the arms of her enemy, forgot that she was a prisoner at Masterson. She responded to him with hungry ardor, standing high on her toes to drink from his lips and weave her fingers through his curling hair.

Her mouth opened to his and his tongue glided slowly, silkenly, over her lips and between her teeth. She accepted the intimate kiss and, as his tongue darted in and out of her mouth, understood the message it conveyed.

The speed with which he aroused her was electrifying. White-hot passion pounded through her veins and she felt an urgent craving for fulfillment. But Gareth meant to take his time, to savor every moment. He lifted his lips from hers and kissed her temples as his hands freed her hair from its net coif. Feeling the silken weight of it, he smiled.

"Your crowning glory," he murmured.

"Black as a crow's wing, or so I'm told."

He lifted a lock of it to his mouth, dragging it slowly over his lips. "It's beautiful. You're beautiful."

He pulled at the laces of her gown. Briar Rose made no resistance as he sent it drifting to the floor. She heard his hiss of indrawn breath as he looked at her nude body, the colored light from the leaded glass casting soft patterns over the swell of her breasts and the curve of her hips. He spanned her narrow waist with his hands, his thumbs reaching down to the hollows where her legs joined her torso.

"Do you know," he asked, tasting the flesh of her throat and shoulders, "what torture it's been, knowing you were under my roof, that I had every right to possess you, yet having to hold myself off from you?"

"Gareth, I . . ." She couldn't finish, not when his lips teased her nipples and his hands were doing such delicious things to her.

"No woman has ever affected me like you do, Briar Rose. I can't decide whether you're the devil's own tool or an angel from heaven." His hands went around to her, bringing her against his hard length.

Briar Rose realized then that the urgency of his desire matched hers. She pulled impatiently at his clothing. She gloried in the feel of him, gliding her hands over the majestic rise of his shoulders and down his torso. It was sheer torment, needing him in this way, wanting him so much that nothing else seemed to matter.

All she knew was what his compelling touch told her: that she was desirable, that he wanted her to feel pleasure. His hands knew just how to caress her; he knew the rhythm of her passion. He laid her on the bed amid the lavender-scented furs and bolsters. Lavender . . . she remembered it from their wedding night and wondered if Gareth recognized it too, for he was being as gentle with her now as he had been then. The light played over his sinewy body as he loomed above her, kissing her face, her neck, her breasts, and then lower, across her middle, which tightened as her skin quivered. His fingers dipped to the soft folds of her femininity and then his mouth was there, his tongue darting, his teeth grazing her until Briar Rose began to tremble.

"Gareth," she moaned. "No . . ."

But he ignored her protest, pressing her back on the bed. The exquisite sensations continued, all the more compelling because of the forbidden nature of his love-making. Briar Rose arched and writhed and spoke his name again and again, both in protest and in supplication. Nearly mad with desire, she begged him to come to her, to assuage the ache she felt.

Gareth sheathed himself in her. A cry was torn from her throat when at last he gave her fulfillment, taking his own release in the wake of her explosion.

They lay panting in a twisted disarray of naked limbs and rumpled bedclothes. Gareth propped himself up on one elbow and gazed down at her. With a finger he traced the delicate line of her jaw, her small, squarish chin, rubbing his thumb over her lower lip.

"How magnificent you are," he said.

She looked away. "I'm not. I did nothing, only lay and let you . . ." She didn't dare finish. "I am weak," she said.

"Nay, lady, 'tis just the opposite. Few men I know are stronger than you."

Briar Rose wasn't sure that was a compliment, but it pleased her nonetheless. Unable to help herself, she smiled at Gareth and touched his bare chest lightly.

"What is all this?" she asked, tracing a hardened scar with her finger.

"An old battle wound. A failure on my part to protect myself."

"You're a young man, Gareth. How is it that you've done so much fighting?"

He looked wistful for a moment. "Masterson fell to me when I was not much older than you. I was in the

King's favor then and he relied on me in the border wars with the Scots. 'Twas a good time, one of many victories, and it saved me from being shipped off to fight the French. I honor the Scots for the way they do battle. There are few things so awesome as the sight of a host of them advancing, half naked, with their weapons flailing, to the strains of Hey Tuttie Tatie."

"It sounds very exciting. And dangerous."

"It is both."

"Do you miss it, Gareth?"

"It's a finer occupation than roaming the countryside on the tourney circuit or performing low deeds for those who will pay my price."

"Like Acacia."

He looked at her sharply. So she still didn't suspect her father.

"My people have to eat."

"I see." In spite of herself, Briar Rose was beginning to understand why he'd stolen her ring. Reflecting on the townspeople who had begun to love and respect her, she wondered if perhaps the ring might do them more good than it did her.

Gareth, however, was thinking of other things now. He leaned over and kissed the pensive frown from her brow.

She knew, as her arms wound around his neck to draw his lips to hers, that all her efforts to forget the blissful times in his arms had gone to naught. She would never forget how he made her feel or how she returned his tenderness with her own caresses. That had always been with her, deeply suppressed at times, but it was there.

"Damn you, Gareth Hawke," she whispered, and he made love to her again.

* * *

Paulus burst in early, groping through the darkened chamber to open the drapes. When the yellow shafts of light fell on two reclining figures, the squire gasped.

"Pardon, my lord," he stammered, backing toward the door.

Gareth propped himself up on his elbows. "Never mind, Paulus. Tell me what brings you here at this hour."

" 'Tis Giles, my lord. I think you should see him straight away."

With that the squire fled, shielding his eyes from the spectacle of a shapely leg dangling from beneath the bedcovers. Gareth grinned after him and then down at Briar Rose, who remained undisturbed by the intrusion. She slept so sweetly. Gareth found himself wishing that every day could start like this one. Carefully he extracted himself from the bed and dressed for his meeting with Giles.

Just as he was about to leave, Briar Rose awoke. Before she quite realized where she was, she indulged in a luxurious stretch, feeling rested and unusually content.

"Where are you going?" she asked a little shyly, flushing as his gaze alit on her exposed leg.

"To see Giles." He dropped a kiss on her forehead and left her staring after him.

Briar Rose forgot her own troubles then. She was delighted that Giles had returned so quickly. Murmuring a fervent prayer that his outing had been a success, she climbed from the bed and dressed hurriedly.

On her way down to the great hall she stood on the landing to look for a moment out the tall, narrow window. The morning sun flashed its blinding light across the thatched rooftops of the town. People were coming out, walking together in small, shivering groups or pushing loaded carts in front of them. Despite a general improvement about Masterson, Briar Rose still sensed a pervasive poverty. Once again she experienced a stab of guilt. Acacia would pay dearly for her ring and the money would benefit the townspeople greatly. And yet to give it up would be to forsake her brave ancestor, Isobel d'Evreux, and to relinquish Briarwood to Acacia . . .

Shaking her head to rid herself of these troubling thoughts, Briar Rose left the landing and continued her descent to the great hall. She froze at the sound of Gareth's voice raised in anger.

"Imbecile!" he roared. "You knew I'd never countenance an illicit trip to Morley!"

"Aye, my lord. But when I learned the wench was alive—"

Briar Rose entered the hall in time to see Gareth pacing up and down, sputtering wrathfully. "Of all the incautious, foolhardy—"

"Maeve!" Briar Rose ran lightly across the room to embrace the bewildered young woman. "Thank God you're safe. I knew it was a chance you'd be willing to take." She kissed Maeve's tear-wet cheek.

Gareth jerked Briar Rose around to face him. "What do you know of this business?" he demanded.

"She knows nothing, my lord—" Giles began.

Briar Rose tilted her chin up. " 'Tis plenty I know, Gareth. I arranged the whole thing."

His eyes widened in amazement. "You did this without my knowledge?"

"You'd never have allowed it."

His anger deepened and, incredibly, Briar Rose thought she detected a look of hurt in his eyes. "You might have tried talking to me about it. If I'd known there was one of Masterson's own still at Morley, I would have made arrangements."

"Why are you so angry, Gareth? Giles was only gone a short time and he's brought Maeve back." As she spoke, Cedric entered the hall, having been roused by Paulus. Speechless with delight, he ran to his love and embraced Maeve with poignant tenderness.

Gareth turned his back on the spectacle as if disgusted by it. He spoke to Briar Rose. "Look again at Giles, whom I'm sure you beguiled into this idiotic scheme with your womanly wiles. What is that on his face, the mark of success?"

Briar Rose recoiled from what she saw on the cheek that had previously been turned from her: a livid burn in the shape of the same brand that had been put on her thigh. The indelible mark of Morley Diocese.

She swallowed. "What—what happened?"

"I think it's obvious," Gareth snarled. "Giles was caught and marked for life because of his indiscretion. He was lucky to get away with his life, and that of the girl." He took her by the shoulders and gave her a shake. "Do you know what you've done? My very best agent, whose every move depends on secrecy and disguise, has been ruined. Now wherever he goes he'll be recognized. You've rendered him useless to me."

"I—I'm sorry. Giles, shall I send for the barber?"

Giles was as bold as ever, even in the face of his master's wrath. " 'Tis not so very bad, is it, my lord? When the burn heals, I can raise a beard to conceal the scar, and none will be the wiser."

Gareth gave a sarcastic snort. "I have never known you to be so easily led by a woman, Giles."

Briar Rose's stepped between the two men. "How dare you attack Giles for showing bravery and cunning! Truly, Gareth, I think you suffer from wounded pride."

He almost slapped her to return the sting of her insult. With tremendous effort he stayed his hand, but not his tongue.

"Bitch! I'm tired of your meddlesome ways. You've caused nothing but trouble since you came into my life. I don't know why I bother—" He cut himself off and signaled to the guard.

"Take her away."

The guard approached, but Briar Rose froze him in his tracks with a strident cry.

"No!" Her expression was fierce. "I'll not be dragged away again."

With one swift movement she bent and tore her ring from its cache in the hem of her shift. She flung it at Gareth. It hit him square in the chest and then fell with a metallic clatter to the floor.

A heavy silence hung in the hall. All eyes were riveted on the small object, though no one moved to pick it up. Briar Rose stared at Gareth, and her bosom rose and fell with angry passion.

Finally she spoke. "There it is. That's what you've been wanting from me for all this time. Take it. You've won."

"The ring is yours, Briar Rose. I shan't take it."

"The time for being noble is past." She nodded at the fallen ring. "If that's the price I must pay for my freedom, then so be it. Nothing is worth my having to remain under the same roof with a tyrant like you. I shall leave as soon as possible."

"There are compelling reasons why you should stay at Masterson." Gareth dropped his voice to a low whisper. "You are my wife—"

"I believe that can be corrected."

She watched him swallow hard. "You're in danger, Briar Rose. Acacia—"

"You lie constantly. I've as good as turned Briarwood over to Acacia. What need have I to fear her now?"

With that, she turned on her heel and left the hall, making for her solar where she would ready herself to leave.

Only Giles was bold enough to brave Gareth's mood.

Gareth's first instinct was to vent all his wrath on Giles. He controlled himself with an effort.

"She'll not let me be a proper husband to her and I'm tired of playing the jailer. What can I do but give her her freedom?"

"Maybe you can convince her, my lord, of Wannet's threat."

Gareth shook his head. "She may not admire him, but he's an old family friend. At least she trusts him. Perhaps she'll be agreeable to marrying him." Gareth grimaced at the idea, thinking of Celestine, and then turned to Cedric. "You will accompany the lady to Tynegate. 'Tis one of the few places she has friends. I doubt Wannet's hunters will find her there. He's probably gone to Windsor for the winter."

Cedric's face fell. He'd only just been reunited with Maeve, and now he was being sent away from her.

"You must go," Maeve said softly, extracting her hand from Cedric's. "We owe her this."

Cedric nodded and embraced Maeve. "Forgive my selfishness. Of course I'll go."

"Why not send the ring to Padwick, my lord?" Giles asked. "Then, perhaps, he'd have his wife call off Wannet's search and provide you with a fat bounty."

Gareth frowned with distaste and stooped to pick up the ring. He pocketed it. "No. The least I can do is keep it safe for her. One day she'll be wanting it back."

* * *

Briar Rose expected to leave quietly. She decided to go to the Wexlers in York, where she'd had her education. Lady Wexler had friends at court; perhaps she could arrange for Briar Rose to find a place there.

But her send-off was far from quiet. At the main gate a throng of well-wishers awaited her. From the kitchen staff there was a generous sack of food. Maeve gave her a pair of dainty tatted garters and uttered her thanks for perhaps the hundredth time. Hal and the other lads presented her with a bag of grain for Dame. Meg and her brothers and sisters shyly offered a hurriedly embroidered handkerchief.

Feeling somewhat embarrassed by the generosity of these people, Briar Rose smiled at the throng. She saw Giles wending his way toward her. She cringed at the sight of his disfigurement, which he'd gotten because of her. Yet his face was not accusing.

"My lady—"

"Giles. How is your cheek?"

He grinned lopsidedly, favoring the injured part. "It'll mend." He drew her aside, leading her to a corner by the main gate where winter bracken showed brown through a thin layer of frost.

" 'Tis madness for you to go off like this."

She shook her head. "No, Giles. This is the only rational thing I've done since I first laid eyes on Gareth Hawke. At last I think I'm over the sickness that drew me to him."

She knew Giles saw the wistful longing in her eyes, which gave lie to her words.

"You may find, my lady, that running away from your troubles will not solve them. And what of Lord Hawke?"

Her answer was bitter. "He has what he wants. I'm just sorry I didn't give in to him earlier."

Giles faced her squarely, his angular, foxlike face intense. "He doesn't have what he desires, my lady. What he wants is you."

Briar Rose felt her heart quicken. If only that were true . . . She thought she might be able to forgive everything else if she knew he loved her.

"Then why does he hide himself in the keep instead of coming out here to call me back?"

"He has a great deal of pride, which you've wounded lately on numerous occasions. He, too, is hurting."

Briar Rose refused to allow herself to feel sympathy for him. "Then he must not want me that badly," she said.

"My lady—"

At that moment Gareth appeared. The rising sun outlined his massive shape, his cloak flowing out behind. His eyes were stormy as he approached with purposeful strides. Murmuring, the crowd gave him a wide berth and Giles wisely stepped into the background.

Briar Rose squared her shoulders. Gareth looked so angry that she had to resist the impulse to shrink from him.

"I didn't expect such a display on my leaving," she said coolly.

He shrugged. "You've made your share of friends here."

"And enemies also, Gareth."

His jaw worked inside his cheek. "I'm not your enemy, Briar Rose. I'm here to give you your ring back."

She shook her head. "It's too late for that, Gareth. I don't want you to have any hold over me at all. Do what you will with it. 'Tis nothing but a bit of gold. In the end I'll have Briarwood, with or without it."

"I wish you'd reconsider, Briar Rose. The world is a dangerous place."

"Gareth, I've found more danger in your arms than anywhere else."

He laughed bitterly and caught her against him. Her gasp of surprise was stifled by his hard kiss. Behind them, the onlookers gave a collective sigh.

"I'm a fool to let you go," Gareth growled.

"You must. If you try to lock me up again, I—I'll find a way to escape, you know I will. I'll send messages to my father, to the King himself if need be."

He shoved her roughly away from him. "Go then, nightingale. Fly away, little bird."

She blinked away tears and hoped no one noticed. The cruelty in his voice was unbearable. She left with a painful lump in her throat and the sound of well-wishers behind her.

"You must be disappointed to have to leave Maeve so soon," she said to Cedric.

He smiled. "Thanks to you, my lady, we'll have a lifetime to be together."

"You mustn't stay with me long. I was thinking I'd go to Wexler, in Yorkshire."

"Pardon, my lady, but Lord Hawke suggested we go to Tynegate."

Briar Rose's first reaction was to refuse any idea put forth by Gareth, but she had to admit it was reasonable. Tynegate was secure and more agreeable than the dark halls of Wexler. She gave Cedric a nod, indicating her assent.

They traveled westward, stopping infrequently and seldom speaking. The frozen moors rolled out before them, punctuated by craggy stands of gritstone and clusters of barren trees. The wind soughed mournfully through the hedgerows. The northern country was colorless, black and brown with shades of gray. The sun was a shapeless yellow mass on the horizon to the right, reminding the riders to hurry, for it would soon be dark.

Dusk fell as they crossed the creaky wooden span over the half-frozen River Tyne. When Cedric called to the sentry, the gate opened like a great, hungry maw and then closed behind them as if swallowing them up. A pair of stableboys scurried up to see to the horses, exclaiming over the white palfrey's beauty.

They were taken to the hall. Kenneth appeared, looking splendid in a parti-colored purple and gold tunic with matching hose and fur-lined cloak.

"Briar Rose," he said warmly, giving her a fond embrace. "This is a happy surprise."

She shook the mud from the hem of her cloak. "I must look a sight. 'Tis not the best time of year to be traveling."

"Winter seems to suit you, my dear. Your cheeks are fairly blooming."

Briar Rose smiled at him. He was such a gentleman, with his pretty compliments and hospitable manner. She accepted a cup of hot spiced wine from a servant and felt herself begin to thaw. As she sat drinking, she noticed that Cedric and Kenneth were speaking together in hushed tones.

Then Rowena arrived, pausing in the entranceway as if to dramatize her own appearance. She was wearing a green embroidered gown and a gorgeous matching cloak. Her brown hair was swept up in a filmy coif of gold net, and her eyes had been expertly painted with kohl. Briar Rose was amazed at the standards of dress Rowena maintained in the isolated keep.

Not surprisingly, Rowena's welcome was more perfunctory than warm. Bluntly she asked, "What brings you to Tynegate?"

"I've left Masterson for good," she said bluntly.

"Fascinating," Rowena murmured, her appetite for gossip thoroughly whetted. "You've had a falling-out with Gareth, then."

"The final one, after many." There was no point in deceiving Rowena and Kenneth. Weeks ago they had witnessed tension between her and Gareth, although she'd been naively in love with him at the time.

"So you are homeless," Rowena said.

Kenneth broke in impatiently. " 'Tis obvious Briar Rose is agonizing over this."

Briar Rose's hand went to her cheek. She was surprised to find a tear there. "Never mind, Kenneth. I'll try not to impose on you for long."

Rowena looked sharply at her brother. Before he could stop her, she demanded, "How will this affect our plans, Kenneth?"

"We'll speak of it later," he said gruffly.

"No, tell me now," Briar Rose insisted. "I would know exactly how I've intruded on you."

"We'd planned on going to court for the Christmas season," Rowena explained.

"Go, then, by all means," Briar Rose said. "Don't change your plans on my account."

"We'll go to Windsor as planned," Kenneth said. "And Briar Rose, you must come with us."

"To court?"

"Certainly! 'Tis a fine opportunity for you."

"But how do you know I'll be welcome there?"

Kenneth laughed. "You should have been presented at court long ago. I'd be proud if you'd allow me that honor."

"Really, Kenneth—" Rowena began.

"I'll hear no more from you," he said to her sharply.

" 'Tis settled then. Briar Rose comes with us to Windsor."

Later in her room—the very room where she had spent that first blissful night with Gareth—Briar Rose lay in troubled sleeplessness. Her life had changed so much since the calm days of summer, and now she was taking yet another reckless turn. She doubted the wisdom of following Kenneth and Rowena to Windsor, but she had no better plan, no better choice. She'd go, and see what fortunes awaited her there.

She balled up a small fist and ground it into the feather bolster on the bed, uttering a vehement oath. Her path was irrevocably altered. She'd lost Briarwood, and everything that went with it.

With all her heart she tried to summon a vile hatred for Gareth. Yet each time she told herself how loathsome he was, other images came back to haunt her: silver-rimmed eyes laughing or warm with passion, a mouth smiling irresistibly, awakening her desire with hungry kisses. The many small kindnesses and comforts that were so maddening in the pleasure they gave her . . .

How could one man mean so much to her? What was it about him that both infuriated and elated, made her want to be near him every moment? Even now a part of her ached for him.

Briar Rose punched the bolster again, hollowing out a spot for her head. Tears wet the fabric and her voice sounded raw with agony as she ground out his name, over and over again.

12

Gareth rode out to the moors every day, skirting the boundaries of his estates. Leafless trees fringed the western boundary, haunted by curlews. Sheep stood in the winter bracken, fat with their coats of wool. The flockmaster raised his hand and called a greeting. It would be a good spring.

Why then, did this empty feeling persist? Gareth wondered. Instinctively his hand went to an inner pocket of his tunic and closed around the Briarwood ring. *Her* ring.

'Tis all I have left of her, he said to himself, and then grimaced at his own softness. He was mooning like a lovesick lad. She's gone, and well rid of you, he admonished himself, but she was in his blood. There had never been a time when he'd felt so alive. Even when she'd infuriated him she'd filled him with passion.

With a stiff will Gareth thrust the troubling thoughts from his mind and rode on, noting where a stone fence had buckled and where a deep rut had become a danger to wandering sheep. It was easier—infinitely so—to dwell on such mundane things, as if they really mattered.

Still, Gareth couldn't forget her. One day, when she'd been gone a fortnight, he found the crest in his hand once again. He didn't remember getting it out; it seemed to appear there of its own accord.

Frowning, Gareth studied the ring. It was old and worn but had been masterfully wrought. The rose, with its seeds and rocks, reflected her beauty, her bounty, and her determined will.

Gareth stooped to the ground and took up a stick. Almost without thinking he began to draw in the dirt. The design that took shape pleased him and that night he committed it to parchment.

He would make a window for Briar Rose. She'd admired his work. Perhaps a gift from his own hands would soothe the hurt he'd done her, at least a little. He found some shards of the glazier's glass from his previous work and labored for hours over it, rendering his design with painstaking skill. When it was finished, he felt inordinately proud of his work, and then put it away. Later, when Briar Rose's anger had abated, she might deign to accept the gift.

The party that left Tynegate in late November was as well-organized as a small army. In addition to Briar Rose, Kenneth, and Rowena, there were two railed carts—one for clothing alone—and a long string of servants and retainers. Despite its size, the group progressed steadily. Before long, the snow-dusted northern moors were behind them.

What lay ahead, Kenneth told Briar Rose, was days of continuous riding along muddy, rutted tracks. They passed through the wild Yorkshire wolds and continued down into Lincolnshire, along the reed-bedded shorelines and great chalk ranges. Finally they passed through the fenlands and farmlands of Berkshire.

At last Windsor Castle came into view. The massive royal residence sat high on a tufted ridge. To Briar Rose it appeared a long medley of stone mirrored in the river Thames: walls, towers, royal and ecclesiastical buildings, with the flag-masted Norman keep dominating all.

"What do you think?" Kenneth inquired, looking pleased at her awe.

" 'Tis most imposing."

With Kenneth leading the way they crossed the water meadows and passed through the town, where the houses crept up to the castle walls. At King's Gate there were numerous men-at-arms in royal livery which bore the leopards of England and the lilies of France. A line of them stood, unblinking, holding gilt pikestaffs in front of them.

An official welcomed them and sent their retainers off to a guest wing adjacent to the keep, which housed hundreds of visiting nobles. The horses were taken to the vast stables. Briar Rose followed Kenneth and Rowena to St. George's Hall, a room of vast proportions. There were raised hearths at either end and the walls were festooned with tapestries and hangings of red and purple velvet.

A number of nobles were there, chatting as they sat at long tables, listening to the tunes of a lone piper or playing at chess or backgammon. They took little notice of the newcomers, being well used to the comings and goings of their peers.

"We look a sight," Rowena muttered, glancing down at her travel-stained cloak.

"Our lodgings will be ready shortly," Kenneth said. "And then, I think, it will be time for the evening meal."

The huge dining hall was lit by torches high on the walls and tall beeswax candles skewered on silver holders. Fires burned in the twin grates and the noise of music and conversation was deafening. Kenneth met the ladies at the great arched entranceway and they took their places in line to be presented.

John of Gaunt, the duke of Lancaster and the King's fourth son, presided over the festivities.

"He's never far from the seat of power," Kenneth whispered to Briar Rose as they advanced down the line. " 'Tis said he covets the throne himself, unlikely as it is that he'll ever take it."

Briar Rose studied the royal prince, in awe of his position. He was a king's son, and John of Gaunt looked it. Tall and imposing like most of his kin, the duke wore a jeweled headpiece and sword. His flowing robe of velvet sported the leopards of England and the spurs on his heels were wrought of gold. Briar Rose thought him splendid. The smile she gave him was genuine when she was introduced as Kenneth's ward.

"Fie on you, Sir Kenneth," he said, "for keeping such a treasure as this a secret." To Briar Rose he said, "Welcome to Windsor, my lady."

They passed into the main part of the hall where the tables swarmed with nobles and rich churchmen. Dulcimer, harp, timbrels, and a bladder-pipe were playing a lively tune. She felt the urge to dance. With each passing moment she was enjoying this court life more.

They sat at a midlevel table and Kenneth offered her a sweet quince from a flat silver dish. "Indulge yourself, Rose. This is quite possibly the best table in England."

She tasted the fruit. "I'm not used to this new name you've bestowed on me, Kenneth."

He waved a dismissing hand, unwilling to launch into a lengthy explanation of how Gareth had told him, through Cedric, that her identity must be protected. He merely said, "It's not wise to reveal all about oneself at a gathering such as this. You'll find that everyone here has a secret or two stowed away."

Briar Rose gave his words little thought as the food and diversions arrived. While a magician performed, the sculpted St. John's bread was served: a meat pasty in the shape of a hedgehog. After this came salmon roasted in wine and onions, tender thistles, spice cakes, and finally, as the shawms signaled the end of the feast, subtleties of spun sugar were presented.

Briar Rose attempted to sample everything, but the food was so rich and plentiful that she finally gave up and watched the mummers and jugglers at their antics. By the time the tapers were burning low, she felt sleepy.

She was about to whisper to Kenneth that she would like to leave, since the duke and his young wife, Blanche, had already retired, when she felt a hand on her shoulder.

"So you are the Lady Rose now," said a voice. "How very intriguing."

She turned and found herself staring, surprised, into the smiling face of Lord Alain de Wannet.

"Good evening," she said slowly, laying her hand in his.

"Come dance the gaillard with me," Alain invited, pulling her to her feet.

Kenneth was about to intercede, for Gareth had sent him a warning about Wannet, but there was no graceful way to do so. He sat, discomfited, and watched as Lord Alain led Briar Rose away, looking for all the world like a weasel who had just captured a plump hen.

"You've caused quite a stir," Alain told her as they moved through the steps. "The duke himself was remarking on your grace and beauty all evening."

"You flatter me, Alain. Surely His Grace has more important matters on his mind." Briar Rose looked up at her partner. She was beginning to reconsider her dislike of Lord Alain. Perhaps she'd not been fair to him last summer. She'd been so taken with Gareth then that no other man could have impressed her. But now she knew something of men. Perhaps she would give Alain a second chance.

"Lancaster is never too busy to notice a comely lady," he was saying. "Especially not during a feast. You'll find, Briar Rose, that people at court concern themselves greatly with such things. And for good reason. As friendships are formed, so are alliances."

"Of course." Briar Rose spun about in his arms, enjoying his attention and darkly handsome looks. "But Alain, there is no beneficial alliance that can be formed with me." The dance ended and they left the floor.

"I don't understand, my dear. Besides being beautiful, you're rather handsomely endowed."

She shook her head. "Not anymore." The pain glimmered in her eyes. "You see, Alain, I have lost Briarwood."

Briar Rose learned quickly that at court, one was judged by one's clothing. She'd never seen such a profusion of cloth of gold, cloth of Tarsus, rich velvets, shimmery silks and satins. She began to despair of her own wardrobe, which consisted of a single warm chemise and surcoat, a pair of slippers and stockings, and her mantle and hood from Gareth. The latter two garments were presentable enough after the mud from the road had been cleaned from them, but the other items were barely appropriate for mingling with the high nobility.

She made no secret of her dilemma. The other

women in the guest chamber found her honesty engaging.

" 'Tis like wearing a banner that says I'm from the provinces," Briar Rose said to Sybil Lowate, a young lady from Kent.

"Then we must set about refining you," said Sybil, happily taking the newcomer under her wing. "I'm larger by half than you, Rose, but let's see if there's something in my trunk we could alter."

"Really, Sybil, I couldn't possibly—"

But the girl would have none of it. She was apt with her needle and soon had her maid pitching in.

To her surprise, Briar Rose learned that John of Gaunt was equally thoughtful. She had no idea how he'd found out about her need, but he sent two lovely lengths of cloth to her, along with his wife's own seamstress.

One brilliant, chilly morning in December, she donned a new day gown of deep gold Spanish merino, caught her hair back in a coif of gold netting, and put on a sturdy pair of new shoes. The diversion for the day was hawking, one of her favorite sports.

Briar Rose followed Sybil outside, where their mounts were saddled and waiting. At the sight of her white palfrey, she felt a familiar stab. Even the smallest reminder of Gareth still knifed into her heart. She wanted so badly to forget him, to forget that whole part of her life. She did her best to get accustomed to court life, filling her days almost feverishly in order to avoid thinking about Gareth, drinking too much in the evenings so she'd not lay awake at night. She thrust aside her thoughts before the emptiness became too great.

The hawking party consisted of the duke of Lancaster and a varied entourage of nobles. Kenneth, Rowena, and Lord Alain de Wannet were among them. The group rode to the nearby heath country, enjoying the crisp winter air and the brilliant sunshine—a rarity at this time of year.

It took numerous cadge boys to display the birds from the royal mews. The wooden frames they hefted on their shoulders bore hawks of all shapes and sizes: the falcon gentle with notched bill, the mewing falcon, the swift-swooping peregrines.

Briar Rose was adept at the sport. Even the men were impressed by the dexterity with which her small hands managed the jesses, lunes, and tyrrits. Each time she let fly a bird, it circled unerringly back to her gloved fist.

"What a turn this sport has taken," Alain grumbled good-naturedly. "Now we've a woman who outshines the men."

The duke laughed deeply, even as he struggled clumsily with the creances. The bird he held took off at a crazy angle and flew aimlessly away. "Perhaps Lady Rose can give us a lesson or two in falconry."

Flattered by his request, Briar Rose obliged. "Look how you hold the lines, Your Grace," she said. " 'Tis not a war-horse you are reining, but a small bird. It requires a far more gentle touch."

Under her patient guidance the duke gave successful flight to a long-winged kestrel.

"By God!" he exclaimed when the bird returned to his wrist. "I think you've done it, my dear Rose!"

"Nay, Your Grace, 'twas your own hand."

"Beauty, wisdom, and modesty, too," he said. "Are you guilty of no fault, dear maiden?"

Briar Rose's throat tightened at the word "maiden." As far as anyone at Windsor knew, she was a maiden—unmarried, a virgin. Lancaster wouldn't be so kind if he knew the truth—that she was the wife of the outlawed Gareth Hawke. She blushed and tried to smile.

Kenneth said proudly, "My ward is a rare prize, is she not, Your Grace?"

Rowena's eyes simmered with fury. " 'Tis a pity," she said, "that Rose is in such dire circumstances. Elsewise she would be quite an asset to the court."

Kenneth shot his sister a warning glance which she imperiously ignored. John of Gaunt frowned. "What's the problem? Come, you mustn't keep it from me."

Rowena basked, gloating in the duke's attention. With false sympathy she said, "Rose is no longer the heiress she once was. She's lost all to her stepmother." Rowena watched Briar Rose's discomfort with obvious relish. She expected the duke to forget the girl immediately now that he knew she had so little to offer.

"Your Grace," Briar Rose murmured, "don't concern yourself over me—"

"Nonsense, my dear. We must do something to help. An advantageous marriage, perhaps . . ."

"Oh no!" Briar Rose cried. "You mustn't!"

"I'll think on it," the duke said, ignoring her protest. "But later. We've not finished amusing ourselves."

Amusement seemed to be the main goal of the nobles at Windsor. Evenings were spent feasting and indulging in a variety of entertainments. When Prince Edward, whom everyone admiringly called the Black Prince, arrived from Bordeaux, the merriment increased tenfold. The heir to the throne—handsome, charming, the hero of Poitiers—was beloved by all.

Alain de Wannet was never far from the royals, or from Briar Rose. To Kenneth's chagrin, he was her constant escort at table. Laying his hand on her arm, he said, "The generosity of the prince and his brother knows no bounds. You must accept their help with grace."

She folded her hands on the table and smiled. "I was advised that a lady should retain an air of mystery about her, but I'm no good at deception." When Alain brought her before the Black Prince, she told him about Briarwood.

"But why did you give it up?" he asked. "Clearly it grieves you to have done so."

Briar Rose thought of Gareth, of how she'd had to escape him before her obsession with him ate her alive. Giving him the crest had been the only way to convince him to set her free. She swallowed hard and looked up at the prince.

"I—I had good reason, sire."

The next afternoon Alain placed a jasper chessboard in front of her and drew forth an exquisite set of jade figures. "Do you play?"

"A little."

Setting up the men, he laughed. " 'Tis well for me, then. I don't excel at chess myself so I must be careful in selecting my opponents."

"You're sure to win this match," Briar Rose admitted, and made the first move with a pawn. They went back and forth cautiously.

"It intrigues me that you've given up Briarwood," Alain ventured.

"It was a necessary move," Briar Rose said, advancing one of her rooks.

Alain looked hard at her and stroked his beard. This was not what he'd expected. If Acacia had the ring, that meant she'd no longer be needing him. It also meant that Gareth Hawke had come through with his end of the original bargain. Smiling, he captured her rook.

"And you consider your action irrevocable?" he asked.

Briar Rose shrugged and moved her bishop ineffectually forward. "I must accept what I've done."

"You give up too easily, dearest. What does Acacia have but a ring, a mere symbol? I should think that so long as you are firstborn, Briarwood is yours."

"Perhaps that's so."

"Prince Edward and his brother John think likewise. Should you marry, Briarwood is yours, ring or no ring."

"You may be right, Alain, but with all due respect to the prince and the duke, I cannot marry."

Alain rolled his eyes heavenward. "Such a jaded heart. Tell me, Rose, why do you shy away from marriage?"

She moved her queen away from her king. "It seems to be more misery than joy."

"You're young to speak that way."

She saw genuine sympathy in his dark eyes and heard the concern in his voice. She drew a deep breath. Suddenly she was eager to share her secret with someone, to unburden herself.

"It all started last summer, when I returned to Briarwood to find that my fiancé had died. I—I suppose I was very vulnerable when I first laid eyes on Gareth Hawke. With all my heart I fancied myself in love with him . . ."

The whole story came pouring out. She blushed with shame when she admitted how easily she'd given herself to Gareth in marriage. She fought tears when she told how she had learned of his betrayal.

Alain carefully hid the enormous shock he felt.

"Good God, Briar Rose, how did you finally get away from the blackguard?"

"I gave the crest to him. I could no longer stand being bound to him. Doubtless he has already dispatched it to Acacia."

Alain shook his head. " 'Tis a rare tangle of deception. My heart goes out to you, my dear. What will you do?"

"I don't know. I considered returning to Briarwood. Much as I loathe the fact, I am a married woman and have every right to inherit. But as soon as the name of my husband is found out, the estate would be brought under interdict. I could never do that to Briarwood."

"There is only one answer, then," Alain stated. "You must rid yourself of Gareth Hawke. You're entitled to an annulment."

Briar Rose felt her heart turn to stone. "But then what? My situation won't change. I'll still be homeless, penniless."

He looked at her archly. "Only until you marry again, and do it properly this time. Think about it, my dear. With a marriage that is sanctioned by Lancaster, the Black Prince, perhaps the King himself, Acacia wouldn't dare oppose you."

It was a tempting thought, to regain Briarwood through a proper marriage.

"I've been unlucky in love, Alain, but perhaps I've been wrong to let feelings count for so much in my life. If and when I remarry, I'll be sure love doesn't enter into it at all." She moved one of her knights. "I believe I'll consider what you've suggested."

He smiled again and placed his queen face-to-face with her king.

"Checkmate, darling," he said.

* * *

Cedric and Maeve stood before Gareth in the great hall of Masterson, their faces glowing, their hands clinging together. Gladness radiated from them. Gareth felt a hollow pang of emptiness, as if the winter wind on the moors had blown through his heart.

Cedric stepped forward and bowed. "My lord, Maeve and I wish to be married."

"I've been expecting that."

"Then you'll allow it? I have the full merchat fee here—"

Gareth waved away the knight's coin and looked from Cedric's eager face to Maeve's bright, hopeful eyes. Only the most unfeeling man would be able to deny them.

"Of course. God keep you both."

"We shall have to go away, my lord. You see—"

"Say no more; I understand." Bitterness twisted Gareth's smile as he added, "There's not been a wedding at Masterson since I was placed under the ban."

"I thought to go to York, my lord. I've an uncle there."

"See the steward before you leave for a gift of silver coins, along with my best wishes."

Cedric snatched Gareth's hand and pressed a kiss on it. Again that emptiness in Gareth made itself felt.

Giles came soon after them. The burn on his cheek was now concealed. The beard gave his wise little fox-like face a look of mystery. "So the lovebirds are preparing to leave the nest for a time."

"Aye. Don't give me that look of yours, Giles. I still say what you did was reckless and ill-conceived."

"I only regret that it precipitated Briar Rose's departure." Giles didn't fail to notice the pain that flickered across Gareth's face. "You think of her still, my lord."

Gareth folded his hands and looked down at them. "By the rood, Giles, I ought to smite you for reminding me."

Giles smiled complacently. "But you won't, my lord, because it's the truth. Tell me, do you love her still?"

"Love!" The word exploded from Gareth like an oath. " 'Tis naught but an annoyance in my life. Best that I forget the troublesome woman and get back to managing Masterson."

"Forget, my lord? Yet you retain her ring—her token, so to speak."

Gareth's hand went to the inner pocket of his tunic. "Aye, this accursed thing. I want no part of it, but she flung it at me and wouldn't take it back." In sooth, he didn't blame her. The ring was a tainted token now.

"If you agree to marry me," Alain said, pressing his suit yet again, "I'll help you get Briarwood back."

Briar Rose laughed her chiming laugh. How quickly she was learning the ways of court life. No one dared take anything seriously here. She hadn't seen anyone betray an honest emotion in days. It certainly made life simpler.

"You jest, Alain." She turned her attention to the archery lanes to watch the knights and nobles displaying their skills.

The stakes in the contest were fittingly high. When an archer's arrow found the bull's eye, the duke of Lancaster would bestow a lavish gift: a jewel, a silver plate, even a royal destrier. This made the tension high and the competition fierce, both in the lanes and in the covered pavilions where the ladies cheered for their favorites.

Although Briar Rose was rapt, watching the display with avid attention, Alain pressed his point.

" 'Tis cruel how you cast me aside."

She turned her flushed face to him. "It's unfair of you to tease me with your proposal."

"But I tease not! I've taken the liberty of making some inquiries about your problem. There is a solicitor from York here at court called David Feversham. James Goodson brought him along to do some business. Feversham's a wily sort and I've had dealings with him that were less than pleasant. But he knows the law and is discreet. No one need ever know that you were married to Gareth Hawke."

Briar Rose glanced down at her hands. But I know, she told herself. I'll never forget . . .

Alain took her hand in his. "Marry me, love. Only then will you be able to claim your rightful inheritance."

" 'Tis kind of you to offer, Alain, but a flimsy enough reason to marry."

"That's how alliances are formed," he insisted. "I think the benefits are obvious."

"For me, perhaps, but what of you, Alain? You've three times the wealth of Briarwood. How would you profit from this?"

He smiled, thinking her impossibly naive. She knew nothing of the intoxicating lure of power, the desire to add more and more to one's holdings. The profits he'd reap were enormous: broad, bountiful estates, a strong keep, a retinue of able knights. And Briar Rose herself—ripe, delectable, with those pretty, pouting lips and smoky dark blue eyes, a body that held out the promise of nightly delights.

But Alain was too wise to mention this. He knew better than to frighten her off by appearing overeager.

When he went to try his skill at the archery lanes, he

exuded confidence. Huzzahs from the pavilions attested to his popularity. The whisperings about his first wife's suicide hadn't tainted him, not after he'd put it about that Celestine was unstable, as many convent-bred ladies were.

Yet all the cheering didn't improve his shooting. His arrows either fell short of the target or flew past it. His pride stung, Alain returned, glowering, to the pavilion.

"Shafts were doubtless poorly whittled," he grumbled. "Should've brought my own."

Briar Rose laughed at his temper. "Come, Alain, admit you didn't shoot well."

"I can shoot as aptly as any man here."

"As well as any man," Briar Rose teased. "I wonder how you'd fare against a woman."

"What a ridiculous idea. I'll allow there are one or two men here who could best me, but certainly no female."

"Very well then," she said, "I shall challenge you myself."

"Absurd. Ladies do not shoot."

"But I do." Briar Rose thought for a moment. "Perhaps I'll give it a try at that. The prizes are quite handsome."

Alain held his temper in check with difficulty. He was appalled that the chit would actually consider such a thing. Then, as he studied the proud tilt of her chin and the firm set of her jaw, an idea came to him.

His voice was silken when he said, "Very well, Rose, I accept your challenge. I'll shoot against you."

She smiled delightedly. "I knew you had a sense of fun, Alain." She moved down toward the lanes.

"What's this?" the duke of Lancaster asked, spying her.

She took his hand, smiling impishly. "I've challenged Lord Alain. He claims he can outshoot me."

"My dear, this is a man's sport. Surely you don't mean to—"

The Black Prince strode forward, laughing. "Give the lady a chance, brother. I hear she excels at falconry; why not archery as well?"

Alain hesitated at the end of the lanes. "We've not discussed the conditions of the match. Surely such an unusual contest demands unusual stakes."

"I quite agree," said Lancaster. "Now, what shall it be? My prize falcon, perhaps? Or a jewel . . ."

Alain nodded. "If Rose bests me, I'll match any prize she wins."

Briar Rose laughed. "That's all very well, Alain, but I've nothing to offer you if you should be the victor."

"Yes, you do, my dear. If I win, you'll agree to become betrothed to me."

Her eyes widened. "Those are high stakes, Alain. This is only a game after all."

"Yet you're so sure of yourself, how could you refuse?"

As Lancaster and the prince waited, Briar Rose reflected briefly on Alain's previous performance. Surely she could manage a bow and arrow better than that! The prizes would help her out of her poverty. She was tired of being a charity case. She tossed her head proudly.

"Those terms are agreeable to me."

There was a collective intake of breath from the crowd when the announcement was made. People leaned forward at the rails when they realized with delight that the very fate of the beautiful Lady Rose hinged on this singular match.

Briar Rose was unnerved by the sudden rapt attention that was focused on her. She stepped down to the lanes with a confidence she did not feel. She was given a bow and a quiver of three arrows.

"I defer to the lady," Alain announced loudly with a deep bow. He affected an attitude of rakish assurance as if he were certain of victory. "You may shoot when ready."

Briar Rose handed her cloak to a page. She flexed the bow a few times, familiarizing herself with it. Then she took aim. This was madness, agreeing to this reckless wager that could have such disastrous results. But her prize would be handsome. She closed her eyes and drew a deep breath. The captain of the archers at Briarwood had schooled her well. There was no reason she couldn't hit the mark.

Planting her feet firmly, she took her shot. The mark was sorely missed and the crowd remained silent. Briar Rose pursed her lips.

Alain made a great show of inspecting his arrows before making his shot. He hit the bull's eye true in the center and turned, smiling, to the cheering crowd.

Briar Rose felt determination take hold. She blocked out the noise of the crowd and concentrated. She was steadier now and her second arrow lodged accurately in the mark. With great satisfaction she heard an exclamation of surprise rise from the crowd.

Perhaps because the stakes were so high Alain rose to the occasion and hit the mark a second time. The onlookers grew tense.

Briar Rose countered aptly, finding the bull's eye with her last arrow. They were tied now; if Alain missed, she'd still have a chance.

Tension was high among the audience as Alain aimed his third arrow. The outcome hinged on his success.

The arrow sang down the lane and lodged in the

bull's eye. For a moment, just the beat of a heart, silence prevailed, and then the crowd burst into a loud chorus of cheers and applause.

"A Wannet! Huzzah! Huzzah!"

Briar Rose barely managed to conceal her dismay. When the nobles demanded that Alain claim his prize, she had only the smallest tremulous smile. She felt wooden, not yet fully aware of what she'd done.

Alain took her boldly in his arms and kissed her hard on the mouth. His lips had the feel of a conquest won.

There was a small, cell-like office in Winchester Tower where, even this close to the high holidays, clerks labored over their accounts. David Feversham was working for Goodson there. When he saw Lord Alain de Wannet, he looked away in distaste. The man who, months earlier, had tried to cheat him was suddenly behaving quite agreeably.

"Let us go someplace else, my friend, where we can talk in private," Wannet said.

Feversham shrugged, knowing he'd be pestered by Wannet until he heard him out. He put his papers aside and they left Winchester Tower and went outside below the town to walk among the barren vineyards of the southern slope.

"I'm about to become betrothed," Alain announced once they were far from the walls of Windsor. "There's a problem. The lady is married and must have an annulment."

Feversham's eyes narrowed. "On what grounds, my lord?"

"You're the expert, Feversham. 'Tis for you to determine that. It shouldn't be so hard. The wedding wasn't performed in the Church, but by a magistrate." Wannet fished in his cloak and took out a folded parchment Briar Rose had given him. "Have a look at this. Surely it's not valid." He also gave Feversham a cloth purse, heavy with coin. "I'll give you three times that much once the lady and I are wed." His velvet cloak billowed behind him as he turned. He paused on the incline. "Can I count on your discretion?"

David Feversham nodded. He stared after Wannet, puzzled and tantalized by the lucrative task.

He opened the parchment and scanned it. There was nothing remarkable about the document. It merely stated that the marriage had taken place, was sworn to and witnessed . . .

Suddenly his eyes were riveted to a signature at the bottom. The name jumped out at him: Gareth Hawke, baron of Masterson.

David had a swift recollection of the man who had, at considerable risk to himself, helped him recover an old loan from Wannet. He'd not forgotten Hawke's honesty, his fearlessness, his sense of fairness.

And now Wannet was asking him to destroy the man's marriage, such as it was. What did it all mean?

David Feversham looked regretfully at the sack of coins he held. He couldn't do it, not unless he was sure it was what Gareth Hawke wanted. He looked at the bride's name. Briar Rose of Briarwood. A name he'd heard tossed about Windsor, yet it told him nothing. But perhaps the woman herself could enlighten him.

Kenneth was no more pleased with what Briar Rose had done than she was. He scowled at her, in a rare surly mood. "So you've found yourself a husband."

She nodded glumly.

"You hardly seem the blushing bride."

Her eyes were huge and despairing. "Oh, Kenneth, what shall I do? It all started as such a silly joke; I'd no idea Alain would take me seriously."

Kenneth clenched his jaw. Gareth had warned him specifically against Alain de Wannet, and Wannet had done exactly as he'd feared. Glowering, Kenneth cursed his own stupidity. He should have kept Briar Rose at Tynegate.

"What about Gareth?" he asked sharply. "Though few know of it, you're still his wife."

Briar Rose shook his head. "Alain is taking care of that. I'll have an annulment soon."

"That's the easy part, Briar Rose. But you still haven't answered my question. What about Gareth? Is it really so simple to sever yourself from him?"

Her temper burst and she whirled on him, startling a nearby footman. "No, Kenneth, it's not simple at all! It's the hardest thing I've ever done. I married Gareth because I loved him. I'd be with him still, even knowing he didn't love me, if he'd just been honest with me. But all I ever got from him was lies, lies and treachery! Don't you see, I *must* leave him to salvage whatever dignity I still possess."

Briar Rose let her temper cool. Her heart still pounded as it always did when she thought of Gareth, but she was slowly regaining control of herself.

"Perhaps some good will come of this," she conceded, trying to convince herself. "Without help, I've no hope of getting Briarwood back. Alain may give me what I cannot win on my own."

"Look to it well, then, and hope that it comes about."

"I shall." Briar Rose fought a pervasive feeling of despair. "I must."

* * *

David Feversham entered the hall amid a deafening cacophony of music, laughter, banging utensils, and loud conversation. He fought his way along the lower tables, scanning the higher ones for Lord Alain.

Wannet was seated beside a woman of heart-stopping beauty. Inky waving hair framed a small, pale face with lips as red as cherries and wide, expressive eyes. Lady Briar Rose ate daintily, barely picking at her food. She glanced from time to time at Lord Alain, smiling tentatively yet looking troubled. She hardly seemed like a girl newly betrothed.

When Wannet turned away to laugh at some jest, she excused herself from the table.

David Feversham hurried to her side, intercepting her under the great archway at the end of the hall.

"My lady, a word with you."

She hesitated, giving him a dubious look.

"It concerns Lord Gareth Hawke."

Something like pain crossed her face. She nodded at the iron-studded doorway.

"Outside. I can barely hear."

They stopped under a frozen arbor in the courtyard. A few servants hurried by and guards stood at their posts.

"I am David Feversham, my lady. Lord Alain has engaged me to see about an annulment."

Her face took on a guarded look. "Can it be done?"

Feversham nodded.

Briar Rose stared at him with huge sad eyes. "So be it." She gathered her cloak around her and moved away.

"My lady, are you sure?"

To his amazement, he saw that there were great tears rolling down her cheeks.

"Very sure," she said, her voice trembling, far from certain. She left swiftly, holding her hand to her mouth as if to stifle a sob.

David Feversham sat in the courtyard for a long time, thinking about the woman. He knew there was something amiss here. Wannet would simply have to wait. Feversham refused to act until he confronted Lord Hawke and found out why on God's earth the man wanted to be rid of the beautiful Briar Rose who, despite her words, obviously loved the man desperately.

13

Briar Rose shivered in the stillness of the morning chill. She crossed the chamber to one of the tall windows, stepping lightly around the sleeping forms of tiring women and handmaidens and looked out over Windsor.

Bathed in the glow of a red rising sun, it appeared enchanted, not a place for mortals. Briar Rose imagined fairies and will-o'-the-wisps darting among the yew trees in the courtyard, and gold-clad knights from another world, clashing in monumental battles upon the distant water meadows.

She sighed and wiped away a tear which strayed down her cheek. If only life could be so charmed, so far from everyday problems. Another tear fell and she let it trickle down until she tasted its salty tang. She couldn't understand herself anymore. Today the banns of her betrothal were to be posted; by all right and reason she should be the happiest woman at Windsor.

Wannet, Stepton, Eagleton, Briarwood . . . It was more than Briar Rose had ever dreamed of having. So why, in her fickle heart, did she long to forsake all and go back to Gareth Hawke? He is a scoundrel and a thief, she told herself firmly. But, oh, what wild adventures they'd shared! Every moment with Gareth had been charged with passion, be it anger or ardor. That was something she'd never have with Alain. No rugged peaks and valleys, no explosive moments . . .

She was so deep in her troubles that she didn't notice the stirrings behind her. She was surprised to see the maids moving about, bringing water for their mistresses and shaking out their gowns.

A ripple of laughter stirred the air. Briar Rose returned to the center of the chamber and caught snatches of conversation.

"It's true, then. He is here."

"Aye, I had it from the royal lodgings."

Rowena approached, fussing with the laces on her shift. "Did you hear, Rose? The King and Queen Philippa have come to Windsor!"

Briar Rose took up a cloth and wiped it about her face and neck, recoiling a little at the chill. "I should have thought the King would make a more flamboyant arrival."

"There's a bit of gossip afoot that he had to come in stealth, as the French are ever after him."

Briar Rose's eyes widened. That King Edward was vulnerable was a thought that hadn't occurred to her. From all she'd heard of the great monarch, he was invincible, laying claim to the thrones of England and France, reviving chivalry throughout the kingdom, legendary already in his own lifetime.

"You mean someone would harm him?"

"That stands to reason, doesn't it? Ever since the King crossed the leopards of England with the lilies of

France, he's made many enemies. As far as the French are concerned, Edward *is* England."

Briar Rose stepped into a chemise of brown silk, one of many gifts she'd received since coming to Windsor. "God be thanked, then, that he's safe at his own castle."

"Assuming there are only friends here," Rowena said.

The chapel was hung with boughs of yew and laurel and holly in readiness for the Christmas season. Beeswax tapers glowed softly, their light reflecting off rich ornaments and painted banners. The precious relics seemed almost alive, shimmering in a golden glow.

When Briar Rose first entered the chapel through the paved cloister, she was amazed at the number of nobles who had crammed themselves inside. Her betrothal ceremony was a thing of little note when compared to the many other events at Windsor. She wondered why it attracted such interest.

And then, as she moved forward to take her place next to Alain, she saw. The King was there.

He could only be King Edward, standing erect in his robe of purple, a jewel-encrusted crown adoring his fair head. Although he was no longer youthful, he still had a regal bearing and handsome mien. He smiled down at his plump Queen Philippa and nodded greetings to the nobles, his subjects.

Briar Rose's knees felt weak as she swept down before him, murmuring, "Your Majesty."

He helped her out of her curtsy with his own hand. "So you are the Lady Rose, of Briarwood."

"Aye, my liege."

King Edward smiled. "My sons Edward and John didn't overstate your charms."

"Thank you, sire."

The King held Briar Rose's hand and turned to Philippa. "I'm told she is adept at hawking and archery."

Briar Rose blushed, remembering the fateful match. "Not quite adept enough, I'm afraid."

Edward laughed. "What a pretty story that was, offering yourself as stakes in the game."

"I—it was an impulsive thing to do, sire."

"Aye, but it worked out nicely, didn't it? You shall wed the loyal Wannet because of it. I won't pretend that it doesn't please me greatly. I've need of more solid support in the north."

Briar Rose faced him squarely with anguished eyes. "Your pardon, my liege," she faltered, "but I cannot say for certain that Briarwood is mine to bring to the union. I—I relinquished it to my stepmother."

"That remains to be seen," Edward said.

At the King's command and in the sight of the most illustrious peers of England, Briar Rose and Lord Alain de Wannet knelt on velvet cushions before a hanging basin of holy water to plight their troth.

Briar Rose felt aloof, as if it were happening to someone else. She barely looked at Alain, barely heard the Latin words that the priest spoke like an incantation. Her face was shrouded by a thin veil held in place by a circlet of silver on her head, and this gave her the freedom to look about, to further remove herself.

She was fascinated by King Edward. The monarch who had all of England at his feet seemed to emanate power.

By the grace of this man, and this man alone, people lived or died. Fortunes were made and fortunes fell; families were elevated or destroyed at the whim of the king. By his will did Gareth Hawke live under the ban, and by his will alone could the interdict be lifted.

This idea intruded upon all other thoughts and Briar Rose gave only the least bit of her attention to the betrothal ceremony. The notion that King Edward might be moved to help Gareth was not new; how many times in the past had she considered it? But now, faced with the formidable king, she found herself doubting the ability of her or anyone else to sway him from a decision long settled.

With one ear she listened to the priest, as if afraid to participate fully. If she gave too much thought to what she was doing, she'd not be able to go on.

Her eye was caught by a furtive movement in the narthex of the chapel. No one else saw, turned as they were toward the altar. Briar Rose continued to watch. The sweet-scented beeswax candles now illuminated the newcomer. It was a monk wearing a drab brown robe. His hands were concealed by voluminous sleeves, his head and face shadowed by a hood. Briar Rose thought it odd that the monk neglected to remove the cowl upon entering the house of God.

Nor did he move like one come to worship. Taking silent but purposeful steps, he edged up the side of the chapel, his back brushing the stone wall and his front touching the rounded sides of the pillars.

It occurred to Briar Rose that the monk had some message for the Black Prince, so urgently did he make his way toward him. No one, not even the prince himself or the people who flanked him, noticed as the cleric positioned himself close behind and leaned forward as if to whisper.

There was a silence and Alain tugged impatiently at her sleeve. Briar Rose was vaguely aware that she was supposed to make a response, but she couldn't speak. Her eyes were riveted on the monk. She stiffened, her kneeling legs growing rigid on the velvet cushion. The monk's hands parted and she saw a flash of silver.

Alain tugged again and hissed something. The stiffness left her and she shot to her feet.

"Sire!" she shouted, shattering the silence of the chapel. She lunged at Prince Edward, forgetting momentarily that he was a royal person. Now he was only a man, one in danger of losing his life, and she had no thought but to help him.

She threw her entire weight against the prince, knocking him to one side and finally to the chapel's stone floor. Mortified gasps arose from every corner of the building.

The scuffle lasted only seconds, until John of Gaunt caught the girl and pulled her away from his brother.

"Have you lost your reason?" the duke of Lancaster demanded, giving her a shake.

Briar Rose had barely enough breath to utter, "That—that monk! He must be stopped!" She pointed a shaking finger at the fleeing man. "Assassin!" she called at the top of her voice.

Although the men-at-arms who were stationed at the door believed, as everyone did, that the girl had lost her wits, they barred the monk from leaving.

"Let go of me," Briar Rose said sharply to the prince and duke.

Taken aback by her order, the brothers relinquished their hold and began brushing themselves off.

She went directly to the monk and groped at his sleeve until she felt the coldness of a steel blade.

She held it aloft for all to see. It was an ugly little dagger with a sharp, double-sided blade.

Prince Edward strode down the aisle, his handsome face livid with outrage. He whipped the hood from the monk's head, revealing a crafty, sharp-featured face.

The head was not tonsured but covered with dark, curling hair.

"This is no man of God," the Black Prince thundered, "but the devil himself come to murder me in the sight of my father, the king."

The intruder seemed to crumple, wedged between the men-at-arms so they had to support him. His face drained to white and he began to whimper.

"Pitié, ayez pitié . . ."

Prince Edward spat on the floor in disgust. "French dog! Take him away and hold him for questioning."

The assassin continued to grovel and plead, yet Briar Rose noticed a wild, avid look in his tear-bright eyes. Those eyes were fixed on the dagger she still held in her hand. Before she realized what he meant to do, the man lunged forward with desperate strength. Lightning-quick, his hand shot out and took hold of the dagger.

Briar Rose staggered back, her hand filling with blood as he dragged it forcibly from her. He turned the knife on himself and plunged it into his own chest.

"Ma patrie . . ." he grunted, dying almost before he hit the floor. *"Ma pat . . .* Ah, ah, *manus domini est!"*

"Sweet, merciful Christ," Briar Rose whispered, her eyes wide with horror as the man's blood crawled across the floor toward the hem of her gown. She stepped back and closed her eyes, feeling the bile swell in her throat.

It was a moment before she could speak to the king. "Forgive me, sire, for attacking your son."

Edward took her hands, heedless of the blood that stained his own, and pulled her around to face him.

"Dear lady," he said, seemingly unruffled by what had transpired, "there is naught to forgive. My sole concern is how I might thank you adequately."

"That the prince has not been harmed is thanks

enough, sire." Briar Rose blushed, a bit discomfited at being the center of such rapt attention.

Alain said, "God be thanked that it's over. Now, shall we get on with the banns?"

"I think not, Lord Alain," King Edward said with a wave of his hand. "We are all agog, and the presence of a madman lying dead on the narthex floor would surely taint the ceremony, would it not?"

"But we've not spoken the betrothal vows—" Alain began, and then stopped at a severe look from the King.

Briar Rose's status at Windsor soared after that. Not only was she the lucky intended of a rich and powerful baron, she was now a distinct royal favorite.

She arrived at her quarters to find a pair of maids placing her few belongings in a carrying box.

"What's this?" she asked. "Am I being sent elsewhere?"

"Aye, you are, my lady," the elder maid replied, dipping her head deferentially. "I'm Nan and this is my daughter Columbine. We're from the barony of Stepton and in your service now."

Briar Rose looked confused. "But I—by whose orders?"

"Lord Wannet himself," Nan explained. "You've no servants of your own, I'm told."

Briar Rose nodded.

"So now you do, my lady. Lord Alain knows we'll take good care of you." Nan gave her a gap-toothed smile. The silent Columbine wore a simpleton's grin. They went back to folding gowns.

Rowena, who had heard the exchange, shot a look of concentrated envy at Briar Rose. "Didn't you suppose your life would change when you became betrothed to

Alain?" She paced agitatedly, her small hands working behind her back. "You may think that Alain is satisfied with you, but in truth 'tis Briarwood he wants."

The words were a taunt, meant to make Briar Rose feel small and insignificant.

Nan stepped between the two women and glared at Rowena. "Now, my lady, don't you be baiting the girl with that sort of talk." The maid gave her a sideways glance. "Folks'll begin saying you're jealous, and you don't want that."

Rowena flushed and scowled at the maid. "Shut up, woman, or I'll send you and your idiot daughter both for a beating!" She whirled away with a flurry of satin skirts.

Sybil Lowate took Briar Rose's hand. "You came here with nothing and now you're a royal favorite, nicely affianced, and an heiress. Surely you can see how that would set Rowena's teeth on edge."

In the days that followed, Briar Rose began to feel like a cosseted pet. She was fawned over by maids, given presents, fed all manner of delicacies. In return she was expected to perform like a trained terrier. Her skill at falconry and archery became legend and the nobles delighted in pitting themselves against her. In the evenings she was obliged to sing for them or play at the harp and wasn't allowed to retire until she'd danced with at least a dozen courtiers.

Her life was a frenzy of activity from the time she awoke until the morning's small hours. Through it all she put on a facade of cheerful insouciance. To ease the soreness in her heart she allowed herself to feel nothing.

Christmas was upon them. Windsor's great halls were festooned from end to end with greenery. Above every alcove and archway there swung bunches of mistletoe, where hopeful maidens maneuvered themselves in order to garner kisses from their favorites.

Briar Rose had spent hours preparing for the feast. The seamstresses placed at her disposal had created a splendid gown. An underskirt of shimmery silver was covered by a heavy violet gown with a revealing square-cut bodice. Alain had given her an amethyst, which winked upon her bosom.

He escorted her into the hall, resplendent himself in a mauve tunic and hose, topped by a flowing satin tabard.

"My lady," Alain said smoothly, bowing low, "I've never seen a sight more fetching."

She inclined her head. "For all that I've been fussed over, I should think they would make me presentable."

The feast was a blur of activity. Conversation was impossible; the noise of music and mummers and clanging utensils drowned out single voices. Relieved by this, she sat back and watched the spectacle of the ceremony.

She was given wassail from the great ornate bowl. There was a great blaring of horns outside the hall and a gay song could be heard. As the men tugging the Yule log entered, the entire company joined in the singing.

"The Yule log burns." King Edward said. "Let it destroy old hatreds and misunderstandings. Let it banish envies and bring us good fellowship for all this year!"

Briar Rose lifted her cup along with the others and for a moment let the monarch's words touch her heart. Would that all wrongs could truly be destroyed, burned away like the log. She found herself wondering, once again, if the King might heed his own words and forgive Gareth . . .

But the merriment around her wouldn't allow her to

pursue the thought. The boar's head and roasted peacock were brought to table.

The eating was interrupted by carols and dancing. The nobles crowded around an enormous pool of liquor called snapdragon. In it floated the "toast": bread and roasted crabs, held up as each noble tried to best his peers by offering a more elaborate tribute to the King.

Briar Rose stood at the edge of the pool, stifling a yawn. Rowena studied her with envious eyes.

Blandly Briar Rose asked, "Are you enjoying the festivities?"

"What a question, Rose! There is no finer celebration on earth tonight. Don't you agree?"

Briar Rose recalled the small, intimate Christmases of her childhood and felt a sudden longing for those days of innocence. Carefully, so as not to offend, she said, "I'm overwhelmed by the ostentation here."

"As we are overwhelmed by you, my beauty," Alain interjected. Loosened by the wine he'd drunk, he freely placed a wet kiss on Briar Rose's mouth.

She pushed him away. "Alain, remember yourself," she said.

"You must get used to the ways of court," Rowena instructed. "Stop acting like a child."

"Leave me be, Rowena. I'm tired of your knowing ways."

"Ah, she has a temper, gentlemen," Rowena proclaimed cattily.

The nobles laughed uproariously and one bold man, an earl, reached forward and pinched Briar Rose on the backside. Incensed, she slapped his hand away and the amusement heightened.

"Come now, love," Alain chuckled. " 'Tis all in good fun."

She spun on him and unleashed a fury that had been building all evening.

"Fun, you call it!" Her dark violet gaze swept the crowd contemptuously. "You call yourselves peers of the realm, yet I've seen beggars with better manners than you!" She ignored the chorus of outraged gasps that greeted her insults and turned sharply to stalk away.

Perhaps it was only an accident, perhaps not; Briar Rose would never know. Rowena's dainty foot appeared in her way and sent her sprawling into the pool of snap-dragon. There was a moment of horrified embarrass-ment as she righted herself and lifted her drenched skirts in humiliation. Briar Rose looked helplessly at Alain, begging him wordlessly to come to her aid with some gallant gesture.

He spoke, a sly amused gleam in his eye. "I must say, gentlemen, that I now prefer the toast to the liquor."

Hearty laughter rang out, sounding like thunder in Briar Rose's burning ears as she stepped from the pool, slogging the liquor over the floor.

She pushed her way through the gathered nobles, intent on storming up to her chamber. Instead she found herself staring into the pale, amused eyes of Grif-fith of Morley.

"You . . ." It was worse than any nightmare.

"I see you've moved on to grander things," Griffith drawled. "Yet your conduct hasn't improved."

Briar Rose spat in his face and heard the collective intake of breath from the onlookers.

"You're among likely company, Griffith. These peo-ple here appear to understand your brand of amuse-ment."

"Seize the wench!" boomed an imperious voice. It was Bishop Talwork, his stony face cold with rage.

"Here, what's this?" King Edward himself had come to see what the commotion was about. He frowned at the sight of Briar Rose, disheveled and furious, her anger matched by the bishop's.

"The woman's gone mad, sire," Talwork explained matter-of-factly. "She insulted your subjects and defiled a man of the cloth." He indicated Griffith, who was wiping spittle from his cheek. "The woman should be taken away. Obviously her reason has left her."

King Edward frowned. "Perhaps we should let the lady speak her piece."

"Nay, sire," Talwork said quickly. "She's a danger to us all and will spoil this most holy of nights with her raving. Best to take her away from here."

Something in Talwork's counterfeit piety, his easy familiarity with the king, caused Briar Rose's control to snap. She faced Talwork and the king squarely, arms akimbo, not caring that a pool of liquor was collecting at her feet.

"You may well wish me gone from here," she said in a clear, ringing voice, "for in my 'madness' I could possibly say something quite damning, couldn't I?"

Only a slight tic at the corner of Talwork's thin mouth betrayed his nervousness. "Stop this ranting, woman. 'Tis unseemly to behave so before the King."

Briar Rose laughed harshly. By now she had every ear in the hall and Talwork knew it. She was well aware that she might easily be punished for her conduct, but she no longer cared.

"Sire, may I speak?"

"Truly, Your Grace—" Talwork began.

"Silence," the King commanded sharply. "Lady Rose has lately saved my son's life. She will be heard."

Briar Rose drew herself up. "Your Grace, I can no longer be silent about this. Morley Diocese is corrupt.

Bishop Talwork and his lackeys make a mockery of your favor and of the holy Church. Indulgences are sold, as are offices. Fornication is rampant; there are dozens of women enslaved there like concubines."

The crowd in the hall gasped.

"These are grave accusations, my lady."

"But they are true. Bishop Talwork has committed all manner of sin in the name of the Church. It must not be allowed to continue. He seeks to expand Morley's holdings. Lately he tried to seize the estates of Lord Gareth Hawke."

The mention of the notorious name caused a stir amid the crowd. A whisper rippled through them until the king called for silence.

Talwork gave a thin-lipped smile. "You see, the woman prattles on about Hawke. It might interest you to know that she was his whore."

The words stung Briar Rose and started new whisperings. She longed to strike that smug, aristocratic face.

"The bishop presumes to know much about me," she stated. "There's no love lost between Gareth Hawke and me. But he's been wronged; I'm the first to admit it."

The king regarded her sadly. "Hawke was a great man once, a good subject, though headstrong. However, he attacked Morley—"

"Please, sire. I know it's forbidden to attack a diocese, but Talwork's men captured his sister and other members of the household. The Lady Mary died and the others were forced into service. Lord Hawke acted as any man of honor would. Talwork plagues him still, long after the trouble. Clerics butchered his horse and then attacked him when he was defenseless on the road, leaving him for dead."

King Edward frowned deeply. "What say you to this?" he asked Talwork.

"Fantastic lies," the bishop asserted.

"I speak the truth!" Briar Rose shouted, her anger renewing itself in the face of Talwork's complacency. " 'Twas my own eyes that saw the murdered horse, my own hands that bound the wounds inflicted on Lord Hawke. And . . ." She paused to shock every eye in the hall by lifting her underskirt high to reveal a naked thigh. " 'Twas my own flesh that was seared by the Morley brand!"

The livid scar on her pale skin matched the cross and serpent emblem that Talwork wore at his shoulder and the amulet that rested on his chest.

Briar Rose dropped her skirt and faced the king. "Forgive my immodesty, sire. At peril of my honor and your favor, I've told you what I know of the corruption at Morley. Now it's for you to consider it."

She left the hall with as much dignity as she could muster in her wet skirts. Had she turned, she would have seen Rowena place a cautionary hand on her brother's arm. She would have seen Kenneth shake her off and stride purposefully toward the king, his hand raised to be allowed to speak.

And, had Briar Rose dared look back, she would have seen a tear of pity roll down Queen Philippa's cheek.

14

"I'm to Windsor, then. The king sent a summons." Gareth was in the armory taking down his shield.

Giles's keen eyes narrowed. "Does it bode well or ill, my lord?"

Gareth shrugged. "That remains to be seen. It does alter my plans. An acquaintance from Ravenscar has offered a good sum for finding a runaway serving wench. It seems she was his mistress. I'll have to send word that I can't help him."

"A pity," Giles said. "We could use the money."

A trace of the old lines of worry appeared on Gareth's brow. The riches from the battle with Morley and Wannet were spent. The knights had been paid, seed bought for the planting season, tithes paid, and stores put by to see them through the winter. But the security of that was temporary.

"There will be other jobs, my lord," Giles assured him.

Gareth flashed a grin at his agent. "You're right. Besides, I think it wise to leave domestic matters alone. I've had my fill of women for a while."

Giles laughed as he knew Gareth expected him to do. His master would never admit to the pining that tore at him. He went through the motions of living yet didn't really live at all.

"When are you leaving, my lord? It would please me to accompany you."

"There's no reason to wait."

He answered the mysterious summons without question because it had come from the king himself, because in spite of everything Gareth was a good subject. They reached Windsor in the full grip of January's chill.

Gareth hesitated when they arrived at the huge eastern gate. Not knowing whether he would be seized or succored, Gareth rode into Windsor. Servants showed him to a private chamber, which surprised him since a multitude of nobles and their retinues were staying at the castle. After he'd bathed and donned fresh clothing, Gareth was taken to a privy chamber in the royal lodgings, where King Edward awaited.

The monarch sat with his retainers and counselors, his priests and pages, his favorite hawk tethered at the back of his ornate chair.

Bowing low, Gareth greeted him.

"Rise, Lord Gareth. I thank you for coming so quickly."

"As you commanded, sire."

"Come here and sit with me so we may talk."

Gareth mounted the dais, aware of the eyes of the king's counselors on him.

"I've wronged you, Lord Gareth. Never should you have been censured. Your attack on Morley Diocese was warranted. The agents I lately dispatched there assure me of that."

Gareth said nothing, although his heart swelled. By some miracle the king had discovered the truth.

"I beg you, sir." Edward said, "accept my grant of mainpern and my most humble apology."

"My liege, I am your servant."

"Fortune smiles on me that it is so. Furthermore, sir, Morley is yours. Every bit of it will be granted to you."

Gareth was speechless. His spirits soared and gratitude shone in his eyes. "My liege, I only hope I can do justice to your gift."

King Edward smiled down at Gareth. "Aye, 'tis Morley you'll have and you may add it to your title. My one stipulation on this gift is that you marry. Only then will it fall to you."

Out of the corner of his eye Gareth saw the counselors nodding sagely. He couldn't fault the King for this requirement. It was logical that he would expect an advantageous marriage in exchange for the grant.

It occurred to Gareth to say that he was married and had been for some months. But, remembering Briar Rose's angry departure, he suspected she'd managed an annulment by now.

He forced a grin. " 'Tis a compelling way to speed me to the altar, sire."

"So I hoped." The King chuckled. "So I hoped. Perhaps here at Windsor you will find what you need. But all has been put to rights," he added, addressing the entire assembly. "I shall soon undertake the less pleasant business of dealing with Talwork."

Just then a page burst in, dancing in agitation.

"Bishop Talwork is gone, Your Majesty!"

"God's wounds," the King swore. "How could it have happened? He was heavily guarded—"

The page quailed at his wrath but continued. "The guards were overcome, sire."

"Send for the captain of the guard," the King responded swiftly. "We'll comb the forests until we find him."

"Can I be of service?" Gareth offered.

King Edward shook his head. "Not now, Lord Gareth. If you're needed, I shall call on you. We'll see you at the feast tonight."

The great hall glittered with lights and echoed with music and laughing voices.

A flash of color amid the dancers caught Gareth's eye. He froze, staring, his heart pounding, when he saw that the shimmery, red-veiled hennin concealed a face he knew achingly well.

Her laugh was as sweet as Gareth remembered. His mouth went dry and his limbs stiffened. He felt as if he'd just been seized by the throat. Not until this moment had he realized how much he'd missed her.

How and when she had come to be here were unimportant. But how the Yorkshire girl who had ridden away from him had been transformed into this dazzling, perfectly poised creature was a matter that filled Gareth with questions.

With a stab of fury mingled with trepidation, he saw that she was dancing with Alain de Wannet. She whirled around again, still smiling, her beauty shattering in its brilliance. Like one overcome by a too-bright sun, Gareth blinked. His chest heaved and the blood pounded through his veins. He felt sick unto death, yet he'd never felt so alive as at this moment.

The incessant pounding, the trembling of his limbs, the ragged breath that rattled in his chest, forced a realization he'd long battled. He loved Briar Rose. He *loved* her. He, who had thought never to feel anything after the humiliation of his censure, was now possessed by a love so agonizing that he felt his eyes burn.

Gareth raked a hand through his hair. When could this have happened? Probably in the first moment he saw her, last summer at Briarwood, when she'd defied convention and ignored all the rumors about him.

Sweet Jesu, he groaned inwardly, how is it that I didn't know? How could I have heard her whisper of love so many times and kept my silence? All the times he'd hurt her, put her off, lied to her, came back with the fury of a winter storm.

He stared at Briar Rose and tried to will her to look at him. If only he could catch her eye, he knew he could convey his feelings to her. If God was merciful, it wouldn't be too late. She didn't see him. He strode across the floor, his cloak billowing behind him.

"I'll finish this dance with the lady," he murmured.

Briar Rose was dumbfounded as her vision was filled by the sight of Gareth looking more handsome than she had allowed herself to remember. She'd never thought to see him again, least of all at court. Yet here he was, so large and imposing, with the light playing off his glorious blond mane and an odd smile curving his lips.

"Greet me, Briar Rose," he said, his big hand pressing at the small of her back. "Have you no word for a knight returned to the royal fold?"

At last she found her voice. "What are you doing here?"

"I could ask the same of you, but I shall answer first. By the grace of our king I've been mainperned."

Briar Rose felt a rush of gratitude. After her outburst at the Christmas feast, she'd not known what the result would be. She'd expected to be ordered from Windsor in disgrace, yet, incredibly, the king had believed her.

"And now you," Gareth was saying, that odd smile

setting her heart to leaping in her chest. "What brings you to Windsor?"

"I came with Kenneth and Rowena. I've been treated most kindly since my arrival."

Gareth winced, thinking of what she'd endured at Masterson. An apology was on his lips, that and a hundred other explanations, but before he could speak, Wannet tried to reclaim his partner.

"Now that you're back in the king's good graces, Lord Hawke, you'll want to renew old friendships. I'm sure the lady will excuse you."

Alain spoke his next words with great relish. "You've no claim on Rose, my lord. The marriage you coerced her into is over."

Gareth longed to drive his fist into that smirking face, but it wouldn't do to commit such an offense so soon after the King had welcomed him back. He turned a face of stone to Briar Rose.

"Is this true?"

She swallowed. He looked so fierce, so handsome. Her throat tightened and she felt the sting of tears in her eyes, tears for what might have been, if only . . .

He gripped her arm and shook her. "Answer me, Briar Rose."

"Gareth, I . . ." Had she really done it? Had she really sought an annulment from her marriage to the man who had conquered her heart so long ago, high on the windswept moors of Yorkshire? She lowered her eyes.

"It's true."

He sent her a burning look of sarcasm. Thank God, he thought, that I learned this before I confessed my love to her and humiliated myself.

"You're well rid of me, 'Lady Rose.' " Turning on his heel, he strode away.

Later, Gareth was haunted by the stricken look on Briar Rose's face. Perhaps he shouldn't have been so harsh with her; how could she have known that the king would forgive him?

Despite his anger Gareth couldn't help but feel a certain wry amusement at the turn things had taken. How forgiving these people were, the very ones who had once shunned him. They were like puppets responding to various tugs of the royal strings that were attached to them.

In another part of the hall Briar Rose was trying—and failing—to keep her eyes off Gareth. She was amazed by his easy grace, the way he handled even the most powerful nobles. She suddenly found him so attractive that she could barely think straight. Everything had changed for him and she was the cause of it. Yet he didn't seem to know that.

Briar Rose gave a troubled sigh. The cost in clearing his name had been dear. She may have lost her home, for surely by now her ring was in Acacia's possession.

Would he ask her forgiveness? Would he try to make amends? She couldn't possibly imagine it, not after the stony look he'd given her when Alain announced their marriage was over. If, by some miracle, Gareth did offer an apology, could she find it in her heart to forgive him? She didn't know.

They didn't meet again that evening. Gradually the company retired. Gareth felt weary to the bone, staying only in hopes of capturing the glittering beauty, whom people called Rose, for one more dance.

Instead he found himself paired with Rowena, whose manner toward him had changed dramatically.

"Felicitations, my lord. You're back among us." She leaned close to speak. "I always knew there had been a great mistake."

Gareth gave her a half smile. Now that the way was clear, the woman would flatter him freely, perhaps try to revive their marriage plans. Wishing that it was not Rowena but another in his arms, he looked for Briar Rose and saw her with Wannet.

"They're a likely pair, aren't they?" Rowena said, following his gaze. "The king himself has sanctioned their union."

Gareth stopped in midmotion, his eyes hard and steely. "What's that? Wannet and Briar Rose are betrothed?"

Rowena laughed gaily. "Haven't you heard? 'Tis the match of the season." She slid her arms up to his shoulders, smiling seductively. "Pity she wasn't more patient. She should have been loyal enough to stay with you, Gareth. If she had . . ." Rowena let her voice trail off, admiring the speed with which he concealed the stricken look on his face.

The next day there was a great hunt in the royal forests that lay beyond Windsor. It was to be the last event of the season, for soon the royal family would disperse to the business of ruling the empire and the nobles would return to their various estates, having had their fill of revelry and posturing before the royals.

Briar Rose wasn't sure what lay ahead for her. She wanted to get to Briarwood as soon as possible and have done with the business with Acacia, but Alain didn't seem to be in much of a hurry.

She joined the hunting party that had gathered in the water meadows beyond the keep. The day was unseasonably warm, like a false breath of early spring. Briar Rose drew her palfrey up when her eye was caught by the sun glinting off a golden mane. Her heart rose to her throat.

Gareth sat his black palfrey proudly, looking as fine and noble as any of the grand company. It was sheer torture for Briar Rose to look at him, for it brought all the bittersweet memories rushing back.

A sad smile curved her lips. Months ago she'd chosen Gareth for her husband and promised to help him clear his name. Now it was done, but fate had taken a cruel turn.

She thought suddenly of Sister Marguerite. At last she understood what the wise nun had been trying to teach her. She must give of herself in order to find happiness. She shouldn't have expected it to come all at once. But she hadn't been patient enough, selfless enough, to help Gareth with no thought for herself. Always she'd expected something in return. It was a lesson learned too late.

When Gareth glanced her way, it startled her. Her heart leaped as she tried to read what was in his eyes. She saw them grow hard and knew he was thinking about last night.

Forcing her eyes away, she positioned herself among the women. The hunt began with a great blaring of horns and the horses surged forward, the king in the lead.

Like a host riding to battle the party thundered into the forest, startling birds from the trees. Briar Rose was glad for the demanding course. She had to concentrate on what she was doing, which spared her from thinking of Gareth. She rode toward the rear, enjoying the almost warm softness of the air as it whistled past her ears. Off to her left was a glistening pool, surrounded by winter bracken on one side and soft, dry grass on the other.

Having given the horse her head, Briar Rose had the sensation of soaring. The feeling was so intense that she didn't notice the fallen log until it was too late. The mare squealed and reared, hooves pawing the air. Briar Rose felt as if a great hand had swooped down and scooped her from the saddle and cast her roughly to the ground. Her breath left her, and she felt herself slipping, almost gratefully, into a faint.

"Oh, God, *no* . . ." The words barely penetrated her consciousness. Then she felt a pair of strong arms lifting her, holding her against a broad, warm chest. She became aware of a familiar scent, of woods and leather and uncompromising maleness. She raised her eyelids and found herself staring into Gareth's face.

Relief softened the lines about his mouth. "God's wounds, Briar Rose," he breathed, "I thought you'd been killed."

"Gareth . . ." She sighed, laying her head against the warmth of his shoulder. Then the words were out of her mouth before she could stop herself. "Would you have grieved for me, Gareth?"

For a moment she thought he was going to laugh at her. "What kind of question is that?"

She shook her head. "Never mind." The truth would kill her. Blushing, she turned the subject. "My horse!"

Gareth nodded to the left. Briar Rose was relieved to see Dame standing by the pool, drinking placidly.

"Thank God," she breathed. "I feel so foolish."

"What were you thinking of, leaving the hunting party like that?"

"I had an urge to go off by myself."

Gareth set her on her feet, watching her closely to assure himself she wasn't hurt. He needn't have worried. She brushed herself off and stooped to pick up her coif.

"They're long gone now," she remarked.

"Let's go sit by the pool, then," Gareth suggested. "That is, if you don't mind my company."

"I—no, I don't mind."

They walked side by side, not touching. A warm breeze swept down and rippled the grasses at the edge of the pool, stirring the images of the trees in the water. Briar Rose sank down onto the grass. She glanced over at Gareth.

She read a dark, agitated rage on his face.

"You're to marry Wannet," he said angrily, seating himself beside her and drawing one knee up to his chest. The sunlight danced across his rugged features. "You lost no time getting our marriage annulled."

Briar Rose's temper prickled. Only Gareth Hawke would be so arrogant to behave this way—so thankless, so full of righteous anger.

"I saw no reason to wait, my lord." She masked her sinking feeling with coldness.

"By the rood, woman, *why?*"

"I owe you no explanations."

"Surely you feel no love for the man."

"Love," she said bitterly. "What is that but some illness of the soul? It has no place in the way of things. 'Twas you who taught me that, Gareth. Am I not an apt pupil?"

Insolently he reached out and tugged at a silken strand of hair. "How wise and sophisticated you've become, 'Lady Rose.' "

His sarcasm stung. "You're dismayed to find me thus," she accused. "No doubt it fed your pride to believe that I sat pining for you. Don't flatter yourself, my lord. Happily I've recovered from that girlish malady."

With a muttered oath he grasped her by the shoulders and bent his head close. "Have you, nightingale?" he drawled. He dealt her a punishing kiss, his lips forcing hers apart, making a mockery of her resolve against him. With one arm he held her captive, wrapped her against his own hard length, while his other hand went to work at tormenting her.

As he kissed her deeply, his hand roved down her back, tracing the curve of her hip before moving around to stroke the side of her breast.

She thought she would be crushed by his embrace. Already she was feeling dizzy. The hand she pressed against his chest was weak, not the protest she meant it to be.

And then, a careless traitor to her will, she felt the beginnings of a response. His hands, his lips, his probing tongue as it traced the outline of her mouth, lit a fire in her veins. His fragrant male scent assaulted her senses and she was engulfed by a desire wilder than any she'd ever felt before, even when she'd been his willing wife.

"Gareth . . . no . . . oh, Gareth . . ."

He stiffened and pulled away, studying their hands. Their fingers were entwined like a lovers' knot. What was it he heard in her words—a curse, or an entreaty? He looked up at her face. Her lips were soft and moist, inviting, but troubled shadows flickered in the depths of her eyes. He disentangled his hand from hers.

"What of Wannet?"

She looked away. "I am promised to him."

He drew up on his elbow and pressed upon her shoulders. "You can say it still, after this?"

Briar Rose closed her eyes, wanting to hide from his probing gaze. "My flesh is weak to you, Gareth."

"What you call a weakness is the very strength of

womanhood. Be true to yourself, Briar Rose. Say you were made for me, for my arms and my lips." He ran his mouth up the column of her throat to her ear, curling his tongue into it, making her shiver.

She knew it was true, but she couldn't forget how he had betrayed her.

As if he'd read her thoughts, Gareth reached out and turned her to face him. "All I sought was to shield you from Acacia's malice. All along I intended to keep Briarwood in your name."

Briar Rose stared at him. "Then why did you hold me at Masterson?"

"I tried to explain. I'd had word that Acacia had set Wannet after you—"

"So you've said, Gareth."

"Aye, and you didn't believe me. I knew he meant to marry you and take Castle Briarwood for his own." Gareth's face hardened. "It appears he has succeeded."

Briar Rose shifted uncomfortably on the bed of grass. The sun was high, streaming down through the bare trees. She'd never believed Gareth's claim against Alain. Still . . .

She faced Gareth. "If I'm mistaken about Alain's character, then I shall not marry him."

"And then? Say it, nightingale. Say you'll have me back."

"I don't know. I've scant reason to trust anyone."

Gareth's scarred eye lowered at her. "Including me, of course."

"You yourself admit that you wronged me. Because of you I am without a home."

"Perhaps not."

Briar Rose hesitated. "What do you mean?"

"Briarwood is yours so long as you retain the crest."

"It's been so for generations."

"I've kept the ring. Acacia doesn't have it."

She raised her eyes to his, searching for deception. There was none. All she saw was a calmness in his expression, a look almost of relief.

"Where is it?"

"I left it locked away in a coffer at Masterson, not wanting to risk carrying it on such a long journey. I didn't know you'd be here. It's waiting to be restored to your finger." He raised her trembling hand to his lips.

With a cry of delight she flung her arms around his neck. "Gareth! I never dared hope. Acacia must have offered you so much, and you needed it so badly—"

"Not badly enough to hurt you, nightingale."

Her eyes were moist and full of all the love she'd ever felt for him. "Gareth, thank you."

"You see, I'm an honest man after all. Can you forgive me, Briar Rose?"

She studied his face, which was lit by the soft winter sun. She knew every crag and plane of that face, just as she knew the scars on his chest and arms. Forgive him? She asked herself. He had deceived her, but now she understood why. Yet, with a flicker of sadness, she realized her stolen heart could never be restored.

"God help me, but I love you still," she said finally, her voice barely above a whisper. "Even more now, Gareth, than when I first laid eyes on you and vowed you would be my husband."

The words kindled a fire in his soul and sent his heart soaring. He felt a sense of rightness about the world that he'd not known since he'd been placed under the ban. His life seemed to smooth out before him.

"Nightingale . . ." he whispered, reaching to gather her again in his arms. He meant to tell her then that he loved her, that he'd loved her from the start, but something made him hesitate.

He dragged himself away from her. It was too soon. His feelings were too raw to give to her just yet; better to let his love mellow in his heart before confessing it to her. He wanted their reunion to be perfect, untainted by shadows. And Alain cast a long shadow. He would stand between them until Briar Rose ended the betrothal.

It was agony to wait, but it would be worth it. Gareth stood, not daring to look at her. It was so damned easy to forget himself when she smiled.

But Briar Rose wasn't smiling. She was confused. "Gareth . . ."

The soft plea was like a knife wound. He clenched his fist and turned away.

When they returned to Windsor, the hunting party was already back. Alain spied them as they entered St. George's Hall, their clothing rumpled, bits of dried leaves and grass clinging to their hair.

He strode forward, tugging at his beard. "Where the devil have you been?"

She looked up and the dreamy haze that had been in her eyes cleared. "Alain! I—I took a spill from my horse and Gareth helped me."

"It appears," Wannet drawled, plucking a strand of grass from her hair, "that he helped himself as well. Goddamnit, Briar Rose, isn't it bad enough that Rowena's told all Windsor that you were Hawke's whore—"

He staggered back against the wall when Gareth's fist smashed into his face. His hand went to his mouth, catching the tooth that had been dislodged by the blow.

"By the throat of God, Hawke," he rasped, spitting blood, "I'll see you dead for this."

* * *

"He means it, my lady."

Briar Rose turned. "Giles!"

He pointed his toe and swept his plumed hat from his head, making a courtly bow to show off his lavish costume of parti-colored turquoise and black. The scar from Morley's brand was disguised by a full beard now.

"What a handsome fellow you are, sir. And *who* means *what?*"

He brushed his cloak aside with a flourish and sat down on the garden bench beside her. "Wannet means to kill Gareth Hawke."

"You lie, Giles!"

"Wannet will never give you up. You'd be the jewel in the crown of his pride."

"That's his problem. I belong to Gareth, and he to me."

"If Alain discovers that you intend to remarry my master, he'll have him murdered." Giles hesitated, then dropped his voice to a whisper. "Alain made that vow to his closest ally. To the king's brother, John of Gaunt."

"Gareth is strong," she insisted. "Alain can't hurt him."

Giles raised an eyebrow. "Are you sure, my lady? Look how narrowly the Black Prince escaped death. 'Twas only yourself between that French dagger and him. Gareth isn't half so well-attended."

She nodded, stiff with fear. "Have you spoke to Gareth of this?"

"Nay, my lady. He'd laugh in my face and declare he'll not be intimidated by any man."

Briar Rose stood up, her eyes flashing. "I won't have it. I'll go to the king and tell him I wish to end our betrothal and marry Gareth. Surely he'll not deny me after—"

"What will you say when King Edward asks your

reasons? That one of his esteemed subjects, John of Gaunt's close friend, is planning murder? A royal favorite you might be, but the line is drawn where blood and family are involved."

She regarded him through pain-filled eyes. She heard again Dame Marguerite's voice cautioning her to put those she loved before her own desires.

"Giles, what should I do?"

"I can't tell you that, my lady. 'Tis something you must decide for yourself."

She searched her aching heart for an inkling of hope, yet there was no way she could have Gareth and shield him from Alain's treachery. And there was no way she could tell Gareth the truth. He would never run from his enemies. She knew her reckless lover would have her even if it meant his own demise.

Gareth had joined the king's men in their search for the fugitive bishop, Talwork, and his companion Griffith. A blare of trumpets announced the return of the party. Briar Rose rushed out on a tide of noble courtiers to watch.

A small contingent of riders wended its way across the outlying meadows toward the castle. The hawk emblem stood out sharply on Gareth's shield. He rode hunched over as if a great weariness had come over him. Paulus, his squire, appeared to be asleep in the saddle. Behind these two came a robed outlaw—Talwork. Apparently Griffith eluded the hunters still. The captain of the guard and a handful of men brought up the rear.

Only dread of the consequences kept Briar Rose from flinging herself into Gareth's arms, cradling his weary face between her hands. A sound, almost a sob, escaped her throat. Alain, who was standing next to her, followed her gaze.

"So," he said, "the mighty hunter returns triumphant."

She bit back a retort. "He has done the king a service."

"Pity he couldn't have done it with a bit more style."

Briar Rose forced herself to feel nothing save a dull numbness. For many long, agonizing moments she waited and watched while Gareth approached with maddening slowness. She felt a flood of tenderness for him when she realized the reason for his plodding. A more vain man would have galloped this last leg of the journey, thundering in with a flourish for the benefit of the onlookers. But Gareth considered the horses instead, which were weary from days of hard riding through the forests.

With a painful lump in her throat Briar Rose recalled the first day she'd seen him, so long ago. During the tourney at Briarwood, while the other knights preened and ordered their retainers about, Gareth had ended the day by servicing his horse himself.

Never again would she be able to speak her love to him, to tell him all that was in her heart. It was almost more than she could bear when his magnificent gray eyes sought her out in the babbling crowd and gladness lit his rugged, weary face.

Biting hard into her lower lip, Briar Rose turned her gaze away from him and placed a hand on Alain's arm in a gesture of forced affection. She turned her back on Gareth and bestowed a proprietary kiss on her betrothed, hoping, even as her heart splintered into a thousand pieces, that her display was convincing.

15

Gareth was in a foul temper when he bellowed for Paulus. The squire came scurrying into the chamber.

"Find me some clean clothes," Gareth said. "I'm going to bid farewell to the King."

"It'll be good to get away from this place, my lord."

Gareth looked at him sharply. "What do you mean by that?"

Shrugging, Paulus said, "She's toyed with you long enough, my lord."

Gareth didn't have to ask who Paulus meant. Ever since he'd returned to Windsor after seizing Talwork, he'd agonized over Briar Rose. He didn't understand her at all. He'd expected a welcoming embrace. He'd even dared dream that she would tell him all had been set to rights and they were free to remarry.

The image of her in the arms of his enemy was seared onto his soul. Had she sunk a dagger into his heart and twisted it, she couldn't have driven the hurt any deeper.

Gareth cursed under his breath. He'd been a fool to

allow himself to believe she'd forsake Alain for him. No doubt his absence had given her time to think, to decide that she'd profit more by marrying Wannet.

Still muttering oaths, he dressed in his finest clothes and went to take his leave of the king.

Alain tarried at Windsor long past the first soft days of spring. He offered up one excuse after another until his mother, the imperious Lady Beatrice, arrived.

Beatrice was unbearable, but at least she kept Briar Rose close to the lodgings they shared. For Briar Rose lived in constant terror of seeing Gareth. She'd managed the initial deception well enough, but she was sure to betray herself if she was repeatedly in his company.

She'd heard that Gareth had tried to leave Windsor. Only a day after returning from the manhunt, he'd made his request to the king, but Edward had refused to let him go. So Gareth spent his days in council while Briar Rose passed the time with Beatrice, hiding from him.

One day at the end of the Lenten season, Alain came to take her to a biblical play that had arrived in Windsor. During a break in the play she followed Alain down to a crowded pavilion where drinks and pasties were being served to the nobles. She accepted a cup of mead from Alain and raised it to her lips.

She nearly choked on the sweet liquid, for when she lifted her eyes, she found herself staring at Gareth Hawke's handsome Saxon face.

It was as if the crowd had peeled away, leaving no one but the two of them. Jesu, Briar Rose thought, holding the cup with both hands to keep it from being spilled by her trembling. Sweet Jesu. It was bad enough that he haunted her every moment, both waking and sleeping. But to see him again, to feel that quaking of her heart, was more than she could bear.

Marshaling all her will, she tore her gaze away and

joined in laughing with the lords and ladies around her. But even as she walked away, she could feel his eyes burning into her, questioning, challenging.

Gareth cursed the whim that had brought him to the pageant. He'd been conferring with the king's captains and advisers for weeks and had wearied of all the talk. He was like a warhorse, eager for action, impatient with the delays.

He had come to the play to escape the frustration, yet here was more to trouble him than he could possibly find in the council chambers. His anger grew as his eyes followed Briar Rose, spinning gaily away on Wannet's arm. The love that had bound them seemed only a dreamlike memory now. She was a different person, the glittering Rose, the toast of Windsor. She spared not even a smile for her rough-hewn lover from the northern shires.

Still, he noticed something odd in her manner. Her eyes gleamed with more than their usual intensity. Her smile was almost too bright. Her laughter sounded forced and her manner was flippant, more like that of the seasoned ladies at court. Had she, then, cast off her coltish charm? Had she finally been seduced by the grandeur of court life?

Gareth tried to forget the encounter, but she stayed with him, wrapped around his heart, his eternal torment.

Any moment, Briar Rose feared, her mask of indifference would crack and she would fling herself into Gareth's arms. It was all she could do to keep away from him, especially during those awful moments when she'd seen him looking at her, the hurt and confusion bright in his eyes.

But she refused to endanger his life. If he grew to hate her, then so be it.

Giles, who was still posing as a French comte, stopped to whisper in her ear. "Well played, my lady."

Stabbed by unbearable sadness, she looked away. And then, as hot tears threatened to spill, she fled to the rolling meadows. Gathering her cloak around her, she noted that it was the one of violet blue. Gareth's gift. The very smell of the white rabbit lining took her back to Masterson, and she felt an unexpected homesickness. How she had hated it there, yet she had somehow come to think of the place as a home. She wondered about Cedric and Maeve, Meg and all her little ones, even Kate. She longed to see them again. Here at court, favors were traded instead of feelings; alliances were formed instead of friendships.

She mounted a rise which gave a splendid view of the first stars of twilight. Leaning her arms on the cool stone of a crumbling terrace wall, she felt a gentle breeze lifting tendrils of hair from her shoulders.

It was a night made for lovers, the air redolent of the season's new growth, the nightingale's song clear and sweet.

She knew not how long she stood there, her elbows resting on the wall, her chin cradled in her hand. Suddenly a pair of strong arms gripped her and spun her about; a firm mouth descended upon hers, a bold tongue plundered the softness beyond her lips.

Gareth! How he had found her didn't matter. That he was here, holding her in his arms, was all Briar Rose knew. She dissolved into his embrace, found solace in his closeness. She felt herself falling into a well of passion, letting herself be enveloped by the sweetness that whirled through her.

She loved him so much. . . . It was impossible to deny it. Yet it was precisely the fact that he was so precious to her that made her come to her senses. She could not indulge herself in his love; the cost was too dear. Slowly, like one awakening from a drugged sleep, she recovered from her state of trembling desire, all the while cursing herself. It would be harder than ever now, but she must turn Gareth against her.

She put all the force of her frustrated passion into the slap she delivered to his cheek, and leveled a gaze of offended dignity at him.

"How dare you follow me," she said. "I didn't invite your attentions."

"Neither did you repel me, my lady," he drawled. "At court they may have taught you that it's unbecoming for a lady to enjoy the pleasures of the flesh, but your response was that of a wanton."

"How am I to react when you steal after me in the dark and intrude on my privacy? I shall call for help." She opened her mouth to alert someone in the field below.

An iron hand clamped itself over her mouth. "Hold your tongue, woman. Have you forgotten who I am? It wasn't long ago that you professed love for me."

When he removed his hand, Briar Rose no longer needed to pretend anger. "You're a brute, Gareth Hawke."

His eyes flashed silver in the moonlight. "Tell me, Lady Rose, what *you* are. Have you lost your senses?"

"Quite the opposite. Let's say my good sense has returned. Your absence gave me time to think. I was a fool ever to have anything to do with you. I am promised to Alain de Wannet, and the king himself has sanctioned us. I'll not go back on my word."

"You were more than ready to do just that before I went off on the hunt."

"I was confused, but I know my own mind better now."

Gareth couldn't believe that this was his Briar Rose. Where was the artless girl who had brightened his days and filled his nights with silken splendor? Where was that unspoiled straightforwardness that set her apart from all others? Suddenly it occurred to him that perhaps she was behaving this way against her will. A desperate thought, but he clung to it.

"Is it some threat, then, that makes you cling to Wannet?"

"How you flatter yourself, Gareth! Do you think for one moment that I would be frightened by idle threats? I was wrong to have welcomed you back."

He placed two fingers under her chin, staring meaningfully into her eyes. "Ah, but you did welcome me, didn't you, nightingale?"

She jerked away. "I've heard about the king's promise. I'll not be your pawn, my lord, in your ploy to get Morley."

He grabbed her by the shoulders and gave her a shake. "Is that what you think? That I'd use you to get the land?"

"It only stands to reason—"

With a bitter oath he shoved her away as if she'd suddenly grown distasteful to him. "You've studied the ways of court well, my lady. Thanks be to God that the king has finally agreed to let me go home. I've had more than my fill of court life."

For a moment he thought he'd struck a nerve, but it must have been the play of torchlight from the field that made her look so hurt. When he glanced at her again, her beautiful features were set firmly, like the face of an alabaster statue gleaming in the light of a rising moon.

Gareth's pride kept him from pleading with her. There was nothing more to be said.

He gave her a last look, long and searching, then turned and left.

Briar Rose watched him, biting her lips to stifle the words that would call him back. As he retreated, striding proudly, his broad frame outlined by silvery moonlight, she felt the very life drain out of her. Yet she held still until he disappeared into the night.

Gareth had been home for some weeks when Giles returned. He laid a sealed parchment on the table. " 'Tis from Kenneth Shelby. Months old, I fear."

Gareth opened the letter, eager for news. He and Kenneth had missed seeing each other at Windsor by a matter of days, Kenneth having been called to London on business. Gareth's eyes flicked over the page. A particular passage caught his eye.

Setting the letter down, he glowered at Giles.

"Ill news, my lord?"

"Why didn't you tell me of Briar Rose's role in my pardon? All along I thought Kenneth had been the one who had convinced the king of my innocence, yet it was she who first spoke for me." He pictured the scene as Kenneth had described it. He saw Briar Rose's humiliation as she was shoved into the pool of liquor, her rage when she came face to face with her tormentors from the diocese, her righteous courage as she exposed the livid brand on her thigh for all to see, her speech moving the queen to tears.

Gareth clutched the letter tightly. He owed all his

good fortune to her. "You should not have kept this from me, Giles."

Giles was not one to quail at his master's wrath, but he felt a stab of guilt. Never had he known two people to love so fiercely. They were kindred souls, Briar Rose and Gareth, alike in courage, in compassion, in fiery spirit. He had seen it from the first. It was hard to imagine one without thinking of the other.

The pain of loss flickered in Gareth's eyes. Neither time nor distance had dimmed it. Gareth was a man half alive, hollowed out as if some vital part of him was missing. His torment was a mirror of his lady's.

"My lord," Giles said, "I have done you a grave wrong."

"What's this? The Fox of Masterson admitting to error?"

" 'Tis no jest, my lord. 'Twas my own doing that Briar Rose spurned you in favor of Wannet."

"Giles—"

"I feared what would happen to you, my lord, if you married her and took possession of Morley. I heard you'd be murdered. I thought it best to keep Briar Rose—the only woman you'd willingly wed—from you. I told her my fears and she rejected you. To keep you safe."

"Safe!" Gareth exploded. He laughed harshly, humorlessly. "So this is safe. This—this living hell. Being deprived of the one thing I want above all else. That is safety?" Gareth laughed again. "What protection I have," he remarked acidly. "Shielded from harm by a woman and a petty court spy."

Giles looked away, cut by the words. "Love does make a man—and a woman—do strange things."

"You shouldn't have presumed to know what's best for me," Gareth said. "Wannet's power is not to be scoffed at, but it is to be defied." He straightened, pulling himself up to his full, magnificent height. The steel of determination glinted in his gray eyes.

He grinned down at Giles. "And defy him I shall."

His first impulse was to go charging to Windsor to reclaim her. But that wasn't possible. The king expected him to remain at Masterson, awaiting the small army he'd been asked to command against the Scots. Besides, Giles had learned that Wannet, too, had been asked to head up a company. By now he was probably marshaling his forces in Yorkshire. Briar Rose would be at one of Alain's estates to keep company with his mother.

"I'll try to find her if you like, my lord," Giles suggested.

Gareth nodded, hoping it wasn't too late. "Do that, Giles. And Godspeed."

Like a caged beast he prowled his estates, training his knights for the summer fighting. When he rode out through the town he was no longer glared at by hungry, accusing eyes. Small children's hands reached up to touch the hem of his tabard, to offer a hastily plucked spring flower and garner a smile from him. This was the Masterson that he remembered from his boyhood. Never, he vowed, would he let his people be deprived again.

Where had it come from, this new surge of caring and concern? He'd always felt guilty about his people, but not until recently had he felt genuine compassion. That, he conceded, was a lesson learned from Briar Rose.

A sad smile curved his lips. She'd shown kindness, caring for the sick as if they were her own, arranging Maeve's deliverance from Morley. She'd made him see that there was more to being a provider than simply bringing money home and doling it out. She'd made Gareth realize a lot about himself, and he loved her for it.

He loved her . . . Had he ever told her so?

A week slipped by, then two, and there was still no word from the king. Just as Gareth was certain he would go mad from waiting, Kenneth arrived. But the army he led was not a fighting force; it was a string of retainers transporting what seemed like a small household. Rowena, glittering and breathless, clung to her brother's arm.

Spying Gareth, she ran to him and flung her arms about him, showering his face with kisses.

Gareth put her off as politely as possible and tried to speak to Kenneth, but Rowena refused to relinquish him.

"I've missed you." She ran her hands over the front of his tunic. "And you, I'm certain, have been feeling the lack of a woman about the keep. Why, look at this place! The servants are slovenly and slow to obey. We've been here an hour and still haven't been shown to our quarters."

"I'll send for someone—"

She placed her fingers lightly on his lips. "I want you to show me, Gareth. Come, I insist."

He looked to Kenneth for help, but his friend had already left the hall. Gareth had no choice but to give in. He took her above the hall to one of the small private chambers.

Rowena positioned herself in front of the door. "And now, my lord," she said, smiling, "I'll allow you to give me a proper welcome." She pressed herself against him.

"I've been thinking about the past, Gareth. About when we were betrothed."

" 'Tis lucky we realized our mistake in time."

"But don't you see, my love? All is well with you now. We can be wed as planned."

Gareth couldn't believe his ears. "Much has happened since then," he told her gently, setting her away from him.

"Gareth, you're not thinking. You *must* have a wife."

"Enough, Rowena. I'm bound to say something to hurt you."

Her eyes darkened. "Are you saying, Gareth, that you won't marry me?"

"Consider it a favor."

She drew herself up, looking haughty. "I was hoping, my lord, that it wouldn't come to this."

"Sadly, it has."

"Oh, I'm not sad yet, Gareth. For you *will* marry me. I thought you might be hesitant, so I took some measures to ensure your cooperation. I've engaged a solicitor to sue you for breach of promise."

A sick feeling twisted in Gareth's gut. "Would you hold me like that, Rowena?"

"Aye. If need be."

"I won't make it easy for you."

"But in the end I'll get my way." She captured his hand and held it to her cheek. "It will be good, you'll see."

"It won't, Rowena. It can't."

She flung his hand away with an angry oath. "It's *her,* isn't it? That—that upstart Briar Rose. You think you love her still. A fat lot of good that will do you, my lord."

"What do you mean by that?"

"She's married, Gareth. She belongs to Alain de Wannet now."

Rowena swallowed, and then smiled as she read the full impact of her lie on his face.

16

Alain's mother, Beatrice was having another of her headaches. She sent Briar Rose for a draught of hippocras.

As she was returning, wending her way through a dark passage, a chill blew in through a narrow window. It seemed that summer had suddenly been interrupted by an intense cold spell.

The wind whistled in again, and this time it carried voices. Briar Rose hesitated, cocking her head. No one but the sentry was supposed to be out on the walk at this hour of the day. She went to the window and, standing on her toes, looked out. Two men stood a few yards away, speaking in earnest tones.

One of them was Alain, his profile with its pointed beard outlined against the blue twilight. Then Briar Rose recognized the other. It was Lionel Beaupre, one of Alain's agents. She strained to hear their words.

". . . managed to avoid capture thus far," Beaupre was saying. "He and his man, Griffith, are hiding out at an abandoned croft beyond the Plain of York."

Briar Rose stiffened. Beaupre was obviously speaking of Talwork, who had escaped from Windsor.

"Perhaps you should go after them, my lord," the man continued. "It would please the king greatly if you were to seize them."

"True, but I think I'll wait. They may still be useful. Now, what have you found out about Hawke?"

"He waits at Masterson to lead a company against the Scots."

"As do we all."

"Ah, but there *is* news, my lord. It appears he's going to be married to Rowena Shelby."

Briar Rose nearly dropped the cup of hippocras she held. The words plunged into her heart like a blade of cold steel. Gareth and Rowena . . . So the old betrothal had been revived.

"Jesu . . ." she whispered, leaning her forehead on the window ledge.

"When?" Alain asked sharply.

"That's not clear, my lord. Surely not before he meets the Scots."

Briar Rose heard Alain laugh, a sinister sound in the gathering twilight. "I'd always planned on killing Hawke. Now I can't afford to wait. I won't allow him to have Morley."

"What will you do, my lord?"

"I'm not sure. I'd love to run him through myself, but I don't think that would be wise."

Coward, Briar Rose thought furiously. She longed to lean out the window and tell him so, but she held her tongue and listened again.

". . . could arrange something that will leave no taint on me. The outlaws from Morley might be just the solution I seek . . ."

Briar Rose strained to hear the rest, but the wind had

shifted, taking Alain's hissing voice with it. She spent a moment composing herself, trying to still the hammering of her heart.

She couldn't help the bitterness she felt. She'd given Gareth up to prevent this exact thing from happening. Giles had promised her that Gareth would be safe if she didn't marry him. So why hadn't he cautioned Rowena?

In all fairness, he probably had. But Rowena didn't care for Gareth as Briar Rose did; no one could love him that much.

"You must come, my lady," a page said, startling her. "There's a woman in the hall to see you."

Briar Rose went to the hall. Her eyes scanned the dais and sideboards, but all she saw was the usual assortment of visiting nobles and household folk.

A stirring at one of the lower tables caught her eye. Suddenly time fell away as Briar Rose rushed into a pair of welcoming arms.

"Janet! Oh, Janet!" Tears sprang to her eyes.

With an intuitiveness born of years of loving service, Janet felt Briar Rose's pain, the months of loneliness and worry, and gathered the girl against her ample bosom.

Finally Briar Rose pulled away. "Let's go to my bower, Janet. Our reunion is not for these eyes."

Once alone, they held each other again. Briar Rose studied the careworn, aging face. "You've come a long way, Janet. And alone."

The woman nodded slowly. "I come in defiance of your lady mother's orders."

Briar Rose let a moment pass. "Why are you here?"

" 'Tis your father, sweeting. He is ill."

She gave a cry of alarm and dropped to her knees beside Janet. "Father! Sweet Jesu, what is it?"

Janet gave a grunt of contempt. "The physician, that Godfrey Pelham fellow, comes daily with his foul concoctions and leeches, bleeding the poor man when the moon permits it. But, in sooth, there is naught to be done. Your father is old, my lady. There's no remedy for that."

"He is dying?" Briar Rose buried her face in Janet's lap. She saw her father clearly, ever loving, ever indulgent. The unique way he had of stroking her hair, the way he always listened when she spoke, as if every word were a gem spilling from her lips. Always when she had run to him in distress he'd been able to soothe her. It was impossible that he'd ever leave her.

She raised a tearstained face to Janet. "I must go to him."

The old woman nodded. "He would wish it, my lady."

Briar Rose was already up and rushing about the room, gathering a few of her belongings. "We shall leave immediately."

" 'Tis night, my lady. Surely we can wait until morning."

She studied Janet, the tired lines around her eyes and mouth, the weary way she lumbered about the room. "I'll go alone. You may rest here, and I'll see you're conducted to Briarwood at your leisure."

"Think of yourself, my lady! No one save thieves and cutthroats would travel by night. What would your father say? He'd dismiss me!"

Briar Rose sighed heavily, hearing the sense in Janet's words. She dropped the bundle she was holding. "I shall wait until dawn, then."

She knew better than to ask Alain's leave to go to Briarwood. She'd done so before, many times, and he had forbidden her to consider it.

She sent a page the next day to tell him that she was going to town. Nan, who had been in her service since Windsor, looked at her oddly as she and Janet prepared to leave.

"Aren't you taking a bit much for a ride to town, my lady?" the woman questioned, eyeing the large bundle Briar Rose held.

"Some things for the almonry," Briar Rose explained hastily. "You needn't pry, Nan."

Nan glowered but said nothing. On impulse, Briar Rose went to Columbine, who was folding the bed-clothes. "I'll see you later," she whispered, winning a broad grin from the girl.

She saw Alain leaving Stepton as she and Janet were getting their mounts. He had a good-sized band of armed men with him, as if he were embarking on some exploit. Briar Rose shivered. There wasn't anyone at Stepton who could be trusted to take a warning to Gareth. But, she told herself, Gareth would doubtless ignore a warning from her anyway.

It was getting on toward evening. Briar Rose and Janet had begun looking for a place to pass the night when a rustling in the hedgerow caused Briar Rose's horse to shy in alarm. Before she realized what was happening, a half dozen cursing, ragged men were upon them. In the instant before a heavy club descended on her. Briar Rose screamed for Janet to run. And then she found herself looking into the malicious small eyes of Griffith of Morley. The club made contact with her temple and she slithered to the ground.

* * *

She came around shortly, jogged by the trotting horse over which she'd been slung. She could see nothing in the darkness, but smelled earthy forest scents and, after a time, woodsmoke. Her wrists and ankles were tightly bound by leather and her head throbbed abominably.

She was taken to a camp deep in the woods, where the outlaws from Morley huddled around a fire. There was an abandoned croft around which a few animals were tethered. Butchered carcasses hung from some of the trees.

A burly man took her from the horse and laid her against a tree, giving her a gap-toothed grin. Briar Rose shot him a scathing glance and looked away.

Talwork came shortly, not nearly so grand without his cloak of ermine and many jewels. "I've waited a long time for this moment, my dear," he drawled. "I've been watching you, but until today you never left Stepton."

"What do you want from me?" Briar Rose demanded.

Talwork laughed. "Need you ask?" Rage burned in his eyes. "You are the cause of my disgrace."

Briar Rose spat at his feet. "Scoundrel!" she hissed contemptuously. "Have you not committed enough crimes already?"

He laughed again. "Not quite, my sweet. Not quite." He made a gesture, and several men, including Griffith, gathered round, their avid faces illuminated by the fire. "Gentlemen," Talwork announced. " 'Tis time the young lady suffers her penance."

Her bound hands were held high above her head and the thongs about her ankles were cut. Strangely, Talwork seemed to want no part of her, not in this way, but he wasn't averse to giving her to his men. He stepped back, his eyes hard and bright with cruelty. "She's yours," he said to his men.

Griffith ran his hand down her length in a rough caress. Bile rose in Briar Rose's throat. She was terrified, yet even that feeling was secondary to the disgust she felt.

A hand was at the lacings of her cloak, poised to draw it from her. Briar Rose squeezed her eyes shut and tried to think of some prayer of deliverance, but her mind was too full of revulsion to think straight. She set her jaw and willed herself to survive what was to come.

Her eyes flew open at the sound of hoofbeats. Curses and the squeals of high-strung war-horses filled the air. Her tormentors scattered, all except Griffith. His tongue flicked out and circled his leering mouth.

Briar Rose screamed again, not in fear this time, but in surprise. A blade sang through the air behind Griffith and severed his head cleanly. His tongue still protruded from his mouth as the head met the ground with a dull thud.

Warm, sticky blood poured over Briar Rose and she recoiled, still screaming, unable to think. A strong arm swept down and drew her onto a horse.

"Alain . . ." she said weakly. "Sweet Christ, thank you . . ."

He shouted commands to his men, ordering them to give the outlaws no quarter. More heads rolled and soon the forest floor was sodden with fresh, acrid-smelling blood, littered with fallen bodies. Briar Rose watched the spectacle with mingled horror and relief. Mercifully, it was over in a matter of minutes.

But not all the rebels had fallen. Out of the corner of her eye, Briar Rose saw Talwork slinking through the shadows. He went to the croft and untethered one of the horses.

"Alain, look!" Briar Rose said, pointing. Talwork disappeared into the forest.

Alain and his men gave chase. Talwork had a decent mount, a palfrey. With a start, Briar Rose realized that it was her own horse, Dame, that he rode. The mare bore him swiftly away from the less-fleet destriers of Alain and his men. The hunt continued until first light glowed on the horizon and the morning mist swirled about the forest floor.

Looking down from her pillion behind Alain, Briar Rose noticed a small stone marker beside an overgrown path. It was a cross bearing the word *"Sanctarium."*

"Alain," she said, "he's heading for a sanctuary church. You'll never be able to touch him if he reaches it."

He cursed and spurred his mount, but the war-horse still couldn't match Dame's speed. They burst from the forest in time to see him arrive at a small parish church.

Briar Rose clenched her fists in frustration. According to the Church law of sanctuary, anyone, even a criminal with blood on his hands, achieved holiness if he passed through the inner portals of a designated church. Once inside, and seated on the frithstool beside the altar, he was immune to seizure.

As Alain's company thundered toward the church, Talwork rang the galilee bell. To Briar Rose's dismay the summons was answered shortly. Talwork spoke briefly to a robed cleric, shoved some coins in his hand, and disappeared inside.

Alain drew his horse up in front of the church and dismounted.

"My wrists," Briar Rose said, holding them out to him. He took out a dagger and cut the leather thongs. They entered the church together.

Talwork smiled at them from the frithstool. He'd already donned the customary black robe with

St. Cuthbert's cross on the shoulder. Only his heaving chest belied his calmness.

"You cannot touch me, my lord," he said to Alain.

"By God, I should drag you from that stool!" Alain shouted.

Talwork sniffed. "At one time we were close allies, both of us united against Hawke. Perhaps, my lord, we could revive that alliance, to our mutual profit."

Briar Rose tensed in the ensuing silence. She knew Alain was out for Gareth's blood, but would he agree to ally himself with an outlaw?

They decided to wait. Talwork couldn't stay in the church forever; at some point he'd have to come out. Wannet and his men were ready to seize him. They settled in the town, making their quarters at a poor tavern. Briar Rose shared a room with the alewife's two daughters, who never spoke to her, being overawed by her rich garments and terrified by the blood that spattered them.

Briar Rose expected Alain to demand her reason for fleeing Stepton. But she didn't see him at all; for he stayed near the church, watching with the patience and cunning of a seasoned hunter. She worried herself to distraction over her father, but Alain wouldn't hear of letting her go. He came back to the tavern only once, summoned by Lionel Beaupre. Briar Rose, who had been sitting by the fire, saw them speaking in hushed tones. She edged closer to hear.

". . . should be here within the hour," Beaupre said.

"Well done," Alain murmured. "God, but it will be good to face down Hawke at last."

Briar Rose shrank back, full of dread. Jesu, they'd set

a trap for him! She forced herself to wait until Alain and Beaupre left and then followed them to the church.

She arrived just in time to see Gareth, riding in tandem with Paulus and Giles, his blond mane gilded by the noontide sun. Lifting her skirts, Briar Rose ran toward them, calling a warning across the hundred yards that separated them. But they couldn't hear her above the thudding of their horses' hooves. They were so intent on reaching the church that they didn't glance her way.

Gareth leaped from his horse, his heart beating wildly. Never had he ridden so swiftly, driving his mount nearly to exhaustion. But the two separate messages he'd received had convinced him that Briar Rose was in real danger.

First Janet, the tiring woman from Briarwood, had arrived with some garbled tale of outlaws who had fallen upon them on the road. As Gareth was puzzling that one out, another messenger had come, this one, curiously, from Wannet. More knowledgeable and coherent than Janet, he'd mentioned a church north of the Plain of York, where Talwork, the outlawed bishop, had taken the girl.

Giles had been dubious, wondering aloud why Wannet had sent for help, but Gareth had reasoned that Alain lacked the cunning to dispense with Talwork and his followers.

And so he had come, not allowing himself to think of what Briar Rose might suffer at the hands of the man she'd ruined. He almost trembled with relief when the church came into view. Without waiting to see if Giles and Paulus were behind him, he burst through the door, sword drawn.

Talwork was there, to be sure, but he was alone and the church was quiet. He sat on the frithstool, calmly reading from an illuminated psalter.

Gareth reached him in two strides. His arm shot out and caught Talwork by the top of his black robe. Twisting the fabric until it strained against the man's neck, Gareth snarled, "Where is she?"

Talwork gurgled fearfully. Gareth twisted harder, bringing him to his feet.

"What have you done with Briar Rose?" he demanded again.

Four knights appeared, the Wannet eagle blazing on their chests. One of them grabbed Talwork from behind, dragging him a safe distance from the frithstool. The other three fell upon Gareth, wielding heavy clubs and their own meaty fists. Dazed by a dozen blows, Gareth swayed and lurched between his attackers, cursing himself for being duped by Wannet.

Alain appeared, his eyes gleaming with victory. Someone entered the church behind him. Gareth couldn't see her face, as she was outlined from behind by the brilliant sun, but there was no mistaking the small, womanly shape of Briar Rose.

She started toward him and then seemed to stop. Wannet caught her against him in a hearty embrace.

"Well done, my dear," Wannet said loudly, beaming down at Briar Rose. Then he glanced back at Gareth, his mouth curled maliciously.

"So here you are, my friend, at last. It seems the nightingale has lured the hawk from his aerie."

Gareth awoke to darkness and the stink of rotten straw and unwashed bodies. Stars of pain winked before his eyes as he rubbed the throbbing lump on his head. He set his jaw, remembering. When Wannet had spoken the scathing words to him, he'd given a bellow of pure animal rage and leaped at his enemy's throat. The knights holding him had knocked him senseless.

"Who stirs?" asked a voice beside him.

With a half smile of bitter irony, Gareth turned to face Talwork, making out a hunched form by the weak light of a high windhole.

"Probably the last man you'd expect as your cellmate, Bishop," Gareth said darkly.

A pause. "Hawke . . ."

"Aye, the very same."

"Your foul hide be damned for what you have wrought," Talwork said. "My only comfort is that you'll suffer the same fate as I."

Gareth laughed harshly. "For a man of the cloth, you're quite unforgiving."

"Do not speak to me of forgiveness, Hawke."

There was a heavy creaking and a metallic groan as the door swung open. By the glow of a smoking rushlight, Gareth made out the hated face of Alain de Wannet.

He drew himself up, steadying himself with one hand on the wall. "My only mistake, Wannet, was that I didn't kill you ages ago."

Wannet gave an arrogant shrug. "Pity you didn't." He stared at his fingernails with studied casualness. "What a snorting stallion you are, Hawke, so hot for Rose that you disdain all caution." Slowly he walked toward Gareth. "Pity she doesn't appreciate your valor."

Wannet fairly strutted about the cell. "I have it all now, Hawke." His dark eyes glittered as he sought to deal a punishing blow to the man he hated. "I wonder if it eats at you that Rose is now mine."

Gareth's mouth went dry. He felt the blood drain from his face.

"Quite a prize is my Rose," Wannet said. "But doubtless you're aware of that. A she-devil in the bed-chamber, lusty as a tavern wench." He gave Gareth a broad wink. "You know that, don't you, Hawke? I'll always regret that you had her first, although she wishes to forget. I'm sure she's thankful that I can show her more refined ways than your animal rutting."

Scarlet rage shimmered before Gareth's eyes as he lunged at Wannet. It took all three of Alain's guards to restrain him.

Wannet preened at his beard. "Watch yourself, Hawke. You'll want to save all your strength for our meeting in the lists."

"What the hell are you talking about?"

"Oh, I've several plans in the offing. First I'll take this Talwork to London to be tried in the ecclesiastical court and get myself a fat bounty. When I return, you and I will do battle, my friend. To the death. 'Tis the only honorable way to settle our differences."

"By the rood, let us fight it out now!" Gareth shouted, twisting in his captors' hold.

Wannet flicked an imaginary bit of lint from his sleeve. "Not so fast, my friend. I'll let you cool your heels here for some weeks until you weaken sufficiently. Then we'll see who is the better man."

Briar Rose's hands trembled as she inserted an iron key into the lock. The key caught and held and then turned with a cold rasp. Shaking, she closed her eyes. Bless you, Columbine, she said silently.

For a fortnight she'd been held captive in her room at Stepton, closely watched by Nan, wondering desperately what Alain had done with Gareth. Just when she'd given up on helping him, Columbine had come with the key and some garbled directions that led Briar Rose to the dank cellars of Stepton.

She swung the door open and stepped inside. At first she saw only darkness, heard only her quick, nervous breath. A sickening stench assailed her nostrils. Then her eyes adjusted to the dimness of the cavelike cell and she made out three dark shapes against the far wall, those of Gareth, Giles, and Paulus.

"My lord," Giles rasped. " 'Tis time to eat."

A harsh laugh was the response. "Eat? Does one speak so to swine when bringing them slop?"

The bitterness in Gareth's voice made Briar Rose wince. All at once she realized the horrors he'd endured in this place, the endless hours of darkness and despair. She rushed to his side and took his gaunt, bearded face in her hands.

"My love, 'tis I, Briar Rose."

He thrust her aside with an angry oath. "What's this? Wannet has sent his woman to torture me now!"

Giles scrambled to his side. "Not to torture, my lord, but to deliver us, if I'm not mistaken."

"We must away," she said urgently. "There's little time."

Giles was already on his feet. He roused Paulus and helped Gareth toward the door. They left the cell, Gareth stumbling between the two men, Briar Rose leading the way through winding corridors. There was a tense moment as they emerged onto the courtyard, but the night was starless and black and no one saw. Alain's men were lax now that he'd gone to London. Moving as swiftly as Gareth's condition would allow, they crossed a broad meadow to a coppice where Dame stood. Alain had recovered the mare after Talwork's wild flight to the Sanctarium.

Gareth was too weak to sit the horse alone so Briar Rose mounted behind him, wrapping a blanket around his shoulders. Thus they rode through the night.

As Briar Rose brought her arms around Gareth's waist, all the love she'd ever felt for him came rushing back on waves of anguish. Smoothing his matted hair, she whispered his name again and again. It was sheer agony just to touch him, to run her hands over his emaciated body. The arms and thighs that had once been thick with vigor now lay limp and immobile. There was a frightening rattle in his chest, and his scarred eye seemed even more sunken in his thin, bearded face.

"My dearest love," she murmured. "How much you've endured. 'Tis all my fault . . ." Her tears wet his back and he stirred.

"Briar Rose . . ."

"Don't speak, my darling. Save your strength." In sooth, she was afraid of what he might say. How could he care for her still, after all the pain she'd caused him?

She and Giles decided to go to Tynegate. It was close, and Kenneth and Rowena were there, having left Masterson when Gareth had.

"He needs time to mend," Giles explained. "He must have tried a dozen times to overpower our guards, and each time they wounded him more."

Gareth swayed atop the horse, having subsided into a half-waking state. His mind was muddled, his thoughts blurred by pain and sickness. Vaguely he realized that he was being taken to safety by Briar Rose.

"What the devil are you doing here?" he mumbled.

Briar Rose winced at his tone. "I am here because you need me," she said simply, and left it at that.

* * *

"Where is Sir Kenneth?" Giles asked.

"He stayed at Masterson after all," the steward explained. "Something about the king's army . . ."

Rowena wasn't long in coming. From the avid curiosity in her bright eyes, Briar Rose guessed she couldn't wait to hear the news. With a start, she remembered that Rowena and Gareth were to marry. It was ironic, endangering herself so that the two could be together.

Rowena stared at Gareth's thin, bearded face, his ragged clothes, his fevered brow. His eyes were dull, uncomprehending. Then she looked sharply at Briar Rose. "And what of you? I thought by now you'd be married to Alain de Wannet."

"I am not. That's not important now. Gareth needs tending."

Through the dull haze of fever, something stirred within Gareth. So Rowena had lied after all. But before he could wonder at the burgeoning hope in his heart, Rowena called for servants and issued brisk orders. A chamber was to be prepared for Gareth.

"The rest of you may stay where you choose," Rowena said. She and Briar Rose watched as Giles and Paulus helped Gareth to his quarters.

"Was it you who rescued him?" asked Rowena.

"I led him from Stepton. Rowena, if Gareth is to remain safe, I must have your promise not to betray his presence here. There are those who oppose his taking possession of Morley." It was all she dared say.

"But take it he will, once he marries."

"If he lives to marry."

"Come now, Briar Rose, you know better than that. He's a young man and won't be long regaining his strength. I shall see to it personally that he recovers."

As the summer days slipped by, Briar Rose felt like an outsider in the elegant, well-ordered keep. Rowena barred her from nursing Gareth, and she had no choice but to defer to her hostess. Giles had gone off on some business, as he was wont to do, and Paulus would have nothing to do with her.

She took to exploring the moors and corries along the river Tyne, riding hard and trying not to think of the uncertain future. She went to nearby Ninebanks, where the busy shoppers and hawkers took her mind from her troubles. Spying a fine bolt of cloth, she thought of Gareth, whose own clothing had been ruined. Filled with a need to do something—anything—for him, she bought some lengths of fabric and found a seamstress to make up the garments for her. In just a few days the woman produced a fine saffron batiste chemise, a tunic worked in heavy fustian, and a surcoat emblazoned with a hawk emblem. For herself Briar Rose resisted a bolt of escarlate and settled for a serviceable blue dress.

On the day the garments were ready, Briar Rose made her way back to Tynegate, full of hope that her gifts would please Gareth and impel his forgiveness.

The household was quiet and Rowena was sequestered with Gareth, as she had been for days. Briar Rose tapped lightly at the door. Rowena stepped outside, her eyes cold. "He's sleeping."

Briar Rose tilted her chin up. "I have something for him."

Rowena reached for the parcel. "I'll see that he gets it."

Snatching it away, Briar Rose snapped, "I shall give it to him myself. Let me by."

The other woman planted herself in front of the door. "You'll only upset him."

Briar Rose's temper kindled. "Who are you to keep me from him? It was I who freed him."

"And it was you who caused him to be taken in the first place. You toyed with his affections like a common whore."

In an angry flash Briar Rose's hand shot out and slapped the woman. "You call me whore, yet how do I know what you do all day in this room with him?"

With a feline snarl Rowena leaped forward and grabbed a handful of raven hair, yanking with one hand and pummeling with the other. She was like a vixen protecting her den, viciously possessive.

"Stop this," Paulus ordered sharply, pulling the women apart. "What is this all about?"

Rowena brushed a lock of disarranged hair from her face, panting with fury and exertion. "The chit tried to force her way into Lord Hawke's room. My only thought was to protect him from her."

Paulus leveled his eyes at Briar Rose. "You'll not be allowed to dupe my master with more of your lies and wily tricks."

There was no reason for her to remain at Tynegate. Guarded by Rowena's possessiveness and Paulus's misguided loyalty, Gareth was more inaccessible to her than ever. And if he'd not asked to see her by now, there was small chance he wished her company at all.

Her heart grew leaden with that realization. Everything had gone awry. There was nothing left of the sweet, gilded dream she'd cherished from the first time she'd laid eyes on the handsome knight.

It was time—past time—to turn homeward, to Briarwood, where she should have stayed after all, should have made a stand against Acacia from the first. If God was merciful, her father still lived, even though a month had passed since Janet had gone to fetch her.

She meant to leave quietly, giving no notice of her parting. Yet despite everything the urge to see Gareth, to look upon him one last time, was irresistible. On quiet feet encased in soft leather boots, she mounted the stairs and tested the door. It swung open with a small creak.

The dawn light that filtered in through a gap in the heavy draperies illuminated the alcove bed. Briar Rose crept closer, her heart thumping as the bed brought back cherished memories of the first time they'd loved, here, in this very room.

She stared at Gareth for a long moment, grateful that he appeared better now, and then she turned and left.

17

It was not a festive homecoming. Briar Rose and her escort rode into Briarwood at dusk, weary and shivering from the persistent summer cold spell. When one of the grooms recognized her, a shout of surprise went up.

Briar Rose didn't linger over the greetings and all the questions. She ran through the great hall and up the wide staircase.

Her father was a dark shape on the bed. Acacia was dressed in yellow, her haughty face illuminated by the hearth fire. Her features pinched into an expression of loathing. "Seize the wench!"

The footman hung back, hesitating.

"Do as I say, Britt."

Briar Rose approached the bedstead, keeping the footman at bay with a look of formidable fury. "Never mind, Britt. I'll not be running away anymore." She spun to face Acacia. "Move aside. Better yet, leave, Acacia. I would see my father alone."

She moved across the dim, musty-smelling chamber

and instructed Peter, a houseboy, to tie back the hangings so that the firelight would permit her to see. Light flooded the bed.

Briar Rose rushed to his side and buried her face against his shoulder.

He stroked her hair gently, as he had done when she was a child. She lifted her face, her cheeks wet with tears.

"My lord, I feared for you so. Janet came to fetch me some weeks ago, but I was detained." She swallowed, not allowing herself to think of Gareth just now.

There was a bit of the old light in his smile. "My dear, you should have known I'd not have the discourtesy to pass away before seeing you once again."

"My lord, you mustn't—"

He waved a thin hand. "I don't mind speaking of death. My life has been full. But I have regrets, Briar Rose. I've caused you to lose Briarwood."

"I'm here to win it back, my lord. I'll not allow Acacia to bully me."

"There's no need for me to bully," Acacia snapped, coming forward. "I've legal claim to Briarwood." With obvious relish, she raised her hand.

Briar Rose gasped. Gleaming on Acacia's long forefinger was the Briarwood crest. She looked in confusion at Acacia, then back at her father.

"I'm sorry, Briar Rose," Lord John said. "I thought Gareth Hawke would honor his promise and send me the ring."

"Send you . . . ?"

"Aye, daughter. I bade Lord Gareth to take the ring for safekeeping. But apparently Acacia offered a larger reward, for she got the ring at Christmastime."

At Christmas . . . The words thundered in Briar Rose's ears. So Gareth had lied after all. At Windsor when he'd said the crest was safe at Masterson, he'd lied. He had already sent it to Acacia and taken his reward. Briar Rose felt her heart splintering. Tears burned in her eyes, but she refused to shed them. She'd cried enough for Gareth Hawke.

Sir Simeon burst into the room, not stopping to apologize for the intrusion.

"The Scots are descending on Briarwood!" he cried. "A band of them was sighted a day's ride distant, on the other side of the river Swale!"

Giles handed his muddied cloak to a servant and went directly to Lord Gareth, who sat on the dais in Masterson hall overseeing the midday meal, studiously ignoring Rowena, who sat at his side. As usual she'd acted against his wishes and followed him to Masterson, insisting he needed further nursing.

"God's blood, look at you, Giles," Gareth boomed. "What happened, did you meet up with the Scots, or did Wannet find you again?"

Giles looked down at his poorly bandaged arm. "You say that in jest, my lord, but you've guessed the truth. I just barely got away from the Scottish marauders with my life."

Gareth frowned. "Where are they, Giles?"

The agent hesitated as if loath to impart the news.

"Well?"

"They've forded the river Swale, my lord. They're headed toward Briarwood Manor."

The mazer Gareth was holding dropped with a clatter. "Holy God, they've gone that deep?"

"Aye, my lord. A good-sized band of them. You can trace their trail by the burned-out, gutted villages they left in their wake."

"Damn! And all the while I kept my counsel here, waiting for word from the king."

Giles cast his eyes downward. "There's more, my lord."

"What? Tell me, Giles."

"Briar Rose is there, at Briarwood."

Masterson became a beehive of activity as Gareth prepared his men to ride against the Scots. According to Giles, they'd be outnumbered, but not one of his men demurred. The archers flexed their bows and honed their arrows, and the knights and squires readied their horses and weapons. A number of men from the town volunteered as foot soldiers, offering spades and pitchforks when all the weapons had been doled out.

Grimly Gareth assembled his company in the bailey, calling orders above a cacophony of voices, braying pack animals, and the groaning wheels of the laden supply carts.

Just as they were preparing to leave, Rowena rushed out and grabbed at the hem of Gareth's tabard.

"This is madness," she cried. "You'll all be cut to pieces! And if you're not, you'll be punished for going against the king's plan."

"Edward's plan be damned," Kenneth sneered, bringing his horse up beside Gareth's. "His hesitation has cost us dearly."

Rowena ignored her brother, looking appealingly at Gareth. "I don't understand," she said. "Why would you risk your men for the sake of a woman who spurned you for your enemy?"

Gareth's face hardened. "If you don't know the answer to that, Rowena, then you don't know me at all."

* * *

For the time being Briar Rose and Acacia abandoned their enmity. With the Scots nearly upon them there was no time for arguing. Supplies had to be laid in, the livestock driven to places of safety, the people warned. Everywhere she went Briar Rose heard frantic prayers and pleas for deliverance.

With her father ailing, the knights had grown lax and were ill-prepared to do battle. Sir Simeon had been designated captain, but he wasn't a forceful leader.

Briar Rose went outside, feeling the persistent chill in the air, to watch Sir Simeon working with his men.

The knights were milling about in disorderly fashion and Simeon was scowling over some plan that had been scratched in the dust. Briar Rose moved closer to hear.

"They're coming from the west," Simeon explained. "We'll need the archers to be stationed all along the western wall and the knights to keep their positions back here, in the outer ward."

Briar Rose couldn't help seeing the folly in Simeon's plan. "We must stop them before they reach the walls, Sir Simeon," she said, startling him. "They've already raided our livestock in the fields. The western slopes have been burned. Our best hope is to divide our forces, leaving some of them at the walls and marching forth with the others."

"My lady, with all due respect—"

"No, listen. Peter stole out to see what the Scots are like. There aren't as many of them as we'd feared. They'll have to cross the river again in order to get to us. I propose we go out and meet them and drive them back to the corries."

"My lady, *please*—"

"Perhaps they're hesitating for a reason. It could be

they're waiting to be joined by others. We'd best strike soon."

Starlight glinted off the metal of Briar Rose's chestplate as she rode down among the men. Simeon gasped, coming to her side.

"My lady, sweet God, is that you in that armor?"

She smiled. "Aye, Simeon. But just the chestplate. I couldn't abide the other things, even if I'd found something to fit."

"This is too much, my lady. I cannot allow you to ride into battle."

" 'Twas my plan, Simeon, and I'll not sit cowering in the keep while you go off to fight."

Simeon argued long, complaining that she unmanned him, but in the end her will prevailed. She rode at the head of the small army, wielding a sword that nearly equaled her own weight. A banner depicting the rose of Briarwood flapped overhead. As they descended into the corry, a leaden rain began to fall. The river, full of stones, was swollen. The army slogged and slithered along the muddied landscape through dark, dripping forests, hunting for the Scots.

At last, in the full dark of the storm, they spied the Scottish camp situated high on a hill. Huts of hide and branches sheltered them and the carcasses of butchered game and stolen sheep hung from every tree.

She heard the rain pattering on her helmet, felt the rivulets pouring down her back. Now that they were facing the enemy she began to feel real fear. The Scots were aware of them now. They came out of their huts and skirled their eerie-sounding pipes. A hail of rocks and arrows rained down on the Briarwood army. Briar

Rose winced when she heard a cry go up somewhere behind her.

Sweet Christ, she thought, what have I done? Will we all be killed here on this dreadful night?

She shouted a command. It sounded strange to her own ears, as if the voice came from someone else, perhaps from Isobel herself. Her men surged forward, the longbowmen answering the Scottish taunts with a flurry of arrows. The mounted knights came up from behind, closing in from right and left, keeping to the battle plan even though their horses slipped and faltered in the mud.

It was almost too dark to see. The only light came from the Scots' camp fires and from a few stars that blinked from between the banked storm clouds. Briar Rose rode among the foot soldiers, trying not to hear the wild howls of the Scots and the agonized cries of the men she commanded.

One of the Scotsmen advanced on her, wielding an ugly-looking club. He swung it high above his head, ready to deal a shattering blow.

"For the love of Christ," someone shouted. "Stop!"

Briar Rose glanced back at Peter, who hadn't left her side since the battle began.

The Scot laughed harshly, menacing the youth with his club. "We don't mean to stop, laddie, until you turn tail and run."

Peter ducked to elude the blow. The Scot laughed again and turned his attention back to Briar Rose. But Peter was still there, clawing at the man's bare arm.

"She's a woman, you lout! Would you lower yourself to smite her?"

Briar Rose saw the man peering at her, the whites of his eyes gleaming.

"By Jesus," he breathed. "A *woman—*"

Peter hurled himself forward and plunged his knife into the bare, corded neck.

Briar Rose grimaced as she heard a gurgle and a curse and saw the man slump to the muddy ground. Peter withdrew his knife and looked in wonder at the blood that slicked his hands.

"I—It's still warm . . ." he said, his voice trembling with horror.

"Go wash your hands in the river, Peter. And forgive yourself. He'd have killed us both if you'd not acted."

Just as she was turning her mount back into the fray, Sir Simeon rode up. His helmet was dented where he'd taken a blow from a club, but otherwise Briar Rose couldn't discern any wounds.

"Ill news, my lady," he shouted above the din. "A band of Scots has broken free of the right flank and is making for the keep."

Briar Rose spied a string of dark shapes bobbing westward. "Hold the rest here, Simeon," she said quickly. "I'll pursue them with some of the mounted men."

By the time Briar Rose's cumbersome party reached them, the walls of the castle were in sight. The rain poured down in a great, drenching sheet, impeding the large war-horses. The Briarwood men were able to fell some the Scots at the rear, but the others were already clamoring toward the gate.

With relief, she caught sight of a number of archers, positioned between the crenels, already firing. They seemed surprisingly well-organized, firing with precision, reinforced from the back by other men.

And then Briar Rose saw the reason why. High on the wall beside the barbican she saw the flutter of a cloak outlined against the stormy night sky.

"Father!" she screamed, digging her heels into her

horse's flanks. The animal bunched its muscles and leaped forward with a squeal of surprise, climbing the bank toward the gate. Unable to move on his own, Lord John of Padwick was being carried in an unwieldy chair, commanding the men of Briarwood as he had in years long past. He was both awesome and pitiable, powerful in his vision of the battle, yet feeble of body and voice.

Briar Rose rode hard toward the keep. Just as she was about to gain the last rise before the gate, her horse took an ill-aimed blow. It reared, giving a high-pitched scream of panic, and cast Briar Rose to the mud. She righted herself in time to see the animal galloping wildly down into the corries. Unable to move well because of her chestplate, she slipped through the mud, grasping at handfuls of sodden grass. Her helmet had fallen askew and she could barely see. Cursing, she tore it from her head and cast it to the ground.

Briar Rose angled around to the left, heading for a water gate she knew of in the northern wall. As she ran toward it, she saw a Scotsman facing down one of the castle hounds that had apparently gotten out of the kennels.

It was an absurd sight, the dog baying and snarling while the man advanced, swinging out with his double-edged sword. Briar Rose remembered that the Scots killed everything in battle, even dogs and cats, because their mysterious old religion warned of a phenomenon called shape-shifting. No doubt the wild, hide-clad man thought the hound was an Englishman transformed.

Briar Rose thought she could slip past the man, but the hound bounded up to leap about her in greeting.

The man swung about, teeth bared. His face broke into a wicked grin.

"What's this I see?" He laughed, grabbing out and capturing a hank of Briar Rose's wet hair. "I dinna think to enjoy the spoils of battle so soon." He drew her to him, still grinning. "Ach, then the battle can wait. I'll have my prize now."

He grasped her about the waist and began dragging her back down the hill toward the forest. Briar Rose screamed and fought and cursed, feeling his greased flesh being rent by her nails.

She looked back at the keep, thinking it would be her last glance at her home. She'd die before she'd give herself to this man. Lightning flashed and she saw her father's chair, high on the wall. Another flash, and the chair was gone.

Briar Rose kicked and bit, feeling the man's grip on her tighten. Above the din of battle and storm she thought she heard more voices and hoofbeats. Her spirits plummeted. The pillaging Scots were now being joined by others. She put all the strength of her fury in the kick she delivered to her captor.

"A she-devil, ye are!" the man howled, clutching at his leg. When she tried to break away, he caught her again, this time bringing her against him with both arms.

"Aye, a real vixen," he muttered, seeming strangely pleased with her. "I like a woman with some fight in her." Slowly, with wicked relish, he began bringing his mouth down to hers. She twisted in his arms, but he held her head still by clutching savagely at a lock of her hair. His other hand tore at the laces of the chausses that encased her legs.

"Please God, *no* . . ." she pleaded, and squeezed her eyes shut.

The Scotsman's laugh turned into a great heave of surprise and agony. Briar Rose's eyes flew open in time to see the man fall back, his mouth gaping. He was dead before he hit the ground; his body was trampled beneath the hooves of a raging, snorting war-horse.

Briar Rose felt the air empty out of her lungs as a strong arm swept downward and scooped her up as if she were nothing. She was thrown roughly across the horse's back, her shoulder making contact with the cold, wet steel of armor. She was jolted to the bone as the horse thundered away.

Only when the war-horse slid to a stop and she was pulled to a sitting position did Briar Rose realize what had happened. It was like waking from a nightmare. For within the knight's gleaming helm she caught the flash of silver-gray eyes.

"Gareth . . ."

He opened his helmet and kissed her swiftly and hard. Briar Rose clung to him, the taste of his urgent mouth bringing memories flooding back. Under better circumstances she would have thanked all the saints of heaven.

Gareth broke the kiss, his eyes boring into her. "I can't say I'm surprised to see you here, like this," he said. He lowered her to the ground. "Your little army has been joined by my own, and the Scots to the west have been driven back up into the hills. I must leave you here for now. There are a few of the devils still pounding at the gates."

"Gareth, take me with you."

He shook his head, wheeling his horse. "Stay here, Briar Rose." She saw his brow darken. "Don't cross me in this."

And he rode away, thundering up to the head of his men.

* * *

Briar Rose couldn't abide the waiting, listening to the shouts and cries and squealing horses. She pushed away the hair that was plastered to her face and started toward the keep.

Her heart flooded with relief. The last of the Scots were fleeing. Most of them were headed for the river. Too late, she saw a small party of them coming in her direction.

As she jumped to one side, she lost her footing and hurdled down a steep bank. She felt her feet slip in the mud, heard herself scream, and landed in a shallow part of the river with a bone-crunching thud. The dark shapes of the Scots advanced on her.

They were shouting, but she didn't hear their words. She plunged into deeper, icy waters and felt the current sweep her downstream. The Swale was so cold that her limbs went numb; her heavy chestplate dragged her downward. Her head slipped beneath the surface several times in succession.

Then the effort of swimming became too much. She gave in to the pull of the frigid water and her panic suddenly disappeared.

The water swirled around her, inky black, filling her mouth, crawling over her scalp like cold fingers. She was suffused with a bizarre sense of peace, drawn to the water as if it were a place of unearthly comfort. She opened her eyes to feel them chilled. Slowly, as the thoughts emptied from her mind, she edged toward that place, closer, closer . . .

She was on the brink, almost there. Then, suddenly, her arm was gripped in a steely hold. She was dragged, against her will, from the velvet emptiness. She struggled and choked, water streaming from her mouth.

Her attacker held her fast. She was engulfed by chills

as she felt herself being hauled up the bank. She fainted with a curse on her lips.

Gareth brought her to the room himself while his men remained outside, driving the Scots to the north to lick their wounds and bury their dead. In his arms the girl felt slight and fragile, her face as still as a death mask. Gareth trembled each time he looked at her. Please don't let her die, he prayed silently. Please . . .

"She must be bathed," Janet said, coming briskly into the room. Lines of weariness gathered about her eyes.

With aching tenderness Gareth took the girl's hand and cradled it within his. Janet and two other servants waited silently by, touched by the concern on his craggy face, the ragged lines of fatigue deepening about his mouth. Even Paulus, who had no love for Briar Rose, was not immune to his master's distress. Not even when his estate was crumbling about him had the Hawk given way to despair, but now, for the first time, tears glinted in his eyes.

A priest came with his rosaries and vials of oil. Gareth whirled on him. "Who summoned you here?" he demanded, placing himself between Briar Rose and the cleric.

The man looked ill-at-ease. "I had word the lady was ailing, my lord. 'Tis best she not be left unshriven—"

"Unshriven!" Gareth roared, his terror mingling with rage. "Get out! I won't have you here, giving up hope, hovering by with your potions and incantations. Get out, all of you!"

The priest and servants scuttled away from Lord Hawke's wrath and, ever so quietly, closed the door behind them. Gareth let out a long, ragged sigh and turned back to the bed.

"All is well, nightingale," he murmured softly. "You're home now."

Carefully, so as not to disturb her, he began removing her clothing. The sight of Briar Rose's lovely flesh mottled by wounds caused fury to swell in Gareth. He cursed the Scots with every vile oath he knew.

When at last he'd freed her of her sweat-soaked small-clothes, he hesitated. His heart rose to his throat as he regarded her supine form. She looked so slight, so fragile. All the vibrance had been burned out of her. Her limbs hung limp and unmoving. Yet never, Gareth realized with a choking cry of agony, had she looked more beautiful to him.

Like a mystic performing some sacred rite, he took up the steaming linens and cleansed her hair of the mud and river weeds and tenderly moved the herb-steeped cloth over her face and neck. Cradling her in his arms, he bent her forward and bathed her back and shoulders. His hands trembled as he sponged her torso, down her legs to her dainty feet. Then he applied a smooth healing bethroot balm to her chest, rubbing slowly, as if the gentle motion of his hands could draw the sickness from her. Finally he clothed her in a light bedgown of soft cambric and laid her back on the bed.

Perhaps he imagined it, but it seemed to Gareth that she rested more easily now. At last he remembered himself. He was uncomfortable in his damp clothing. He stripped down to his chemise and braies and drank a cup of wine. He seated himself by the bed and gazed at Briar Rose as if he couldn't fill his eyes adequately with the sight of her.

There was no prayer fervent enough, no promise sincere enough, no supplication desperate enough to express his feelings at that moment. His fears for Briar Rose, his guilt over what had happened to her, ate at him.

He didn't know how long he sat there, tormented by his thoughts. When he looked up, he could see stars winking in the sky and the fire burned low in the grate. Unfolding his great frame, Gareth built up the fire and came to stand beside the bed.

A force too great to resist drew him to Briar Rose. She looked so small and weak, so achingly fragile. He climbed into bed beside her and pulled the coverlet up over both of them. Gareth laid close, cradling her head on his shoulder and wrapping his legs snugly around her.

Take my strength, he begged her silently, wishing his own vigor could somehow flow into her, healing the sickness. Aloud he whispered, "Take all that I have, nightingale."

Through her fevered slumber she responded to him, nestling her thin body against his hard length. Gareth gritted his teeth against the terrible emotions that shook him and held her close.

He was forced to face the possibility of losing her. To never again see the laughter in her blue-violet eyes or taste the sweetness of her rosebud lips, never again to spar with her, to hear her infuriating, endearing jibes—the thought brutalized him like a bludgeon blow.

He awoke the next day to find Janet peering at him, frowning. Propping himself up on one elbow, he circled his arm protectively around the sleeping girl.

"No doubt you're shocked to see me lying with another man's betrothed," he said, his voice gritty with sleep.

Janet shrugged. "I'll not judge you, my lord. 'Tis between you and my lady to forgive each other. From what she told me, there's a lot of forgiving to be done."

For two more days he stayed with her, allowing no one near her. Her waking moments were confused delirium. She babbled disjointed phrases, speaking of Briarwood, of Acacia and Wannet, of Griffith and Talwork. It all made little sense to Gareth.

He managed to feed her broth and water but little else. The herbal remedies provided by Janet seemed to do nothing, but he continued bathing her damp brow, her neck, her limbs, which seemed to grow thinner and weaker with each passing hour.

On the third day Gareth felt her slipping away from him. The restless thrashing of her body ceased. She spoke no more and would take no nourishment. Gareth watched in dread as the flush of fever left her cheeks and her color became ashen. Her hands felt cold and clammy. Her chest rose and fell with alarming rapidity and shallowness. Her face was a mask of death, unmoving, drained of color.

His shoulders shaking with barely controlled sobs, Gareth went to the chamber door and opened it.

"Fetch the priest," he said roughly to the page who waited there. Never had it been so difficult for Gareth to admit defeat.

The cleric came hesitantly. Gareth stepped aside, muttering, "I'll not deny her your prayers any longer."

The priest drew out his rosary and stood over the bed.

Briar Rose swallowed and winced with pain. A wisp of hair seemed to be tickling her nose. She wanted to brush it aside, but her hand felt too heavy to move.

Vaguely she was aware of a peculiar smell which teased her mind with its familiarity. A voice droned nearby, faint at first, but growing stronger.

"Per istam sanctam unctionem . . ."

Briar Rose felt a touch of fear. It was the prayer of extreme unction, which cleansed the souls of the dying. The familiar scent was incense. Her eyes, ears, mouth, and hands were being anointed with olive oil.

Slowly she dragged her eyelids open. The light pierced her eyes painfully. She saw the priest, his face a pale oval, his attention riveted on the beads he held loosely in his hands.

With an effort she turned her head slightly on the bolster. The motion made her dizzy, but momentarily her eyes focused on a figure hunched upon a stool. *Gareth.* It was Gareth as she'd never seen him before. His great fair head was cradled in his hands, fingers splayed out like the points of stars. His shoulders had an uncharacteristic droop. And—surely her eyes deceived her—his cheeks were wet with tears.

Suddenly it became of overriding importance for her to reassure him, to comfort him in his despair.

"Gar . . ." Her voice had the rasp of disuse. "Gareth . . ."

He raised his head and turned to her slowly, as if afraid of what he might see. Then he was kneeling at her side, her head cradled in his big hands, his lips devouring her now-cool cheeks.

Briar Rose was overwhelmed by his outpouring of love. She clung to him, thankful to be alive. All her questions could wait for another time.

Gareth guarded her well after that, rarely leaving her chamber, barring Acacia from seeing Briar Rose and deflecting the girl's questions about all that had happened. He was terrified of the large blue bruise that stood out at her temple; Janet had warned him that any upsetting news could cause her to lapse back into illness.

Briar Rose was too weak to get up and had to satisfy herself with Janet's reports that her father was recovering from the wild night of battle. Gareth evaded her other questions and for once she didn't press him.

She knew it was a false truce that had gone up between them. But for now she found herself enjoying Gareth's care. Never had he been so tender with her, so attentive. He sat at the bedside and held her hand and spoke of the coming season and his responsibilities to his estates.

She listened to his plans and dreams with her heart in her throat. At last, all she had wished for him was coming true. He'd been mainperned and was back in the good graces of the king. He attended Mass freely. Gareth had but to marry, and Morley would be his.

To *marry* . . . Briar Rose winced. At times she was sure he loved her and would declare for her.

It was all so confusing. The moments they spent together were sweet, but nothing was said of their future. Many times she longed to speak of her true feelings, but uncertainty won out and she kept silent. Still, she couldn't help the small flame of hope that flickered within her when Gareth was near, smiling, speaking so gently, almost like a lover.

18

Inevitably, the fragile truce between them had to be tested. Within a fortnight Briar Rose was well enough to move about the keep, visiting her father. Acacia chose this time to take her women and retainers to Padwick, on the coast beside the Narrow Sea.

"I cannot believe she's giving up on Briarwood," Briar Rose told her father, sitting on the edge of his bed.

"She went to Padwick, I think, because of Gareth Hawke. There's something going on between them that I cannot fathom. It's as if Acacia fears Hawke."

"I don't know why she should fear him," Briar Rose said bitterly. "After all, he did exactly as she wished."

"Are you sure, daughter? Sometimes things aren't quite as they seem."

She could see that her father was tiring, almost drifting off as he spoke. "You're right, my lord. Gareth has evaded my questions long enough."

She found him in the stableyard instructing a company of his knights to return to Masterson now that the fighting was done. Throwing back her shoulders, she approached.

"Gareth."

He swung about. "You shouldn't be out, Briar Rose."

Her blue-violet eyes blazed with a vehemence he remembered from days past. "At times I think you wish me to malinger like an invalid. I am well now, yet you persist in coddling me."

How could he explain that his fear of losing her was so great that he dared not let her go? As long as she remained in her chamber she was his, depending on him for her every need. The moment she was declared healthy she was free to send him away. That was what Gareth dreaded above all things.

"Well, my lord?" she asked heatedly. "Will you hear me out?"

He nodded and took her arm, leading her from the stableyard into the bailey, to a greening arbor near the dovecote.

Briar Rose placed her hand over his and for a moment Gareth thought he saw a flicker of the girl as she'd once been, a full year ago when they'd first met. But she lifted his hand and removed it as if it were a thing of distaste.

"I want some answers, Gareth. I've kept my silence long enough. And please, no more lies."

Her distrust cut him sharply. "Ask me, then," he said quietly.

"Gareth, where is my crest?"

"At Masterson. I told you—"

"No more lies, I said! Do you think me so stupid and gullible to believe that, now that I've seen Acacia?"

"What does Acacia have to do with this?"

"You know the answer to that. You gave her the

crest, didn't you? After all your promises, you sent her the ring."

He shook his head, frowning. "Nay, Briar Rose, Acacia is the one who lied. I never gave her the crest."

"Damn you, Gareth, I saw it on her finger with my own eyes! She herself told me—"

He sent her a quelling look. "She's tricked you, nightingale. If she wears a ring, it must be a forgery."

Briar Rose stopped. She hadn't considered that possibility. Jesu, but she hoped it was true. Slowly, in a gentler tone, she said, "Acacia is easily capable of such a trick."

"Of course she is. That explains why she took herself off to Padwick. She knew I'd expose what she'd done. 'Twill be easy enough to prove her deception. I'll send to Masterson for the ring."

They walked together in silence for a time. "I want to believe you, Gareth," Briar Rose said at last. "I think that I do. Time will tell, won't it?"

"Aye, nightingale. I don't blame you for distrusting me."

She didn't deny it. Although she felt more at ease with him, there was yet another troublesome matter.

"I've heard you're betrothed to Rowena Shelby," she said softly.

"Briar Rose, it's the last thing I could wish for, but Rowena talks of suing me for breach of promise."

"I never thought you to be a man easily manipulated."

"I could say the same about you, Briar Rose. And I could ask you similar questions. Even while you accuse me of bending to Rowena's will, you are betrothed to Alain de Wannet. He's proven himself a poor protector, allowing you to be set upon by the Morley outlaws, but I don't see you castigating him for it."

Briar Rose wanted to hurt him, to avenge the way he'd ravaged her heart. She drew herself up. "There's no love between Alain and me, but when I had no home he took me in. And 'twas he who saved me from the outlaws."

The hurt she'd meant to deal him found a home, lodging squarely in his heart. He could have turned the hurt back on her, reminding her of her part in luring him to the Sanctarium, but he didn't. There was no point in dredging that up.

"So where does that leave us, Briar Rose?" he asked gently.

A bird trilled in the arbor and sweet summertime scents wafted through the air. But inside Briar Rose was cold, like an empty well.

"There is no 'us,' Gareth. Our marriage is annulled and we're both promised to others. All that remains is for you to leave here and get to the business of running Masterson, and Morley when you come into possession of it. As for myself, I have Briarwood. All I ask is that you send me the crest, if indeed you have it."

He started to say something, but the jewellike hardness that rimmed her eyes stopped him. No amount of begging in the world would sway her now.

"You'll have it," he said quietly.

Briar Rose tried to feel relieved that he was leaving at last, but her heart still pounded at the thought of him. And then fluttered madly when his departure was delayed.

A small contingent from Masterson arrived, led by Giles. Along with some retainers and a pair of knights, he had Maeve in tow.

Briar Rose met her in the hall. This was a different

Maeve from the sad-eyed, hollow-cheeked girl she'd met at Morley. This Maeve had the bloom of health in her cheeks and her belly was big—nay, huge—with child. Cedric, who had come to Briarwood with Gareth, stood proudly at her side.

Briar Rose embraced Maeve and tears sprang to her eyes. "It seems I weep constantly," she apologized. "In sooth, I'm happy to see you."

"And I'm happy to be here, my lady. I couldn't stand waiting at Masterson, away from this husband of mine."

"You should have waited, Maeve," Gareth said, striding into the hall. "We were planning to leave at dawn."

Briar Rose sent Gareth a dark look and turned back to the girl. "Of course you must stay, just for a few more days. How long until your confinement?"

Maeve blushed and smiled softly. "At least a month. And I've never felt more healthy. The journey was easy on me."

But that very night proved Maeve's calculations incorrect. Just as Briar Rose dropped off to sleep, Janet scratched at her door.

"It's Maeve, my lady. She's having the baby."

Wrapping herself in a robe, Briar Rose followed Janet to the small chamber Maeve shared with Cedric. With nervous hands, she struck flint and lit a lamp. Instantly she saw that Maeve was in the throes of a birthing pain, her face ashen and contorted, her breath coming in quick gasps.

The pain receded and Maeve stared with terror-filled eyes. " 'Tis too early," she gasped. "Oh . . ."

Briar Rose held her hand and let Maeve grip it through the pain. "Where's Cedric?" she asked.

"He—he went to fetch Lord Gareth and to find someone to help . . ."

Briar Rose pursed her lips. Her first thought was of the physician, Godfrey Pelham, but then she remembered that Acacia had taken him to Padwick. "There's a midwife in the village," she said. "I'll get her myself."

Maeve nodded. "Hurry, my lady. I cannot bear this alone."

Briar Rose threw a mantle about her shoulders and flew down to the stables. On the way, she met Cedric and Gareth.

"Go to your wife, Cedric," she ordered. "I'm going to fetch a midwife."

Cedric fled toward the stairs, muttering disjointed prayers under his breath. Gareth stayed with Briar Rose.

"I'll come with you," he said.

Together they rode down into the town, stopping at a small house by the river. Mistress Lyons grumbled at being roused so abruptly, but she was a good-natured soul and promised to come apace.

They rode back to the keep and went to Maeve's chamber. Cedric murmured words of comfort as Maeve braved another pain. It was a touching scene, dimly lit and as tender as a church painting. Briefly, Briar Rose felt a stab of envy. It seemed that Maeve had all she longed for: a loving husband and, very soon, a babe of her own. She glanced back at Gareth, who stood in the doorway, to see if he had a similar reaction. But his eyes were hard as he stepped away from the door.

Maeve was able to smile. "My mother was known to have short birthings. Perhaps it will be so with me."

The midwife confirmed this. "The pains are hard and fast," she pronounced, her hands working over a length of linen. "It won't be long." Then she turned to Cedric. "Begone with you, sir. 'Tis women's work we have here tonight."

"Nay!" Maeve exclaimed through gritted teeth. She gripped his hand so forcefully that Cedric's eyes widened and he settled himself again at the bedside.

Briar Rose made herself useful, responding to Mistress Lyons's terse orders. She and Janet, and even Gareth fetched warm water, pots of herbs, endless serviettes. Two hours crept by, then three . . . At last Maeve released an animal cry.

"Bear down, girl," Mistress Lyons instructed. "Use all your strength."

Briar Rose stared in rapt fascination as Maeve's face turned an angry red and she made strange gurgling sounds in her throat. While the midwife called encouragement, she arched her back and heaved mightily, again and again.

Briar Rose's arm ached from holding a bowl lamp high. She gave it to Janet for a moment and went to the door, wiping her face.

Gareth hadn't left the screens passage. He was pacing up and down, almost as nervous as Cedric.

"God's blood," he said hotly. "It sounds as if you're torturing her in there."

" 'Tis the pain of birthing," Briar Rose said, oddly touched by his concern. "We've done everything possible to see to Maeve's comfort."

"She sounds bloody uncomfortable to me," he fumed.

"Don't worry, Gareth. 'Twill be over soon."

Janet's whisper brought her back into the room. "My lady, look. 'Tis God's greatest miracle."

Briar Rose brought her hands to her bosom. She was suffused with sweet warmth as she watched the birthing. A perfect baby boy was born, flailing his slippery limbs and bawling lustily.

"Your son, sir," Mistress Lyons said. The twinkle in

her eye belied her brisk manner. She swaddled the babe in clean linen. "A mite undersized but a strong one just the same. Hold him now while I tie off the cord."

Awed by the sight and touched by the look in Cedric's tear-bright eyes, Briar Rose handed the midwife a length of thin-spun silk and watched as the pulsating cord of life was tied and then cut.

"God keep him," the woman pronounced.

Gareth burst into the room as if he'd not been able to stand the suspense. "I heard a cry—" he began, and then stopped short. His eyes seemed to melt and his voice softened to a whisper. "By the Mass," he breathed. "What have you there, Cedric?"

The knight grinned crookedly. "A boy child." The baby calmed immediately upon being cradled in his strong arms and Cedric repeated the midwife's blessing. "God keep you, my son, my Giles."

Briar Rose couldn't tear her eyes from Gareth. He seemed fascinated by the baby, peering almost shyly at the little wizened face, reaching out tentatively to touch a tiny hand.

Maeve smiled weakly. "Giles . . . after the man who brought me to my husband. As fine a knight as his sire, he'll be." She reached for the babe.

She stopped in midmotion with a gasp of pain and confusion. Her eyes sought the midwife, questioning.

"Afterpains. Oft as fierce as the birthing ones."

"But I feel—sweet, merciful Lord—" Suddenly Maeve bore down as she had before, with the same intense concentration, the same animal grunting.

The midwife, who until this point had exhibited an immovable calm, gave an exclamation of surprise. " 'Tis yet another babe—a twin!"

Gareth watched, awestruck, as the second baby came

into the world. There was something so beautiful about it that it was almost holy.

Maeve's daughter's thrashing and wailing matched that of her brother, although she was smaller and more delicately made. Maeve and Cedric wept openly, thanking God and all the saints for the dual gifts of Giles and his tiny sister, whom they insisted on calling Rose. Bowing deferentially, Cedric begged Briar Rose and Gareth to be the children's godparents. It was awkward, being paired in peoples' minds when they were so far apart, but they both accepted the responsibility without hesitation.

Proud of her handiwork, Mistress Lyons tidied up.

"Come," she said to Gareth and Janet and Briar Rose. "Our work is done."

Briar Rose nodded and followed them to the door. Pausing there, she looked back at the new family. They were oblivious to her now, absorbed in the children. Bathed in the amber glow of oil lamps, Maeve appeared as serene and sweet-faced as a Madonna, Cedric as loving and prideful as any man she'd seen. Longing mingled with her happiness for them, and her heart cried out for all she could not have.

Janet brought mead and bread from the kitchen and they sat together in the hall. The keep was quiet except for the occasional and curiously jarring cry of a baby.

"Never seen the likes of that," Janet remarked. "Twins! I should have guessed it. The girl was too big for just one."

"Is that why they came early?" Briar Rose asked the midwife.

"Aye. We'll keep a close watch on them, for the early ones are sometimes weak of lung."

"Giles and Rose aren't at all weak," Briar Rose insisted vehemently.

Gareth drew on his mead and chuckled. "You're probably right about that. If they're anything like their namesakes, there's nothing weak about them."

Briar Rose couldn't help smiling at him. They'd just witnessed a miracle together and the experience softened the hard edges of the barrier that stood between them.

The midwife yawned and Janet stood up. "I'll show you to a room, mistress, so you can be near if you're needed."

They left Gareth and Briar Rose alone in the hall. An awkward silence strained between them.

"I thought to leave today," Gareth remarked.

"But what of Maeve and the children? They won't be fit to travel for some time."

"I'll leave Cedric and a few others."

"I see." Briar Rose knew she should go back to bed, but she didn't feel the least bit sleepy.

Gareth must have felt likewise. He stood up, moving agitatedly. "I'm going out," he announced. "The air in here is oppressive."

Bleakly she watched him walk down the length of the hall toward the door, thinking that she was the cause of his oppressive feelings. But he stopped and turned to her.

"Come ride with me, nightingale. I could do with your company."

The night was clear, the sky studded with silver stars. A bird's call went up and was answered as Briar Rose and Gareth rode out to the moors.

Briar Rose felt wonderfully free, her unbound hair

streaming out behind her, her body unencumbered by heavy clothing. She wore only her bliaut and cloak.

Proudly she showed him Briarwood, pointing out the fields and frowning at those that had been burned by the Scots. She took him into the forest, where as a girl she'd played and hunted. The leaves rustled richly in the late summer night.

They came to a fragrant clearing at the river's edge. "There's a cave over there," she said, pointing. "I used to hide there from my tutors when I didn't feel like working at my lessons."

Gareth smiled, imagining her as a child. She would have been a bright imp, full of mischief.

"Just before I left for Wexler," she continued, "I put a token in the cave." She frowned. "I'd forgotten all about it until now."

"What sort of token was it?" Gareth asked.

"You'd probably think it silly."

"I'd like to see your cave, Briar Rose."

A playful gleam came into her eyes. "I'll show you the cave, Gareth, but you'll only get to see the token if you get to it before me." She dug her heels into her mare's flanks and lowered herself over Dame's strong neck. She thundered across the clearing, Gareth close behind.

They'd almost reached the cave when Dame's hoof caught in an unseen divot. The mare stumbled to a halt.

Both Briar Rose and Gareth dismounted. Gareth took the mare's bridle and walked her a little way, studying her gait. "Lame," he pronounced.

"Is it very bad, Gareth?"

He shook his head. "She'll be fine, but you'd best not ride her for a while. Let's walk to the cave and let her rest a bit."

It was smaller than Briar Rose remembered. Then

she realized that the cave hadn't changed; she had. She was a woman now, not the blithe, breathless girl who had whiled away the hours so long ago.

Gareth bent low to enter the dark hollow in the bank. "So this is where you hid and plotted wickedly against your tutors."

Briar Rose laughed. "They were always patient with me. Too patient, perhaps. I was a spoiled child." I should have had some rowdy older brothers to take me down a peg or two."

"If you'd had brothers, they'd have spoiled you just like everyone else, Briar Rose. You make a man want to do that to you."

She sucked in her breath. "Gareth, you mustn't speak to me that way."

"What way?"

"Like—like—" Like you care for me, she finished silently, but she refused to tell him so.

Noting her discomfort, Gareth turned the subject. "Where is this token you told me about?"

Briar Rose felt herself blush. " 'Tis nothing, Gareth. A silly thing—"

"Why don't you show me and I'll judge for myself. You may be many things, Briar Rose, but you've never been silly."

Near the back of the cave there was a small projection of rock, like a shelf. She felt her way to it and found her token secreted exactly where she'd hidden it three years earlier.

"It's a tapestry," she said, handing it to Gareth. "I spent years learning how to weave, but in all that time I only produced this one thing. I thought it so poor that I never showed it to anyone, but I liked it all the same. Weaving is a strange art; you can't see the results until it's done. It was as if my hands envisioned what my eyes could not."

Gareth went to the mouth of the cave. Dawn was breaking, blue on the horizon. He turned the small tapestry over and studied the picture.

It was a raven-haired girl and a knight on their wedding day. They stood together bordered by twining roses. The girl—needless to say, Briar Rose—was gowned in spun gold and pearls, looking like a jewel, shining with innocence. Her hair was unbound and her fingers were laced with those of the groom. Gareth's eyes moved to the knight. He was curious about this one. What man had Briar Rose envisioned as a husband those three years ago?

He was tall and broad. His head was bare. The features were strong, yet there was a look of peace in his eyes and his mouth was gentle. Gareth knew it was only his own foolish longing that made him recognize something of himself in the tapestry knight.

Gareth was silent for so long that Briar Rose grew nervous. If he'd laughed and made sport of her work, she would have understood. But he was pensive, his features soft, his scarred eye seeming to droop even more than usual.

"A little girl's dream," she quipped. "I was going to give it to Hugh, my betrothed, but when it was finished I realized he'd not like it."

"Why not?"

"The groom. I tried to make him look like Hugh, but something went awry. Hugh was much smaller, closer to my size. And he was dark-haired. So I hid it away, along with the dream, I suppose."

Gareth let the tapestry fall to his side. "What do you dream of now, nightingale?"

She faced him squarely. "I dare not dream at all."

That hurt. He wished there were some way he could call back the girl who, in wistful innocence, had woven this tapestry.

"We'd best get back," she said. "Give me the tapestry. I think it should stay hidden away." She took the tapestry, replaced it, and went to the mouth of the cave. In the burgeoning light of dawn a gleam caught her eyes. Stooping, she picked up the object.

She nearly dropped it as if she'd been burned. It was the Morley amulet, the serpent twisted around the cross. A tremor of cold shuddered through her.

Gareth took the object from her. She heard him hiss with anger as he recognized it.

"They've been here," Briar Rose whispered.

Gareth looked around quickly. Seeing the fear in her eyes, he reached out and stroked her hair gently. "Don't worry, sweeting. Talwork has been taken to London by Alain and Griffith is undoubtedly lost without his master, as are the others."

"Griffith is dead," Briar Rose said, pushing away her fear. "So are the others. I saw Alain's men kill them."

Gareth pressed his mouth into a hard line. "For that I'm indebted to the man." He sighed wearily. "It was much easier to hate him when I thought he meant you harm."

Briar Rose laid her hand over his. "Gareth, I'd like nothing better than to see this enmity between you two ended. Alain—"

"Let's not speak of him," he interrupted curtly.

Briar Rose nodded, only too happy to comply. The day was perfect, the sun glowing gently in the east, a light mist swirling across the ground. If shc tried, she could imagine that nothing was amiss in the world.

Gareth went to the horses and walked Dame a little

way, testing her foreleg. "She's still favoring it," he remarked. "You'd best ride with me."

Briar Rose started to say that they could walk, but she was weary from lack of sleep. She let Gareth help her into the saddle, trying not to let her heart leap at the feel of his big hands spanning her waist. He tethered the mare's reins to his own and mounted behind.

A lark's song rose up as they crossed the clearing and entered the forest. The morning sun sent pink rays slanting through the trees, dappling the soft earth of the forest floor. Briar Rose had been sitting stiffly in front of Gareth, battling the terrible longing she felt at his closeness, but the sounds and smells filled her with a sense of peace and she leaned back against him.

Gareth closed his eyes tightly. Her softness tantalized him; the scent of her hair brought back memories that were better left tucked away.

He brought his arms up and placed them around her middle, drawing her against him. Burying his face in her hair, he said, "You're wrong about the tapestry, nightingale. I think, somewhere deep inside you, is a girl who dreams still."

"No . . ." she protested. "Gareth, you mustn't hold me like this."

"By the stars, Briar Rose, I'd be sinning against nature if I didn't!"

Hearing his voice crack with emotion, she swiveled around in the saddle, bending one leg and hooking it over the cantle. His face looked tortured.

"Gareth, what do you mean?"

"How can you not know?" he said, his voice still rough with passion. "I love you, nightingale. I think I've loved you from the first."

The words swelled and echoed in her heart. "Jesu, Gareth. If this is another of your lies . . ."

But she knew it wasn't. She read the truth in his eyes. She was the one who'd lied when she told him she had no dreams. Her dream had never left her. Through all that had happened, she'd never stopped hoping for the miracle of his love.

Their lips melted together, saying all that needed to be said. Briar Rose savored the taste of him, moved her hands up to caress his neck and to weave her fingers into his hair in a way that had once been familiar to her, and was familiar still. With a groan of longing Gareth pulled her all the way around in the saddle so that she was facing him. The well-trained horse didn't falter at the shifting on its back.

Their next kiss went deeper, tongues meeting and darting, tasting and twining together. The world shrank away and there was just the two of them, embracing intimately, recapturing the feelings that they'd both denied but hadn't ever lost.

Briar Rose offered no protest when she felt him remove her mantle. Nor did she stop him when he untied her bliaut at the top and slid it down over her shoulders, baring her flesh to the soft morning air. She watched in wonder as his hands, trembling slightly, moved over the pink-tipped mounds, palms rubbing lightly. Then he slid her garment lower.

"Sweet God, but you're beautiful," he said, looking down at her thighs, which were parted over the horse's back.

Slowly she opened the leather jerkin he wore and then his chemise, running her hands over his chest. Fire pounded through her veins. A frankly carnal lust added its heat to the smoldering love she felt. There was something inexpressibly erotic about riding this way, half naked, the horse's warm body moving slowly beneath her.

Every inch of her was on fire, ignited by his hands and mouth and the love words he whispered in her ear.

"Gareth," she breathed. "Stop."

His head came up, a stricken look on his face. "Would you deny me now, Briar Rose?"

She smiled at his confusion. "No, my lord. Indeed, I would *have* you now, but you'd best stop this beast before he grows resentful and bucks us off."

He paused to devour her lips one last time before dismounting. When he lifted her from the saddle, he paused again, holding her aloft, so that her breasts were even with his lips. He held her pressed between himself and the horse, moving his mouth over her flesh until she gave a ragged cry of urgent need.

Slowly he let her slide to the ground, giving her bliaut one last pull so that it fell away, exposing all of her. Briar Rose helped him shed his clothes and they lay back on the pile of fabric, flesh against flesh, mouths joined, their bodies crying out to be united.

Gareth loomed above her, his face framed by a hood of broad leaves. He told her that he loved her again and again and Briar Rose answered with her body, sheathing him in her.

Their passion rose and crested to a high peak of pleasure. Briar Rose had never felt so fulfilled. Gareth loved her now and that made all the difference. Not only was her body sated; there was a warm plenitude in her heart that made her want to sing with joy.

She saw her feelings mirrored in his silver-rimmed eyes as he held her gently. They stared at each other for a long moment, their hearts quieting, the forest blossoming around them.

"Marry me, love," Gareth said.

She felt her heart rise to her throat. "I already did that, once upon a time."

He shook his head, raining kisses over her face. "It will be different this time, nightingale. No secrets, no lies. A proper Church ceremony for all to see."

"But what about Rowena and Alain?"

"The two of them be damned, and the king, too, if he objects. What say you, Briar Rose? Will you be my wife?"

An assent was on her lips, but she couldn't bring herself to say yes. Not yet, at least. Things were happening too fast. She'd been hurt too many times before to rush headlong into this.

Gareth read the hesitation in her eyes and cursed himself for testing her faith in him so many times.

"Don't answer me now, Briar Rose. I don't blame you for being cautious."

"Gareth, I—"

He placed a finger gently over her lips. "Let's go back to the keep and see how our godchildren fare. And then I'll go to Masterson and get your crest, and find some way to dispense with Rowena. When I return, perhaps you'll be ready to tell me what I long to hear."

19

Briar Rose sat beside her father in the bailey where a table had been set up for receiving the Michaelmas rents. Gareth had been gone three weeks and she missed him sorely. It was as if some vital part of her were lacking, and she was only half alive.

A great glove, its fingers and thumb stuffed with wood chips, hung from a pole in front of the keep, signaling the start of fairing time. A goose was roasted and refeathered to be paraded through the hall. Everyone partook of goose and ginger at the great feast, for it was believed that whoever ate goose at Michaelmas would not lack for luck throughout the year.

Yet it seemed to Briar Rose that her luck ran out only hours after the feast. A group of very unwelcome riders came to the main gate.

Alain. She had managed to put him from her mind for a good while. Yet she knew this meeting was inevitable. She met him in the inner courtyard as he strode toward the great hall. He stopped walking when she spoke his name, his eyes hard with anger.

"Welcome to Briarwood," she said, taking his arm and leading him into the hall.

"Is that all you have to say to me?" he demanded. "By the throat of God, Rose, I risked myself and my men to save you from the rebels. And you thank me by running away in my absence!"

"How could I possibly allow you to starve Gareth Hawke to death?"

"He wouldn't have starved. In due time we would have settled our differences with swordplay, as befits men of honor."

"How can you speak of honor, Alain? You are the most cowardly, underhanded—"

His hand snaked out, and he grasped her upper arm. "Who are you to speak of being underhanded, Rose?" He tugged at his beard in frustration. "I cannot fathom why. I've treated you well, opened my home to you when you were homeless, offered you a place as my wife—"

"You've never understood me, Alain. I love Gareth Hawke. No matter what you offer me, no matter what you do to keep us apart, you won't be able to change that."

Alain couldn't bring himself to admit defeat. He drew her against him and put his face very close to hers. "Your pretty speech doesn't move me, Rose."

Lionel Beaupre rushed to his master's side.

Alain gave him a questioning look. "Well?"

"He's coming, my lord." The agent withdrew.

She saw a sinister glint in Alain's eyes. "What—"

"You heard Beaupre. Your lover is on his way here. I wouldn't want you to be without your crest when we're wed."

"No—"

"Call your women to get you gowned to receive Hawke."

"I won't do it, Alain."

His fingers bit into her arm. "You will, my sweet. It would grieve me to harm your father, but if I must threaten you in that way, then so be it."

"You're mad," Briar Rose said as Nan and Columbine fussed over her hair and dress. It was absurd being gowned like this for the occasion of betraying Gareth. Yet Alain had come prepared with her maids and gowns and even some of the Wannet jewels for her to wear.

Alain gestured at the courtyard where, shortly, Gareth would ride in. The garden was a blaze of autumn color, shimmering in the sunlight. "Looks peaceful down there," he said casually. "Hawke will have no notion of the archers hidden beyond the walls." He laughed. "Think of it, Rose. A hundred arrows aimed at his heart. And they'll find a home if you try to warn him, if you betray so much as a quiver of uncertainty."

"You'd cut a man down in cold blood?"

"That, my dear, is up to you. If you cooperate and play your part well, Hawke won't be touched."

Briar Rose was chilled by the hatred she saw in Alain's eyes. "What do you want me to do?"

" 'Tis simple. All you have to do is inform Hawke that you need your ring for our wedding next week."

"And if I refuse?"

"Hawke will die. Think of it—his body bristling with arrows—"

"What if I cooperate, Alain? What will you do then?"

"My quarrel with Hawke will be at an end. In marrying me, you'll slay him as surely as I might have done with a sword."

A shout from the bailey announced Gareth's arrival. He was with Kenneth and his squire. Briar Rose caught her breath when she spied Rowena.

Smiling triumphantly, Alain led her down the stairs.

"I'll not be a good wife to you, Alain," she vowed.

He shrugged. "Don't be tiresome, Rose. Eventually you'll grow used to me."

"Like your first wife did?" she demanded.

He sent her a venomous look. "Celestine was unstable. I had nothing to do with her suicide."

"Damn you to hell, Alain," she said as they stepped from the hall.

Her eyes found Gareth and her heart began to pound painfully. He had dismounted and was walking toward her and Alain. Rowena clung to his sleeve. Quiet fury seemed to emanate from him.

A hush gathered as the milling people in the bailey recognized the black and gray hawk on Gareth's tunic.

Gareth disengaged himself from Rowena's grasping hand and looked with steel-hard eyes at his enemy.

"I had hoped I'd seen the last of you, Alain."

"Let's forget our differences for now, my lord. There's much bad blood between us, but that will be settled today, as my betrothed will soon tell you."

All eyes turned to Briar Rose. A murmur of confusion rippled through the crowd.

Gareth's jaw tightened. "Get on with it, Alain. Say your piece."

"I'll defer to Lady Rose."

He stepped behind her and nudged her forward. She tried to look at Gareth but knew that if she did, she'd dissolve into tears.

"Say it," Alain hissed into her ear. "Say it, or watch your lover fall."

She swallowed and passed her tongue over her dry lips. "Alain and I are to be married next week. I shall be needing my ring."

Gareth froze, his face contorted with rage. Rowena took his hand, stopping him from leaping at Alain's throat.

He ignored her and looked at Briar Rose. His eyes bored into hers, searching, questioning.

She faced him squarely. " 'Tis true, Gareth. I've made up my mind."

He backed away, dazed and furious. He fumbled in his pocket and drew out the ring. The gold gleamed dully in the sunlight. He dropped it into her hand and left, calling for his horse.

Two days later Briar Rose rode with Alain and some of his men up into the moors surrounding Briarwood. He'd said he was interested in seeing the land, but she could see the cold ambition in his eyes.

A pair of travelers were on the road far below. One was a poor crofter, dressed in a hooded robe, and the other wore a gold circle on his sleeve, the mark of the Jewish faith. Briar Rose couldn't see the crofter well, but the Jew's dark features were vaguely familiar.

Briar Rose twisted the reins nervously in her hands. She looked down from the moor, battling a dreadful feeling of hopelessness. The manor stood upon its grass-covered knoll, embraced by the River Swale. The walls gleamed in the soft autumn light and the distant church bell tolled richly.

"Briarwood . . ." she whispered. She heard a faint shout within the walls of the keep. Briar Rose swallowed. The Scots had been driven away, she told herself. Still . . .

Alain called after her, but she paid him no heed. She clattered through the gate and didn't stop until she was inside the bailey. She found Simeon and gave him her mount. "My father?"

"He's all right. He's in his chamber."

Briar Rose exhaled loudly, relieved. "I must go to him."

"Of course. But my lady—"

"Yes?"

" 'Tis your stepmother. She's returned. At this very moment she is in the chapel with her group of manorial officials."

"What for?"

"The hallmote, my lady. She's making her daughter, Bettina, heiress to Briarwood."

Briar Rose burst into the chapel. The small gathering stood round the baldechine. Father Sabius murmured a prayer as the master of ceremonies held out a stick, which symbolized the transfer of the peerage to the young heiress, Bettina. Acacia's green eyes glittered as she took hold of the rod.

"And now the crest, my lady."

It gleamed dull yellow on a purple velvet pillow.

"Stop!" Briar Rose said.

All eyes turned to her. Acacia blanched and her hand flew to her mouth.

"What's the matter, Acacia?"

"You—you're—"

"I'm here. And just in time, it seems. I'm surprised at you, Acacia. I thought you'd finally realized that your place is at Padwick."

"Briarwood is mine," Acacia said desperately.

"Nay, lady," boomed a voice from the back of the chapel. There stood Alain, looking perfectly calm.

Acacia's eyes narrowed. "I thought you'd dealt with the girl."

He laughed. "So I have, Acacia. Unfortunately for you, 'twas not in the way you'd planned. I intend to marry Briar Rose. She'll have the manor."

"But you promised me—"

"I honor only my own ambitions."

Acacia's mouth twisted with rage. "You low, cheating whoreson!"

The clerics and officials shuffled uncomfortably and Acacia hesitated. She suddenly seemed to realize that all her plans had gone awry. She let out a shriek and threw herself at Briar Rose.

"You! It is all your fault!"

Alain and the captain of his guard acted quickly, pulling the raging Acacia off Briar Rose. The older woman's gaze of fury bored into Alain as she was helped from the chapel by her women.

Little Bettina was wailing in her nurse's arms. Briar Rose nodded to the nurse, who gratefully withdrew.

Alain came and took her hand. "I'm sorry."

She nodded. "I'm going to see my father."

"My lord, you've a visitor."

Gareth glanced up from the rent sheets he was studying and frowned at Paulus. "I told you I'm not seeing anyone."

The squire looked agitated. "He's waited all day, my lord. He says it's a matter of great importance."

Gareth scowled. "Have I not made myself quite clear? I've work to do—"

"It concerns Lady Briar Rose, my lord."

The sound of her name caused a cold fist to clench around his heart. Against his will, he nodded. "Send him in."

David Feversham entered shortly. "I've been looking for you for many months. I'd have found you sooner, but I was imprisoned for some time on false charges. Giles found me in York and managed to get me free."

Gareth extended his hand. "You are welcome, David."

Feversham swallowed. "My lord, I'm afraid I've been presumptuous with a matter that concerns you. But since you settled that loan for me, I've felt indebted to you. I only hope I've done the right thing."

"Tell me."

The solicitor's nervous hands set a well-creased document on the table before Gareth.

" 'Tis the record of your marriage to Lady Briar Rose. Lord Wannet charged me with the annulment."

Gareth felt as if an old wound had been reopened. He'd be a lifetime forgetting Briar Rose. "Why do you bring me this, David? Surely there's no need to—"

"Because, my lord, there has been no annulment. You are still married."

Gareth slammed his fist down on the table. "By the saints, is this business never to be finished? The woman is to marry Wannet within the week."

"Then you must stop her, my lord. Bigamy is a serious crime."

"Why didn't you do as you were charged, David?"

The other man swallowed. "I bear no liking for Wannet. I didn't do his bidding because—because I—"

"Come on, my friend. Out with it."

"The very mention of your name brought tears to her eyes. I couldn't simply destroy your marriage without your consent."

Gareth gripped the edge of the table until his knuckles whitened. "No. No, David, you must have been mistaken. God knows, I tried to make up for all the grief I'd brought her, but in the end she couldn't forgive me. She humiliated me by announcing her impending wedding to Wannet before all of Briarwood."

"I beg your pardon, my lord, but I wonder who was more humiliated that day."

Gareth swung around to face Giles, who had arrived with Feversham. He knit his brow into a frown. "How long have you been lurking there, Giles?"

Giles shrugged. "Long enough. As I was saying, you were not the only one who suffered a blow to his pride. You spent all spring at Tynegate with Rowena."

"I was an invalid, damnit! Briar Rose didn't come to see me all the time I lay abed with the wounds her betrothed had dealt me. I doubt she cared whether I lived or—"

"She did, indeed, my lord." Paulus stepped into the room, his face pale and contrite.

"Good God!" Gareth exploded. "Is this whole business to become a matter of public debate? Who else is out there listening in?"

Rowena came and stood behind Paulus, Kenneth with her. For once there was no trace of guile on her face, but some sort of reluctant acceptance.

"Gareth," she said, her voice quiet but firm, "I think what Paulus is trying to tell you is that Briar Rose cared very much for you. Not a day passed that she didn't try to visit you when you were ill. But we—Paulus and I—kept her away."

Gareth felt his insides turn to stone. He passed his hand over the fine weave of his fustian tunic. "Why are you telling me this, Rowena?"

She dashed the tears from her face. "It's time I

stopped fooling myself, Gareth. I'd like to think I've lost you, but that's not quite true. I cannot lose what I never possessed in the first place. Once, you belonged to Celestine, and then to Briar Rose. But never to me."

Gareth looked around the room at all the expectant faces. He drew his brows together and stared with a pained expression at the marriage record on the table. "What the hell am I going to do about that?"

" 'Tis a promise you made, my lord," David Feversham said. "Duly inscribed and witnessed."

Gareth tried to beat down the hope that sprang forth in his chest like a blossoming flower. He mustn't allow himself to hope. The disappointment that was sure to follow would be bitter.

Giles took up the marriage document and placed it in Gareth's hands.

"Go to her, my lord. It's the only way."

Huntsmen provided venison and a suckling pig was slaughtered. The cook, Lawrence, sent workers scurrying in all directions, preparing the feast. The great hall was swept and scrubbed and festooned with colorful boughs of changing leaves.

The dressmaker, brought by Alain from Yorkshire, was in Briar Rose's solar on the morning of the wedding. Janet was shaking out the trousseau that had been prepared for her when she was to marry Hugh Tesselwaithe.

"Acacia came poking about, looking to see if any of the gowns were suitable for her," Janet said.

Briar Rose lifted her arms so the dressmaker could smooth the sleeves of her wedding dress. "How is Acacia now?"

"She's taken to her bed. It won't be long until she skulks off to Padwick. Still, she seems . . ."

"What is it, Janet?"

The woman shrugged. "Never mind. Just be careful, sweeting." She began brushing out Briar Rose's long, gleaming locks and weaving them into a single elaborate plait in the back.

Briar Rose was suddenly nervous. Although she lacked a new bride's trepidation, she was aware that hundreds were already lining the walls of the bailey, gathering outside the chapel to see her. She fidgeted as Janet and the dressmaker fussed over her gown.

The underskirt was of filmy gold fabric covered by a wide, split overskirt of heavy cream silk, shot through with gold filament. Thousands of tiny seed pearls adorned the square-cut bodice, forming the shape of a rose. Gold braiding adorned the sweeping oversleeves, which had dagged edges and revealed a glimpse of gold tissue beneath. The dressmaker drifted a gauzy veil over Briar Rose's head and held it in place with a circlet of gold and pearl-encrusted combs.

Briar Rose tried hard to smile. Bathed, scented, and arrayed like a princess, she descended from her solar to make her way to the chapel.

"Were you seen, Lord Hawke?" Padwick asked, gesturing Gareth closer to his bed.

"No. Everyone seems to be busy with the wed—with the preparations."

Padwick nodded. "Good. How are you going to reckon with Wannet?"

Gareth's face hardened. "A direct confrontation is best. I've had enough of underhanded maneuverings."

"Well said, my lord."

"Where is Wannet now?"

"In his chambers."

Gareth went to the door. A pair of footmen were coming in with a large chair to transport Padwick to the chapel to witness his daughter's wedding. Gareth paused and turned back.

"My lord, are you sure about this?"

The old man nodded slowly. "I know my daughter well, Gareth. She doesn't want to be Alain's wife."

Gareth made his way to Wannet's chamber. It had to be true. God, it had to.

The door was ajar. Alain was being clothed in brilliant red by his men, pulling a fine-toothed comb through his pointed beard and fussing over his fingernails. Gareth strode into the room, his sword clanging against the doorframe.

The little comb fell to the floor and Wannet blanched. *"Hawke . . ."*

Lightning-quick, Gareth drew forth a dagger and pressed it to his neck.

Alain tried to cover his trembling with bravado. "What mean you, Hawke, by coming here?"

"I'm here to stop you from marrying my wife."

"She's not your wife. The marriage was annulled!"

"Not so, Alain. I have the document here, still intact."

"By God," he snapped, "I'll kill Feversham. . . ."

Gareth shook his head. "Give it up, Alain."

He leaned against the wall of the chamber. "There was a time, Gareth, when I hated you. But now I think I'm merely tired." Alain smiled. "You're a persistent bastard."

"I love the girl. There's nothing I wouldn't do for her."

Alain nodded. "You loved Celestine, too, and it was I who won her. We're even now."

"I'm not doing this to get even."

The church bell tolled. Alain went to the window and looked down at the surging crowd in the courtyard. Then he turned back to Gareth. "You had best go, my friend, if you're to take my place at the altar for the nuptial Mass." He twisted the crest ring from his finger and held it out. "You'll be needing this."

Too late, Gareth saw Alain nod to his squire. The door flew open, and half a dozen knights raced to Wannet's defense. At the same time Acacia flew into the room, a dagger in her hand.

A blade flashed. The church bell continued its rusty tolls. The ring bounced across the floor with a metallic clatter.

"My God!" someone shouted. "He is killed!"

Briar Rose stepped out into the bailey. The throng quieted at her appearance. Somehow, as she moved along the way that had been cleared for her, she remembered to keep a smile on her face.

The chapel doors had been flung wide. Earlier, she and Alain had met at the church porch to plight their troth. All that remained was the nuptial Mass. There was no turning back now.

She stepped inside and drew in a shaky breath. A lutenist strummed and sang of love everlasting. Incense filled the air. Candles cast a dim, golden glow over the chapel. Glancing up, she noticed that high above the altar the windhole had been glazed. Not with plain glass but a colored picture of the rose of Briarwood with its scarlet petals and golden seeds and craggy base. A wedding gift, probably, she told herself. But what hands could have wrought such a beautiful piece of work?

She remembered another bit of glasswork. Gareth's hawk. Could he? . . . She shook her head. It wouldn't do to march up the aisle with tears in her eyes.

The small space was crammed to the walls with people who turned to stare at her. Faces swam before her eyes. Her feet felt leaden, unable to move. Strange, she thought. What was Giles doing here, and why was he grinning so broadly?

"Come, my lady," whispered a voice at her elbow. "The groom awaits to celebrate Mass with you."

Her eyes widened. "Kenneth!"

"You don't think I'd let you walk down the aisle alone?"

With that, he took her arm and accompanied her to the altar. Her amazement grew as she recognized some of the onlookers. The Wexlers had come with other nobles from neighboring shires. Maeve and Cedric jiggled their babies to quiet them. And there were Kate and Meg, freshly scrubbed and smiling. Even Paulus was present.

And then she saw her father. He'd been brought on a litter and was propped up by bolsters. When he caught her eye, he smiled. Acacia was nowhere in sight.

Briar Rose could barely see Alain, for all the guests were leaning out into the aisle, admiring her fabulous dress. She caught a glimpse of his figure at the altar. Odd, but he wasn't wearing his usual red. His tabard was black, trimmed with silver. Somehow he seemed taller and broader. Briar Rose shook her head. She was imagining things.

Finally she and Kenneth reached the altar rail and she came face to face with the groom.

A small cry leaped from her lips. Her knees buckled

and she fell against the broad warmth of his chest. The lutenist's song grew and swelled in her ears.

"Steady, nightingale," he murmured. "One would think this was the first time you married."

"You—"

"Aye, my darling." Silver-rimmed eyes smiled down into hers.

"But Alain . . ."

His gentle fingers reached beneath her veil to brush the creases from her brow. "David Feversham never got our marriage annulled. Besides, how could I let you marry someone else when my heart cries out for you alone?"

Tears flooded her eyes. Suddenly, all she'd ever dreamed of was coming true. "Gareth . . ."

"I love you, nightingale. Don't make me live my life without you."

She turned slowly to the wedding guests to see if they were as shocked as she was by this turn of events. But all she saw was smiles. Alain stood near the back with his retinue. A hasty bandage adorned his shoulder.

Gareth looked grave for a moment. "Your stepmother. I'm not sure who she meant to attack, but her blade found Wannet. At first we thought the wound was mortal, but he survived. The man has more lives than a cat."

Rose-gold sunlight glinted through the new window, warming Briar Rose's face. She smiled up at Gareth. "A wedding gift?" she inquired softly.

"Aye, love. I gave you nothing the first time. Will you accept it?"

She swallowed hard. She had only to do what had been in her heart since that very first day she'd laid eyes on Gareth Hawke.

Trembling, she placed her hand in his. He gave her a

look of fathomless love as, ever so gently, he slipped the Briarwood crest on her finger. Then he turned and held her hand up for all to see.

"Behold, the lady of Briarwood!"

Bending low amid the loud outpouring of approval, he said, "And more important, the mistress of my heart." She lifted the veil from her face. The shining look of love he saw in her eyes nearly brought him to his knees.

His lips descended on hers in a kiss that made her his for all time.